BAD BET

BAD BET

by

Roger Longrigg

Hamish Hamilton
London

First published in Great Britain 1982
by Hamish Hamilton Ltd
Garden House 57-59 Long Acre London WC2E 9JZ

Copyright©1982 by Roger Longrigg

British Library Cataloguing in Publication Data

Longrigg, Roger
  Bad bet.
  I. Title
  823'.914[F]   PR6062.0516

  ISBN 0-241-10760-1

Typeset by Pioneer
Printed in Great Britain by The Chaucer Press
Bungay, Suffolk.

CHAPTER 1

Newmarket Heath seemed limitless. In fact it is limited by the Devil's Dyke far in front of the grandstand, by the London road far behind it, by the trees sheltering the National Stud far to the left, and by the yellowish outcrops of Newmarket town far, far to the right. But these bounds were invisible in the clammy mist of that October afternoon. It gave one a sense of going racing in the middle of Salisbury Plain — in the middle of the ocean, or of a sodden Sahara. It gave one a feeling of detachment, isolation, irresponsibility. It gave one an idea that it might be wise to give the last race a miss, and get away out of it home to the fire.

The tall, gaunt grandstand was crowded. Many noses were blue and some were dripping. French was heard, and Irish, and a scattering of American, and all the accents of the United Kingdom. Voices were *forte* in greeting, *fortissimo* in the last furlong of a race, *mezzoforte* in the exchange of lubricious gossip, and *pianissimo* in the transmission of inside information. Sniffing was drowned by sneezing and sneezing by coughing. The lenses of binoculars became misted. Whisky Macs were much drunk in the bars.

Ralph, third Viscount Hadfield, stood stocky and bonhomous by the Jockey Club enclosure in the stand. He was used to this sort of thing — impervious — rather preferred bad weather than otherwise because it kept a lot of layabouts away. But he wondered about his American friends, on such a poisonous afternoon. Well, they knew their way about. If they wanted brandy, God knew they could afford it. It went against the grain for Lord Hadfield, entertaining them, to pour drinks for a man who could buy him out twice over and not notice. But it had to be done. They were powers in the thoroughbred world, massively financed, with tentacles everywhere. That enormous place in Kentucky, that army of stallions — it made Lord Hadfield sick to think of it. He was rich himself, but he *deserved* to be rich. It made them worth a few drinks. If it hadn't, they wouldn't have had the drinks, not at Lord Hadfield's charges. He didn't think he was mean, but he admitted in private to being realistic. He never gave unless he was buying. His ancestors had done very nicely on the same principle.

He saw two of his Americans. He saw Matthew Carver and the girl, Carver's daughter, crossing towards the rails to have a bet. It wouldn't be a big bet. It wasn't Matthew Carver who was rich. He was a good fellow and a clever fellow, a popular bloke and a man everybody trusted, but he had one ghastly drawback. He wasn't very rich. On the other hand he was influential. His advice was often sought and sometimes followed. Lord Hadfield saw the two of them, father and daughter, being greeted several times as they threaded the crowd towards the rails. Of course, people knew that this was a fellow who could get them nominations for their broodmares to the best stallions in Kentucky, who could put them in the way of buying fabulous yearlings before they got to the sale-ring. Naturally everybody knew him, and naturally everybody said hullo.

Lord Hadfield saw the Carvers intercepted by Rollo Hampshire, probably because the old boy liked the look of Carver's girl. Being a duke, he thought he could get what he wanted, and being a duke he was usually right. Jovial reunion. Introduction of girl to Rollo. Girl unabashed. Met dukes before.

Lord Hadfield was amused to notice that the duke and the Yank (was that right? was a Kentuckyan a Yankee?) were identically dressed, to the button. Buff-coloured covert-coats, of the kind a sensible fellow buys off the peg in Aquascutum or Burberrys, and a fool has made by his tailor. Brown felt hats from Lock or Herbert Johnson. Shirts in small checks, from Turnbull and Asser or Harvey and Hudson or Marks and Spencer. Silk ties, muted foulard pattern. Tweed trousers, browny-green; jackets doubtless matching but invisible. Brown brogues, highly polished, muddy. Yet Carver looked American. Impossible to say why or how. Normal haircut. Normal face. Anglo-Saxon type, English ancestry. English wife, come to that, not that the nationality of his wife would affect his face. Her character might. From what Lord Hadfield had heard of that wife's character, the poor chap ought to be looking haggard. But he seemed fit and cheerful. He was fifty, fifty-two, a few years younger than Lord Hadfield. He looked less. Good digestion, clear conscience.

2

Lord Hadfield had a good digestion, too. He left his conscience alone. He didn't bother it, and he didn't let it bother him.

Another couple joined the Carvers and the duke; then another. They were having a kind of cocktail-party there in the Members' near the rails — quite a nuisance for people trying to get to their bookies. The other couples might have been attracted by the duke, or by Matthew Carver, or by the girl. She was a great girl, a sweetie, a lovely little thing, curly dark hair, blue eyes, sticky-up nose, cheeks pink in the weather, laughing. Completely American, in spite of her English mother. Pity, in a way. Waste.

The horses were going down to the mile start. The starting-stalls were almost invisible in the mist. It was a straight mile, and the colours would be impossible to identify until they got below the distance. Lord Hadfield remembered with amazement the days — not so very long ago — before the loudspeaker commentary.

And there was the other American, George Whyte, tall, younger than Carver but looking older, looking unhappy, wearing the same clothes but as though they were fancy dress. Fish out of water. Shy. Dull. Introduced by Carver to Rollo Hampshire and the others. Shook hands all round. American thing, foreign thing, not usual in England, not on a racecourse. You nod and say, 'How do you do?' Americans shake your hand and say, 'How are you?' Seems to demand a reply. Ridiculous way to go on.

George Whyte was Matthew Carver's partner; as a matter of fact you could almost say he was his boss. He was the money, the land, the buildings, the major share in all the bloodstock, all that fantastic empire. He was the one to get close to. But you couldn't. Lord Hadfield had tried. It was thoroughly vexing that the fellow one liked was quite poor, and the fellow who was rich one didn't like. Silly state of affairs. Ironic. Perverse.

'That,' said Lord Goring, 'is Matthew Carver. The older man is the Duke of Hampshire. The tall man is George Whyte. The girl I don't know.'

'The others?' asked Prince Ghalib al-Jilani, in his near-perfect upper-class English.

'Of no importance. A small owner-breeder and a stipendiary steward.'

Prince Ghalib nodded. He was interested only in big game, and the trophies his white hunter was showing him were Rowland

Ward specimens indeed. He was a student of bloodstock and high society. In the one he had been successful, thanks to good advice, a lifelong familiarity with horses, and a personal income greater than that of a medium-sized country; in the other, in spite of advantages of which he was thoroughly aware, he had been disappointed. He had not been treated as a leper by the British and French aristocracies, but he was not welcomed as a friend and equal. It was hurtful.

For example, he had visited Lord Hadfield's private stud near Newmarket. He had seen the mares and foals. He had given the stud-groom his usual tip — £25. Lord Hadfield had been very affable and had offered him his choice of three foals. Ghalib reckoned himself a fair judge, and he knew the going prices. The foals were moderate and the prices extortionate. Ghalib was not that much of a snob. Hadfield was a Viscount, but the family was not old as desert Arabs counted age. Ghalib declined the foals, extremely politely. Hadfield did not, after that, invite him to stay for lunch. He should have done so. On the telephone the previous day, he had all but done so. The invitation was implicit. 'Buy a foal and you can have lunch with an English lord' — that was the line. Hadfield was not the real thing, though he was a Viscount and a member of the Jockey Club.

The Duke of Hampshire was the real thing. So, oddly enough, was Matthew Carver, about whom Ghalib had read in the *Thoroughbred Record* and the *European Racehorse*. His family had been established in Kentucky longer than Hadfield's in Suffolk. An English duke was slapping him on the back at this very moment. It was possible for an American, a certain kind of American. It should be possible for a prince of the royal blood.

Everything Ghalib could do he was doing. He was thirty-five, tall, athletic. Women were apt to say that he looked like one of his own hawks, aquiline, almost beautiful in a predatory way. His hair and eyes and heavy eyebrows were black and his skin almost white. His lips were thin but his smile broad. He had been to the most expensive orthodontist in Wimpole Street in his childhood; since his schooldays at Harrow he had been to the most expensive dentist in Harley Street. His tweeds were built by Huntsman and his shoes by Lobb. Everything else he wore was handmade, silk, and French. He was not scented except for a slight, correct whiff of Trumper's 'Coronis' on his hair. He was as right as he could be. He was not slapped on the back by the Duke of Hampshire.

Goring was a help but not a great help. He was a lord but he was poor and a professional bloodstock agent. That was what he called himself; other people called him a horse-coper. He was not even his own master. He was the British representative of a French agency, through whom Ghalib was negotiating the purchase of some broodmares. He was obliged to hold Ghalib's hand; he was paid to do so; they both knew it. Many introductions on the racecourse resulted, but few invitations. Goring looked like a weasel, an animal Ghalib had never seen but clearly imagined.

Ghalib looked with hunger at the party Goring pointed out to him. The duke was laughing, though he had in other ways the look of a drunken mute at a funeral. Matthew Carver was laughing. He had hazel eyes and light brown hair and he looked as though he played squash. The girl was laughing. She was standing with her back to Ghalib, laughing at something the duke was saying. The horses were going down into the murk at the start of the straight mile. The loudspeaker was naming them as they passed in front of the grandstand. The girl turned to look at them. Ghalib saw her face for the first time. He felt the familiar, savage tug of lust. He wanted that girl.

An unknown, ancient author, quoted by al-Ishaqi, had given the definitive account of female beauty in the eyes of an Arab: 'Four things in a woman should be *black*: the hair of the head, the eyebrows, the eyelashes, and the dark part of the eyes; four *white*: the complexion of the skin, the white of the eyes, the teeth, and the legs; four *red*: the tongue, the lips, the middle of the cheeks, and the gums; four *round*: the head, the neck, the forearms, and the ankles; four *long*: the back, the fingers, the arms, and the legs; four *wide*: the forehead, the eyes, the bosom, and the hips; four *fine*: the eyebrows, the nose, the lips, and the fingers; four *thick*: the lower part of the back, the thighs, the calves of the legs, and the knees; four *small*: the ears, the breasts, the hands, and the feet.' Ghalib, educated in the West and in the brothels of the West, preferred the narrow hips and slender legs which he saw the girl had, and the blue eyes which were vividly visible even at a distance. But al-Ishaqi himself could not have faulted the redness of the middles of her cheeks.

The law at home, in the Emirate of Halat al Bhudi, specified death by stoning for adultery and a hundred lashes for other fornication. Ghalib neither approved nor disapproved of these penalties: they were Islamic law and therefore the law of his land; they were immutable. But not in Europe. When Ghalib changed his clothes, on board his private jet, he did not forget the *ash-Shar,* the divine law revealed to and by the Prophet, but he put it on a shelf. He did as the Romans did, and he did it better because he was richer.

Ghalib wanted to meet the girl immediately, and to find out her name and where she lived. He wanted to meet Matthew Carver and George Whyte too, equally badly, though for different reasons. He wanted to meet the Duke of Hampshire out of a simple and innocent desire to be acquainted with English dukes. He told Goring so. But Goring did not feel able to break into the group, for none of whom had his agency acted and with none of whom had he more than the barest racecourse acquaintance. Pointing them out, he had given an impression of familiarity. Challenged, he stammered and stumbled and temporised. He seemed to be in a bad temper about something.

Goring was indeed in a bad temper.

He didn't like nursemaiding a Wog in public, even though the agency had made and would make a great deal of money out of this particular Wog. But it was not he, misunderstood and misused Goring, noble and deserving Goring, who would make the money. It was fat Henri de Cheminade, guzzling and showing off over there in Paris. That was manifestly unfair. Everything was unfair.

It was unfair that a Wog entrepreneur should have an income of millions and he, aristocratic and honourable Goring, a miserable salary from that fat Frenchipoo.

It was unfair that Hadfield had tried to sell a foal direct to Ghalib, without going through the agency. Even though he failed. He had *tried* to be unfair. It was typical of the rich.

It was unfair that Matthew Carver, who was not very rich, should be in partnership with George Whyte and the rest of that syndicate of multi-millionaires. He, expert and perspicacious Goring, should have been asked to join George Whyte's syndicate, replacing as Carver was supposed to do the financial contribution with his judgement and his contacts.

It was unfair that some damned interfering busybody had brought his mother to the races, all the way from London, dowdy and twittering and gushing, an intense embarrassment, an imposition. He saw enough of her at home. She wanted him to

6

introduce her to everybody, to all the glittering turf personalities she had read about in the *Daily Express*. She should have known better. He knew better. He couldn't imperil his standing by parading a mother like that. He couldn't understand his father having married her. She didn't fit as a peeress. She didn't fit anywhere, except at the kitchen sink. Even there she was always complaining.

Lady Goring was complaining, but not aloud. Never aloud. She only looked as though she had just complained very loudly indeed, and was on the point of doing so again. Her feet hurt, her back hurt, her feelings were hurt.

Edith Calverley had persuaded her to come, given her a lift. 'It's time you had a change, a bit of an outing. See some new faces, have a bob or two on your fancy.'

But Edith's car bounced. It was too small and light for a long journey. The drive gave Lady Goring a headache. The traffic was heavy and the visibility bad, so that Edith got into a sulk. They arrived a bit late, so they had a very long walk from where Edith parked the car. Then Edith thought she had done enough, providing the transport. Poppy Goring had to buy her own Day Visitor's badge. It was terribly expensive — six pounds and something. She had to give the man a cheque. She was shocked. She had not been racing for years and she had had no idea that they charged so much simply for letting you in. And she had thought she was Edith's guest. She thought that was the understanding. They went Dutch for lunch, too — racecourse sandwiches that gave Lady Goring indigestion. Then Edith had completely disappeared. It was like racing with Freddie in the old days, her charming and selfish husband. He always disappeared with his cronies, leaving her to spend the afternoon alone. At Ascot he bolted into the Iron Stand — no women admitted — and stayed there all afternoon drinking brandy-and-soda with glamorous clubmen whom Poppy never even met.

Once upon a time she had known Newmarket well. They stayed with the Hadfields for the races. She never saw Ralph Hadfield now. She had lost touch with nearly all Freddie's friends. She had lost touch with Newmarket, too. She had forgotten her way about. She thought they had changed it. There were new escalators and some new buildings. It was confusing and overcrowded. Everyone else knew where to go but she was lost

7

and puzzled. She thought Bobbety Bobs might have taken her under his wing. She called him that when she saw him. It was her private name for him, ever since he was little. He should have liked it. He was all she had and she was all he had. They lived together and she slaved for him. She was glad to. It was a mother's privilege. It was a pity they were so poor. He minded. He blamed her. Naughty Freddie had not been careful with money. The estate had gone and the London house and the cars and the pictures and the stud and the bloodstock. The broodmares fetched terribly disappointing prices at the auction. Perhaps they were not as good as Freddie had thought. It was hard for Bobbety.

Lady Goring found a place to stand where she could see the next race. She wanted to sit down but there was nowhere to sit. None of the names of the horses meant anything to her, and few of the trainers and jockeys. Few of the owners. It was all a new lot since the days when she came with Freddie in his chauffeur-driven Bentley.

She saw Bobbety Bobs in the distance with his client, his Prince Something. Of course he was here on business. He worked very hard. Perhaps she should not have expected him to look after her. She tried to help him in his business. She tried to get him to invite his clients home to the flat for dinner. Foreigners liked that, being made welcome in your home. But he never asked anybody home.

The race started, far away in the fog. Nothing could be seen. People at home, watching on their televisions, would be seeing much better. Lady Goring passionately envied them, not because she was interested in seeing the horses but because they were sitting down and warm.

She raised her race-glasses as the horses came into view at the bushes. She saw not one field of horses, but two. Every horse was duplicated, one image a little behind and above the other. They were Freddie's glasses, and he had dropped them too often on the concrete steps at Sandown and Lingfield and Windsor, at York and Doncaster and Ayr.

Matthew Carver was enjoying himself. He did not allow the sombre company of George Whyte to mar his enjoyment. He was excited. He did not object in himself to the childish quality of becoming excited. He preferred people who could be excited. He disliked the blasé pose of some of his richest friends, who never admitted to getting a kick out of anything. He liked the capacity for excitement in Rollo Hampshire and Ralph Hadfield and in his daughter Clare.

His reunion with Clare, here this afternoon on the racecourse, was the very best thing among many good things. He had not seen her for weeks. She had been with her mother in London, and he had only just crossed to England. She was the one he was closest to, of his three children. It was inevitable. When Mollie decided that she hated America and Kentucky and Matthew, the others were young enough to need their mother, and young enough to be uprooted without disaster to their education. But Clare was in the middle of high school and headed for college. Consequently, Matthew had one American child and two English children. It sometimes gave him a sense of disorientation, even of schizophrenia.

Clare was a great joy to Matthew. Her only problem was keeping out of trouble. Not drink or drugs or crime or bastards, but harebrained escapades which always seemed to send larger shockwaves further than anyone could have predicted. The time she visited the junior college in Vermont in the role of a Persian princess, olive-skinned and flamboyant, and had the President and the Dean of Students grovelling and toadying, until she could no longer keep a straight face and blew her own cover with helpless laughter. The time she burgled a men's dormitory on another campus, and executed an astonishing mural with aerosol paint-sprays. They valued the mural now — would not let the college redecorate the wall — but there had been awkwardness then.

None of it was evil but all of it was fraught with far-reaching and unpredictable consequences. You needed a seat-belt when Clare was around. She got away with murder because of the way she looked. She had inherited her mother's small-boned elegance but not, thank God, her massive, her almost magisterial, lack of humour.

Another reason for Matthew's enjoyment was simply being back at Newmarket. 'Headquarters', the English called it. It was some years since he had set foot on this ancient track, this almost holy turf. It was utterly different from any American track, and pretty different from any other European track. Only the Curragh remotely resembled it. Looking across the misty plain, it was easy to imagine Boudicca's Iceni camped, arming themselves for the last, hectic, savage resistance to the Romans. You could see pawky James I with his falcon on his wrist; Charles II on his favourite hack Old Rowley, busy inventing modern thoroughbred racing; Queen Anne, Frampton, Flying Childers, Fred Archer . . . Only a very unimaginative visitor, or a very ignorant one, could fail to be excited by the reek of this glorious history.

It was different from any other track in its huge expanse of grass, its bleakness, its thronging ghosts, the extraordinary way they ran the long-distance races from some invisibly remote point, almost straight, furlong after furlong, towards the grandstand. This was a test of a profoundly different kind from the tight, flat, three-quarter-mile dirt circuits, turning always left-handed, of America. The turf had been undisturbed since Boudicca's chariot-horses had grazed it. Everything here was differently named, differently managed. The shouting bookmakers. The metal annual badges. The horses coming for the day, and then going home to stables maybe at the other end of England. The people subtly different in dress and manner, and very different in voice.

Yet the absolute essence was the same, gloriously the same. The gut-tugging gallantry of the thoroughbred horse, the most beautiful living creature in the world. The most expensive living creature. The money tied up in that moderate-sized field of moderate horses now cantering down to the mile start — a million dollars? Three million? And in the big race the following day, the Champion Stakes, any one of half a dozen of the runners might be worth ten million dollars.

Beausoleil might be worth that and a great deal more. Beausoleil was reason enough, on his own, to have brought Matthew and George Whyte to England. He was probably the best mile-and-a-quarter horse in Europe. He had won the English Two Thousand Guineas, and three Group I races in France. As a four-year-old he had won the Eclipse Stakes at Sandown and the Benson and Hedges Gold Cup at York — a race which was the graveyard of so many glittering reputations. He was being retired after the Champion, and syndicated for stud. Matthew and George Whyte thought they wanted shares. Neither had seen the horse in the flesh, but they knew his pedigree and his racing form in minute detail. It was necessary now to see him as an individual, to see how he ran. Matthew was excited at the prospect. This might be a really great horse, who might become a really great stallion. One share — one fortieth part of the animal — might be cheap at $300,000.

The syndication was being managed by Henri de Cheminade and his Agence Fille de l'Aire. That was all right. Henri was not Matthew's favourite personality, and his English sidekick little Robert Goring seemed, on slight acquaintance, a dismal little prick. But they weren't buying them. Just giving them George Whyte's cheque.

The point about Beausoleil was not only his absolute excellence as a racehorse. It was also his particular breeding. He traced in tail-male to the mighty Nasrullah, like so many middle-distance champions, via a grandson re-exported to Ireland. On his sire's side he also represented the famous Nasrullah-Princequillo nick, a combination of bloodlines which had again and again proved itself so successful — which made both lines more influential than either could have been on its own. This blood was freely available in America. George Whyte's Cragrock Farm was full of it. But on his dam's side, Beausoleil represented a complete outcross, a potential injection of blood of the highest class almost totally unavailable to American breeders. That was what they would be buying, that Franco-Irish exotic strain, with speed and stamina both close up in the pedigree. Matthew had a hunch this would make another nick. He could not logically justify this belief, though George Whyte, being George, had tried to pin him down to fact, to computerised analysis of the genetics. To a cautious and self-aware extent, Matthew played hunches. There was good precedent. The great Federico Tesio had not bred Nearco by the book. There was an element of magic in it — faith — superstition.

There were other elements, too, firmly enough in the record to satisfy even George. Both Beausoleil's sire and his dam gave evidence of prepotence. As a result of line-breeding — the appearance of certain ancestors twice or more in the pedigrees — they had doubled genes controlling certain identifiable characteristics, which made them breed exceptionally truly, which made them 'stamp their stock'. It was highly probable that Beausoleil had inherited prepotence with the rest of his stunning qualities. He would breed good horses from bad mares and great ones from good mares.

Matthew had a good mare himself, at home in Kentucky —

one of the few animals of which he was sole owner — that he hungered to send to Beausoleil. He could see a Kentucky Derby winner out of that mating. He could see a filly out of that mating becoming one of the influential mares of thoroughbred history.

It did no harm to dream. Without dreams there would be practically nobody in racing and nobody at all in breeding.

Matthew would not know completely how he felt about Beausoleil until after he had seen him. But he knew how he expected to feel. It was exciting.

As well as this Beausoleil negotiation, Matthew and George Whyte would go to the yearling sales, held during both the Newmarket October race weeks. They might buy. If they did, it would only be the very best. It would be George Whyte's money, other money from other associates in various countries, and a little bit of Matthew's money. Buying yearlings was the greatest gamble of all. The margin of error could be reduced, but not to anything within a shout of vanishing-point. Even Vincent O'Brien, the wizard of County Tipperary, had had his abysmal failures. Far fewer than lesser men, because the margin *could* be reduced. George Whyte trusted Matthew to reduce it. Then he signed cheques. It was a good working arrangement. The horses might go to Kentucky, or stay in England to be trained. The partnership kept a few horses in training at Newmarket. It was smart to diversify, with dollars and sterling sitting on a perpetual seesaw. It was fun. And some horses were evidently suited by grass and gentle turns. Some could only act on a right-handed circuit, like Ascot or Longchamp.

Matthew had studied the catalogue and marked certain lots — yearlings by Northfields, Habat, Petingo, Blakeney, Nonoalco, all well enough bred to win a classic. The one he liked best was by Mill Reef, the American-bred who had won the Epsom Derby and the Prix de l'Arc de Triomphe for Paul Mellon, and now stood at the British National Stud. He had a very strong feeling about it, another hunch. But sight unseen he would not have bid a lead nickel.

Meanwhile, another excitement on this cheerful afternoon was that one of their horses was running, though it was only a minor excitement, because the horse had no chance of winning and would not try to do so. Fred Cottle the trainer had been clear about this on the telephone. 'He's a big baby, Mr Carver. He hasn't grown to his strength. I want to get one run under his belt, so he can see what a racecourse looks like and get an idea of why he's taken there. Then put him away for the winter. I wouldn't have bothered you to come and see him, but since you're here I'm glad you'll see him. He might make up into a nice three-year-old, but even next year don't expect him to be winning before June. One day he might be anything.'

Matthew was sure all this was absolutely sound. It was a godsend to deal with somebody direct, abrasive though Fred's manner could sometimes be. The colt was by High Line, a once-unfashionable stallion whose manager could hardly give nominations away — until he made history one bright afternoon at York, in a gale-force wind, by siring four successive winners. Nobody had ever seen such a thing before.

Matthew, Clare and George Whyte went to the top paddock where the saddling-up boxes are. They saw Fred Cottle, looking every year a little more like a pickled walnut or a leprechaun carved out of wood. He had once been a very skilful jockey whom not everybody absolutely trusted. Like many jockeys he had taken out a licence to train; like not so many he had been pretty successful. Not in a class with Jack Jarvis or Gordon Richards or Harry Wragg, but much better than average. He had seventy-five horses in his yard, a good staff, a deeply conscientious wife, and no virus for four years. What he wanted — what he had never had — was a classic winner before he retired. This was no secret. It was true of most other trainers in Europe.

Matthew greeted Fred Cottle as an old friend, and George Whyte greeted him as an old servant. Matthew wondered if this was as obvious to Fred as it was to himself. He imagined so. He had heard trainers say that their greatest problems were not with horses but with owners.

Matthew introduced Fred to Clare. Fred was shy with Clare, though not Clare with Fred. Fred was correct in word and manner, but pawky, reserved, abrupt. He would have preferred Clare not to be there, Matthew thought. Racing was a man's business. Women were distracting and dangerous. They were hysterical. They raised their hopes too high and they were bad losers and they blamed everything except their horses. That would be how Fred's mind instinctively worked. It was common enough, but it was silly in a country with so many great racing ladies, including a passionately involved and deeply knowledgeable Queen.

Aces High appeared in the top ring, rugged, not yet saddled, led round by the lad who looked after him. 'Did' him, as they said. He looked fit to run, but Fred Cottle could be trusted on a point like that. Certainly it was desirable to show him the track at least once as a two-year-old. The Rules of Racing said that every horse had to be ridden to win every time it ran: but nobody would apply the letter of that law to an overgrown, inexperienced baby.

'He's no more beautiful than most of his half-brothers,' murmured Matthew. Fred Cottle looked at him in surprise. Matthew remembered this other and most annoying semantic difference. In America, 'half brother' meant 'by the same sire'. In England and Ireland it meant out of the same dam — what America called 'uterine brother'. There was no convenient way of saying 'by the same sire' in English English — you had to use all those words. Some things English were better than some things American, Matthew thought, such as the granite attitude to drugs. But this phraseology was definitely an exception.

'Handsome is as handsome does,' said Fred Cottle.

Matthew remembered that Fred had bought the animal, at the previous October sales, on his own initiative, and passed three-quarters on to the partnership. George Whyte had two legs, Matthew one, Fred himself one. George Whyte and Matthew had broken all their usual rules, and bought their shares unseen on Fred's strong recommendation. It was fair enough. Fred was an excellent judge, the colt was cheap, and the arrangement reduced the training bills. The colt was not, therefore, a horse to be rude to Fred about. Matthew regretted his remark. Even men who looked like pickled walnuts had their sensitive spots, and Fred thought very highly of the High Line blood. Matthew drew him out on the subject, so that Fred could justify his faith in the ultimate merit of the horse, so that he could feel better about Matthew calling him ugly. They got into the higher flights of pedigree, of probable preference for sharp or galloping tracks, hard or soft ground, middle or long distances. Clare was interested but out of her depth. George Whyte listened attentively, frowning.

Fred Cottle sketched out his tentative ideas about the colt's three-year-old programme, inviting Matthew's opinion and comment.

Clare knew that George Whyte owned half the horse, her

father only a quarter. The funny little brusque, gnarled trainer should have been saying all this to Mr Whyte. Should at least have included him in the conversation.

Clare wondered if Mr Whyte minded being left out of a discussion in which his should have been the dominant voice. She tried, as she often did, to think herself into another person's mind. She found it impossible to think into George Whyte's. He was an android, something made of rubber on a wire frame, with a computer inside. A computer which had had an unhappy childhood.

Aces High was led away to be saddled. Fred Cottle went with him, picking up the tiny racing saddle on the way from the travelling head lad (a phrase which had to be re-remembered, Matthew thought, every time he came here).

A crowd had collected by the small ring, and surrounded the adjoining main parade ring. There was a fair hubbub of talk and of sniffing, and a lot of complaint about the weather. Between the asphalt paths the grass was churned into mud. Matthew waited, with George Whyte and Clare, for Aces High and Fred Cottle to reappear. He expected to see everybody. He did. Rollo Hampshire, loudly wishing them luck. Ralph Hadfield, who also had a runner in the race. Little Robert Goring with a tall, very handsome Levantine.

Aces High and Hadfield's runner were led into the main ring, joining the dozen horses already there. Aces High, new to all this, was nervous and on his toes, tossing his head, sweating lightly between his hind legs. Matthew, George Whyte, Clare, Fred Cottle, Hadfield and Hadfield's trainer followed the horses into the ring, as though inspection of the owners and trainers was as necessary a facility for the crowd as scrutiny of the horses.

Hadfield's trainer was an elegant fellow called Nigel Hughes. Matthew would not have sent a horse to Hughes, though Hadfield thought well of him, and he trained for other rich owners. He was in the greatest contrast to his fellow professional Fred Cottle. He was what had been known in the old days as a 'society trainer', an Old Etonian who had served for a few years in a famous cavalry regiment, ridden a few point-to-point winners, attached himself to a celebrated stable as Assistant Trainer, at a nominal salary, and then used his abundant contacts to set up in business for himself. There was no problem about his licence. He had an uncle in the Jockey Club.

Hughes did not run his stable on a tight rein, as Fred Cottle did. In spite of his time in the army, he was not a disciplinarian. His lads were scruffy. He gave an impression of slap-happiness, of excessive trust and good nature.

Ralph Hadfield's horse was favourite, and on the formbook deserved to be. He had run twice, respectably, without winning. He had the experience and he was at last fully wound up. He still got the maiden allowance — he was getting eight pounds from the three winners in the field. It should be his day. Everybody said so. Matthew gathered that Hadfield had had a small bet and Nigel Hughes a large one.

Like Aces High, Lord Hadfield's horse Green Camembert had been walked from his box to the racecourse stables during the morning. Green Camembert's lad hated the walk. He was wearing his new shoes, seventeen quid in Newmarket High Street, and they were maybe a bit narrow, and the heels were so high they forced his toes to the front. The sodding horse nearly trod on one shiny leather-look upper.

The lad was called Darren Finn. He looked Irish but he came from Ipswich. His Dad was a brickie and his Mam had gone off with a lorry-driver's mate. He'd done his year in Borstal for nicking lead off a roof. A fag with marbles in his mouth, what they called a Career Adviser, said being so small and light he might get a job in a racing stable. At the age of nineteen he'd had six jobs. He was never going to make it as a jockey. Still, there were rewards. This job with bloody Hughes was the best. Newmarket. More opportunities at a big training centre for a likely lad to do himself a bit of good. Darren never thought Hughes would have taken him on. But he never checked all the references. Trusted his own judgement. Darren could do the wide-eyed crap. Stupid shit, he deserved to be ripped off.

The bloke in the pub, whose name Darren never did know, said what was his horse's chance in the two-year-old race? Bloody certainty, said Darren. With a bucket of water just before the off? says the bloke. Can't promise, said Darren, the buggers watch you. Tip me the wink in the paddock, says the bloke — just a little nod if your horse had a nice long drink.

There was a tenner down, and another tenner if the horse was beat.

16

The bloody snoopers at the Equine Research Laboratory couldn't detect bloody water.

Darren made sure his horse was short of water all morning. Saved carrying it. Gave him a lovely big drink in the racecourse stable. Had to pick his moment, during a race. It went down quick. Horse was as thirsty as buggery. Gallons went down. That would stop him like concrete on his feet.

Darren led his horse round the parade-ring, going along behind the one the Yanks owned. Stuff them. Without seeming to, he looked out for his friend in the crowd. He saw him, in a brown fur hat. He gave his little nod. Then he nodded some more, like exercising his neck, like he had a stiff neck. When he looked again the bloke had gone.

The man in the brown fur hat hurried from the paddock into Tatts. He went to the rails which divide Tatts from the Members'. The credit bookmakers, facing into the Members', had their backs to him. He went to one called Trevor Plimsoll. He appeared to have a bet with Trevor Plimsoll. Certainly Plimsoll's clerk appeared to be writing something down in his book. It was not evident that he had retracted the tip of his ballpoint.

The man in the fur hat sauntered away, as though pleased he had had his bet. Trevor Plimsoll laid bets against Green Camembert, offering his more important customers 5 to 2, half a point better than the odds of 2 to 1 generally on offer in the ring. In a number of cases the half point made a difference of several hundred pounds.

Nobody noticed that Trevor Plimsoll was not laying off any of his heavy commitment against Green Camembert. Normally he would have hedged at least part of his liability. There was no change in his lugubrious yellow face or in his nasal voice.

He hedged all his bets against the second favourite.

Prince Ghalib al-Jilani decided it was time he had a bet. He had done plenty of racing in France but little in England. He betted heavily, but sensibly. He had started betting in France after he had begun to feel at home on the French turf — after he knew something about the form and breeding of the horses and the personalities of their owners, trainers and jockeys. He did not yet feel quite at home on the English turf but still he wanted to bet.

He saw Lord Hadfield in the paddock with his trainer Hughes. They looked pleased with life. They looked like men who thought their horse was going to win.

Ghalib asked Lord Goring about Green Camembert. Goring said it was a racing certainty at the weights and on its form at Catterick and Wolverhampton.

The horse itself looked fine. Ghalib was a good judge of both fitness and conformation. It walked torpidly round the parade-ring, in contrast to the excited, overgrown animal in front of it. This was probably good. A placid temperament, an indifference to noise and crowds and bustle, conserved all a horse's nervous and physical energy for the moment when the stalls open.

Ghalib wanted to back Green Camembert, and to do so he wanted to open a credit account immediately with a rails bookmaker.

Goring said that this was probably not possible with any of the leading firms, for a stranger, a foreigner, because Ghalib would not be able immediately to supply references acceptable to the bookmakers. If he was going to bet more than a few pounds, they would want a banker's reference or one from another bookie.

'But there's a smaller man I happen to know pretty well,' said Goring. 'He'll oblige anyone I vouch for.'

Goring led Ghalib to the rails and to Trevor Plimsoll. He had a brief, low-voiced conversation with Trevor Plimsoll. Ghalib politely withdrew out of earshot, since he was himself being discussed. Trevor Plimsoll felt able to extend the hospitality of his organization to Prince Ghalib, on Lord Goring's recommendation. Bills or cheques would be sent care of Lord Goring at the London office of the Agence Fille de l'Aire. A card and a copy of Trevor Plimsoll's rules would be sent. Meanwhile Trevor Plimsoll was happy to extend unlimited credit to His Highness.

His Highness had £5,000 to £2,000 on Green Camembert. This was a little bet. He was feeling his way.

The jockeys came into the paddock, tiny and garish. Fred Cottle's stable jockey came up to the owners and trainer and touched his cap. He was a calm dwarf, never in the top six but never out of the top dozen. Fred gave him no pre-race instructions. None were needed. The jockey knew the horse and the situation as well as his governor did. This race was part of Aces High's education, no more than that.

Aces High went down to the start with his head cocked hard to the right, looking with astonishment at the crowd. He had never seen a crowded grandstand before, or heard the braying of the bookies and of the loudspeaker commentary.

Green Camembert went down stolidly, hardly raising a canter.

Matthew Carver found his hands trembling, idiotically, in the excitement of running any horse in any race. He knew that, as far as Aces High was concerned, this was not a race but a rehearsal. Even so he was excited. He did not understand why anybody bothered to have anything to do with racing, unless this moment filled you with adrenalin and butterflies.

Clare's face was pink with excitement and with the cold.

George Whyte watched everything with grave attention. He was permitting matters to proceed. He gave his tacit consent to the running of the next race. It was impossible to tell what he was thinking. It did not seem that he was excited.

Aces High was slowly out of the stalls. He ran very green, wandering all over the immensely broad straight course from his low draw on the left almost to the far rails and back again. After three furlongs he got the idea, took hold of his bit, and ran with resolution up the stand rails. He finished with plenty left, in the middle of the field, not having been touched with the whip. The whole operation had been thoroughly satisfactory, and the jockey had done exactly as he should. Aces High had enjoyed himself, after a baffled beginning. Next time out he would be a different animal.

Green Camembert, profiting from his experience, broke quickly from his draw in the middle, ran prominently for a furlong, lost his place, went backwards through the field, and finished last but two.

Trevor Plimsoll was pleased with Lord Goring, and Goring was pleased he was pleased.

Friends are so important in a hard, unfriendly world.

Lord Hadfield looked angry, and Nigel Hughes mystified and a little sick.

The Stewards' Secretary knew Green Camembert's previous

form and had seen one of his other races. He drew the attention of the Stewards, as his duty was, to the discrepancy in the performances. The Stewards ordered a dope-test, and interviewed Hughes and his jockey. They did not accept Hughes's explanation because Hughes could give none. The jockey said the horse went down dead and came back deader. He tried to wake him up, but he didn't persist with the stick because the horse felt completely wrong. It was obvious to the Stewards, who knew them both well, that both trainer and jockey had expected the horse to win and were authentically mystified.

'It's just possible, sir,' said Hughes, 'that the horse hates Newmarket because he's trained here. I had a filly three years ago who was a stone better anywhere away from home.'

This suggestion was noted but not generally believed.

Clare was hailed by the young married couple who had given her a lift to Newmarket. She introduced them to her father and to George Whyte. They were pleasant, Matthew thought, but more English than enough. They reminded him of some of his wife's relatives. He offered them drinks, but they were meeting another friend in another bar. There was a complication about Clare's lift back to London. They hoped this would be solved over the drinks. Clare accordingly went off with them, arranging to meet her father later in front of the grandstand opposite the winning-post — the kind of arrangement that always seems foolproof in prospect, and often fatally non-specific in baffled and lonely retrospect.

Clare was told she was meeting someone she would like.

Matthew and George Whyte were in turn hailed by Lord Hadfield. He was hiding his anger, suspicion and sense of betrayal under his brushed-and-combed mask of good sportsmanship. All who saw him marvelled. No trace of disappointment did he show. A very parfit gentil sporting Peer of the Realm. A good loser.

Hadfield glimpsed simultaneously old Poppy Goring, whom he had known pretty well in the days of her husband's greatness. She had been all right then, if a bit dimmed and dwarfed by Freddie. It was unfortunate that he had left her without a bean. It was typical of Freddie. But it was no good trying to keep up with people who had dropped out. It was not really a kindness. They couldn't cope with the journeys and the tips and the incidentals.

They couldn't return hospitality. They couldn't dress themselves. Old Poppy couldn't dress herself. In the ordinary way, it would have been a kindness to pass by on the other side. But Hadfield hailed her — far too long since we've met — what fun to see you here — do you know my American friends? Mr Carver, Mr Whyte, Lady Goring. A drink? Of course you'll have a drink, Poppy, you too, Matthew, you too, George.

Green Camembert? Luck of the game. The going. Over the top. Too late in the season. No good squealing.

In giving drinks Lord Hadfield was not giving. He was investing in his image. It was only a couple of quid and it was money well spent.

Lady Goring was flustered. She had been all alone with her headache, her aching feet and back, her indigestion. Suddenly she was besieged by cheerful well-dressed men. Well, two of them were cheerful. It was like the old days, like Freddie's day. She was startled to be made much of by Ralph Hadfield. She was abashed to be addressed with respectful formality by the elegant Americans.

Ralph led his party to the small bar halfway upstairs in the grandstand, the one sternly and ludicrously called 'Members' Bar' because everyone is admitted. He bought drinks as though he liked doing so. He did not buy a bottle of champagne, but small gins and whiskies.

Lady Goring found herself, in the crush, beside Mr Whyte. She attempted conversation, as she had been brought up to do. He hardly attempted to reply. She was aware of his eye, almost imperceptibly flicking up and down her shabby tweeds, her inexpensive shoes, her knitted woollen hat from a Women's Institute sale. He excused himself abruptly, and moved away to talk to Ralph Hadfield. He left her alone by the bar with her unwanted drink and her aching feet.

Lady Goring was not as hurt as she would have been a few years before. It had happened so often.

The other American materialised beside her. She was too disheartened to make conversation. He made it. It seemed he knew her Bobbety Bobs. He said nice things about Bobbety.

He said, 'I'm absolutely exhausted, Lady Goring. I see two chairs over there which have just been vacated. If I don't sit down I shall fall down. What do you think?'

It was perfectly obvious to Lady Goring that Mr Carver was not in the least exhausted, but that he saw she was. She nodded vigorously, spilling her drink. She sank with passionate gratitude on the plastic seat of the chair. They had a pleasant chat about Bobbety Bobs, Ralph Hadfield, and the afternoon's racing. Lady Goring really enjoyed the conversation.

'You see, we've been asked to this dinner-party in Exning,' said Clare's friends. 'And . . .'

'And you want to go,' said Clare, wondering how she was getting back to London.

'Well, we really rather urgently do. What we'll do is ring up and see if we can bring you. At worst they can only say no. But I expect they'll say yes, as your Pa is staying with the Hadfields.'

The connection was illogical, but Clare understood it. It was the way her mother reasoned.

'I have to get back to London tonight,' said Clare. 'My mother . . .'

'Oh dear. There's Tom. Hi, Tom! What's your cordial? Do you know Tom Kavanagh, Clare Carver? Her Pa had a horse in the third.'

'Which one?' asked Tom Kavanagh.

'Aces High. My father only has a leg.'

'I noticed him. He'll win a race.'

'Not this year.'

'No. Maybe not next. He's a big fellow, isn't he? He might make a jumper, another Heighlin. Can I ride him?'

'Do you ride races?'

'Not as many as I'd like. I'm always sucking up to owners. I'll suck up to your father, if you'll kindly advise me what to say.'

Tom Kavanagh was dark, like Clare herself, small though not as small as herself, with grey eyes and an open, weatherbeaten face. He looked as though he had been rained upon, blown upon and sunned upon every waking minute for twenty years. Since he was seven. He looked about twenty-seven. When he smiled his eyes almost closed and a kind of triangular dimple appeared in his right cheek.

Clare's friends nervously and circuitously approached the subject of a lift.

'My car is terrible,' Tom said to Clare. 'Hardly to be dignified with the name of car at all. Its best days were many, many years ago and many, many owners ago. The springs in the seats go twang and dig you in the behind. But I'd far rather not drive all that way on my own. You'd really be doing me a favour to come. I had to warn you about the springs. Honour demanded it.'

'Do they really go twang?'

'Like a harp. A dozen harps.'

'A musical ride,' said Clare. 'That's nice.'

Matthew Carver thanked Lord Hadfield for the drink, and took his leave of Lady Goring. She was too grateful for the unimportant, the habitual courtesy he had shown her. He felt slightly a fraud, earning so much gratitude for so little.

He went down the stairs and out on to the grass in front of the grandstand. Talking to Fred Cottle and the jockey while Aces High was unsaddled, then drinking with Hadfield, had used up the half-hour between races. There was no time to see the next lot in the paddock. It was no deprivation, in this weather.

'Been looking for you, Matthew,' said a voice. 'I was going to call you this evening at Ralph's, but I'm glad to beard you in person.'

Matthew turned to see a familiar, grubby-looking man, not quite perfectly shaved, with unpressed trousers and a stain on his hatband.

Another horse-coper. Or, as he would say, bloodstock agent. A good deal grander in his trade than poor little Goring. Major Sir Merivale Lucas, Baronet, late of the Coldstream Guards, now head of the MidAtlantic Bloodstock Agency. Traded on his name and title. Quite legitimately. Goring tried to do the same thing, but Lucas was better at it. He had offices in London and New York, and he specialised in Anglo-American and Irish-American deals. He was a fixer. He was useful. He had had many dealings with Matthew Carver and George Whyte and their associates.

It was funny that he had never learned to shave or brush his hair or press his trousers. 'They called him "Scruffy" Lucas in the army,' Ralph Hadfield had once told Matthew. 'It drove him mad then and it drives him mad still. That's why his wife always calls him "Scruffy". It amuses her to drive him mad. It's the only fun she ever gets.' Ralph's stories were rarely altogether true, and never altogether kind, but this one had the ring of truth.

'Do you remember, ten years ago,' said Lucas, 'breeding a filly by Hedgerow out of Sweet Afton?'

'Yes, of course,' said Matthew. 'I sold her at Keeneland.'

'And they called her Meadowsweet, and she won five races. Do you know what's happened to her now?'

'No. I'd like to. I hate losing touch with my foals.'

'That's what I thought, and that's why I wanted to talk to you. Never mind the race, this is much more interesting. She went to stud at four, then changed hands a few times. She went to California for two seasons. I daresay that's why you lost touch. She's had some good foals, though not by top-class stallions. Nothing outstanding. No stakes winners. But the new owners think a lot of her. She's gone to Virginia, to a place called Fox Hill. Somerset County. Do you know it?'

'I've heard of Fox Hill,' said Matthew. 'Yes, sure I've heard of it. But not for a long time. I thought it had been out of business for years.'

'It was, but it's been revived. I'm acting for the owners in Europe. Looking for fillies that might make broodmares, mares in foal, the usual thing.'

'I wish them luck.'

'Yes, so do I. I love seeing a historic set-up re-restablished. The house is beautiful, breathtaking. You know those eighteenth-century Virginia houses. Fox Hill is a gem. Thomas Jefferson had something to do with it. Would you like to see Meadowsweet again?'

'Yes, very much.'

'Well, the owners would be tickled pink if you went there. It's more or less on your way home to Kentucky. You'll like the barns and the farm manager. You'll like the foals, too. Meadowsweet's got a very nice yearling colt. You'll want to see that. You might want to buy it. And then, you know, there's this . . .'

Matthew waited. Lucas seemed to be wondering how to phrase his next point.

'You and George and your mates have an awful lot of stallions, Matthew, and they're all in Kentucky. I know it's no great distance nowadays, but owners of mares very often pick a local stallion just because it's easier, just to save the hassle.'

Matthew nodded. It was silly but it was true.

'Have you thought how many broodmares there are in Virginia? Think of Rokeby alone. Think of all the farms round Middleburg and Upperville. You might have a great success with a stallion in Virginia.'

'That's possible.'

'And you might find Fox Hill just the place to stand him.'

'That wouldn't be my sole decision, as you know. But I might look at the place. I would like to see Meadowsweet again.'

'You do that, Matthew. I really wish you'd do that.'

Everything Lucas said was sensible. But Matthew wondered why he said it. Why he was so energetically espousing the cause of an unimportant stockfarm 3,000 miles away. Matthew guessed that either there was a strong personal reason, or Lucas owned a share of Fox Hill. The latter seemed more likely. Lucas didn't seem a man who did things for personal reasons. What he liked was money.

Matthew did not at once decide to go to Fox Hill, but he did not decide not to. He was intrigued about Lucas.

There was one more race. Clare watched it with Tom Kavanagh. He seemed determined to keep her close by his side. She was agreeable to this arrangement. She was curious about him, and she felt his curiosity about her. She knew she attracted him. She wondered if he knew how much he attracted her. It was satisfactory that they were to have an enforced two hours together, in the car with the twanging springs.

She met her father as they had arranged. He kissed her, and said, 'I guess I won't see you here tomorrow.'

'Why not?' said Tom, smiling at Clare so that his eyes almost disappeared and the triangular dimple appeared.

'Well, *why* not?' said Clare, feeling on her own face an equally broad smile.

'How long have you two known each other?' asked Matthew Carver, smiling also.

Clare gestured largely, indicating a lifetime's intimacy, or the utter unimportance of time.

Prince Ghalib al-Jilani saw, in the car park, the unknown girl he had seen with Matthew Carver. She was with another man, a young man, walking briskly through the darkening and dismal afternoon, among cars, towards a car. Ghalib was not interested in the young man. He was very interested in the girl, more even than before, because of the light and supple and bouncy way she walked, because of her slenderness and the unconscious arrogance of her carriage.

'Thoroughbred,' murmured Ghalib, who was a good judge of conformation and fitness, of breeding and performance.

In the car, amid the imagined twanging of the springs in the seats, they were able to begin to satisfy their curiosity about each other. They talked alternately or together, each answering questions but more anxious to ask them. Tom made no secret — could have made no secret — of his interest in Clare. She was uncharacteristically cautious. She did not want her heart to show vividly on her sleeve. Not yet. She had been taught by her mother about pride, and she strove to remember the lessons, although to her mind the pride that mattered was about quite different things. She had been hurt before by her emotional impulsiveness. She was not introspective, but it was impossible for her not to know that much about herself. But she did not think she would ever become a truly careful person. She didn't really want to. She didn't like truly careful people.

Tom learned that Clare spent most of her time in America but some in England. She did not say, but revealed, that the tug of war was sometimes agonising. Her parents were still married, but they very rarely saw each other.

'It makes a career pretty well impossible,' said Clare. 'So I do odd jobs in New York or Lexington or London or someplace, until I spin off again. I don't mind that. I don't want a career. I don't have *time* for a career.'

She realised she might be giving an impression she did not intend, so she added, 'I can't afford not to have a career, actually, but I still don't have one.'

Clare learned that Tom had been born in the West of Ireland, brought up in County Meath among hunters and thoroughbred horses, educated in England at Ampleforth and Cambridge. He had worked for three years as assistant manager of a big public stud in Kildare, but the stud had just been sold and the job disappeared. He was in England looking for a similar job. He didn't want to be a trainer. His passion was for horses rather than for racing, and especially mares and foals. His race-riding was strictly amateur, enjoyable, peripheral.

'I think it's insanely brave,' said Clare.

'So do I,' said Tom heartily. 'So do I. I'd think I was a hero if I wasn't always so bloody terrified.'

'It's braver to do something if you're frightened than if you're not.'

'I know. I tell myself that. It's funny how absolutely unconvincing it is.'

In the long term, Tom wanted to manage a really top-class thoroughbred stud. 'Breeding farm to you, or stockfarm, or whatever you call it.' Such jobs existed, but there were few of them. You needed contacts. Tom had a good many, mostly through riding in races, but they were not at a glittering international level. He had had a gentleman's education, but there were no lords in his family and his father was a country doctor.

'I'll be your contact,' said Clare.

CHAPTER 2

After the racing, Matthew Carver and George Whyte collected
Fred Cottle, and the three of them went to the Mercedes George
had hired. Matthew drove them into Newmarket, and they picked
up the vet whom Fred most trusted. They went out of Newmarket
on the Bury road, and after a few miles they rolled through the
unimpressive gateway of the Gallypot Stud.

The Mill Reef colt was boarding there for the sales, though he
had been foaled in Yorkshire and reared in Somerset. This fact
had been advertised in the leading sporting journals of a dozen
countries. He could be inspected by appointment. He had been
inspected, by dozens of trainers and agents. Matthew had made
his own appointment by telephone, from the Hadfields'. George
Whyte came along because most of the money was his; Fred
Cottle as a courtesy, and because he might possibly train the
animal; the vet because no inspection of a horse of any age is
complete without a check of heart and lungs.

They were expected. They were welcomed without enthusiasm.
The stud manager had no personal interest in the Mill Reef colt,
who was simply using them as a livery stable. These were almost
the last of the potential customers to come. Other people could
look at the colt in his box at Park Paddocks, in the paddock
outside the sale-ring, or in the ring itself.

The light was switched on in the loose-box. They looked in
over the half-door. A compact bay looked back at them with a
placid lack of interest. There was a hayrack above his head. There
was a wisp of hay in his mouth, which he was meditatively
chewing; there was hay in his mane.

Matthew stared for a long moment.

At this stage all he could do was eliminate the obviously
hopeless. He could see any glaring fault of conformation. It saved
time and trouble. There was nothing obviously wrong with this

colt and much that was obviously right. That was all that could be said, while the animal was munching hay in a loosebox.

'Do you have a light outside here?' Matthew asked the manager.

'Yes,' said the manager sadly. He had been expecting the question, but hoping it wouldn't be asked.

He turned on a big light over the door of a nearby box, which flooded the small stable-yard with a kind of damp radiance. A groom, who looked to Matthew like a cross between Snoopy and Fred Cottle's grandfather, appeared. He clipped a strap to the colt's leather head-collar, and led him out into the yard.

'Just have him stand there for a minute, please,' said Matthew.

He walked round the colt slowly, several times. He inspected it from every angle. He was looking critically, analytically, for specifics, and he was waiting for a mystic voice to tell him that this would be a champion. Precisely, he looked at the slope of the shoulders, those crucial shock-absorbers which have to be at exactly the right angle; the spring of the ribs, for depth in front for heart and lungs, and not too rapid a tapering towards the loins; for hocks of a strength and conformation to propel the whole weight of the horse forward with every stride; for a perfect proportion between forelegs and withers, and between all parts and all other parts; for an elegant setting-on of head on neck and neck on shoulder . . .

Nobody said anything. Matthew seemed to go into a trance. He knew he was making the stud manager bored and impatient, and probably late for his tea. He was sorry about that, but he would not be rushed.

He asked the groom to lead the baby round: round and round, one way and then the other.

He was seeing the skeleton articulating under the skin and the unformed muscles. He was visualising the muscles that would be developed in forearm and second thigh and quarters, by feed, work, strapping. He was visualising the whole machine, in six or eight months' time, at full gallop.

He heard the mystic voice, speaking from his own gut, and the voice said that this was a champion.

The vet checked respiration and heart with his stethoscope. It was unlikely in the last degree that he would have anything to report.

Even as Matthew watched the vet prodding at the colt with the stethoscope (which the horse seemed to enjoy), he thought of the extraordinary mumbo-jumbo on which some buyers relied. Measurement here to be exactly half measurement there. No white on a leg. Theories about ears and manes and feet. Some of this was altogether rubbish, and some largely rubbish with an element of value, like the Bruce Lowe numbers and the 'dosage' system for assessing pedigrees. To Matthew himself his own judgement seemed largely instinctive, but he knew it was acquired. It was experience. The voice was experience. It came from the gut because that was where experience settled, and produced a reaction which seemed emotional and instinctive.

They thanked the groom, and Matthew tipped him. They thanked the stud manager. They drove away. They swore the vet to secrecy, which was rude but needful.

'We must have him,' said Matthew.

Fred Cottle sat in the dark in the back of the car, beside the vet, in an agony of suspense.

England or America?

Fred respected Matthew Carver's judgement and he respected his own. He thought this colt was a Derby winner. He wanted to train him very badly indeed.

Matthew Carver was speaking. He said, 'I heard or read someplace that they sent Mill Reef to England because he had slightly long pasterns. They figured he'd go better on grass.'

Fred Cottle wanted to shout — Yes! A horse with long pasterns will break down, digging into the dirt on those tight turns! And this one's got his sire's long pasterns! Keep him here! For Christ's sake keep him here!

'It's not a fault,' said the vet. 'You can't fault Mill Reef in any way.'

'You can't fault this colt,' said Matthew Carver. 'But he has long pasterns, and I think we'd be smart to keep him here.'

A bird sang in Fred Cottle's leathery heart.

'Do you agree, George? He can go to Kentucky when he retires.'

George Whyte nodded, which was pointless in the dark. He had not noticed the long pasterns. He knew what Matthew looked for, but his own eye saw only a horse.

They dropped the vet at his home and Cottle at his yard, and drove to Hadfield, near Mildenhall. They found Ralph Hadfield squatting in his study surrounded by pieces of paper. He was trying to plan matings for his mares. He consulted Matthew, George Whyte was standing there, serious and attentive, but Hadfield consulted Matthew.

'This one,' he said. 'Almost unraced. Third in the Guineas when she wasn't fit, then got the virus and never ran again. Look at the breeding. She's got a yearling by So Blessed, filly-foal by Grundy, and in foal to Blakeney. What do you think, Matthew? Where would you send her, supposing nominations grew on trees?'

Matthew looked at the pedigree and at a photograph of the six-year-old mare. Wheels turned in his mind and patterns formed, of inbreeding to the very great at three or four removes, of outcrosses to complementary lines.

His mind went click.

'Beausoleil,' he said.

'Ah,' said Hadfield. 'Ah. I'll talk to that fat crook Henri.'

'You can talk to little Goring,' said Matthew.

'Yes, but I don't want to.'

Tom Kavanagh dropped Clare in a cavernous street off the Cromwell Road, outside the building where her mother's flat was. He asked her to ask him in for the drink he said he deserved, and he asked her to come out to dinner.

She thought for a moment, her face unusually solemn. She said she would not ask him in, or come out to dinner. She did not explain.

But he was picking her up in the morning, to drive her all the way back to Newmarket, in the car with the twanging seat-springs.

He drove away puzzled but exulting, to the house of the friends with whom he was staying in Fulham.

Clare walked up the one flight of stairs, drably carpeted in a pattern once jazzy and encouraging. There was a smell of half-remembered magnificence, and of dust and boiled vegetables. Clare tried to keep her heart from sinking, at the thought of the evening ahead with the mother she loved.

The weather changed during the night. The dawn was clear.

The sky gave promise of a kind of last effort of summer, like the capering of a senile man, or the crimson mouth of a dowager. The horizontal sun affected to promise more than it could possibly deliver. Matthew Carver viewed the bright dawn with suspicion. He always viewed English weather with suspicion, and especially during the Newmarket April and October meetings. It was another example of instinct deriving from harsh experience.

He was brought a cup of tea at six-thirty, this being deemed indispensable for anyone starting any day. He shaved in water that had not yet been heated by Ralph Hadfield's arrangements, the time-clock on the boiler being set for civilized hours. Ralph said it saved him £200 a year, which paid the training-bills for one horse for two weeks and two days. He enjoyed calculations of that kind, but it was hard on early-rising guests. Unusually, Matthew regretted not using an electric razor. Shaving with soap and a blade made him feel clean and fully awake. There was, perhaps, an element of puritanism in this, of ritual self-scraping to propitiate a jealous Old Testament God. That would fit with the ethos of his bible-thumping ancestors, who had gone from Yorkshire to Rhode Island in order to live undisturbed in the glow of hellfire, and only then, somewhat relaxed in fervour, crossed by the Cumberland Gap with their dogs and horses, and staked out their acres of Kentucky.

Matthew dressed casually and warmly. He went downstairs, seeing no one. He drove off in George's hired Mercedes. He stopped a little short of Newmarket, on the Norwich road, where other cars were parked.

To the left rose, vastly and gently, the stretch of ancient turf which is Warren Hill and Long Hill, part of the fractured empire assembled for the Jockey Club by Admiral Henry Rous 120 years ago: the 'Bury Side' gallops, which with the 'Racecourse Side', the 'Limekilns' and the 'Railway Lands' comprise the Newmarket training grounds. Charles II was painted here, sitting in a little pavilion, watching the horses of noblemen and gentlemen being given their 'breathers' in heavy clothing, in the liveries of their coats of arms, by training-grooms and riding-boys. Then all was amiable improvisation. Now only certain strips of ground can be used on a given day, marked by little dead bushes stuck into the turf and daily moved. Trainers are allotted times and places by the Jockey Club Agent, and pay an annual gallop-fee for each horse in their yards.

Fred Cottle was due at 7.30. Matthew was a little early.

Other strings of a dozen or three dozen horses were circling before their work, or cooling off after it. No mechanical walkers here. Strings were leaving the gallops in Indian file to go back to the pampered tedium of their stables all over Newmarket. Other strings were arriving by the minute. Some of the trainers arrived in cars big or little, and stood watching their teams work. Many rode hacks, often broken-down or useless thoroughbreds once the stuff of somebody's dreams. One rode a dainty Arab stallion, and one a big cob like a Welsh farmer's. The place was swarming with horses in the early glitter of sunshine: incalculable numbers of scores of millions of dollars' worth. The same might be seen at Lambourn and Malton, on the Curragh and at Chantilly. Nothing like it could be seen in America, where there is no such thing as a training centre, except a racetrack where some horses are visiting. To Matthew it was the big magic. Ancient, as efficient as tomorrow. The horses pounded up the slope, singly or in twos and threes or small batches of two-year-olds, at intervals of a few seconds.

Nobody used a stopwatch. Another striking difference. What was valid on unvarying flat dirt was meaningless on this resilient, growing, ever-changing turf.

The occasion was public. Anybody could come and watch. A few people did — owners, the 'Newmarket men' of the sporting press, once reviled as touts and hunted from their hiding-places with bloodhounds, and the simply curious, the simply marvelling, like Matthew.

Fred Cottle arrived in his Jaguar, and stumped across the grass to where Matthew stood. His head lad arrived a moment later on horseback, followed by the file of titupping racers. All the lads and stable-girls wore crash-helmets. All the horses wore rugs with 'F.C.' in the corner. The head lad had the list, given him by Fred the night before, of exactly what each horse was to do in what company. The horses went to the far end of the gallop and began circling. The head lad sent them off. They hurtled up the long slope, on wet grass which was touched with silver by the sunlight, the lads like lizards on their necks. Fred had no need of a copy of his list. He knew every horse in his care as though he had given birth to it.

Then Matthew followed Fred's car to Palgrave Lodge, on the edge of the town, a 'racing-box' built for himself by a nobleman in the year of the Indian Mutiny. It had been inhabited by a succession of trainers since the nobleman's bankruptcy in the year after the Mutiny. It was really much too grand for Fred Cottle but it went with the stable-yards, the covered school, and the schooling paddock for the jumpers. Fred's furniture, Fred himself, were dwarfed by the high ceilings and doors and splendid, ugly Victorian fireplaces. He looked like a bantam in a peacock's cage. He was dwarfed by his wife, too. To Matthew, she was stately in a sociable way. She seemed to him to have come from a higher, or at least a more pretentious, starting-stall; but he knew that the complexities of English social grades were impenetrable to an outsider.

Matthew had breakfast with the Cottles, bacon and eggs and toast and marmalade, and coffee from a silver pot which was undoubtedly a gift from a grateful owner. The dining-room was lined with pictures of horses, as were the hall and all the passages. Matthew wondered what happened to a trainer when he had no more room on his walls for his winners. Presumably he retired.

Outside, fleetingly visible from the dining-room windows, the morning bustle of the stable was in full swing — the daily disciplined chaos of mucking-out, feeding, watering, grooming, cleaning tack, breaking out bales of hay and bedding, mothering seventy-five fragile and valuable animals every one of which was a little bit different from all the others.

After breakfast, Matthew and Fred watched three young steeplechasers being schooled over the practice fences. Fred was unusual among the leading Newmarket trainers in having a few jumpers. He did it partly from pure enthusiasm, partly to keep the wheels professionally turning during the winter, partly to oblige a few important owners. Matthew was one of these — important in influence if not in investment. He always tried to have at least one jumper in training in England. He had one now, owned in partnership with Fred, a five-year-old Irish gelding called Poetaster, bought as an unbroken three-year-old 'off the field' in County Roscommon, so far unraced, expected to make his début in a novice 'chase in December. Like many Irish horses, he was a natural jumper. He hardly had to be taught.

'After one race, we'll never have to school him again,' said Fred.

He was being schooled now, by a rider as Irish as himself, over scaled-down copies of steeplechase fences and over flights of small hurdles. He pinged them with energy and enjoyment. Matthew's half had cost him only £2,000. He might get that back, and the training and racing expenses, but he did not bank on doing so in a sport so shot through with chances and accidents. At the end he had, perhaps, a nice hunter worth a few hundred, or a trainer's hack, or a cripple. There was no possibility of the vast increase of value which might come with Beausoleil or the Mill Reef yearling. You went into jump racing for pure sport. Any other approach was folly.

'I'd like to get Mr Whyte interested in National Hunt racing,' said Fred.

'I don't think you ever will,' said Matthew.

Matthew went straight from the Cottles' to Park Paddocks, Messrs Tattersalls' establishment on the edge of the town at the racecourse end. He was correctly dressed for the sales, where most men wear Husky jackets and tweed caps, and most women wear headscarves. There were already a lot of cars in the steep and serpentine car-park, and a lot of horse-boxes, and a lot of people.

Yearlings were transferred in their hundreds from horse-boxes to Tattersalls' stables. When their numbers approached, they were taken out and led round outside. People lined the rails, scrutinising. People had drinks in the bar under the seats inside. People were photographed by men from agencies. A board outside showed in lights the number of the lot currently under the hammer. A loudspeaker carried the auctioneer's voice outside.

The Mill Reef colt was expected to come up at 11.30.

Matthew saw George Whyte. He saw Goring and his Levantine. He saw Ralph Hadfield with his trainer Nigel Hughes, and almost everybody else he knew in English racing. There were several Frenchmen he knew and several he did not, some evident Texans and equally evident Californians, and a sprinkling of cold-looking Arabs.

Matthew and George Whyte were joined by Fred Cottle, who was leaving his head lad to oversee the second lot on the gallops, as he had to do most days in the summer when he went himself with his horses to the races. They saw the Mill Reef walking around, lovely by daylight as by lamplight. There was a stir of interest. There were other Mill Reefs in the sale, but this was the one the pundits liked.

Matthew, looking at the colt, heard again the voice from his gut: 'Yes. We must have this one.'

They went inside, and found seats near the arch where the horses were led in, in full view of the auctioneer. Matthew was excited and he saw that Fred was excited. George was George. There were two lots to go before the Mill Reef, sent up by the same Somerset breeder. They were nice but not glamorous. The bidding hung. Matthew had leisure to compare this, one of the world's very greatest sales, with the others. Essentially it was exactly the same as Keeneland, and attended by many of the same people. The weather was notably different, giving the crowd a notably different look. This circular arena was different, and very handsome. It was warm. Matthew remembered the old sales-ring here, roofed but open; at the December sale of foals, a man could get hyperthermia during the sale of a single lot.

Here there was room for the horse to be led round, quite a distance round and round, all the time it was being auctioned. At Keeneland it could be turned, but no more. It stood on a little stage, above the audience, like a character in a Goldoni play, with the auctioneer still further above, like another character in the same play. The Tattersalls system was better. A greater difference was in reality quite unimportant — the voice and delivery of the auctioneer. The Englishman barked the bids as he got them, and rather hectored his bidders. 'I'm selling at £34,000. It's against you on the left. He's too cheap. £35,000, will you?' He spoke. He didn't intone. He had none of the sing-song, bubbling, non-stop, ritualistic, incantatory quality of American auctioneers. It was a pity. It didn't make any difference to the business done, but that chant added a kind of crazy magic.

The Mill Reef colt came in. There was a buzz of attention. Matthew felt his palms wet and his mouth dry.

It would have been a good thing to have had an agent bid for them anonymously, and to hide their own interest. Everybody here knew that George Whyte could afford any price. His visible participation — even if Fred Cottle did the bidding — would surely send the price up. But George would bid. He always did. It was something Matthew dimly understood.

The bidding started at a totally unreal figure, and was quickly carried up to £100,000 by equally unreal contestants.

Lord Goring came in at £300,000. It was evident that he was bidding for his Arab.

Goring fought off one well-known agent, then another (who bid by wagging his pipe up and down in his mouth), then a French trainer (who bid with his cigarette-holder). The price began to approach the highest ever paid for a yearling at public auction in Britain. Goring seemed to himself and to everyone to have secured it, at a price just short of the record.

The colt walked round and round, placid, seeming to be quite aware that he was the centre of attention, seeming to enjoy it.

George Whyte bid, by way of a folded newspaper. The auctioneer did not immediately see him, but one of the alert young men flanking the rostrum picked up the bid and told the auctioneer about it. Goring bid, by nodding briskly, equalling the record. George bid, nodding. There was a soft, electric hum of intense excitement. The colt was the calmest creature in the building. The lights blinked on the board, almost simultaneously with Goring's bid. George bid. There was a rustle of murmured speculation. A lot of people did not recognise George. Almost nobody knew Ghalib.

Translated into dollars, Goring's next bid just about equalled the current Keeneland record of nearly $2,000,000. George bid. Goring conferred with his client. He looked like a determined weasel, and then like a miserable weasel. He turned his back on the auctioneer.

Somebody came up deferentially to ask George his name, because the auctioneer did not immediately recognise him. His name was recognised and his bid was known to be good.

George's moment of glory was soured. They ought to have known who he was. They knew who Matthew Carver was.

Matthew agreed to take a one-eighth share in the Mill Reef yearling. It was all he could afford. It was far more than he could afford, but he foresaw great joy and great profit.

The colt was to go at once to Palgrove Lodge. Gently, patiently, Fred Cottle and his men would break him. He would run on the bouncy grass of England, and never, never risk those pasterns on dirt.

Fred was not given to showing his emotion. But he could not restrain, or even diminish, the huge grin that split his pickled-walnut face.

Ghalib was disappointed. But George Whyte had had the look of a man prepared to go on for ever. Ghalib could afford to go on almost for ever, but there came a point when a price became unreal. Ghalib had not made a fortune by buying at unreal prices. He shrugged, and considered other yearlings on his short-list.

Goring felt sick with anger. He had been betrayed by Ghalib and by George Whyte.

Matthew and Fred Cottle had drinks in the oddly tawdry bar, reminiscent of bars on English provincial station platforms. George Whyte did not care to join them. He remained in his seat, cynosure of some eyes.

Fred was allowed to confirm to a couple of journalists that the colt would be joining his string, and would race for a group of owners headed by Mr George Whyte of Kentucky. Matthew confirmed his membership of the group.

Fred was congratulated, with unconcealed envy, by fellow trainers.

It was quite obvious to the journalists, and would appear in their columns next day, that this sensational purchase joined the pattern for which the group's operation was known. You bought a yearling of the very highest class, at the very highest price. You won races of international importance and celebrity. You syndicated it for stud at a cost to the subscribers which represented a massive appreciation of the value of even the most expensive yearling. You turned a million dollars into six or eight or ten million in two years, a bigger and faster profit, free of all tax, than anybody could make in any other way.

If you won the big races.

To the rest of the world, the operation had two great merits. Since winning big races was the essence, all the horses always ran absolutely openly; they ran to win. Betting coups, even the biggest, were trivial compared to the seen merit of a horse. Honesty *was* the policy. Secondly, it was perfectly agreeable to the group to sell perhaps thirty-five of the forty shares to thirty-five different people. Some of these thirty-five would sometimes sell nominations — lease, in effect, their share of the horse for one season to another breeder. The effect of this was to make a great stallion widely and internationally available. All you needed was money.

The operation had one demerit in the eyes of the world. Men as rich as George Whyte and his friends cornered the market in the best. Nobody else could compete. There was bound to be envy and resentment. The long purse is courted but not loved.

In his euphoria, Fred Cottle told Matthew that he had on his own initiative bought a yearling two days before, at the very beginning of the sales. It had been sent up by a breeder only just admitted to these sales, and consequently given the worst position in the catalogue, at the very beginning, before anyone had arrived, before serious business had begun.

It was bad luck for the breeder but it was good luck for somebody.

The colt was sprint-bred pure and simple. It was a February foal, born unusually early, and consequently well advanced for its theoretic age of one year. It was the perfect 'early sort', one to pick up a sequence of races at the beginning of the season, and maybe in the South of France before the English season began.

A horse of this class was of no interest to George Whyte.

Matthew liked owning some horses he could call entirely his own. It was exciting and rewarding to be associated with great horses far beyond his financial class, but it was nice to have humble and independent fun as well. He said that, if he liked the horse, he would buy it.

Back to the races, respectably dressed, in a fitful and chilly sunlight. The parade-ring at 2.45, the runners for the Champion Stakes. Beausoleil. A bright bay with a white blaze, a little bigger than average. A midsummer sheen to his coat. Matthew knew exactly what he was looking for, here in the paddock, and when the horse went down to the start, and in the running of the race, which he won with contemptuous ease. Matthew was looking at conformation, temperament, action, stamina, finishing-speed, courage, fidelity to the bloodlines he represented. He was looking for a physical individual who measured up to his pedigree, and an athlete who measured up to his form.

It was all there. The gut-voice expressed what the eye saw.

There was a hint of savagery in Beausoleil's eye. This was the reverse side of the coin of indomitable and heritable courage. In a ding-dong finish on a punishing uphill straight, a horse with such an eye would fight, and fight, out of pride, out of arrogance, out of anger. Many very great racehorses and stallions had had this eye — Aureole, Nasrullah, Ribot. Matthew well remembered in the late 1950s keeping well out of the way of Ribot's teeth and hoofs, when he saw him at Dormello. Ribot became the most important sire of middle-distance horses in the world. Beausoleil had that potential. But he would need very firm and patient handling when he went to stud.

George Whyte accepted Matthew's certainty. He said he would take up all available shares in Beausoleil, though he would probably not keep them all.

Matthew sought out Lord Goring. Goring's Arab politely withdrew, but not far. The conversation was brief, and satisfactory to both parties. Some shares were still available, at $500,000. This gave Beausoleil a value, almost exactly predictable, of $20,000,000. Goring would immediately contact his boss in Paris. Matthew was available to go to Paris. He would conduct any needful negotiations on behalf of the purchasers, as Henri de Cheminade was conducting them on behalf of the owner.

Goring felt that Matthew Carver was really no more than an agent, really no better than himself.

From a public telephone in the grandstand, Goring called Henri de Cheminade, reversing the charges, in his apartment in the Avenue Victor Hugo. He reported the conversation with Carver. Henri replied in his soft, fat pussy-cat voice, in the excellent English which his trade required. He said that Carver should come to Paris the following day, and the day after that, Monday, should present himself at the Haras du Coq, near Calvados, at noon. There its owner and Beausoleil's owner, the duc de Montfermainbrey, would be; and there all day Henri de Cheminade would be.

Henri wanted to get back to his mistress, an impatient Senegalese with purple gums and watermelon hips; but Goring had more to impart.

'Our Wog wants to buy a stud,' he said.

'Find him one,' said Henri.

'As a personal negotiation? I mean —'

'You mean, if Ghalib pays a buyer's commission, do you get the commission? That depends on the size of the commission, *mon petit.*'

'The other thing is, he wants to buy into George Whyte's

syndicate.'

'I would like to myself. Why does he want to? He's rich enough not to need partners.'

'It's something to do with a girl. He's discovered who she is. I don't know who she is.'

'What a funny reason. I think it is not possible. They would have Ghalib as a partner if they wanted his money, but they have plenty of money. Far too much money. Everybody knows that. Did you buy the Mill Reef colt?'

'George Whyte bought it.'

'There you are.'

Someone had seen Matthew Carver talking to Lord Goring, immediately after the Champion Stakes. Someone overheard Goring talking on the telephone to Paris. Thus the whole Press Room knew that George Whyte and his friends were planning to cap their purchase of the morning with a part of Beausoleil.

The man who did the TV interviews between races heard within minutes. He sent his runner to sniff out Matthew Carver. The runner found him, as he expected, by the top paddock. He was in a crowd of people who included George Whyte, and a very pretty girl, and a young man with a brown face and a wide Irish smile. Lord Goring was just leaving this crowd, and rejoining a tall Arab unknown to the runner.

Mr Carver was agreeable to being interviewed on television. Mr Whyte agreed with him that their group had no secrets from the British television audience.

On the face of it, it was odd that the TV interviewer did not want George Whyte. But nobody seemed much surprised that it was Matthew Carver he asked for.

Matthew did not think deeply about this unimportant eccentricity. If asked, he might have said that George didn't like that kind of thing, was shy in front of the cameras, preferred to let Matthew act as spokesman, as he had so often done.

George Whyte thought, *Why not me?*

After the fourth race, Matthew went to the television interview room overlooking the paddock. He discussed briefly with the interviewer, a jockey turned journalist, what they were going to say to each other.

'I believe Jodie Parrish has someone to talk to us,' said the linkman.

'Thank you, Reg. Yes indeed.'

Matthew introduced. Nods and smiles on both sides. Interviewee removes hat to reveal thick, slightly unruly light brown hair.

'Welcome back to British television screens, Mr Carver, and now tell us first of all about that epoch-making moment this morning.'

'The epoch won't last very long,' said Matthew, 'if prices go on as they are.'

'Very true, very true.' Confirm the colt will stay in England to race. Popular decision. Confirm will be trained by Fred Cottle. Fred, earlier interviewed, over the moon.

George Whyte, watching the interview on a screen in one of the bars, did not think Matthew was handling it well. He was not giving enough publicity to Cragrock Farm and Stables, to the syndicate, to George Whyte.

'Would I be right in guessing, Mr Carver, that you were impressed by Beausoleil's performance this afternoon?'

'Sure. He went right away from a high-class field. I'd say it was highly impressive.'

'And?'

'And —' Matthew grinned — 'you're asking me to make a statement that would be a little premature. I am going to Paris tomorrow. I do have a date to meet the owner of the horse and the agent managing the syndication. That will show you we're interested. More than that I can't say, until maybe Tuesday.'

'Quite understood.'

Time for a quick word on a completely different subject. The interviewer not wishing to pry, but this a matter of great interest in the thoroughbred world. Briefly, rumour hath it that a major financial partner in the syndicate for which Mr Carver is speaking has dropped out. Is this true?

This is true. Too well known to deny. But Mr Carver not presently empowered to reveal the name. No, they have no plans as of now to bring in another partner. Obviously that will be discussed. Something to be kept under review. Such a step not to be ruled out. If and when it happens it will be no secret.

'Nothing we do,' said Matthew Carver, 'ever is secret, or

intended to be. We operate in a goldfish bowl.'

'A big goldfish bowl,' said the interviewer, and they both laughed.

Mutual thanks, smiles, goodwill; the interview terminated as the runners for the fifth race came into the paddock.

Ghalib and Goring were watching the interview on a screen in another bar. They turned to look at each other, the same supremely obvious thought in both their minds.

'I've just had a very good idea,' said Goring. 'Excuse me for a minute.'

Henri de Cheminade extricated himself from the damp black arms which were trying to meet round his waist. Naked and obese, he sat on the side of the bed with the telephone in one hand and a black breast in the other. A black hand toyed distractingly with his cock, but business was business.

'First,' he said, 'you must persuade Ghalib to buy shares in Beausoleil. I will make sure they are available to him. That will bring him into inevitable contact with Whyte and his friends. Then, to discuss this and other things, Ghalib shall come to Paris and to the duc's on Monday. There he shall meet Carver, under my — my chairmanship, if you like. *Ai! Qu'est-ce que tu fais, diable?* It will be a nice calm meeting in a quiet place, you know, with time to talk. Better than the hurlo-burlo of the races. Is that quite right? Hurlo . . . *Assez, folle! Ca va te frapper aux yeux . . .*'

'Won't mother want to see you?' said Clare.

'What do you think?' said Matthew.

'You know she has a new apartment.'

'Of course I know.'

'Sure. I guess you paid for it . . . You seem awfully calm about it.'

'I am calm about it, honey. One thing I try to be, in the whole mess, is calm.'

'I know you do. So do I.'

'But I do want to see Jamie and Liz. I can't stand them being strangers, almost foreigners. I must see them.'

'Yes, you have to. And I have to go.'

'With Tom Kavanagh?'

'The seats of his car go twang. How can I resist that?'

CHAPTER 3

Matthew Carver and George Whyte drove back to London after the races on Saturday, over the hospitable protests of the Hadfields.

Lord Hadfield wanted a nomination to Beausoleil.

George Whyte was catching the morning Concorde to New York, where he had an appointment that would have surprised his friends but not his family.

To Matthew Carver he said simply, 'I have an important business appointment in New York,' expecting an answering curiosity of which Matthew showed no trace.

In spite of his conversation with Clare, Matthew telephoned his wife at the new number Clare had given him. He had not seen her for nearly a year. He was concerned about her. Clare's account of her had been guarded and ambiguous: not the way Clare usually talked. Mollie was still doing her prison visiting but she had given up her Transcendental Meditation.

Mollie had made herself totally independent of Matthew in every regard except money. He was not to feel responsible for her. He was to pay the bills: nothing else. She had made that clear years before, in conversation and in her own letters and in lawyers' letters. But you do not choose a sense of responsibility for other people. If you feel it you have it. With exhausted irritation, with pity, with admiration for her honesty and courage and with despair at her relationships with people, Matthew would feel responsible for his wife until one of them died.

If Clare's account of her mother had been open, cheerful, optimistic, Matthew would have consulted his conscience and probably let well alone. As it was, he knew he had a duty to see her, to make sure that her flat was all right and her health was all right and her life was all right.

He telephoned as soon as he got back to his London hotel room. Clare answered. She told Matthew to hold. Matthew heard indistinct voices at the other end, Clare's and Mollie's. Clare, not Mollie, came back to the telephone. She said her mother was too busy to talk. She was too busy to see Matthew, either before he went to France or after he came back.

Matthew asked for his younger daughter.

'Liz went away a few days ago,' said Clare. 'With friends, I guess. She's still away.'

'Where?'

'Mother doesn't know exactly.'

Matthew was displeased. From the little he had seen, he was more than dubious about the way Mollie had brought up Liz. He did not think an impetuous, jobless, directionless, half-educated nineteen-year-old should disappear for days, with nobody knowing where she was. He did not say any of this to Clare, which would have been pointless and disloyal.

Matthew resigned himself to not seeing his wife or younger daughter. He arranged by telephone to see his son. He arranged through the hotel to hire a small British Ford the following day.

Matthew drove to Oxford on Sunday morning. He looked forward keenly to seeing that holy city again. He had spent a year there in 1951-52, on a Rhodes Scholarship, earning a Ph.D. with a historical thesis on the origins of the thoroughbred horse. His tutor at Magdalen had started by mildly deploring, ended by virulently hating, this field of research. The research took Matthew to Newmarket and the Jockey Club library, and to private libraries in Yorkshire and Gloucestershire, his visits always timed to coincide with race-meetings or convenient foxhunting appointments. That winter from Oxford he hunted with the Bicester and what was then the South Oxfordshire and with the University Draghounds, riding perilous hirelings. He rode with honour but without glory in two point-to-point races. He made a great number of friends, a number of whom remained so thirty years later.

At the Magdalen Commemoration Ball of 1952 he met and was bewitched by a solemn, slender girl two or three years younger than himself. She was the Honourable Mary Bardsley, called Mollie by everybody. It seemed that her father was Viscount Wincham. Matthew had by this time too wide an acquaintance

45

with the aristocracy (and too deep a knowledge of some of it) to be impressed by this connection: but he was deeply impressed by Mollie. He took her out in a punt at dawn. Dawn is cruel to most faces after a night of drinking and dancing. Mollie sat flowerlike in the punt, her skin like the petals of a magnolia, her eyes solemn with wonder, her clear voice hushed in the misty and pearly daylight.

She was with a party. She abandoned her party. They had strawberries and cream for lunch. After four hours' sleep, she looked like a snowdrop, a white narcissus, a spray of apple-blossom. She had studied domestic science at the famous establishment at Winkfield. She had studied the piano to an advanced grade. She preferred ballet to opera, the city to the country, blue to all other colours, cats to all other animals. Her smile was hesitant. She agreed calmly to see him again, and gave him the address and telephone number of her father's London house.

He made a tentative effort to kiss her, before she went back to London in the evening with her friends. It was altogether abortive. She turned away sharply, not in rejection but in unawareness. He kissed a mouthful of long, pale hair.

He discovered in her, during the weeks that followed, qualities perfectly invisible on first meeting: almost paradoxical; incongruous in that gentle and faultless exterior. He had wondered, with guilty disloyalty, whether there were not something a little insipid, milky, soft-cored, about this ethereal girl. But he discovered certainties beside which his own convictions seemed like caramel. There was a rock in the middle of Mollie — duty, conscience, morality. She knew exactly what she believed. The sharpest knives of argument bounced, blunted or broken, off her certainties. It was oddly impressive, oddly moving, to hear this pale and slender young girl disposing calmly of world figures as though they were juvenile delinquents. Matthew himself was a man of strong morality but half-formed, little-examined beliefs. Mollie's strength was reassuring. She would give any man backbone, though she looked as frail as a windflower. She had a smack of his own Puritan ancestors, of the Endicott in Hawthorne's stories.

The term had ended; his Oxford year had ended. He lingered on in England because of Mollie. He haunted her family's house. Her father was affable. Her mother never knew he was there. He kissed her with more purpose and more success. At first she submitted without response. Then she responded with vehemence. He thought there was fire as well as rock under the cool ivory, under the creamy petals.

His father had an accident, getting his horse fit to hunt with the Iroquois in October. They jumped one of the big Kentucky creeks; the horse missed his footing on the landing side, and came down on the rider. The saddle-tree broke John Carver's pelvis. Matthew was on an airplane next day, a B.O.A.C. Stratocruiser, and home the day after that. He had to take over immediate management of his father's affairs. They consumed about two-thirds of his time. He would have gone crazy in the remaining third, twiddling his thumbs and thinking about Mollie. He began to commute between Lexington and London. It was expensive and exhausting and exciting.

Mollie said 'Yes' in November.

Matthew presented himself to Lord Wincham. It came as no surprise to his Lordship: Mollie had already told him that it would happen and that he was to give his consent. But it came as a complete surprise and a severe shock to Lady Wincham. 'An American. We really know nothing about him. We know nothing about his family. Our only child. Four thousand miles away.' Lady Wincham's certainties were like Mollie's. It was most evidently from her that Mollie had inherited or learned them. An irresistible force met an immovable object, in the Winchams' gloomy drawing-room that evening. Neither mother nor daughter raised her voice. Lord Wincham gestured with his eyes to Matthew, and they tiptoed out of the room. They drank whisky in Lord Wincham's study. He invited Matthew to call him 'James'; but said he had better wait to be asked before calling Lady Wincham 'Sylvia'.

The battle was unresolved. Matthew left the house without seeing either of the duellists. He dined at the club of which he was a visiting member, and went home to the room he rented in Bayswater. He did not know what to think, and he had had too much to drink.

Mollie was there. She had been there for two hours. She came up to him and kissed him, for the first time taking a physical initiative. He felt her breasts, small and hard and high, through her blouse and his shirt. She moved them. She intended him to feel them. She pressed her groin against his inevitable erection.

She rubbed against him. It was unbearably exciting. It was far more exciting than with any other woman in the world, because this was cool and self-possessed Mollie, pale and virginal Mollie, now goading him, now giving him an invitation which was tacit but which was louder than a trombone.

He took off his own coat and tie. She stood watching gravely. He embraced her. He felt her breasts and her thighs. He began to unbutton her blouse. His fingers were trembling. He had difficulty with the buttons. She undid the buttons, those down the front of the blouse and those at the cuffs. She took off her blouse and unhooked her bra.

'Come on,' she said.

She was naked before he was. Naked, she pulled the cover off the bed. She lay down on the bed, watching him as he finished undressing. He was embarrassed by the swinging and bouncing of his urgent cock. He thought she could never have seen such a thing before. She looked at it solemnly. She did not look frightened, or avid, but serious.

She was as beautiful as he imagined, as he had driven himself half insane, four thousand miles away, by imagining. She was bird-boned. Her shoulders and hips were narrow, her legs exquisitely slender. Her breasts were small but perfect. There was no smile on her face.

He lay beside her and began making love to her. He stroked and kissed her breasts, and presently stroked the soft triangle of hair between her thighs.

'Come on,' she said again.

Those were the only words she had spoken. He had not spoken at all.

She rubbed his cock. He was startled and delighted. He had to push her hand away, or he would have exploded. It went back, not fondling but vigorously rubbing. She was not ready. But she pulled him on to her and opened her thighs below his pelvis. She steered him to the lips of her cunt. With her hands on his buttocks she pushed him into her. She was tight and dry. He thought he must hurt her. He thought she must be giving herself a brutal and disastrous introduction. He tried to look at her face. She hid it in his shoulder, in his neck. With unexpected strength she continued to pull him down on to her and into her. The tightness was more than he could stand; so stimulated, he came almost at once. Far too soon. Calamitously soon. His own juice lubricated her so that he moved more easily inside her. He prayed that he might stimulate her before he lost all urgency, all usefulness to her. It was no good. He felt his own flabbiness inside her. She moved her pelvis and he slipped wetly out of her.

'You did finish?' she said, as calm as though she was asking for a cucumber sandwich.

'Yes. I'm sorry, darling. I . . .'

'I didn't expect it to be so quick.'

'It shouldn't have been. It won't be, next time.'

'Oh, I don't know. Now I must get back.'

'Shall I see you home?'

'No. You're a bit drunk.'

As they went downstairs she said, 'Now we won't have any more of Mummy's nonsense.'

Nor did they. But he was not asked to call her Sylvia.

James Wincham leered at him the next time they met. He was always thereafter an ally, though never a reliable one. Matthew's own boy was named after him. Mollie's decision, and perfectly reasonable. Always called Jamie at home. Mollie's decision. 'Jim' more usual in America. 'Jamie' a very Brit ring. Well, he was a Brit boy. Jim or Jamie — it was profoundly unimportant but it was another thing that Matthew found distancing, imperceptibly increasing the gulf between himself and his family, increasing their foreignness to him and his to them.

Love-making with Mollie improved. She said that she came. She must have done so, since she never in her life lied about anything. At least, she must have considered that she did so. It was not obvious to Matthew.

Matthew neared Oxford, coming in on the dismal approach from the east. He had arranged to meet Jamie at the Mitre. Had the boy been at the university, he would of course have gone to his rooms, in college or in digs. But he wasn't, nor ever likely to be. Mollie had taken him away from his hideously expensive boarding school, for reasons which were never quite explained to Matthew. Mollie did not justify her actions. Since she knew she was right, it was a matter of no importance what anybody else thought. Or, perhaps, the decision about Jamie's removal had been taken by the school. Jamie had been sent to a crammer, chosen, perhaps, because of the lustre cast on it by the neighbouring university. The idea was that he should cram for his A-Levels, the crucial examination taken at the end of what

Matthew would have called high school. 'A' stood for 'advanced'. If they really meant advanced, Matthew thought, Jamie might as well stay at home. Mollie's idea, as Clare had glumly reported, was that Jamie should achieve so brilliantly in the examinations, spurred and groomed by the crammer, that he would get a place in a leading university. Cambridge? Bristol? Edinburgh? Matthew wanted to discuss all this with Jamie, since he was not going to get a chance to do so with Mollie.

He also hoped to find out why Jamie had left his school.

'Hullo, Daddy, good to see you.'

It was good to see Jamie, too. It was good to walk with him through the autumnal magic of Oxford.

Jamie was dressed very much like many of the undergraduates they saw — tweed jacket, turtleneck, jeans, sneakers. His hair was down to his collar but not down his back. Like Clare, he had inherited his mother's narrow bones, but he was much taller, taller than his father. He tended to move, as such boys do, like a puppet inexpertly manipulated: legs and arms seemed to throw themselves out from the centre without volition or purpose, at which moments his cuffs climbed his forearms and his jeans his calves. His strength and co-ordination had some way to go before they caught up with his stature. He was coltish. He was like the High Line colt who had run two days earlier at Newmarket.

Matthew thought he looked a little thin and tired. But Oxford, for all its beauty, was a place with a lousy damp climate, foggy when the rest of Britain was shrivelling in sunshine; and maybe the crammer was making him work.

Jamie suggested lunch in Woodstock, at the Bear. As they drove there, Matthew asked him about his leaving school.

'Hopeless sixth form,' said Jamie, in his clear, arrogant, upper-class English voice. Really it was extraordinary to have a son, his own son, speaking a language so different from his own.

'What I call junior and senior classes in high school,' said Matthew.

'Do you? How bizarre. Anyway, we decided I'd only get decent A-Levels and a chance of Oxbridge if I came to a joint like this.'

'To what end, Jamie?'

'To the end of being an educated human being.'

Jamie continued to talk thus, sensibly and conventionally and without giving the slightest hint that he knew where he was going or what he wanted to do with his life.

'Mummy says,' said Jamie, 'I can always get a job with Cousin Alaric Wincham.'

'Good God. As what?'

'Yes-man, I suppose.'

Matthew laughed, a little guiltily. The present Viscount, Mollie's first cousin, was a fat young man with political ambitions who, at dinner parties and all other gatherings, expected general silence to fall whenever he opened his mouth.

It was probably true that Mollie could make him give Jamie a job.

Matthew asked Jamie how he was fixed for money. Jamie was evasive. Matthew gathered that Mollie kept the boy very short, out of policy rather than poverty, but that Jamie contrived to supplement his allowance by doing odd jobs. He was not specific about the jobs. He hinted at pubs and clubs and discos. Matthew assumed he was a waiter or washer-up; he was not built to be a bouncer. Matthew offered his son some money, but Jamie turned away the offer gruffly, almost gracelessly. Matthew was not offended because he thought he understood. Jamie knew very well that Matthew was the sole support of his English family; that although Mollie had inherited a small fortune in trust she never spent her own money but only Matthew's, on the grounds that he had undertaken to support her. Jamie was reluctant to sponge on his father; he simply lacked the maturity to say so gracefully. Matthew was pleased and proud.

They lunched expensively. Jamie ate little.

'I had,' he said, 'a breakfast copious to the point of gluttony.'

Matthew hoped this was true. At the same time he wondered if there was a single boy of Jamie's age in the United States of America who would have expressed himself with that mock-pompous elegance.

Jamie drank little, but that little brought bright patches of red to his cheeks. Perhaps he had inherited from his mother what was almost an allergy to alcohol.

Matthew, feeling slightly bloated, suggested a walk over the downs. Jamie demurred. He had played football the day before and was tired and stiff and bruised.

'Do they make you play football or do you choose to?'

'I want three volunteers, you and you and you. No, of course I choose to. *Mens sana in corpore sano.* You didn't know I could be so learned, did you?'

'Education,' said Matthew, 'is a wonderful thing.'

Thanks to the miracle of supersonic travel, George Whyte was in New York before he left London. He was in excellent time for his meeting.

Early Sunday afternoon might normally be thought an odd time for a business meeting; but the company he was seeing was, for him and its other clients, prepared to stay open and operative twenty-four hours a day, Sundays and public holidays included. Lee V. Lowe Associates would have welcomed conferences at midnight on Christmas Eve, at dawn on Easter morning.

The office was on the seventh floor of a building in the middle forties between Madison and Park. It was a good address, but the office was cramped and sunless. Lee V. Lowe would have preferred to have met George Whyte in the Oak Bar at the Plaza, the King Cole Room, the Four Seasons. But George Whyte insisted on the office. Lee V. Lowe wanted to be seen with George Whyte, but George Whyte did not want to be seen with Lee V. Lowe.

Lowe was an independent Public Relations and Personal Publicity Consultant. 'Associates' was a lie. There was only one associate and she was a middle-aged secretary from the Bronx. Lowe's client, on paper, was Cragrock Farms and Stables. This justified the fee George Whyte paid. It satisfied the auditors and the revenue. Many major thoroughbred breeding establishments advertised regularly in the *Thoroughbred Record,* the *European Racehorse* and similar journals, trumpeting their yearlings, their stallions, their facilities. Cragrock advertised, in large and tasteful colour pages placed by Lowe but designed by Mrs George Whyte. This was a visible and respectable publicity effort. It was the tip of an iceberg, whose unseen submarine mass was known even in the most general terms by only a few, and in detail only by George Whyte and Lee V. Lowe.

Lee V. Lowe wanted to be rich, all right all right, but above all he wanted to be *in*. He wanted his to be one of those names which, mentioned in connection with a restaurant, *prove that the restaurant is in.* He wanted to be mentioned in Roger Angell's annual poem in the Christmas number of the *New Yorker*. It would go so well:

'Let's raise a glass and call cheer-ho
To Joseph Papp and Lee V. Lowe.'

He had arrived at the current form of his name after studying the precedent of that accomplished and popular actor the late Lee J. Cobb.

He came from Brooklyn.

He was thinnish and thirty-five; he had large, scrubbed hands and a drooping moustache nicely poised between banditto and brigadier-general. He smoked Gauloises and drank Campari. His suits were those advertised as having the English look, his shoes the Italian look, his ties the French look. He sometimes wore a flower in his buttonhole, having seen Mr David Ogilvy doing so. He tried a hat like Mr Quentin Crisp's (itself owing much to the late Cecil Beaton) but he could not get it to stay on at the extreme angle affected by those noted aesthetes. His conversation was modelled on *Private Lives,* the successful younger set in Los Angeles, and quotations from newspaper interviews with Mr Terry Southern, Mr Truman Capote, Mr William J. Buckley and the late Kenneth Tynan.

His clients included a very old actor, a very young actress, a rock group, two restaurants, a gay bar in the Washington Square neighbourhood, and George Whyte. He had been recommended to the last as a joke, but neither of them knew this. His method was less the printed handout than the personal message.

He did not know that the person he wanted to be never existed except in the minds of people like himself.

The person George Whyte wanted to be existed, in fair numbers, in many countries, instantly recognisable. It was Matthew Carver, with money.

'The popular Kentucky gentleman and sportsman.'

His gifts to gentlemanly charities, scrupulously anonymous, were leaked. He was photographed on horseback, with his arms round the neck of a weanling foal, and giving rides on his own back to underprivileged children. Mentions of his distinguished collections (porcelain and sporting art) were shoehorned into the highbrow glossies.

On this occasion George Whyte gave Lee V. Lowe a full briefing about the record-breaking purchase of the Mill Reef colt, and the probable purchase of the shares in Beausoleil.

'Lovely stuff to you and me, Squire,' said Lee V. Lowe with his serious face. He put on his joking face and said, '*But will it hit a home run with Mr and Mrs Front Porch?*'

The private jet was waiting for George Whyte at LaGuardia. The pilot saluted and the steward helped George up the steps. No photographers were present.

They flew over Pittsburg, and then directly to the airstrip on Cragrock Farm. For a man as careful as George Whyte, this facility was ludicrous. Flattening the rolling ground had been a massive and messy operation, rendering a large acreage hideous until the grass came back. It was a terrible waste of pasture. The Blue Grass Field on the edge of Lexington was a few minutes from Cragrock by car. George Whyte had often been asked by the insensitive why he wasted so much ground so pointlessly. He never gave a satisfactory reply. There was none.

The airstrip made learned observers think of that eccentric Duke of Portland who, disliking the scrutiny of his tenants, caused underground carriage-drives to be tunnelled beneath his park, in several directions from Welbeck Abbey, so that he could arrive and depart unobserved. Of course he was rich, too.

The pilot had radioed for a car. The car was there. It did not drive George at once to his house, but to the nearest of the farms. The farm road was surfaced like a superhighway. It snaked between the black fences of the hundred acre fields, all gently rolling in the humpy countryside, the grass yellowed by the season. The lovely white post-and-rail had been replaced, after the successful development of a superior new black preservative: and after an accident — not there, but on another farm — when a half-million-dollar yearling broke a foreleg between rails. All the fences now had a special, resilient heavy-duty wire mesh, zigzags between horizontals: not nearly as pretty, far more expensive, believed safer. Many of the huge fields were naturally watered; all the rest had artificial streams or ponds. Time was, small boys had been allowed to fish in the streams.

The farm road's extravagantly-broad mown verges were lined with thousands of young trees, chosen by Mrs Whyte for their foliage and habit. The fields were dotted with old trees, shade for the stock, relief for the eye. If a twig fell it was anxiously removed; when leaves fell they were raked and carted. The tallest and most elegant of the trees were locusts, with white-blotched trunks. They lost branches in gales. George Whyte did not resent the expense of the young ornamental trees of the roadside. They showed positively. He resented the cost in man-hours of removing the fallen branches of locust-trees. That showed only negatively.

The grass was constantly reseeded and copiously limed. Droppings were never picked up, as they were off the tight little paddocks of England. From time to time a chain was dragged over the grass, mashing or pulverising the droppings and spewing them broadcast over the surface; then that field was rested until all was sweet again. The prodigious amount of available ground made this right. All Cragrock methods started from the hypothesis of vastness.

Mares grazed, a few with late foals still at foot, but most with their foals now weaned and taken away. Out of their sight and earshot the weanlings grazed, in uneasy bunches, many disconsolate, feeling orphaned, not yet with the girlish skitter of fillies which have found a substitute in company for mother-love, not yet with the nascent aggression and rivalry of colts. George Whyte looked at them without feeling the feelings of mares and weanlings. He noted the condition of the fences.

He noted with irritation the condition of the stone walls, which stood intermittent and useless outside the fences, slave-built a century and a half before, vulnerable to passing trucks, their sloped and mortared coping-stones apt to topple and litter the verges. They were the only man-made things on Cragrock older than George Whyte himself. Local opinion demanded their preservation. Lee V. Lowe urged it. George left the matter in his mental pending tray.

The car passed the empty foaling-barn, a perfect circular palace, the plan borrowed from Rokeby and the English National Stud. Mrs Whyte had chosen the Skeaping bronze on its great marble plinth in the centre, and the old-fashioned roses geometrically bedded about it. Other barns for mares, mares and foals, weanlings, dotted this part of the farm, which extended to 1,500 acres. All had been built or renovated during the previous five years. All were of stone. The previous buildings had been wooden. Wood was warmer and cheaper. Perhaps it represented a fire risk. George Whyte, contemplating his barns, remembered the epitaph of the Emperor Augustus: he found Rome a city of wood, and left it a city of marble. The Cragrock barns were not built of marble, but the breeding-sheds and lunging-pits were floored with marble chips.

The yearlings were in a different section, in another 1,000 acres, with their own long barns in a style of qualified classicism. A few had gone to the Select Sales at Keeneland in July. None not selected went to any other sale. The yearlings had all been broken in August. Soon, within a month, they would be ridden on the training-track which belonged to this yearling section. It was a half-mile circuit, coarse sand imported from another part of the state and worked to be soft and safe. There were four practice starting-gates. The yearlings would be ridden by grooms hardly heavier than jockeys, who loved them and treated them tenderly. When they went to Bert Duffy the trainer, much of his work would have been done for him.

The car proceeded to the crown of Cragrock, the 500 acres of the stallion station. There were forty-six resident stallions. Their total value could be computed, on the current cost of shares or nominations in each. It pleased George Whyte to compute it. The figure was well over $500 million.

Almost all the stallions were housed in small new barns, four horses to each, ten palaces arranged to form a little city of aristocrats and their servants. Curved, exotic wood lined the ceilings of each stall, like misplaced parquet flooring. The mangers, polished wood rimmed and bound in metal, were triangular fixtures in one corner of each stall. Some farms fed Derby-winning stallions out of buckets on hooks, believing money was better spent on horses and people, believing that even Derby winners were happy to eat out of buckets. George Whyte was glad that other farms took this view. No one could fail to note the difference.

In the midst of the city was its temple, the breeding shed, two years old, featured in architectural magazines. Nothing had been spared to make it the ultimate combination of beauty and utility. Any mare not successfully impregnated on its tanbark-on-marble-chip floor, against its rubber-padded leather-bound walls, was ungrateful and perverse. It was a pity it was only used for a third of the year.

The car stopped by the new lunging-pit being built at the far end of the block of barns. George got out. He wondered why no work was going on. He remembered it was Sunday. He worked on Sunday; he had been working in New York. Others lolled. There was much to be said for the old days.

The building was to be beautiful, unique: essentially, simply two fenced circles under a roof, in which two stallions at a time could be exercised on the long rein in bad weather. Any large shed with a dirt floor would have done, any old garage or aircraft hangar, with a load of tanbark on the floor. But the architect had given this building something of the lines of a pagoda, carried out in the materials of a yacht. As with every part of Cragrock, there was accommodation for spectators — there would be deep leather seats in galleries at each end, as in the breeding-shed, as even in the foaling barn. With the immediate landscaping, the building when complete was to cost just over $1,000,000. Not all George Whyte's public-relations expenditure went to Lee V. Lowe.

Round the elliptical building, and radiating from it, vermilion paths had already been laid, narrow for persons, broader for the horses. They were made of pulverised brick. They were an extra cost for which the architect had pleaded. He said they were practical as well as useful, and he had aerial photographs taken. Down one of the paths, from the lunging-pits, came Will Stevens the Farm Manager, most important man at Cragrock after George Whyte himself. He was tall, fair, neat, and deeply serious. He looked young for the job; everybody knew he was the best in the world. The men shook hands. Will Stevens was polite but not humble.

'Work's up to schedule,' said Will. 'You'll be able to give a dance in there Christmas time.'

'I have a house for that,' said George Whyte.

Will allowed himself to show excitement about the Mill Reef colt and about the Beausoleil rumours.

George Whyte went on to the training-track, a circular mile of dirt, even more expensive to lay out than the airstrip: another luxury, but an explicable one. Some stables survived entirely in racetrack barns; life for men and horses was rootless. Cragrock Stable lived at home between meets and between seasons. This was one of the reasons Bert Duffy, the trainer, considered he had the best job in the world. A job he would on no account put at risk. George Whyte appreciated the result without being aware of the cause. Not for Bert the abrasive directness of Fred Cottle over there in Newmarket. Not for Bert any directness, unless he knew Mr Whyte agreed with him.

They agreed about Master Mariner, a two-year-old now put away for the season. They agreed he was potentially the best horse in the stable, a candidate for the most important stakes of the following year, including the classics.

Bert Duffy was excited about the Mill Reef colt and Beausoleil, although one would do his racing in England and the other had finished with racing. One day he would be training the progeny of both. If he went on as he had; if he never let his tongue run away with him.

George Whyte got out of his car for the second time, because there were people watching. A Kentucky sportsman of the old school unbent among his grooms, and cast a knowing eye at his horseflesh. He was sparing of comment. But what he said was sound. Clearly: since Bert Duffy warmly agreed with him.

Looking at Master Mariner in his stall, George Whyte was reminded of something so nauseating, so infuriating, that he felt for a moment close to vomiting.

Like much else in the stable, and like most of the breeding stock, Master Mariner was owned in partnership. George Whyte two legs. Matthew Carver one leg. Frank Harding one leg. George wanted to cut that leg off. He wanted to cut several bits of Frank Harding off. He abruptly ended his visit to the stable, and laboured to recover his tranquillity during the short ride to the house.

George Whyte's grandfather's original house had been small and spiky, traditional in a dreadful tradition. His father's had been much better. It had not required demolition, but merely concealment under extra layers. The position was a huge advantage, a hilltop, great trees, the new white classical façade gleaming between the trees, smiling down at the new formal garden and the new wild garden and the urns and statues.

The last few yards, the stroll between car and steps, gave George particular and undiminishing pleasure. The house was now so very tall. The portico was so very white and wide and deep. The taste was flawless and the scale enormous. These two were the essence. It was hard to say which gave more joy.

George strode into this magnificence aware of looking and acting the part. America had an aristocracy. It was politic to deny this in public but it was honest to recognise it in private. The Whytes were not old as some New England and Virginia families were old, but outstanding people were ennobled in every generation. The Howards and the Percys and the Cecils had been

58

commoners once. George's grandfather started as a commoner. He spelled his name 'White'. He came to Kentucky from Chicago with his meat-packing fortune in 1891, a piece of history not referred to in George's presence by those anxious for his favours. He elevated himself to one of the lower degrees of the American peerage. George's father had a more expensive education, he employed a better architect, and he began raising thoroughbreds. Barony became Viscountcy. Cragrock became a seat. George himself, inheriting in 1960, had enlarged, embellished, beautified. Cragrock became a palace, and the Viscountcy a belted American Earldom.

And the Earldom had its Countess: Jean McLaren Whyte, daughter of a Baltimore banker and Master of Foxhounds, jewel in the diadem. She dwelt on an icy social peak. Many people would have said that there no longer was such a thing, in an age of relaxation and recession. They had not met Jean. She was like that wife in O. Henry — you wanted alpenstock and thermal underclothing to approach her. George was proud of her. She was exactly right.

'Hullo, George,' she said, with her cool smile, happening to cross from arch to arch of the gigantic pillared hall as he came in.

'Hi,' said George.

For he knew that to be casual, undemonstrative, was right for American Earl and Countess. So Old Etonian Dukes behaved, when reunited with their Duchesses.

Jean was dressed for the country, in tweed skirt, cashmere twinset, textured stockings, very shiny brown brogues with medium heels. A string of pearls was her only jewellery except her wedding band, an eternity ring, and plain gold studs in her earlobes. Her hair was dark, naturally waved, of medium length; she wore it back from her face, as though she thought that to conceal any part of her face would have been unkind to the groundlings. They should see their Countess. She was worth seeing, pale, with a high-bridged nose and high forehead, straight eyebrows over grey eyes, a determined chin humanised by a not-quite-central cleft.

What was formidable about Jean to most people was that she exuded a half-conscious consciousness of superiority. She was too smart not to know she was a queen. She could unbend with no loss of dignity. Queens can.

What was formidable about her to George was that none of this was an act. She was what she seemed to be, without effort. It was a trick he was still trying to learn.

He followed her into the small library (there was a big library, too) where a fire burned in an Adam fireplace from a bombed house in Harley Street. Harold the butler had brought in the drinks on a tray. Jean had dismantled George's father's bar, and emptied the bottle-cupboard in his study. What you did about drinks was have the butler bring them in on a tray.

'Did you buy whatever it was?' said Jean, accepting a drink from him and sitting down, graceful as a tweedy panther, in a chair by the fire.

George told her about the Mill Reef yearling and about Beausoleil.

'Did Matt Carver choose them?'

'They practically chose themselves. They're both superb.'

'I heard Clare's over there with the Prison Visitor.'

'The what?'

'Your friend the Honourable Mollie.'

'Clare. Yes. She came to the track.'

'Looking beautiful?'

'I didn't notice.'

'Oh, George!'

'I was looking at horses. It was important. These were gigantic decisions.'

Jean burst out laughing. She laughed with abandon but without loss of elegance. It was another trick George had not learned. He did not know what she was laughing at. He guessed that, if she explained, he would not understand. She was departing from the script. She was always doing it. Almost everybody did it. It made George irritable and baffled. This scene had been written before it was played, and it was the return of the conquering hero. But Jean laughed.

George never surprised himself. He knew what to do and say in all normal situations, in the role of gentleman-sportsman of Kentucky, in the role of American aristocrat. He was predictable after the event if not before it, because he did and said the right thing. Jean never did or said the wrong thing, precisely, but she was constantly unpredictable. She did not *try* to be unpredictable. It was not a thing she worked at. It came naturally. It was the same with her children — their two children — and to a lesser extent even with his own deeply beloved sister.

George was far from admitting that there was anything wrong with himself, even when he lay awake in the middle of the night. But there was certainly something different about him. He felt like an alien. It might have been the burden of greatness but it seemed like the burden of dullness.

Doris Bernard the secretary came in. She did not knock. None of the servants or any of the staff knocked on the doors of downstairs rooms. It was Jean's rule and it was absolute. Almost every new servant had to be broken of the abominable bourgeois habit. Some of the children's friends had to be broken of it, too.

Doris fluttered into the room, because she knew no other way of moving. Locomotion, at any speed and in any direction, involved vague waving of the hands, birdlike darts of the head, and gasps of continual astonishment.

'Oh, Mr Whyte!' she said breathlessly. 'Welcome home!'

'Thank you, Doris.'

'There's such a stack of mail! Just in these few days! Would you like it now, or leave it to the morning?'

'The morning. I've had a pretty long day. You know I was out of bed at four in the morning, our time.'

Doris goggled with astonishment, with sorrowful sympathy. She was thirty, fluffy, pretty, chocolate-box, given to tulle and pastel colours and very pale pink lipstick. Jean had found her through a top agency in New York. The fluffiness and fluttering might be deliberate, or natural, or something which had started deliberate and become natural. It amused Jean, because Doris's brain was as hard and sharp as a knife and as quick as a spider. Her memory was prodigious. She took an awesome load of work on her shoulders, having over four years grown from being Jean's personal secretary into an integral role in the management of house, farms, stables and estate.

Maybe, thought Jean, she thinks being that efficient has to be unattractive. Doris was far from unattractive. She had no sex life, as far as Jean knew. She was married to her job, to her manifold jobs.

Doris Bernard had no sex life at that moment, but she planned to resume as soon as Alicia Whyte came home for the Christmas vacation from her college in Vermont. She was nineteen now. Doris had kept her hands off, with ferro-concrete self-control, for fear of frightening the girl. The fear receded with every week.

College brought you up against things. Even if it didn't, you had to pretend that it did. Chicken was the worst thing to be.

For months Doris had intrigued to get the bedroom next to Alicia's. She devised an unanswerable argument to do with insomnia and distracting creaks in other bedrooms. For three years Doris had had that room. She had drilled peepholes. For three years she had watched Alicia dressing and undressing, and seen the development into maturity of those generous pink breasts, the firming definition of those adorable nipples, the luxuriance of that blond besom of pubic fleece. One languid afternoon, towards the end of the summer vacation, she had watched Alicia masturbate, lying naked on her back on the bed, fingers gently and then urgently thrusting in and out between her thighs. Doris had almost screamed with her own longing and excitement; her own simultaneous masturbation, as she squatted by her peephole had been one of the best she ever remembered.

It was beautiful to think of the things she could teach Alicia. She knew about the front. Doris bet she didn't know about the nerve in her ass in back. She might have had her nipples kissed, but not the way Doris would kiss them. Doris would have her screaming and writhing and gushing. In a few weeks' time. And nobody guessed.

The money in this job was good and growing, the power was good and growing, and soon there would be warm wet pussy and kisses sweeter than wine.

Into the small library, having heard that her brother was home, ran Alice Whyte Harding. Like Jean, she was undemonstrative, but she did not carry it to such austere lengths. Her kiss on his cheek could be heard across the room, over the crackling of the scented apple-wood in the fire.

Alice was in her middle thirties, ten years younger than George and five than Jean. She looked like a hazelnut with money and dress-sense — light brown hair cut short and sporty, tanned face and hands, clear hazel eyes. Her features were regular and pleasing. She was attractive. She could look beautiful. But her face and bearing too vividly expressed her mood and health. If Jean was marble, Alice was glass, sometimes glowing with inner warmth and content and well-being, sometimes drab, almost fly-blown, greyly revealing 'flu or misery.

She had glowed like the apse of Chartres rendering the evening sun when, ten years before, she had married Frank Harding. The light had faded. The glass looked discoloured and cobwebby. The charming handsome Californian, the brilliant horseman and yachtsman, many times a millionaire from his family's chain of hotels: he was a fag.

It made George feel ill with disgust.

He and Alice had been close as children, in spite of a gap in their ages which gave them different schools and friends and activities. She was important to him then because she idolised him; naturally, since he was fifteen years old to her five, and twenty to her ten. With her, aware of worship, George felt strong and confident. They remained close, even after Alice went to the Coast. With her as with no one else he still felt relaxed and real. She was the one he didn't have to act to.

Like George, Alice had been brought up with horses, and retained her childish love of them. That had been one of Frank Harding's excellences — his own passion for the turf, his lovely Sanguesanta Thoroughbred Ranch in the green middle of the state. Naturally Frank had come in with George and Matthew Carver; naturally he owned halves or legs of many of the Cragrock mares, and shares in many of the stallions. Naturally, after a slightly messy divorce, he would not be investing further with George Whyte's group. Nor would George have touched a cent of his money.

This was, of course, what the British TV interviewer had wanted Matthew Carver to talk about. For a bad moment, George had thought he was going to tell about Frank. Luckily he had had more sense. He said too much, but he stopped short of disaster. The Whyte family tragedy was no fit subject to be flaunted and vulgarised on television.

Frank's investment had been heavy, and it had been very useful to George. George had not stayed rich by tying up too much personal capital in a perishable and unpredictable commodity. Probably another partner would have to be found, another abundant source of fluidity. Carver had hinted so on TV: improperly, but accurately.

Alice showed much more interest than Jean in the Mill Reef colt and in Beausoleil.

Jean was glad that Alice had come back to Cragrock. Alice might eventually want a place of her own, here or in New York or abroad, but for the moment she seemed settled at Cragrock. It was a good thing. She had taken a beating. She had looked terrible immediately after the divorce in midsummer. She looked better already, transformed. She might get married again. Jean hoped she would, but not too soon, from all points of view. Matt Carver would be the sort of thing, someone civilized and kind and with no problems of hormone balance. If he only got shot of the Prison Visitor. Meanwhile it was good to have Alice at Cragrock. She was chic and cultured. She did them credit. She diluted George. George undiluted was more and more difficult for Jean to bear.

They had not yet reached separate bedrooms, but they were hurrying towards that point.

Jean lived from month to month, hour to hour.

She told herself that she could not stand the cold, meaningless marriage and the cold wet fish in her bed another minute. But she was hooked.

Her father was a vigorous sixty-seven. He had plenty to give her but he gave her nothing. She did not expect much in his will. He had four other children, none of whom had married a multi-millionaire.

She loved her children. Really she did. She knew she did.

What made life tolerable — month to month, hour to hour — was being fucked by Will Stevens. A rod like a crowbar. A harsh gingery bush like coconut matting. He had decent manners, and he took baths. He was qualified, educated; he was a professional, not a peasant. Muscles. B.O. — nice B.O. — a man who was doing something real that made him sweat, and the acrid, honourable smell of sweat was in no way contemptible or repellent. She liked him at noon in high summer, slippery with sweat. She impaled herself on that crowbar, and she had her cake and ate it.

George had never sprung a sweat in his cold fish life.

They were terribly discreet. Nobody, nobody knew anything about it.

Fortunately Jean liked it in long wet grass or on the bare boards of a barn or on stiff, abrasive bales of straw. It was more un-George. They had never fucked in her bed or in his, or in any motel. That would have been insanely rash.

She responded to Will with ferocity and shamelessness. She astonished herself. It made a nice change. She did not need him every day, but when she needed him she needed him.

She knew it could not go on for ever. There were cracks all round the structure, and any one of them could blow any minute. She lived from month to month and from hour to hour.

Six p.m. in Kentucky. Eleven p.m. in ancient, dreaming Oxford. Eleven p.m. in the rooms in the Banbury Road shared by Jamie Carver and Mario Vianello. Fix time. Mario was mixing three-quarters of a grain of heroin with a little water in a bottle that had contained aspirin.

The arrangement had been made by the fathers of the boys, for the good of both boys, for the safety and welfare of both boys. Matthew Carver and il conte Ottaviano di Vianello were old friends, fellow luminaries in the empyrian of international bloodstock breeding and dealing. Ottaviano was a major power in Italian bloodstock and no puny one in the world. He bred on a considerable scale, keeping mares in France and America as well as Italy. His horses raced in Italy, France and Germany, and sometimes in England and Ireland. He was passionately proud of his horses but even prouder of his son, at eighteen the oldest of his eight children. Mario had always had the best, still had it, would have it. He deserved it. He was the best. Uncommonly in his own generation, though commonly in his parents', he had had an English nanny. His spoken English was fluent. But he was bad at writing it. He was in Oxford to put this right. Matthew, knowing the plans for Jamie, had put Ottaviano in touch with Mollie. The boys had met and liked each other.

They still liked each other, and Mario's influence on Jamie was calamitous.

Jamie didn't know where Mario got the stuff. He got more than he needed. He sold the rest, heroin, coke, pot, amphetamines, pethidrine, speed. That was Jamie's part-time work, in pubs and clubs and discos. That was what paid for his own fixes.

Mario lit a candle, and heated his pill-bottle over it. He watched as the four one-sixth-grain tablets dissolved.

Jamie said, his voice a little unsteady, 'My father wanted to give me some money today.'

'How much?'

'We didn't discuss that. I wouldn't take it.'

'What a funny boy you are.'

'Not really. He gives my mother enough.'

'But she doesn't give it to you.'

'She does sometimes. Out of the blue. A great dollop. A cloudburst after months of drought. I never seem to hang on to any of it. She says, "Give yourself a treat," so I do. Aren't those bloody things melted yet?'

'Soon. I need it too, you know.'

'I told my father I'd been playing football.'

'In Italy,' said Mario, 'football is a thing of beauty and artistry. It is ballet. Here it is committing fouls in the mud.'

'I wouldn't know,' said Jamie.

CHAPTER 4

Alice rarely mentioned her life in California. She did so now, but elusively: 'What I miss,' she said, 'is having my own horses, racing in my own colours.'

George nodded. Frank Harding was a filthy pervert, but he was definitely generous. He had given plenty of horses to Alice, to race for her until they retired to breed.

Surely a George Whyte could be as generous as a Frank Harding.

Surely the script called for a big gesture. Not 'This calls for a celebration', but something near it. A welcome-home gesture. A munificent gift. It was unavoidable. The script wrote itself.

George offered his three-quarters of the Mill Reef colt as a welcome-home present to Alice.

Alice jumped up and kissed him and instantly accepted. Since he was visibly deriving pleasure from making the gesture, it would have been churlish to refuse, even to hesitate.

'Name,' she said. 'I always loved naming them. Right out of the breeding, nothing whimsy or private. Mill Reef out of what?'

'The mare is called Velvet Paws,' said George.

'That sounds a little whimsy and private,' said Jean.

'Mill Reef out of Velvet Paws,' said Alice. 'Velvet. Smooth. Plushy. Purple. Flossy. Floss. Mill on the Floss.'

'Cute,' said Jean.

'Long,' said George.

'A little long,' said Alice. 'I do get bored with these *sentences* people hang around horses' necks. Why not just Floss? I like that. Floss.'

'Sounds like a filly,' said George.

'No, I don't think so. Why does it sound like a filly? Flossy would, because that's short for Florence or Flora. Floss. It's a perfectly legitimate name out of the breeding. Floss. When does Floss get here?'

'We kind of decided to keep him in England,' said George.

'For heaven's sakes, why?' said Jean. 'What fun would Alice have, owning a horse she never saw?'

George was easily persuaded. The decision had not been his but Matthew Carver's. He had consented then out of . . . good manners, maybe, good nature. If Alice became three-parts owner of the colt, she could have it run where she liked.

'Fred Cottle will have to be told immediately,' said George. 'He wouldn't have a Telex. I don't want to call and talk to him. Not at this hour.'

'Call him in the morning,' said Alice.

'You can't call trainers in the morning. Matthew Carver knows him better than I do. Better if he breaks it to Cottle. He's in Paris tonight, at the Armorique. He can fix the transport, too.'

George rang. Harold materialised at the door. George asked him to get Doris Bernard. Doris fluttered in, astonished but game. George dictated a Telex to be despatched immediately to the Hotel Armorique in Paris, for the urgent attention of Matthew Carver.

Matthew was tired after driving to and from Oxford, and then flying to Paris. He was worried about Jamie's health, more worried about Liz, annoyed with Mollie, concerned in case Clare should burn her fingers again.

The last thing he wanted, when he came back to the hotel after dinner, was a Telex from George Whyte giving him thoroughly unwelcome news and a thoroughly disagreeable task.

It was late — 11.30. But Matthew knew Fred Cottle's routine. The old guy would be having his last drink in front of the fire. Matthew had been there too often, between eleven and midnight, drinking weak whisky-and-water, not to know the Palgrave Lodge routine.

Matthew hated what he was about to do. But he only had one leg of the horse. George Whyte was paying the piper.

The hotel switchboard put him through in seconds.

Fred Cottle sounded gruff and cross and a little blurred. He might have been dozing in front of his fire. He might have had an extra whisky or two.

Matthew did not try to wrap it up. No sugar could hide the

bitterness of this pill to Fred. He was not a man to be bullshitted at any time, and least of all with bad news.

It was tempting to say that Matthew himself was acting under orders, acting reluctantly and against his own judgement, passing on a message simply. Tempting: but that would have been moral cowardice. It was neither wise nor honourable for one owner to blackguard his co-owner to their trainer. In speaking to Fred Cottle, Matthew had to accept, if only tacitly, his share of responsibility for the decision.

'Very good, sir,' said Fred Cottle, the bitterness thick in his voice.

He never called Matthew 'Sir'.

'Fucking American rich fucking cruel stupid treacherous fucking Americans,' said Fred Cottle, sitting stupidly with the dead telephone in his hand.

Potentially the very best horse he'd ever had in the yard.

They'd promised. They'd made him a promise. Lying bastards.

A man struggled all his life. A rich shit on the other side of the world snapped his fingers, and —

They were fools. They were ignorant cunts. The colt would never stand up to American training and American tracks. Carver should know that. He did know it. He was sacrificing the animal.

Everyone knew the colt was coming to Fred. He said so to all his mates, he said so to the world on fucking TV. Now they changed their minds. It looked as though they lost confidence in him, in his integrity, his professional ability. It made him look a fool, a failure.

He gave himself another drink, and another. He never drank so much, late at night. It wasn't safe. He'd been very lucky, once or twice, getting into a scrape after a piss-up and getting away without being recognised. But tonight was special. He'd never had a kick in the balls like this.

His wife called from upstairs. He didn't want to face her, not with this, not just now. He called back something, anything. He had another drink. He needed air. He staggered out of the house, drunkenly weeping with rage and disappointment and betrayal.

He walked aimlessly into the centre of Newmarket. The streets were almost empty. There were a few cars. He turned off the High Street into the dark back streets. He lurched and snivelled.

A little bit of his mind knew that he was over-reacting to something that had happened to every trainer in history. To George Lambton, with Hyperion. But drink and resentment of callous, stupid Americans drowned this fragment of realism in a bath of gall. He was in a state to commit any folly.

He was in a state to commit the folly to which, at long, long intervals, some disgusting demon drove him.

In a back street the door of a house opened. A group of teenagers left the house, left some kid's party with records and Coke. Three boys went off in one direction, two girls in another. The girls came towards Fred Cottle, who was leaning, sweating, blubbering, against a lamp-post. The girls were thirteen, fourteen. Dumpy little things. They neared Fred.

The demon took hold of his hands. The demon unbuttoned his coat and the top of his trousers. The demon pulled his old cock out of the front of his underpants, and waved it in the faces of the girls.

The girls screamed and clutched each other and ran back to the house of the party.

'Sweet Christ,' said Fred, appalled, terrified, disgusted.

He turned and did his best to run, buttoning himself clumsily as he went.

Ivy Cottle had heard the telephone ring. She had sensed, rather than heard, the four or five heavy, unusual drinks. She had heard him go out. She heard him come in. She heard his harsh, laboured breathing. He had been running. Running away.

They had been married for thirty years. She knew him through and through. She had a sick, blurred idea of what had happened, and a sick fear of the future.

From the girls, the police got a surprisingly good description of the dirty old man in the street. A local reporter got it, too. It was entirely desirable that the description be given publicity, that the public be warned. The description would be given prominence in the paper.

Unfortunately, every stable and stud in the Newmarket area employed dozens of small, gnarled men who looked like ex-jockeys and who had whisky on their breath at midnight.

70

The same evening, Lord Goring attended Prince Ghalib al-Jilani to Heathrow. There was no real need for this. Ghalib had hired a chauffeur-driven Rolls, and the chauffeur knew the way to the airport. But Goring was indefatigable.

What he wanted was something a little clearer, a little more specific, in the way of instructions to find Ghalib an estate where he could breed horses. England? Ireland? Price range? The house? How many acres? Existing stables and other buildings?

Above all: what were Ghalib's notions as to the commission payable to the agent who found him his property?

It was in order to pursue this subject that Goring continued to place himself at Ghalib's disposal at the Savoy, in the car, and at the airport.

The situation was intimately familiar to Ghalib. He was an entrepreneur himself. When the rulers of his insanely rich little country — his uncles and cousins and brothers — decided for reasons of prestige on a new deep-sea port, refinery, suspension bridge, children's hospital or university music school, Ghalib found the architects, engineers, contractors. He introduced them to the relevant ministers (Princes all), and with greater or lesser fervour urged their claims. He substantially increased their financial estimates by dint of costing in his own commission. Contenders not armed with a slush-fund he blocked from the race, by words dropped here and there, by the non-arrival of letters and the disconnection of telephones. He conducted his *pourparlers* more adroitly than Goring, and the scale was incomparably greater. But the arrangement was familiar. The smell was familiar. Not a stink. The reverse. Honey and flowers. Sweet oil, lubricating the wheels of commerce.

Goring learned: Ghalib had reckoned on England, but was agreeable to considering Ireland; he had no fixed notions as to price; he wanted an existing period house of architectural merit, attractive outlook, main services, good communications, and the existence or potential of an airstrip; not less than fifty acres; existing stabling an advantage, if of the highest quality, but not mandatory. And, yes, an equitable commission would be forthcoming to the finder of the right property.

Ghalib lifted off knowing that, if Goring didn't find it, it wouldn't be for lack of trying.

Goring had expected a lift back into central London in the

71

hired Rolls. But when he came out of the Number 2 Terminal, the long grey battleship had gone.

He took the underground train. He violently resented the necessity of this. Ghalib should have ordered his driver to wait for Lord Goring. The driver should have known that it was his duty to do so. Nobody knew how to behave. The working-class louts on the train had no idea how to behave. His own father had betrayed him. The stately home he should have inherited housed handicapped children, snivelling and incontinent, disgusting. His mother continued to betray him by being poor and dowdy.

Had he had a lift in Ghalib's Rolls, he would have put in a chit for expenses: Taxi from Heathrow, £8. Taking the underground instead, he would put in a chit for expenses: Taxi from Heathrow, £8.

He went back to the Bayswater flat to which the treachery of others reduced him. He heard his mother banging about in the kitchen. He went straight to the telephone. He began making enquiries about English and Irish stud-farms coming on the market.

Lady Goring, dispiritedly scouring saucepans, heard him clearly through the cardboard walls of the flat. Bobbety Bobs was still working! So late, and on a Sunday night! It was wonderful how hard he worked. He never stopped! He overdid things. He needed a nice long rest. He needed feeding up.

She couldn't help overhearing what Bobbety Bobs was saying on the telephone. She had no wish to eavesdrop on his business. She had been taught, as a toddler in the nursery, that that was a wicked and unworthy thing to do. She retained in her simple heart this and all other nursery lessons. Truth. Kindness. Fair play. Consideration to those less fortunate. St Paul said that the greatest of the virtues was charity, but to Lady Goring it was fair play. She knew this might be mocked, by clever modern people. But she had been brought up to hate cheats, and she hated them. Naughty, charming Freddie had never cheated, never ever, on the turf or at the card-table or at the billiards-table, or even when selling a horse. He would have scorned to do so. He had pride. Bobbety Bobs had inherited that same pride. Well, he must have, surely?

Having spent all day with her mother, Clare Carver felt able to go out to dinner. Tom Kavanagh came for her at 8.30, in the car with the twanging springs. Clare did not ask him in for a drink. Her mother was already eating — consuming, without evident enjoyment, a mixture of ill-assorted leftovers. There was spaghetti which had become burnt, and resembled leather shoelaces; cabbage which had been boiled to death; some gnarled lumps of unidentifiable meat, looking like chips of ancient timber dislodged with an adze. Clare's mother considered it a duty to finish off leftovers, and she never shrank from her duty.

All day she had been talking about her younger daughter Liz. Clare was also worried about Liz, who should not have disappeared without a word days before. It was, indeed, selfish and inconsiderate. But Mollie Carver refused to make contact with the police or any hospital. Instead she speculated interminably about where Liz might be, and with whom, and what sort of trouble she was in. Clare was thankful to get away, to get back to the twang of the car-seats and the cheerful, oddly exciting company of Tom.

Clare warned herself not to become too excited too soon. But his eyes disappeared when he grinned, and he was funny and gentle.

They dined, late, in the welcoming unpretentiousness of Bertorelli's, though Tom had first suggested somewhere much more expensive.

They were still curious about each other, though they had talked nonstop from Newmarket to London the previous day. Clare found herself being defensive about her mother, with the awkward, irritated, loving loyalty which had been part of her whole life. Tom was not in the least defensive or secretive about his own family, who sounded fun.

'Only my old, old cousin Maribell has let me down dreadfully,' he said. 'She's got chronic bronchitis, owing to having smoked sixty cigarettes a day for sixty years. So they have to find a better climate. She can't stand another winter in Ireland. Which means my old, old cousin Terence is going to put his stud on the market. Breeding farm to you. Nice place. Two hundred acres of the best grazing in Tipperary. I was hoping to manage it for them. They'll hate leaving it, but of course they're right. Cousin Terence will be lost without it, but he'd be lost without Maribell. They still hold hands.'

'How sweet.'

'Yes, it is. Do you think one of your father's millionaire chums might be interested?'

'How much?'

'A hell of a lot. That's the trouble, with things as they are everywhere. At least a million.'

'Dollars?'

'Pounds. That land is worth something near £5,000 an acre, and the house is early Georgian.'

'Do you go with it?'

'That's too much to hope for.'

'Arabs seem to buy most things,' said Clare. 'Would your cousins sell to an Arab?'

'They'd sell to the Wild Man of Borneo, for the right price.'

'I'll call the Wild Man of Borneo. I'll earn my commission.'

When he dropped her outside her mother's building, he kissed her for the first time. It was a demure peck, on the cheek.

She covered the place with her fingertips, nursing it, as she walked upstairs.

Fat Henri de Cheminade was summoned, that same Sunday evening, all the way out to the Haras du Coq. He would have gone for any client, actual or potential. He would have gone at greater speed for any millionaire client; faster yet for any client who was a millionaire duke; and for the duc de Montfermainbrey he fairly flew.

He wanted the Agence de Fille de l'Aire to manage the duke's racing and breeding interests. He wanted to manage the stallion Beausoleil. Stallion management was not the least profitable of a bloodstock agent's activities: but, to date, a miserably small part of Henri's. The great international agencies managed squadrons of stallions — the British Bloodstock Agency, with its branches all over Europe and in America, and its stallion advertisements in the bloodstock magazines which always struck Henri as tastelessly boastful; and in its day, before the much-mourned death of its owners, the spectacular Anglo-Irish Agency. You bought and sold shares and nominations; you approved or debarred mares. You earned commission on every negotiation. Since there were forty shares — forty potential nominations every year — there might be hundreds of negotiations over the period of the stallion's active stud life, each share changing hands for at least a million francs, nominations for a quarter of a million. People would be scrambling for nominations, pleading to have their mares approved as worthy to visit Beausoleil. Much more than straight commission could be earned. *Douceurs* were part of the business. A big company like the B.B.A. didn't do that kind of thing — couldn't, wouldn't. In many ways, thought Henri at the wheel of his Renault 30, small was beautiful. He patted his paunch as he drove, amused at the conceit.

He was more displeased than surprised when he was sent round to a side door, and when the duke received him in an office in a wing of the château.

The duke, emaciated and beautiful, was in his electric wheel-chair, a swift and silent vehicle which incorporated many refinements of his own devising. He helped himself to aged Calvados from a flask in a socket in the right-hand arm-rest of the chair; he drank from a little silver cup in a socket in the left-hand arm-rest. He did not offer Henri any Calvados, because, he said, Henri must drive safely back to Paris, and drunkenness on the roads was a grave and growing evil.

Henri knew the duke was mean about his Calvados, which was home-made and would have cost £150 a bottle in a restaurant.

There was a white pekinese on the duke's lap, which snuffled gently at the heady aroma of the spirit. The duke stroked him continually, and appeared to address all his remarks to him, although the subject under discussion was the syndication of Beausoleil.

Henri reported Lord Goring's conversation with Mr Matthew Carver, at Newmarket the day before. The duke was agreeable to selling the available shares to the group which Mr Carver represented, subject to satisfactory answers to certain questions which he himself would ask. And, subject to those answers, he was agreeable to Mr Carver's visiting the following day.

Henri de Cheminade's manner, throughout the interview, was a good deal different from that familiar to Lord Goring, the Senegalese, his wife, and his hundreds of professional acquaintances. Normally he cultivated a certain flamboyance. He wanted it to be said of him that he had *panache*. But a sensible man used exaggerated respect in his dealings with elderly millionaire dukes. Henri was profuse in his admiration of the white pekinese, and of the aquatints of Victorian racehorses which lined the walls of the office.

It worked. The duke made a clear, a beautifully unequivocal

undertaking that Beausoleil would remain in France, and under Henri's management. Henri would have liked this in writing, but it was not a suggestion he fancied making.

Henri drove rejoicing back to Paris for his rendezvous with Prince Ghalib al-Jilani.

A man with the partitive — a man with a 'de' to his name — should be a gentleman. All his long life, the duc de Montfermainbrey had been entirely prepared to do business with the *bourgeois,* with the *canaille,* with grooms and grocers and bankers. That was one of the reasons he was so rich. But he disliked being invited to confuse tradesmen with equals.

He was conscious of having inherited more than titles and millions and houses. He, and his duchess, and a very few other representatives of the ancient *noblesse de l'épée,* were the custodians of civilization. It was as simple as that. Art was important. Manners were important. The French language was important. Caste was crucially important, because on it depended the survival of all else — appreciation and patronage, gentle manners, the purity of the language. A man with a 'de' to his name was by no means by that token the duke's equal, but he was allowed — he was obliged — to address the duke with an air of dignity. He was not obliged to crawl. He was obliged not to crawl.

The fat man crawled. When the syndicate was discussed, a gross grocer's cupidity gleamed from his little pig eyes. He rubbed his hands and smiled; he was flatulently flattering about Ju-luh, and about the prints which hung in the office because they were not good enough to hang in the rooms of the château.

The duke had to look away from his obsequious, obscene performance, and keep his eyes on Ju-luh, who *was* an aristocrat.

Such a man brought the partitive into derision. That was very bad. It was more than an affront. It was a threat, a canker. A promise given to such a man was not worth the Calvados-scented exhalation which sustained it.

The duke was a devout Christian, a man of unimpeachable honour, the custodian of civilization, and a cynical old monster.

He sent Cheminade away. Then he whispered in his wheel-chair back to his duchess, who sat in amazing lace in her wheel-chair by the fire in the small blue salon. On her lap was her white chihuahua Chantal. In the arm of her wheel-chair was her flask of *eau de vie de fraises de bois,* home-made like the Calvados and tiny quantities of which were distilled from vast numbers of wild strawberries picked on the estate.

'I believe he invented his "de",' said the duke.

'More than one President of France has done the same thing,' said the duchess.

'Is that to excuse him?'

'To accuse him by association.'

'He needs no association to stand accused. He is a provincial butcher selling his managerial services like slices of debased liver-sausage.'

'Dismiss him.'

'No. He is clever and useful. I like employing disgusting people because my hands are unfettered by respect or conscience.'

'Your hands,' said the duchess, smiling gently, 'have never been fettered by respect for anybody except me, and if you were born with a conscience, you chopped it off and buried it seventy years ago. I imagine it manures the strawberries from which this evil liquor is made.'

The duke smiled back, and they drank together.

Prince Ghalib al-Jilani had business in Paris — his real business, which financed the horse business and the social business and women and other marginalia. Since it was Sunday evening, he did not go to glass and steel offices to discuss tenders under the scientific strip-lighting, but to private apartments in very good streets.

He saw a civil engineering contractor, a manufacturer of electrical components for automated dock machinery, and a man whose company made equipment for hospitals. The interviews were brief and relaxed because, in all three cases, both sides had good news. Ghalib's news was that he had already made well-received representations to his uncle the Emir, his cousin the Prime Minister, and his half-brother the Minister of Works. The news of the French gentlemen was that their colleagues — those it had been unavoidable to inform — had agreed to a re-submission of the tenders which took Ghalib into account.

No one said that, if the tenders had not been revised and re-submitted, the contracts would have been awarded elsewhere. Words were not wasted. Courtesy held sway.

Ghalib went back to his hotel to wait for Henri de Cheminade, better than ever able to afford shares in Beausoleil, a stud-farm in

77

Ireland, and such other investments as Henri might drag across his nose.

The duc de Montfermainbrey — indifferent to the hour, indifferent to the convenience even of men whose rank approached his own — made two international calls.

He called the Duke of Hampshire, at home near Petersfield, whom he had known since the war, and whom he saw every year at Longchamp and most years at Chantilly and Ascot.

The Duke of Hampshire was on his way to bed, though not actually in bed, when the internal telephone buzzed in his dressing-room, and a sleepy servant told him there was a call from Normandy. His mouth full of toothpaste, and a Wisdom toothbrush in his other hand, he picked up the other telephone.

'Rollo? It is delightful to talk to you. What a charming invention the telephone is. Some of my contemporaries affect to despise it, on the grounds that it has destroyed the art of correspondence. I cherish it on precisely those grounds. Ever since an episode in the early summer of 1921 I have been wary of committing my feelings to paper, but I am perfectly prepared to share my most intimate emotions with the bakelite instrument of Mr Alexander Graham Bell.'

His English was as fluent as Henri de Cheminade's, and much more accurate. His voice came down the wire to the Duke of Hampshire like a flute — a bass flute, made of boxwood seasoned in aged Calvados, staccato or legato, now high now low, more heavily inflected than any Englishman's English, almost actorish, almost ludicrous.

'Did you ring me up in the middle of the night to sing a hymn in praise of the bloody telephone?' asked the Duke of Hampshire, swallowing toothpaste.

'Partly that. Partly to ask your opinion of a gentleman — an American gentleman, if the paradox does not startle you into incoherence — with whom I am informed you are well acquainted. A Mr Matthew Carver.'

The Duke of Hampshire said that Matthew Carver was indeed a gentleman, a charming fellow, an excellent sportsman, very popular, of the highest repute on and off the turf of two continents.

'He's got a smashing daughter, too.'

'Smashing? What does she smash?'

'All hearts.'

'That would have been of more relevance to me in the summer of 1921, when, no doubt, I would have committed indiscretions to paper . . . Thank you, old friend. Have you personally entertained Mr Carver in your house?'

'No. I don't suppose he wets his bed or rapes the housemaids or eats peas with his knife, but I can't tell you from personal observation. Try Ralph Hadfield.'

Lord Hadfield was in bed, sitting up reading a Georgette Heyer and wondering how writers got hold of such damned ingenious complicated stories.

He was not at all cross at being disturbed, much as he was enjoying his book, because it gave him an excuse to smoke. His wife disliked his smoking in bed, but nobody could object to a fellow smoking while he took an overseas telephone call.

He confirmed what Rollo Hampshire had said about Matthew Carver's reputation and popularity. The family was old as American families went (it was much older than Hadfield's). Carver was house-trained. He did not get drunk at meals, burn holes in the drawing-room carpet, introduce uncouth games after dinner, or make long-distance telephone calls in another fellow's house without paying.

Lord Hadfield did not forget, at any moment during the conversation, that he himself wanted a nomination to Beausoleil. He did not mention it. It might have influenced the old frog's attitude to what he himself was saying about Carver. At the same time, all that he said about Carver was sincere. Lord Hadfield was capable of sincerity, and indulged it occasionally, in order to keep in practice.

Henri de Cheminade took Prince Ghalib al-Jilani to a private club near the Opéra where baccarat was played for stakes that would have made a billiard-ball's hair curl. On the way, he promised Ghalib shares in Beausoleil — one, two, even three — which he was now in a position to do as he was officially managing the stallion.

'This will bring you into contact with some charming guys,' said Henri, showing off his English, 'great friends of mine, maybe you know them already? My pal George Whyte, my pal Matthew Carver. One thing leads to another. A little bird says they maybe want some investment. You maybe come in on yearlings, maybe broodmares. You'll meet my pal tomorrow, my old buddy Matthew Carver.'

Ghalib saw himself being slapped on the back in the paddock at Newmarket by the Duke of Hampshire.

At the club he lost a modest sum but acquired, by Henri's good offices, a plump young blonde who called herself Cosette. She said this was because, all her life, she had been one of *les misérables*. Ghalib thought she was a well-fed *misérable*; he thought her skin and hair were clean.

She was astonished, later in the night, at his endurance and at some of his preferences. She stole his watch when she left, believing him asleep. He saw and ignored the theft. She had given him an excellent hour, and he had other watches.

Before he slept he performed the ceremony of *ghusl*, the meticulous washing enjoined by the Koran: 'If ye are polluted then purify yourselves.' The Prophet himself said, according to Ali, 'He who leaves but one hair unwashed on his body, will be punished in hell accordingly.' It had been difficult for Ghalib's ancestors to obey this law, on the arid coastal plateau of Halat al Bhudi. But it was no hardship in a modern hotel bathroom.

Matthew Carver was another to be disturbed that night, after he had gone to bed, by the telephone. He was pleased. He was painfully wakeful, worrying about his son's health and his younger daughter's disappearance and his elder daughter's susceptible heart and his wife's . . . about everything concerning his wife.

He would have been glad of distraction from anyone; he was delighted to be called by Epaminondas Makropulos, whom he was delighted to find in Paris. Epi was as rich as George Whyte, but not dull; as cheerful as Rollo Hampshire, but not stupid; as careful as Ralph Hadfield, but not mean; as passionately keen about thoroughbred racing and breeding as Matthew Carver himself. He was a banker of long-established family, not a self-made ship-owner. Nobody mentioned this distinction, for fear of annoying ship-owners, but nobody forgot it.

Epi's bloodstock interests were divided between France and America. (He would have raced in England, too, but for the 15% Value Added Tax on the purchase price of horses; in France they calculated it on carcase value.) He owned shares in five of the stallions at George Whyte's Cragrock Farm, all purchases arranged by Matthew. His half-dozen American mares, chosen with

Matthew's help, were housed at a fine modern farm near Middleburg, Virginia, a tenancy negotiated by Matthew.

They asked after each other's health. Epi forbore to ask after Matthew's wife.

He came to the point: 'I am in Paris, but yesterday I was in England.'

'Like me.'

'Like you, but instead of appearing on television I was watching it. I watched the Newmarket races, although I was in a meeting with three lawyers at the time. I won forty pence from one of the lawyers. Come to think of it, he never paid me. Lawyers! My own lawyers! I saw Beausoleil's race, and I saw you talking about Beausoleil.'

'Ah.'

'Ah to you, Matt. I saw that horse win at Longchamp, but I was not sure that he beat anything wonderful. I wanted to see the Champion Stakes before I made up my mind about him, because he had to beat some *very* good horses. Well, now. I like the pedigree, those outcrosses, and everything about that horse. I like that look of arrogance. He is a tiger. Did you ever see Nijinsky before a race? His expression said he couldn't be beaten. Beausoleil has that look. He runs that way. I have mares in Virginia and mares in France that I would dearly love to send to Beausoleil, and you said you were maybe buying a part of him. I have found out where you are staying by remembering where you always stay. So?'

'So I'll be better able to answer this time tomorrow, Epi. I'm seeing your friend Henri de Cheminade — maybe the old duke too — and I hope we have a deal by evening.'

'Good. You and I will dine together, and plan a sensational series of classic victories. Probably I will have a girl for you.'

'I'm too old for girls.'

'When you say that,' said Epi, shocked, 'it shows how badly you need one.'

The morning was brilliant, and warm for the time of year — a blessed contrast to the rigours of Newmarket Heath two days before. Matthew Carver drove a small hired Renault (which could have fitted into the trunk of Henri de Cheminade's Renault) the flat, fast 150 kilometres to Calvados and to the Haras du Coq.

The country rolled gently. It looked extremely lush, the grass still brilliantly green. It was watered by many rivers, and by thousands of tributory streams. All the fields were hedged or fenced with post-and-rail. There was no wire to be seen. It was a land of horses and apple-trees. It gave a feeling of continuous occupation, continuous discipline of nature by man, over an immense period. It reeked of wealth.

No scars showed of the bitter struggles over this countryside after D-Day. The shell-holes had been filled up and the farms rebuilt. The new buildings looked like the old buildings — nobody had a taste for glass and concrete, and the mild, moist climate encouraged mosses and lichens to give a kindly patina to new bricks. The turf had grown over the bomb-craters.

Matthew saw the barns of le Coq before he saw the château, and the paddocks before he saw the barns. He drove very slowly along a needle-straight driveway with broad, mown verges. He went between paddocks fenced with post-and-rail not tidily new and white but greyish and rustic. Many of the paddocks were peopled by huge, ancient apple-trees, under which grazed weanlings, yearlings, mares. There were three distinct stable-blocks, each built round three sides of a well-scrubbed square. They were not ancient buildings, but they were far from rawly new. They were built in the black-and-white half-timbered style popular, because thought to be English, among Norman land-owners two generations ago. (Matthew laughed suddenly, remembering the story about all the French fox-terriers called 'Stop' because it was chic to give your dog an English name.) Not much activity was visible, but there must have been a large and industrious staff: everything was as tidy as though swept with dustpan-and-brush and trimmed with nail-scissors.

The drive curved, pierced a closely-planted orchard of younger trees, and unrolled respectfully towards the château. Matthew stopped the car to inspect the house: he might not have time later.

It was not very large — it was not the original or principal seat of the ducs de Montfermainbrey — but it was grand out of all proportion to its size. It was not a house for a modest man. It was tall for its area; arrogant; relieved from cockiness only by age. The south front, which Matthew approached, had square towers at each end and an hexagonal tower in the middle, pierced by an enormous door. Terraces, heavily balustraded, hemmed the square towers, which were covered in a broad-leafed creeper. The roofs, of the main house and of all three towers, were so steeply pitched that they almost doubled the height of the building; windows speckled them, diminishing in size with height. Ornate finials crowned all the corners of all the roofs, suggesting medieval aerials for the reception of television signals from some magic source. A lawn of about three acres ran to the brink of an exactly rectangular pond, itself of about ten acres, the longer sides of which were embellished by superbly purposeless colonnades. Among the cool pillars ramped wistaria and vines. Matthew guessed at the art and effort which achieved this careless effect; it made him think of a woman paying fifty dollars to a hairdresser in order to look windswept.

There was an open courtyard of *pavé* on the north side of the château, where a few cars were parked. Matthew left his car among them, and wondered on which of a dozen visible doors to knock.

A curious humming noise, as of expensive machinery, caused him to turn. At high speed a wheel-chair approached him, followed by another. Both gleamed with varnish and nickel, like Edwardian yachts. In the leading chair sat a very old man who could not have been anything but a duke, aquiline, with chalk-white skin stretched drum-tight over high cheek-bones and a formidable chin, eyes of a hard clear blue, and a mane of silver hair under a deerstalker hat. The hat by itself was sufficiently ducal. In the second chair, approaching at equal speed, was a woman who must have been close to eighty and was still a great beauty.

The wheel-chairs whispered to a halt, side by side, almost nuzzling Matthew's trouser legs. He took off his hat (the hat he had worn at Newmarket races).

'Monsieur de Montfermainbrey?'

It was not the easiest of French names for an American to pronounce with absolute correctness, with its contrasting vowel-sounds and its tricky internal Rs. Matthew hoped his stab did not sound too rawly Middle Western.

'You must be Mr Carver,' said the old man in perfect English. 'How do you do? It is so good of you to have come so far. We were about to make our daily tour of the paddocks, so called because we do it once a week. You may prefer to immure yourself at once with the good Cheminade, or you might be interested to compare our slapdash and amateurish management with your highly scientific methods in Kentucky.'

'I would very much like to come with you, sir,' said Matthew.

'I am glad. Cheminade has all his life waited, agog, for the opportunities which he is now being offered. He can wait a little longer.'

A curious procession — wheel-chair, pedestrian, wheel-chair — skirted the rectangular pond towards the nearest paddocks, while the duke discoursed about grass.

'As far as we know, not one square centimetre of our turf has ever been disturbed. Nor has it ever been fertilised artificially. We are careful not to over-graze, and the grass is naturally and sufficiently enriched by rotting windfalls from the apple-trees and by fallen leaves. Of course the calcium and the necessary trace elements are present. We flirt with modernity to the point of having periodic chemical analysis. Do you like that yearling filly?'

Matthew did, very much.

'Not Solomon in all his glory could buy her. She will visit Beausoleil in three years' time, after she has won the Prix de Diane.'

The American had no false partitive, if there was an American equivalent to such a thing. The duke thought perhaps it was 'Van', though what he had long ago seen and heard of Vanderbilts scarcely bore out the theory.

The American's clothes were better, for this particular day's particular activities, than those most French aristocrats would have chosen. Some would have walked round the paddocks (or declined to do so) in dove-grey flannel and little urban shoes; some would have overdressed the Anglophile sporting role with tweed knickerbockers, Inverness capes, and tiepins with horses' heads.

His manner was good, combining confident equality with respect for age and eminence. Visiting Englishmen often achieved this delicate balance, by dint of what was clearly instinct or a lifetime's training; the duke had heard that the qualified democracy in the Officers' Mess of a first class British regiment taught young men to forget rank while never forgetting it. It was not a lesson many Frenchmen had the opportunity to learn. It was not obvious to the duke how Carver had learned. The duke tried to picture the Officers' Mess in a first class American regiment, but the image was elusive.

Carver was in startling contrast to Henri 'de' Cheminade.

After a murmured aside to his wife, in which he formally asked her permission to take a somewhat audacious risk, the duke asked Matthew Carver to luncheon. 'A simple little snack. A picnic.'

Matthew had been wondering about lunch. He was relieved to accept. He was anxious to see the inside of the château.

'At one o'clock, my dear fellow. That will give you an hour with the good Cheminade and his friend whom, after seeing him briefly from a distance, I confess I should not like to meet in a dark alley.'

'I would not like to meet Cheminade in an alley dark or light,' said the duchess. 'There would be no room to get by.'

Matthew Carver laughed, but he was surprised at the malice with which these beautiful old people spoke.

Matthew was directed to the office. He found Henri de Cheminade alone, with his feet on a table. Henri struggled to his feet, with a look approaching panic, but relaxed when he saw who had come in. He was relieved to be able to adopt his usual role of *boulevardier,* to keep like Cyrano his *panache* in his bonnet instead of hiding it humbly under the table. With Americans, his sophisticated bonhomie took on yet brighter colours, broader strokes, so he could be sure they didn't miss it. There was almost an orchid in his buttonhole, a tilted white hat, a cloudy cane. He was Sidney Greenstreet impersonating Maurice Chevalier.

All this wasted a certain amount of time, but the details were simple. Beausoleil was to be syndicated in forty shares at $500,000 each. This was (give or take a few points in the dollar-pound rate) almost exactly what the Aga Khan had charged for shares in Shergar, after Shergar won the 1981 English Derby. Shares in Lyphard were changing hands, at that moment, for $900,000; but Lyphard was established as a getter of world-class horses, while investment in Beausoleil was still speculative.

The duke was retaining ten shares. Of the remaining thirty, eighteen were already committed by Henri, with the duke's approval, to various French breeders, some of whom had enjoyed the right of first refusal for many months. Of the twelve thus left, three were promised to Prince Ghalib al-Jilani, a gentleman comparatively new to the European turf.

In his first season, Beausoleil would cover forty mares. A few years before, this would have been unheard of: first-season stallions were limited to twenty mares or fewer. Kentucky breeders were the first to decide that it was silly to limit a horse at the peak of his youthful virility, and their example was patchily followed. It made a great financial difference. Once he was established, Beausoleil's tally could be raised to fifty or more. That made a great financial difference, too.

Matthew immediately committed George Whyte to the purchase of the remaining nine shares, for a little under five million dollars.

'Will he stand here?' Matthew asked.

'Oh no, dear boy. The old sweetie would never 'ave a stallion 'ere. We'd need another yard for visiting mares, stallion box, covering yard, and all that jolly rot. Besides, too many people would be coming 'ere all the time, disturbing 'is repose.'

'Where, then?'

'That 'as still to be arrange. Of course it will be in this area, one of the big studs. I will 'ave some talks and do some vettings and make some decisions.'

Matthew nodded. He foresaw with some gloom shipping his own mare all the way from Kentucky to Normandy, and boarding her here until she was certified in foal. It had become entirely normal, but it had not become cheap. The duke's retention of ten shares — itself a normal decision — guaranteed that the majority of the shares were controlled by Frenchmen, which guaranteed that the horse stayed in France. Well, it was the same set of genes, wherever they were injected.

Henri excused himself, and came back a moment later with a tall man in his middle thirties, extremely handsome, whom Matthew recognised as Goring's companion at Newmarket.

After a few minutes of rather careful conversation, Matthew was favourably impressed. When Ghalib spoke of horses, he let his passion show. He adored them. He was not blasé. As ever, Matthew the enthusiast warmed to another.

'I love my Arab ponies at home,' Ghalib said, 'sweet-tempered and handy and brave as lions. And of course they are the ancestors of your horses. But these animals of yours! A horse like Beausoleil! I felt almost sick at Newmarket. I felt I had been given a great privilege, you know, just to see him win that race.'

This made more sense to Matthew Carver than to Henri de Cheminade.

Another careful conversational phase, prompted with a sort of sly ebullience by Henri, allowed Matthew to get the message that Prince Ghalib had a great deal of money to invest in bloodstock, and was interested in subscribing to an existing American operation. He was impressed by American horses and American management. He saw the wisdom of the syndicated purchase of yearlings and broodmares, because the scale could be so great. You gained in flexibility; you reduced the margin of error. Did Mr Carver not agree?

Mr Carver did agree, since he and George Whyte had been operating on these principles for years. This was known to Ghalib, because it was known to everybody. Ghalib was sending out feelers.

Matthew had not discussed with George Whyte the recruitment of a new partner. What he had said on television was true: no decision had been taken; they would talk about it. The disappearance of a major contributor on whom they had relied — George's grossly unsatisfactory brother-in-law, not now to be mentioned without oaths — might make George want another source of capital. Or he might decide to cut back. Or go it alone. If someone else was to come in, Ghalib seemed as good as any. He had the money, he had the enthusiasm, he already owned a piece of Beausoleil, and — not an overwhelming factor, but not a contemptible one — he was a congenial guy. Matthew liked him.

That was as far as things could be taken at that moment. But they could be taken much farther, quite fast, as soon as Matthew got back to Kentucky and talked to George Whyte.

Ghalib wanted things taken as far as possible as fast as possible. Matthew Carver at close quarters was even more impressive than at a distance. He was lunching with the duke and duchess. Ghalib, a prince of the Blood Royal, was not asked into the château. Henri de Cheminade, evidently a kind of nobleman, was not asked into the château. Ghalib wanted to be Matthew Carver's confederate, his intimate. Doors now shut would open to him. Hands now firmly in pockets would slap him on the shoulder.

He would get on intimate terms with that beautiful, that miniature, that insanely attractive daughter. This was not an overwhelming factor in directing the investment of several million dollars. But it was not a contemptible one.

Partly instinctively, partly from hearsay, partly from the evidence of what he saw and heard in the duke's office, Ghalib found in himself a deep respect for Matthew Carver's judgement. Henri de Cheminade was not a fool, or ignorant; he had not done at all badly by Ghalib. But he was not infallible and Ghalib did not quite trust him. He was in a mood to think Matthew Carver was infallible; and he did trust him.

Henri de Cheminade watched with mounting joy the visible birth of friendship between Ghalib and Carver. He was not losing a client. He was gaining one — a multi-headed and massively-financed one. He was expanding into America with Ghalib, and he was pulling American investment into France, and through his own hands, with Beausoleil.

He had to hush Ghalib up at one moment. The Arab began to tell Carver about the place he was looking for, the *haras,* the farm, the stud. He mentioned an interest in Ireland. Fortunately Carver did not know Ireland well, and had heard of no estates being sold there. Henri turned the conversation adroitly to the subject of Irish whiskey, asking Carver, in all innocence, why it was spelled differently from Scotch whisky.

Henri felt a glow of loyalty to Lord Goring, whose commission he was protecting. It was a sensation the more precious for its rarity, like the duke's aged Calvados.

Which, after a luncheon unimaginably remote from snack or picnic, Matthew was drinking with almost incredulous enjoyment. The duke watched the astonishment on his face, and laughed gently, as one who sees the effect on a nice child of a nice surprise.

Matthew mentioned Epiminondas Makropulos and his interest in Beausoleil. Of course the duke knew about Epi, a prominent international owner-breeder; of course he had met him at Longchamp and Chantilly and Deauville; of course, on slight acquaintance, he liked him.

'If I may venture a personal remark,' said the duke, 'I am not surprised that you and he are friends. I would have expected that you would be congenial.'

'Yes, it's curious. Epi and I have nothing in common, yet we have everything in common.'

'Including a regard for my horse. Well then, I have a suggestion. I have one suggestion that will lead to others. Before I commit myself to serious indiscretion, may I have your assurance that this will be, for the time being, entirely confidential between us? Good. I have retained ten shares in Beausoleil. I expect to send two mares to him in the spring. No more. The other mating plans are made and in some cases paid for. In the ordinary way I would authorise the good Cheminade to sell the eight nominations. He is rather visibly hoping that I shall adopt that orthodox course. It is, in truth, partly the crude visibility of his hope that prompts me to adopt a different course. Would your Greek friend be interested in leasing eight shares?'

'Yes,' said Matthew instantly.

'Of course he will pay as though for annual nominations, at the going rate for nominations. The arrangement will be terminable by either side in respect of any share or number of shares.'

'Yes, that must be right.'

'I think so. I might want to send three or four mares to Beausoleil the year after next. He might conceive a violent distaste for the horse. But meanwhile the shares are his. I expect he will in turn sell some nominations?'

'I doubt if he would send eight mares to one unproven stallion, sir. Even yours.'

'I doubt it, too, and I doubt if Makropulos will lose on the transaction.'

'He'll be over the moon.'

'It is a great pleasure to me to send him there. Of course you must tell him, but I beg you will tell no one else. There are strong reasons for this. Personal reasons.'

Matthew nodded his promise.

The duke's reasons were that he had informally but quite plainly promised nominations to various breeders, before the Champion Stakes, at a figure much lower than they would now realise. So much does one really significant victory affect values. He had wanted a bird in the hand. He now had both the birds that had been in the bush, firmly transferred to the hand. He had no hesitation in mentally tearing up a series of mental contracts. But he did not want to be seen doing it.

The white pekinese Ju-luh was placed by a servant on the duke's lap. He fondled its ears as he went on, 'I imagine it would be convenient for your colleagues and yourself if Beausoleil went to stud in America.'

'Yes, it would, of course. But that hardly seems possible.'

'No? I think it becomes possible.'

Matthew did sums in his head. He did not see how it became possible, unless Epi, Ghalib and the duke himself all wanted Beausoleil to go to America. Their shares, added to George Whyte's nine shares, just outnumbered the French shares.

Well, Epi might easily prefer Beausoleil to stand in America. He had more mares in France, but better ones in Virginia. After this morning, it was possible to sense that Ghalib might like the horse to go to America, and himself with it. And, for reasons Matthew could not fathom, there was a hint that the duke wanted the same thing.

'Henri de Cheminade was quite clear to me this morning —' he began.

'If he was quite clear about the future of Beausoleil, he was arrogating to himself a standing in the matter to which he is not at all entitled. No firm arrangements have been made.'

'He thinks they have, sir.'

'His wish is the father of his thought. What a bestial parentage! No, no, my dear fellow, Cheminade has no claim on me. He is intriguing for a position for which, in all charity, I do not believe him quite competent. The fact that he is pathetically anxious to manage Beausoleil — and much else of mine, if I read the look in his eyes — gives him, alas, neither the right nor the ability to do so. It was wrong of him to give you the impression that I had appointed him to any capacity. Let us try to believe that he did so inadvertently.'

'Hum,' said Matthew, uneasily remembering the morning's conversation.

'I can think of much better hands into which to entrust my darling.'

'Whose?'

'Yours. Don't look so surprised, my dear fellow. You must be aware of your own reputation. Whereas the good Cheminade is probably unaware of his . . . But this is also an aspect of the situation in which I do beg your absolute discretion.'

The duke was happy to stab Henri 'de' Cheminade in the back, as punishment for his presumptuous partitive, his obsequiousness, his greedy grocer's eyes. But he did not want to be seen doing so. The wound, when observed, would appear to have been caused by other hands.

The duke was not motivated solely by contempt. He had respectable reasons. He thought the horse would earn more money in hands which he had reason to believe were expert. He thought he would go on earning longer and, by covering better-selected mares, increase Beausoleil's value by dint of the quality of his foals. He thought the horse would earn more in America than in France.

He thought about Beausoleil's welfare, too, most seriously and sincerely.

As Matthew was taking his leave — and introducing a note of stately formality which had been quite absent from the lunch-table — a telephone rang. The call was for him, from London. He was puzzled. It was his daughter Clare. She sounded unhappy. His heart sank.

She said, 'I knew where you were, because I was with you when you fixed it up, at Newmarket.'

'Sure. Is there a crisis?'

'Yes. Were you going to fly right back home from Paris?'

'I am going to fly right back home from Paris. Your mother doesn't want to see me, I saw Jamie, Liz is who the hell knows where, and I'll see you soon anyway. I have no reason to go back to London.'

'You must come,' said Clare miserably. 'It's about Liz.'

'Oh God.'

'Mother says she's in terrible trouble. Mother says it's your responsibility, and you have to come here to fix it.'

'Can I talk to your mother?'

'She's too upset to talk.'

'All right,' said Matthew, as they both knew he had to. 'I'll come.'

He drove back to Paris with a mixture of feelings, all disagreeable.

Mollie had taken Liz away from him. Mollie was responsible, if anybody was, for whatever was wrong with Liz. It was violently unfair and illogical to blame Matthew for Liz being fatherless, for her being a delinquent or a runaway. But Mollie did not deal in fairness or logic.

It was not her fault. It was how she was. You fought down resentment, fury, because *that* was unfair and illogical, and the effort gave you a gut-ache.

It was unfair of Mollie to make Clare do the dirty work, make a call which was certain to be so unwelcome. None of it was any of

Clare's business, and she was one person in the world who couldn't be blamed for Liz. Mollie would have used emotional blackmail on Clare, unconscious of what she herself was doing. 'I thought children were proud to help their mothers in times of unhappiness.'

It was highly inconvenient to go back to London. The extra flight and the nights in a London hotel were damned expensive.

God knew what mess Liz had got herself into. God knew what follies Mollie had triggered by her bullying, or encouraged by her lavishness and laxity. Her approach to bringing up the children was a disastrous alternation of the two. She might have ruined Liz's life. Liz was a very pretty kid, a little overweight, blonde like her mother, precocious yet childish. She sometimes dressed up to look like jailbait. Maybe that's what Mollie had turned her into.

The superb lunch knotted itself into a jagged flint in Matthew's gut. A splendid and successful day was ruined.

CHAPTER 5

Clare in London hung up. She looked across the room at her mother's averted face. She felt the familiar mixture of desperate, defensive love and almost ungovernable irritation.

From where Clare stood by the telephone table, she could see the row of photographs in silver frames which cluttered up the dwellings of almost everybody in England Clare knew who remotely resembled her mother. There were photographs of Clare herself, Liz, Jamie, the Wincham grandparents; there was a photograph of Clare's mother on her wedding day. The way she looked explained a lot. She was a beauty, slender, graceful, solemn, a fairy princess.

Clare looked, with an ache at the way things had turned out, from photograph to subject and back again. It was more terrible to look at the photograph, because it promised something so wildly different. The slenderness had become scrawny. The small-boned, pensive face had become lined and pinched, and the translucent skin had faded and coarsened. What remained was the solemnity.

Clare looked from photograph to subject: from nymph to martyr. Was she a do-gooder when that shutter clicked? Active or only potential? Did she become one because the marriage broke up? Did the marriage break up because she became one?

Clare thought her mother was the only person who was tireless and always tired.

She was a bad chooser of apartments. This one was so dark you needed a light at noon, in the kitchen and in this stuffy sitting-room and in the passage. The sitting-room could have been tolerable with scaled-down furniture and strict unfussiness. It would have been lighter, and seemed bigger, with simple drapes and a plain, shallow pelmet. But the curtains were immense, grandiose brocade, with a pelmet like that at the Royal Opera

House. They stifled the room, defeated it, darkened and shrank it.

'Did you take over those curtains when you moved in?' asked Clare suddenly.

'No, of course not. They wanted me to buy the ones they had, but I refused. They were skimpy cotton things, curtains for a bedroom, for a maid's bedroom.'

'You bought those?'

'I had them made at Harrods. I knew what the room needed.'

'Wow! They must have been expensive.'

'One must be prepared to pay for the best.'

'Sure, if one can.'

'Your father can. I shall send him the bill, of course. I have not looked at it myself. I shall give him the bill when he comes here tomorrow, on his way to deal with Liz.'

'I don't know how he'll do that, as she won't speak to anybody.'

'He is a man. He is her father.'

'No doubt about that.'

'None,' agreed Clare's mother seriously. 'He will go to the — crouch, I think they call it.'

'Squat.'

'What a disgusting word. Notting Hill. A dreadful neighbourhood. A gang of Trotskyists. Blacks. Paying no rent. Refusing to be evicted. Creating utter squalor.'

'We don't know any of that.'

'I don't understand you.'

'We don't know they're black, or Trot, or squalid.'

'I had hoped for loyalty from you, Clare. I had hoped I could depend on a helpful attitude.'

'What would be helpful would be a social worker.'

'Some ignorant provincial, easily hoodwinked, useless. I won't have interfering bureaucrats meddling in our private affairs.'

Clare wondered whether the social services were rejected because they were too effective or not effective enough. There was no point in voicing this.

Meanwhile it was true that Liz had refused to talk to her mother or to read any message from her; and she had told Clare, quite politely, through a Pakistani intermediary, to please go to hell and leave her alone.

Much of Mollie's information was inaccurate, though it

contained truth.

They called themselves the Happy Valley Commune. They varied around two dozen in number, including several mothers with young children, some born in wedlock. Three were black. The only declared Trotskyist was a Wykehamist who lived with, and off, a girl who worked in a Kentish Town record shop.

Liz moved in with Ali, whose family came from Phulji in central Pakistan, whose father was a baker and mother a teacher, who had himself got a place at Keele University. He had a vague, unfocussed intention to work for his degree. But he was too lazy to pick up a book and open it; too gentle to compete in the demure struggle to get on a bus. He and Liz had met, in August, at a sweltering concert given by a group called Kennedy's Latin Primer, advertised as 'carrying punk to putrescence' but actually tame and banal. Ali and Liz had shared a joint and later a patch of turf in Battersea Park. He said she was the first blonde he had ever fucked and she said he was the first poet she had ever fucked.

That was what he was: a poet. He kept starting poems to Liz's lips and hips and so forth.

She moved in with the Happy Valley after a row with her mother which her mother didn't notice.

Ali was underfed. Liz fed him. The Wykehamist introduced her to a photographer who paid her quite well for posing for peculiar photographs. The black boy and the Maltese who posed with her had no difficulty in feeling and showing the required physical excitement. It was easy money, as long as the studio was warm. Liz never saw the photographs. She correctly imagined they were sold in the back rooms of Soho shops. It made her giggle to think of any of her mother's friends seeing them and recognizing her. She felt little embarrassment and no shame. She needed to buy food for Ali, and she could make money more quickly this way than any other. She had to be quick about it, because she had to get back to look after him.

There was a positive and negative side to all this.

Positively, she cared about gentle, dreamy Ali and she found that, in looking after someone who needed looking after, she was doing something of merit for the first time in her life. Positively, she was glad to help the mothers with their babies. Positively, she felt free and adult.

Negatively, the gigantic virtue of the squat was that it was not her mother's flat. She was out from under.

Positively, being fucked on a dirty mattress by a coffee-coloured layabout was quite nice. Negatively, its charm was that it would have caused her mother to give birth to a set of ovenproof dishes.

Ali knew all about Liz's mother — the whole commune did. She risked being a bore on the subject. He asked her about her father.

Liz shrugged. 'I don't know what he'd say. Probably nothing. He doesn't give a fart for us, for my brother and me. If he did he'd see us sometimes.'

Liz had been better taught than she knew.

At the Armorique, Matthew Carver found a message from Epaminondas Makropulos. He bathed, changed, had two drinks in his room from the bottle of duty-free Dimple, and took a taxi to the Ile de la Cité. The restaurant off the Rue Harley was unknown to him. Another of Epi's discoveries. Epi sniffed out the very best, in food and hotels and horses and pictures and girls, like a highly sophisticated Périgord pig rootling for three-star truffles.

Epi and Matthew had a reunion in which neither observed George Whyte's rule about undemonstrative greetings.

The restaurant was very small, and in general effect brown and soothing. The checked table-cloth lent a cottage air which the menu and the prices dispelled.

They were joined by a girl — one of Epi's girls — who had been, probably metaphorically, powdering her tiny button nose. Epi introduced her as Tanja Dekker. She was Indonesian, with a Dutch grandfather, brought up in Amsterdam because her name and blood were not popular under Sukarno's régime. She was a miniature, smaller than Clare, a startling beauty in a slit silk sheath. Her grip was surprisingly firm when she shook hands with Matthew. Her hand looked too small and frail to hold an egg-spoon, but she was stronger than she looked. Her English was fluent and almost unaccented. Her smile was broad and cheerful. She looked uncomplicated and happy. Epi's girls usually looked happy, and they had plenty to be happy about.

There was no other girl. There was no girl for Matthew. Matthew was relieved and disappointed. Epi had found him other girls in other cities, by some grapevine of his own, who combined beauty, intelligence and complaisance in remarkable measure.

96

Ordering dinner for his friends was one of Epi's skills and hobbies. His conference with the *patron*, in French too rapid and idiomatic for Matthew to follow entirely, resulted in a meal of awesome complexity and subtlety for Tanja and Matthew. Epi himself had a slice of terrine, a plain grilled sole, and fruit. He drank a young, chilled Sancerre from the upper Loire. Matthew was not surprised. Tanja evidently knew him well enough not to be surprised. There was nothing wrong with Epi's figure or digestion or any of his appetites, but he had gone through luxury and out the other side, into simplicity. He was austere in his personal life. He was often Spartan. He did not visit austerity on his friends. He enjoyed their enjoyment. The great luxury he indulged was the smooth running of the wheels of his life, planned, organized, time-saving, every activity profitable or specifically enjoyable, the machinery powered by his will and lubricated by a great deal of money. Girls like Tanja were another indulgence, but they were not nearly so expensive.

'Of course I will lease Gaston de Montfermainbrey's shares,' he said. 'And of course I will not send eight mares to Beausoleil in his first season, and of course I shall make a profit when I sell the nominations. What a good and clever friend you are, Matthew. Will you take him to America?'

'It begins to look as though we might.'

'I hope you will, speaking as I always do entirely selfishly. The outcross will be more relevant to me there. I suppose he will go to Cragrock?'

'Cragrock is pretty well full.'

'That is no problem. Dear George will conjure up another palatial stallion-box.'

'Maybe. I think he thinks forty-six stallions is plenty.'

'Then stand Beausoleil in Virginia, for a change. I make this suggestion simply because my own mares are there.'

'Virginia. That's just what Merivale Lucas said.'

'Did he? I wonder why. Does Scruffy own a piece of a farm in Virginia?'

'That was how it struck me, yes. A place called Fox Hill, somewhere near Somerset.'

'Ah.'

'You sound as though you know it.'

'Quite well. Scruffy doesn't own any part of Fox Hill. But still I begin to understand.'

'They have a mare I bred. I half-promised Lucas I'd go and look at the place.'

'Do that, Matt.'

'Prepare me a little.'

'It is the kind of Virginia house where they make the martinis twice a day and the beds twice a year.'

'Then I won't go there, and sure as hell Beausoleil won't.'

'You might do much worse, really. The barns are fine, the grazing is excellent, and the manager is a guy I would steal tomorrow if I could.'

'That sounds a little better.'

'The house is worth going a long way to see.'

'Beausoleil won't be living in the house.'

'There is one other feature I should mention.' Epi paused, smiled, and said, 'The owner is a man called Peter Collin. He has a sister, who is married but lives there. Her husband is an invalid of some kind. Maybe crazy. Yes, I think crazy. Actually, Peter Collin is crazy too, but not quite crazy enough to put into an institution.'

'This is a funny blurb you're writing,' said Tanja. 'A crazy owner with a crazy brother-in-law.'

'But the sister,' said Epi, 'Ah, the sister. She is called Rosanna.'

'I have to go all the way to Somerset because a crazy man's sister is called Rosanna?' said Matthew.

'No, she could be called Beulah or Beryl or Gladys. The reason to go is because she would have the statue of Zeus on Paphos doing handsprings. She would draw the stars from the sky and cause the trees to bow down in worship. She is quite a pretty lady.'

'Don't you go there,' said Tanja to Matthew.

'No doubt she is the reason Scruffy Lucas likes the place so much,' said Epi.

'Scruffy having an affair with this lady?' said Matthew.

'Impossible. She can choose the very best. I don't know if she does, but I am very sure she can. Like Tanja.'

'You are too vain to live,' said Tanja.

'Well then, like me.'

Matthew laughed. His curiosity was mildly aroused. But he was unimpressed by the sound of Fox Hill. Tanja was right. Epi's blurb was distinctly equivocal. But he did want to see his mare Meadowsweet again.

Matthew excused himself, after his second cup of coffee.

'You like my old friend?' said Epi to Tanja, with the manner of one expecting the answer 'yes'.

'Very much,' said Tanja. 'He is clever and gentle. His manners are good. He is quite unlike an American, but he could be nothing but American. Why is that?'

'Women tell me he is attractive.'

'Yes, of course. Especially just now, I think.'

'Why just now?'

'Because he is so sad.'

'Does that make him more attractive?'

'To every woman, perhaps not. To me yes. And not every man is more attractive when he is sad. It depends on the man and on the reason. A cruel or selfish or weak man might be even less attractive when he was sad. He might be sad because he was not cruel enough, or because he had given something away. I think your friend is not cruel or selfish. If he is weak it is only a little bit and not in an evil way. Why is he sad, Epi?'

Epi told her what Matthew had told him, about Clare's call and Mollie's demand and Liz. He told her the little he knew about Mollie, and the much he guessed. He too had, of course, noticed the occasional heaviness in his old friend's manner, his abstraction, the worry and irritation in his eyes, even in the midst of a happy dinner and a successful negotiation.

Epi's account upset and angered Tanja. She was angry with Matthew Carver's daughter for behaving so selfishly and thoughtlessly. She was angry with Mrs Carver for being so unreasonable and unfair. She was angry that, between them, they had made this attractive man unhappy.

Epi saw Tanja's anger because he saw almost everything. Knowing her, he knew that she would wish to comfort Matthew, to give him at least a short time of self-forgetting joy. She would want to comfort almost anybody who was unhappy, and more particularly any close friend of Epi's, and most of all a man she found physically and mentally attractive.

Epi esteemed and enjoyed Tanja, and he was generous to her. He did not consider that he owned her. Indeed, she had a greater sense of being owned by him, or at least expensively rented.

He said, 'Anything you can do for Matt Carver will be a kindness to me. That sounds like a letter you write, to a friend in a foreign city, if another friend is going there. You are not supposed to stick up the envelope, but your friend who takes it is not supposed to read it. I am very fond of Matt, you know. I don't like seeing him in this miserable, uptight condition.'

When Matthew came back from the john, he found that the bill had been paid and Epi had left.

'He remembered an engagement,' lied Tanja.

'At this time of night?'

'This is a very good time for engagements. Do you have one?'

'No. Do you?'

'No. Isn't that sad? Two of us deprived.'

Matthew looked across the checked table-cloth at the perfect little ivory face and the shy, expectant smile.

So they went off together in a taxi, and she responded to his kisses with enthusiasm, and her body inside the thin silk was like a snake, lithe and wriggling and everywhere.

They were leisurely, almost tentative, in his room. She refused a drink. He did not want one. He took off his jacket. She snuggled on his lap. She was no longer a snake but a puppy, a kitten. They talked. He heard about her life as a model in Amsterdam and London and New York. She heard about his home in Kentucky. She asked delicately about his family, because she really wanted to know.

She expected, from other nights with other men, the therapeutic opening of floodgates, the painful and blessed lancing of the boil. But this gentle American was laconic about his children and silent about his wife.

He was loyal.

The bitter floodwaters built up still behind the dam, and the unlanced boil festered with anger and worry and guilt.

Words slid into actions, friendly, unembarrassed. His body was muscular and spare. Hers was a clinging miracle.

It didn't work. Nothing worked.

Tanja tried everything she knew, with lips and teeth and clever little fingers, and nothing worked. They dressed in silence. She would not let him see her home.

'That woman has castrated him,' said Tanja sadly to Epi. 'I don't know what she has done, but she has cut off his balls.'

'Poor Matt. And with you. How humiliated he must have felt.'

'Yes, I know. Instead of making things better I have made them worse. And of course I have an ache in my gut.'

'Nobody has cut my balls off,' said Epi.

'I know, darling. Where are my friends? That's reassuring for a girl.'

Matthew's last waking thought, before one of his rare Mogadons took hold, was of Fox Hill. Barns good, Epi said. Grass good. Manager good. House good. All right, so all that was good. Pretty woman. Neither good nor bad. Neutral. Irrelevant. Two crazy men. Bad. Scruffy Lucas involved. Bad bad. Make drinks all the time, beds never. *Bad bad bad,* as Kipling's dog said about the kitchen cat.

He was going to have to do a lot of things he didn't want to do, such as going to London and seeing Mollie. Going to Fox Hill was one thing he didn't want to do that he didn't have to do.

The builders and carpenters and painters, the plumbers and electricians and tilers, the garden contractors and roadmen and lumbermen, were aghast at the extent of the work they all faced at Fox Hill. For their bosses it was a bonanza — a full order-book for the foreseeable future.

Some of these craftsmen knew a little about architecture and architectural history, and for them it was a privilege to work on the place. Fox Hill was the most beautiful house they had seen after, perhaps, Monticello. It was built about 1760, at a time when Virginia was very rich and ostentatious and sporting, and also educated in the European taste. The owner hired an architect who had been to Italy and studied the work of Palladio. Fox Hill's columns, porticoes, pilasters and pediments were more redolent of the Veneto than of the English countryside from which most Virginia colonial houses derived. The effect was of classical grandeur made gentle, even delicate. A further Italianate note was struck by the principal outbuildings, the coach-house and stables. These were squared up with the main house and in architectural unity with it, and the stable clock-tower echoed, in a smaller and elongated form, the main portico on the west front of the house.

The place was in a shocking mess. It was unspoiled by any modern changes, but it was in a sad condition of neglect. Everyone in the neighbourhood knew why. Old Charles Collin had died in 1965, of brandy and foxhunting. His son was only twenty-five then, away somewhere, unwilling or unable to take on such a ball and chain. He might have let it, but the local word was that he never bothered — never got around to it. He was remembered as a dreamy kid who spent his time sitting around. It seemed that was still how he spent his time. So the house stood empty for sixteen years, except for caretakers who kept goats in the big dining-room and pigeons in the bedrooms. There were broken windows, rotted sills, sagging gutters and yawing drainpipes, flaking plaster, peeling paint, mess, straw, rubbish inside and out; and, indoors, lovely antique wallpapers tattered and fluttering, curtains in shreds, broken mantles, choked chimneys, cracks and fissures, missing floorboards, ceilings with ominous stains and walls showing a tendency to bulge.

Young Peter got to nearly forty, and decided, so the local word was, to settle down in the ancestral home. He brought his sister. Her husband's money might have had something to do with that. Big works began. The Phillipson money might have had a good deal to do with that, too. Now the basics were pretty well done, the structural work and the plumbing and wiring. There was still a hell of a lot to do.

One thing screamed to be done which nobody knew how to do or had the material for. When you went in by the main west entrance, you found yourself in a lofty hall which, scaled down and modified, was modelled on the great Palladian church of San Giorgio Maggiore in Venice. From it, four gigantic doors opened into the principal rooms. These doors had always been covered in leather, a special sort of leather dyed green and rivetted to the oak with thousands of brass studs. Now the leather was hanging in tatters from the studs, a messy and pathetic sight. Peter Collin had, with an unusual show of energy, charged himself with the responsibility of finding a man who could find the leather and fix the doors.

The garden had once been famous. Of course in that kindly climate, on that lush soil, sixteen years had produced a jungle. This had not been an early priority, but they were getting at it now. The old geometrical beds and parterres were uncovered, the paths cleaned up, a lot of invasive undergrowth hacked away and burned, so that on summer evenings the Fox Hill gardens looked like a vision of hell. New trees were planted in avenues suggested by the eighteenth-century drawings of the place. The grass tennis-court needed a power scythe before its exact position could be determined. It still had to be mown close. A start had been made on the ruinous drive, which threatened the suspension of every vehicle that used it. Nobody had hit the topiary yews yet. Nobody could make out what the shapes had once been. Peter Collin and his sister had screaming arguments about that. They both said they remembered exactly, but they remembered differently. Their old black nurse joined in the screaming, most times. She said she remembered better than they did, but the tree-surgeons still didn't know where to start.

It was an entertaining place to work, but a fellow was liable to get confused.

A carpenter was beginning to replace some warped shelves in the library, one of the big rooms off the hall, a place that even in the racket of reconstruction had a cathedral solemnity. The carpenter unloaded books off the warped shelves and carried them down his ladder to stack them in the middle of the room. There his troubles began. The little old string-bean man they called Jefferson, a kind of lodger or permanent guest (nobody outside the family could make out his exact position), was passionately interested in the dusty old books. He got horribly in the carpenter's way. He was up the ladder when the carpenter needed it, or spreading the neat stacks of books all over the floor, or just being distracting by his nonstop yap. There was no shifting him. The carpenter started with tactful requests, and finished with brutal rudeness, but it all bounced off Jefferson. He didn't hear, or he took it as a joke, or he was so used to rudeness that nothing penetrated.

The carpenter quit early. He was his own boss. He was paid by the hour. They trusted him to tot up the hours fairly. Any more of Jefferson would tickle up his duodenal. He packed up his tools and went out to his pick-up, parked behind the house and in front of what had been the coach-house. They used it as a garage. Mr Collin, Peter, the one they called Peach, was trying to back a car into the garage. The carpenter's truck was a little in the way, but not much. There was no problem about getting the car into the garage. For Mr Collin there was, though. It was as if he'd never driven in his life, or was blind, or drunk. He was like a drunk, roaring the power and then stalling, swinging the wheel too hard or not hard enough, lurching backwards by letting in the clutch too suddenly, stalling, starting, lurching forwards, hitting one side of the broad doorway and then the other, knocking out his tail-lights and denting his wings.

Then, going forward too fast and heaving his steering-wheel too far to the left, he hit the carpenter's pick-up slap dab on the driver's door.

There was a bellow of rage from inside the car. The carpenter thought he was the one entitled to bellow with rage. Mr Collin got out of the car. He had a lot of trouble doing that, not because the door wouldn't work but because he wouldn't work. His expression said that he'd undertaken a pretty gigantic and hazardous mission, getting out of the car and standing on his feet. None of his limbs seemed to obey, unless he thought about it and used maximum will-power.

He got on his feet in the end, and stood looking apathetically at the stove-in side of the truck and the stove-in front of the car. He was tall and thin and stooped, but he had a pot belly. Probably because he never took any exercise, and because he was always eating candy. Nobody ever saw him without a candy-bar, crunchy or chewy, chocolate-coated, young kids' candy-bars. He left the paper wrappers wherever he went, just dropped them. Sometimes somebody picked them up. His face was smooth, pale, pasty. It looked like some kind of dough, like the stuff you start with when you make home-made spaghetti. You couldn't say what colour his hair was. It was colourless. There wasn't much of it, though he was hardly forty. The funny thing was, he could have been a handsome man. But everything about him was a little out of true, like the warped shelves in the library. You could immediately see he was his sister's brother, though everything about her was exactly right. He was blurred, she was in sharp definition. He was bent, she was straight. He moved like an unco-ordinated giraffe, she like a healthy cat. His weight was distributed for maximum clumsiness, awkwardness, hers for maximum elegance and beauty.

'Your truck?' said Mr Collin to the carpenter.

'Yes, sir.'

'Shouldn't be parked there. Blocking the garage. Dumb place to put it. Caused an accident. I might have been hurt. You'll get a pretty big bill for this.'

'But you could see it! It didn't get invisible!'

'How could I see it when I was reversing into the garage? You look backwards when you reverse. At least, you cause a hell of a lot of damage if you don't. Do you *deny* I was reversing into the garage? Of course you don't. You have more sense. More honesty.'

The carpenter said he accepted no responsibility, and would be sending his repair bill to Mr Collin. But before he finished a glazed look came over Mr Collin's face. He was not listening. He began to walk away, belly and shoulders forward, butt jutting.

The carpenter decided he would never come to this crazy establishment again. Until he remembered they owed him nearly $600.

Peach Collin marched, with his invariable combination of dignity and elegance, away from the artisan and his mouthings. He had better things to think about. Philosophical speculations of a magnificent audacity waited to be explored. Peach needed to sit down in solitude. He made for the little pink room (awaiting redecoration) where he did most of his thinking.

He passed his sister Rosie on the way; or rather, at full gallop, she passed him. Rosie was often galloping. Not always, but often. Hers was not truly a philosophic soul. It was not hers to watch, from the empyrean, the scurrying and struggles of the ants. She was not precisely one of the ants — she was a Collin of Fox Hill — but you had to take that on trust. She *acted* like one of the ants. She was dressed in filthy sweater and jeans and sneakers. Her hair was a mess from galloping around. She was carrying a paintbrush in one hand and a leather halter in the other.

'Which horse are you going to paint?' called Peach to her retreating back.

'The paint-horse,' said Rosie.

She trotted away towards the barn where the broodmares were.

Peach was glad to have her at Fox Hill. He loved her deeply, even though she was restless and sometimes nagging. She nagged him about the leather for the doors. She nagged him about having some trees felled, so she could build another barn she said she needed. Peach had accepted — nay, insisted upon — responsibility for these matters. Anybody else would be apt to get the wrong kind of leather, or cut down too many trees. The philosopher-king therefore descended from his mountain to assist and direct the groundlings. In time there would be leather, the right leather of the right colour, tacked in seemly fashion to the doors. In time the trees would be abolished. He had said so.

Rosie's nagging was counter-productive. Each time she mentioned leather or trees, Peach postponed action. She was always in too much of a hurry, except when she stopped. Then she stopped completely, and even Peach appeared energetic in comparison. Rosie was a creature of extremes, thought Peach with affectionate tolerance, temperamentally unable to maintain, like himself, an even, unhurried, gentlemanly progress through the landscape of life.

Peach's gentlemanly progress never took him as far as the horses. That whole area was delegated. He had been taught to ride as a child, but he disliked being so far off the ground; he disliked the impact of the ground on various parts of his body when, in spite of high skill, grace and courage, he parted company with his mount. Rosie's riding had been widely praised, and she was always winning cups and rosettes. To set store by such baubles was not the mark of the superior intellect.

Peach characterised himself as a spiritual Diogenes. Fox Hill was the hell of a tub. He was really superior to Diogenes, in that he did not need, for spiritual abnegation, the crude symbolism of deliberate poverty. Besides, he honoured Fox Hill with his stewardship. He honoured Tim Phillipson by allowing him to finance certain trifling and inexpensive improvements.

Tim Phillipson had been another one who collected trophies. He was always riding in races, and usually winning them. All illusion. Evanescent glory. Reality lay elsewhere. The Buddhists had it right. Peach resolved to study Buddhism. It was a question of finding the time. Tim was lucky, lying in that bed with plenty of time to think. His galloping days were over. Tim's steeple-chasing was one of the things that had attracted Rosie. She hadn't exactly married him because he had won the Maryland Hunt Cup, but it influenced her. It did not influence Peach's attitude to Tim one way or the other. Other things did. Peach saw in Tim a man of absolute excellence, the only man in America worthy of Rosie, worthy of being admitted to Peach's own intimate friendship. Tim, Rosie and Peach formed a triumvirate of nobility which, most of the time, they found it kinder to hide. Peach would have done anything for Tim. He did what he could. He let Tim know, by Rosie, that he was his friend and brother until death. He didn't actually ever go to see Tim. Rosie was always going over to the sanitorium, but Peach knew better than to submit his own finely poetic soul to such an experience. He would have given Tim money if he had had any money, and if Tim wasn't rich enough for all of them.

Peach lowered himself into his thinking chair in his thinking room. A casual observer might have supposed him half-asleep, daydreaming, or in a state of suspended animation. But his brain was churning. He contemplated the cosmos. His imagination tracked comets, and penetrated nebulae. He ate three candy-bars, which were in a drawer of the table by his chair. They were thinking candy-bars. He hardly noticed he was eating them, so far and fierce were his thoughts. The wrappers fluttered forgotten from his fingers.

The four of them met all together for the first time that day at dinner — Peach, Rosie, Cousin Thalia Collin, and Jefferson Dill the resident scholar and poet. The other three had some kind of meat and salad. Peach had a big, sticky butterscotch dessert for his first course. Then they all had apple pie and cream. Peach nearly always had something special. His old nurse Hazel kept the cook up to that. Hazel knew what he needed. He had to replace the energy he used up in thinking.

Cousin Thalia was actually first cousin to Peach and Rosie's father. Her father had been the younger son. She had spent most of her vacations at Fox Hill as a child, in the twenties and early thirties. She regarded Fox Hill as her home. She often said so. Peach was not sure if he himself or Rosie had asked her to come and live here, or both of them, or neither. Now she was here she would stay, there was never any doubting that. The effort of getting rid of her would be so horrible that it was not to be contemplated. Meanwhile she contributed culture and advice. She had also contributed Jefferson Dill.

Jefferson Dill rented an apartment over the coach-house. He joined the family for dinner. He was a writer. Peach had not read, or even seen, any of his books. As his name suggested, he came from Charlottesville. Where Cousin Thalia had found him, and why he had installed himself at Fox Hill, were mysterious to Peach. He imagined he had been told, and the explanations were so boring he had forgotten them. Jefferson Dill was doing research for a history of Fox Hill, which was to be published privately at Tim Phillipson's expense.

Both Cousin Thalia and Jefferson Dill ate with astonishing appetites. Rosie went easy on the crust of the apple pie and on the cream. She drank most of a bottle of hock. Jefferson Dill drank bourbon. Cousin Thalia drank a mixture of cider vinegar and honey, advised by her chiropractor. She suffered from an unusual deformity of the neck, about which she often boasted. The cider vinegar had a penetrating but not displeasing taste. Peach drank malted milk, made by Hazel the way he liked it.

Peach was wearing his father's plum-coloured velvet jacket with a white silk turtleneck, black evening pants, and slippers embroidered years before by Rosie for her husband. Tim had no use for them now.

Cousin Thalia was wrapped in some large, anonymous garment to which Peach referred vaguely in his mind as burnous, yashmak, caftan, muu-muu or tent.

'The colours,' said Cousin Thalia, 'derive from a painting by Marc Chagall. But I dare not suppose you are familiar with his work.'

'Ma Shag-all,' said Jefferson Dill, with high-bred derision. 'Marshall Hall. Marcia Balls. I cannot *look* at any painter after Reynolds.'

Jefferson Dill was wearing a blue denim jacket, white canvas pants, and heavy leather sandals over woolly white socks. Something on a thong dangled round his neck. He had a stiff whitish crewcut. He looked more folksy than he sounded. Peach judged that he tipped the scale at exactly half Cousin Thalia's weight. The nature of their relationship was obscure to Peach. He never actually thought about it. He never thought about either of them, unless they were present, and sometimes not then.

Rosie had bathed and changed, to Peach's relief. She didn't always have time, after galloping round the gardens and farm. Sometimes she didn't have the energy, though she had spent the day in a chair. There was no predicting what Rosie was going to look like — dead-end kid, Tugboat Annie, groom, or duchess. Tonight she was wearing a long crimson velvet dress with a big gold watch as a pendant — their grandfather's half-hunter, on a black silk ribbon. Her hair was informal but not untidy. Its blackness framed the light tan which survived from the summer into October. The crimson suited her colouring. Her eyes were a brilliant green. Peach felt proud when he looked at her. He wished Tim could have been here to see her. But letting Tim out, even just for a day, had become a bad idea. Rosie looked less than her thirty-two years when her face was mobile, when she was talking or laughing or listening. In repose her face sometimes looked older. When she was thinking about Tim she looked older and even haggard. Peach could not bear to look at her or talk to her at such moments. It did her no good for him to be miserable too.

'Somebody,' said Rosie, 'was trying to tell me something about a car or a truck. With an aggrieved note in his voice. But I was designing a gate at the time, and I didn't pay close attention.'

'Interruptions by the illiterate are worse than the onslaughts of stinging insects,' said Jefferson Dill. 'I was plagued myself today, by a carpenter, when I was trying to work in the library.'

Peach opened his mouth to tell Rosie about the fool who had left a truck parked where it was impossible not to hit it. He remembered that the car had been borrowed by Jefferson Dill from somebody fool enough to trust Jefferson Dill with a car. When he spoke to Rosie, therefore, it was in the language they had devised in his youth and her childhood, which continued to be useful on many occasions.

'Ben-Huriot macked prole-wagon,' he said.

'Pee-weach on bridge?' she asked.

'Commanding admiral.'

'What Ben-Huriot?'

'Pickle.'

The language was expanded, like all good languages, as occasion demanded, by new words, including names for new people. 'Pickle' for Dill was not subtle or inscrutable, but Jefferson Dill never seemed to realise he was being talked about. It was true that, like Peach himself, he was not given to listening.

'Pickle hep?' asked Rosie.

'Who cares?' said Peach, reverting to clear.

Fox Hill belonged to Peach, and Rosie's husband paid the bills. But the directing intelligence was Hazel's. They all knew it, though they didn't always admit it. She did what she'd always done — looked after her babies and kept them out of trouble. It was lucky for them she was still around. Nothing would have got done without her.

The idea of little Peachie thinking those trees was clipped to look like chess-men! The idea of little Rosie saying they was clipped to look like animals in a coat of arms! They was clipped to look like the animals in Barnum and Bailey's circus. It was lucky

Hazel was there to put the men right about that.

It was she who called Peter Peach when he was tiny, and Rosanna Rosie when she was tiny. She *invented* those kids. Peach wouldn't have been the Peach of today, or Rosie the Rosie of today, if Hazel hadn't guided them all their lives. They were still her babies. Peachie was a peach. So gentle. Never gave a person any trouble, unless he had a drink. Then he was like his Pa. And Rosie was a rose, a lovely wild white rose in the Virginia meadows!

That Tim Phillipson was almost worthy of her, until he got boils on the brain. Handsomest son of a bitch, for a white man, Hazel had ever seen. Of course he looked Hazel's way. All men did. They couldn't help themselves. She always locked her door when he was around. She pitied his helpless yearning, but she wasn't set on stealing Rosie's man. She wasn't like those bad women Bette Davies used to play on the movies, always stealing another girl's man.

It was her tits they liked. Not that many had seen them. She'd let Peachie play with them when he was little. They had some happy hours, Peach and his Hazel, Hazel and her Peachie.

All the workmen around the place wanted her. She saw the lechery in their eyes. A person wasn't too old at sixty. There was lust all around, indoors and out. The place was a regular Sodom and Gomorrah. You could almost see the lust, coiling around corners, like it was a sort of purple smog. You could feel it. You could feel hot eyes on your ass when you walked past any of the men. But none of those uppity workmen was going to mess around with Hazel. She locked her door against all of them. She locked it against Jefferson Dill, too, horny little bastard. He wanted to get her into that apartment, off by herself, helpless and alone. You could tell by the look in his eyes that was what he wanted. Hazel wasn't going in there to be drugged and raped, no sir.

Rosie was a worry, married to a man who wasn't a man any more. She must be missing it cruel, waking up in the night and nobody there. One day a man was going to come by, a real man. The sooner the better, though Peachie wasn't liable to think so.

Cousin Thalia Collin was casting pearls before swine, wearing her Chagall-inspired robe and bothering to explain it to them.

Fox Hill should have been dwelt in by people of discernment,

110

taste. Peter was a pot-bellied philistine, and Rosanna half the time a kind of wild hoyden and half the time a painted whore. They had no business in a historic mansion. Their grandfather had no business being her father's elder brother. There was trickery in that. It was unfair. It was a disaster. Her Uncle Charles Collin had been a drunken hobbledehoy, forever roaring about after foxhounds and spending all his money and killing his poor wife by neglect and *having children*. If Peter and Rosanna had not been born, Thalia would have inherited Fox Hill and made of it a Mecca of culture and civilization.

Concerts. Operas. Modern paintings. Decoration to accord with a liberated modern spirit as well as with history and tradition. What a challenge that would have been, and how few could meet it as Thalia could have met it!

Not for nothing was she named for a muse.

The slant of her topmost vertebra was an unusual, a distinctive deformity. It was not visible. Doctor Moss intimated that it was something aristocratic, like the haemophilia of the Russian Imperial Family. It was prevalent among the very oldest European noble families. No doubt from them, her ancestors, she had inherited it. Not the Collins, but her mother's family, the Dobins of Richmond. A name somewhat similar, but how different! People had to be taught how to pronounce it correctly. They were apt to say 'Dobbin' instead of 'Doe-been'. Of course it came from the French d'Aubigne.

Thalia had not waited for an invitation from Peter and Rosanna to make her home at Fox Hill. It *was* her home. Her grandfather had owned the house, her father had been born and reared in it. She had more right there than the legal owner because she was worthier. She deplored the British inheritance of primogeniture. Among her aristocratic French ancestors, her residence at the headquarters of her family would have been automatic. She chose to follow that part of her pedigree. She moved in as soon as the house was re-opened.

It was lucky for them all she did, and lucky for posterity. Her advice was not sought as it should have been, but she gave it freely and gladly. They little knew how indebted they were to her, for ideas she had sown in their minds, for dreadful errors averted. Though fate had treated her so shabbily, she gave generously of her brain and taste.

She had expected Jefferson Dill to be more help to her, and

111

more of a companion. That was why she had contrived the arrangement. But he was reclusive and waspish. He was probably behind with his rent, but Peter was too inefficient to realise it. At least Jefferson knew that Thalia was the name of a muse. The muse of pastoral poetry. Of comedy, too, but her Virginia namesake did not identify herself with comedy.

Jefferson Dill was deliberately waspish. He modelled himself on Juvenal, Swift, Voltaire. He was the eternal satirist. He mocked the pretensions of the world.

He had other models, too — the great French poet François Villon, the great Welsh poet Dylan Thomas. He had said so to Thalia. She had thought he was referring to his poetry — to *villanelles* in the manner of Villon, to audacious free-verse rhapsodies in the manner of Thomas. He was not. He was referring to his soul.

To Villon, everything was allowed, because he was a poet. Any theft, any lie, any betrayal was allowed, because he was a poet. Jefferson Dill met this precious nugget of literary history when he was quite young, and it profoundly influenced him.

To the morality of Dylan Thomas, as reported by a man he met, he came later. His informant was a British critic visiting the University of Virginia. He had known Thomas in London at the end of the war. It seemed his poetry was breathtaking but he was an exacting friend. To him anything was allowed because he was a poet. He moved into the houses of his friends, and stayed indefinitely, paying nothing, unwashed, squalid, there of right because he was a poet. He could vomit in anybody's lap, seduce anybody's wife, because he was a poet.

Jefferson Dill had not been clever at seducing people, or very interested in it; he did not really want to vomit for any reason anywhere — he found it uncomfortable and undignified and it made him cry. But he added the poet's right of rent-free living to the rights recorded of Villon, and Fox Hill suited him excellently.

He had never made any money. As a young reporter he had despised the people he was sent to talk to, the clerks and cops and firemen. As a publisher's reader he had despised every book he was given, and the tastes of every editor. As a teacher he had despised most of his material and all his pupils. A few of his poems had been printed. As a novelist he was unpublished and as a playwright unperformed.

112

But he did keep trying.

He went back to the library after dinner that night. Although he dined with the family, he did not as a rule spend the rest of the evening with them. He was occasionally asked to do so, by Thalia. It was not quite clear how he stood, in regard to making use of the sitting-rooms and armchairs. Anyway, he wanted to go to the library. The place would be peaceful at last. He wanted to look some more at the early volumes of the *Annals of the Fox Hill Hounds,* editions limited to a few dozen copies, printed in Charlottesville intermittently from 1800 until the War betwen the States.

He really was researching a history of Fox Hill, which he saw as a microcosm of the history of the South. He could see the review in the *New York Times*: 'It is hard to know whether to admire more fervently the depth of Mr Dill's researches or the limpid clarity of his writing . . . A book indispensable to an understanding of . . . Has enriched not only our knowledge but also our literature . . .'

It seemed that when foxhounds were kept at Fox Hill — American hounds, with a few couple later imported from England — parties assembled to ride after them stayed in the house for weeks at a time. This was in the grand Virginia tradition of Lord Fairfax, George Washington, the Chichesters of Fairfax County, the McCartys of Cedar Grove. The parties were brilliant and unruly. As Bishop Meade said (a note which delighted Jefferson Dill), 'The race must end in a dinner, and the dinner must end under the table. The day's hunt must be followed by a night's debauch.' Things were, perhaps, more seemly after the Revolution.

Jefferson Dill turned to the volume for 1819-20, the first produced after a gap of some years. He came on a passage which leapt joyfully at him out of the page: which was to change his life and other lives.

'Among the sportsmen assembled under the Fox Hill roof at the commencement of the season's sport, was a Colonel Catchpole of Williamsburg, a gentleman of notable joviality and jocose spirit, and a great favourite with the ladies. Colonel Catchpole revealed to the company that he had but lately returned from an extended visit to Ireland, where he had relatives. He had there ridden to the County Kilkenny Foxhounds of Sir John Power, and been extended after the amiable custom of the place the hospitality of Sir John's roof. What distinguished this particular gathering, by the Colonel's account, was an annual dramatic performance, in the highest style of skill and elegance, rehearsed during the season and presented near its end to a large audience who travelled considerable distances for the experience. This jocund venture, known as the Kilkenny Theatricals, was directed every year by Mr Richard Power, brother to Sir John.

'Even as Colonel Catchpole spoke, there was a stirring of interest among his auditors — a kindling of optics both male and female! And, in sum, the resolution was forthwith adopted by all present that the "Fox Hill Theatricals" should present a dramatic entertainment in respectful and grateful imitation of the glorious Hibernian precedent.

'Colonel Catchpole, owing to his experience of the matter, was charged with preparing the Work, assisted by many of the ladies and gentlemen of the company. Costumes were designed and made in the sewing-room of the Mansion, and scenes built and painted in its workshops. On the fourth day of March, all fashionable Virginia assembled at Fox Hill, and were regaled by the first and only performance before an audience of *Grandma Reilly's Secret, or, How Too Many Cats Were Let Out Of Too Few Bags,* a farce-comedy-extravaganza, with songs and ballets specially composed.

'The audience responded with hilarity and, at the conclusion of the piece, with applause which seriously threatened the windows of the Great Hall; after which it was unanimously resolved to make of the event an annual affair.'

But there were no further references to the Fox Hill Theatricals. It did not become an annual affair. Perhaps Colonel Catchpole was indispensible. He was not mentioned again, either.

Jefferson Dill picked up the massive old book, and hurried to the small sitting-room which the family used while the house was being redecorated. They were quiet. Rosanna was doing silk embroidery and drinking brandy. Thalia was reading a popular author at whom Jefferson Dill spat. Peter was just sitting.

When he burst in on them, Rosanna and Thalia looked at him with surprise and Peter with apathy.

He began to read to them. He gripped them. He thought he would, and he did. Thalia was agog. Peter looked more animated, more excited, than Jefferson Dill had ever seen him look. Rosanna seemed amused. There was no need for Jefferson Dill to make the

114

suggestion. It made itself.

'Where do we find a play?' said Peter.

'I have a play,' said Jefferson Dill. 'With a little tinkering I believe it will be ideal. There's a fine part for Rosanna, and a great comedy part for Peter, and a major character role for you, Thalia. Of course we'll need a few other people.'

And so the Fox Hill Theatricals were reborn.

CHAPTER 6

Rosie was not much interested in getting up on a stage and showing off in public. She had been a public figure, and she had enjoyed it, and it was done with. She had been a teenage celebrity in show-jumping, dressage and hunter-trials. She had some good wins, but she knew quite well even then that her fame had as much to do with the way she looked as with the way she rode. Then she was a kind of celebrity in the first three or four years of her marriage to Tim. People said they were the best-looking couple in America. They were nowhere near the richest, but they were rich enough to do what they wanted. They owned good steeplechasers and travelled and drank and gave parties and went to parties. It turned sour.

But Dill's ridiculous bit of history really lit a fuse under Peach. For that reason, if for no other, Rosie went along with the project. It was practically unknown to see the old boy excited. It was good for him. He needed shaking up. He was far too young to be in a rut, and the rut was far too deep. Other people went along in their ruts. Darling old Peach simply sat in his.

It would be fun to have hounds at Fox Hill again. It would be difficult, as they were in Mrs duPont Scott's Montpelier country. Tim might have liked a pack of foxhounds, in the days when he was still Tim, but it was one of the very many things they had not had time to get around to. The might-have-beens. There were so many. Like kids. Rosie was not sure she would have been a good mother, but Hazel would still have been a good nurse. Who could have guessed that the marriage, giving the word any real meaning at all, would last such a tiny time?

The foxhounds were not reconstructed in the Reconstruction, but after a long, impoverished hiatus the thoroughbreds came back. Fox Hill Farm was really re-established by their grandfather in about 1920. He was successful on a small scale for twenty years. His son, their father, was unsuccessful on a large scale for twenty-five years. But when he died the farm stayed alive. The house was empty but the barns were populated. Only just. Three, four or five mares, and one stallion, Corporal. Twenty years old now. Once a steely grey, now almost white. Charles Collin's great grey hope, when he bought him just before he died. Charles did not live to see how calamitously unsuccessful Corporal was as a sire of thoroughbred racehorses. But he got nice half-bred show-horses and hunters. It was very small business, but it kept the farm alive.

Corporal was a very gentle old horse. He was a kind of pet of Ed Lindsey's family, and Ed still rode him bareback most mornings.

All over Virginia, at shows and gymkhanas and one-day events and in the hunting field, you saw nice-looking grey not-quite-thoroughbreds. Corporal's seed, broadcast far and wide. Like many much more important horses, he was certainly prepotent. He infallibly transmitted absolute lack of racing ability, and he nearly always transmitted his colour.

Corporal kept the farm alive, and Ed Lindsey kept it alive.

Ed had seemed as old as a rock to Rosie when she was a kid, in the late fifties. He had been an enormous help to her, as a teen-age competitor. He taught her more about riding than any of the expensive instructors her father sent her to. Except dressage. That he never understood or cared about.

It was not at all clear how Ed and his family lived, all those interregnum years. In a sense you could say they were living rent free, in quarters over the weanlings. Keeping chickens and ducks and a cow on the Collins' land. But almost the only money coming in would have been old Corporal's stud-fee, and it must have been a very low fee. There was plenty of grass, and they made their own hay, but it must have been a problem paying for the hard feed, even with only three or four head.

Rosie remembered from her childhood Ed's extraordinary gentleness and patience with horses. Of all the lessons it was the hardest one for her to learn. She still found herself forgetting it. Not Ed, not ever. He could calm a stallion that would try to kill anybody else, nurse a mare that was sick or sorry, break a weanling so gently that the baby had no idea it was being taught and disciplined. He looked like a black gnome — he was as black as any black Rosie had ever seen. He looked like an old hitching-post, or one of those half-life-size carvings that carry a tray or a lamp. But he was tough and intelligent. He was loyal and honest. He had a great memory and a great eye. He was a godsend. He had made the past possible and he made the future possible.

Rosie was passionately determined, from the first moment of coming back to Fox Hill, to rebuild the glories of the old days. There were lots of reasons, and the biggest was inside herself. She wanted something to lose herself in, so that her heart, rebroken once or twice a week, had a chance to heal. There were things going for her. Ed had kept the barns in good repair, and thanks to her father's lavish ideas they were good barns. She spent a quarter of a million of Tim's dollars on broodmares, after long conferences with Ed, and inspections and haggling, and visits to the Keeneland sales during which she had to exercise a self-discipline foreign to her nature. She spent a lot more of Tim's money sending the mares to some of the best available stallions in Virginia and Kentucky. There were six yearlings and eight weanlings now. They planned to sell the colts and keep the fillies. They were building the foundations.

What they wanted now was a high-class stallion. It was feasible. They had plenty to offer in the way of situation, buildings, facilities, grass, skills. They had to make the place attractive to one of the syndicates that controlled important stallions. So there was fresh paint on the fences, closed-circuit TV in the foaling-barn, infra-red ceiling heaters in the big barn where the mares with early foals could run around.

Rosie threw herself into all this, and for hours at a time she forgot Tim, sitting like a tired old man in a chair by the window of his room, never looking out of the window, picking at the rug over his knees, talking of things he was not doing, people he was not seeing, letters he was not writing.

There was the question of an assistant and successor to Ed. He was over sixty. He had twinges of rheumatism, and there was dark talk of arthritis in one hip. He said he'd never retire — never want to retire — but there were going to be things he couldn't do. After a dozen interviews, Rosie hired a local man called Rick Field, very well recommended by a neighbour. He was white, thirtyish; he didn't mind working under a black because he knew enough to see how much he could learn from Ed. He made no secret of wanting Ed's job ultimately. That was fair enough — it was why he had been asked to come and why he wanted to come.

118

He was so good with the mares and foals that Ed could safely have left the whole foaling routine to him. But of course he didn't.

Of course he didn't. He wanted Fox Hill to be the kind of farm where a mare threw ten healthy foals in ten years. There had to be some luck in a record like that, but a man could increase the luck and reduce the bad luck. Getting up at four in the morning in February to crouch in a foaling-box, that was part of reducing the bad luck.

During all the solitary struggling years, Ed had been sustained by one hope. Rebirth. The family back and the place buzzing. It wouldn't be Peach, not down here in the barns. He never had cared about horses. But Miss Rosie, pretty as a flower, brought up to love horses and loved them. Ed never taught anybody who learned so quick. Never saw anybody sit a horse so graceful. She'd come home and the glory-days would be back. It just needed Ed to keep the place going, kind of skeleton staff doing necessary maintenance until the day. When he needed help he got it from the neighbours, from Miss Viola Biggs of Mount Malcolm. Ed didn't care if you called him a caretaker, a steward, a squatter or what. He was keeping the place in repair for Miss Rosie.

Corporal paid some of the bills. People wanted a sound, steady, sweet-natured animal, they knew where to come for the sire. Neighbours paid the rest, when he tended injured horses or handled difficult ones. He gave a few riding lessons, built jumps, mended saddles, clipped horses, and helped out in different ways. It was a pretty full life. He never could get away. There was no time for vacations and no money for them.

Ed had been born sixty and more years after the abolition of slavery, and he had not been born at Fox Hill. But he knew the sense of being tied to a place for life. He did not feel it was something he chose. The feeling he had was that the place had chosen him, history had chosen him.

He thought when Miss Rosie got married, they might come and live at Fox Hill. But it seemed Mr Phillipson came from a different part of the state, where he had his own place and his own horses. It seemed they travelled all over, to New York and Europe and the Far East. Ed had cards Miss Rosie had sent from places he never heard of. He tacked them up in the room he used as an office.

Now things were turning out better than Ed had dared to dream.

The barns were painted up real pretty, and there were new flower-beds planted in the middle of the yards, and every bit of cracked woodwork and every crumbling brick was replaced, and every bit of metal was polished, and the glass was clean and complete and all the lights worked and all the faucets, and there was new fireproofing and all the mouse-holes filled up, and the missing tiles replaced in the roofs, and there wasn't a thing any of them could think of that still needed fixing. Every foot of the fencing had been checked and rails replaced where needed, and Miss Rosie was having fancy new gates hung. All the grass was raked and cleaned up, and the weeds dug out by hand. No chemical sprays. Trees were lopped and trees were felled and other trees were planted.

Miss Rosie hired an assistant for Ed, a quiet young white guy called Rick Field. Miss Viola Biggs of Mount Malcolm knew all about him. The idea was, Ed would teach him what he knew. There was plenty Rick could learn, and he worked at learning it. But the most important thing he didn't have to learn. He already knew it. Ed watched him with the mares and young stock, and he stood with his hands behind his back and let them rub their noses on his neck, and then, very slow, stroked their necks, and by and by gave them nuts or carrots from the palm of his hand — no rush, no noise, no hassle. If there was other work to be done it could wait. That was exactly right. Miss Rosie had found the right man.

The new mares were very expensive, but they were what Fox Hill needed. They had class pedigrees and good racing form, and some of them were already dams of winners. The best to Ed's eye was Meadowsweet, Kentucky-bred around 1971. Meadowsweet had a yearling and a weanling and she was in foal again. Ed intended her to be a mare that foaled ten times hand-running without a hitch.

People came. That was a big satisfaction, seeing their faces and hearing what they said. They all knew Fox Hill in Mr Charles's day. Pretty soon they'd all know it again. Seemed they liked everything they saw. Seemed they were truly impressed. There was a British Sir came, Sir Lucas something. He was mighty impressed. He was doing business for Miss Rosie. There was a

Greek gentleman with a name Ed couldn't get his tongue round. Ed had never met a Greek before, and he reckoned it was his loss, if they were all like this Greek. He was a friendly gentleman. He knew about horses, breeding and feeding and all about them. He got right in there with the young stock, looking at them and feeling their bone and letting them almost knock him over with their affection. Ed thought his opinion of the place was worth having. It was a high opinion. He liked what he saw. He said so, to Ed and to Miss Rosie. He'd tell people what he thought, and they'd listen. That was good.

Be nice if they could stand a really good stallion. That was the thing to aim for. Then they'd be in business. Miss Rosie had the same idea.

Rick Field had been learning his trade all his life. His family came from Somerset County, but they'd gone north, the other side of Middleburg. His father had been an assistant farm manager, a man soft with horses but hard with kids. Rick had been made to work early mornings, evenings, weekends, even when he was in high school. He wanted more education but there was no way he was going to get it. Working with horses was his education.

Once, when he was small and skinny and pretty frail, his father had him exercising a nappy, half-broken colt on a lunging rein, using the long whip in his other hand just to keep the colt moving and have him lead with the inside leg. It was a bitterly cold morning. Rick had lost his gloves. The old man said that was his own fault, he could hold the rein and the whip without gloves. He could, but it was agony. He was almost crying with the cold of his hands and ears. The cold made him feel weak, and the weakness made him feel scared. If you hurt yourself when you were very cold, it hurt worse. Everybody knew that except the old man, who never felt any pain or fear and despised people who did. Rick's fingers got so numb he dropped the lunging rein. Slack, the rein got caught in the colt's forefeet. He stumbled. He didn't fall. He realised he was free. He bolted round the field, the rein trailing. It was dangerous, because any moment he might catch his feet in it and come down and maybe break a leg — hundreds of thousands of bucks' worth of thoroughbred suddenly a valueless carcase. The colt turned and came at Rick, galloping. With part of his mind Rick knew that a riderless horse doesn't gallop right at a person and knock him down. He stops or swerves. Nobody ever heard of a riderless horse knocking over a person he could see, except in a panic and bolting, or a horse that had run out in a race, but was still racing along with the others on the wrong side of the rail. Rick knew he just had to stand still, and the colt would see him and avoid him. But he was too cold to think clearly. He lashed out at the oncoming colt with the long carriage-whip. The thing hit him across the face. He did what he would have done anyway — swerved and avoided Rick by a couple of yards.

The worst thing about it was that the old man saw. Came out of the barn at that exact moment, and saw not the cause of the blow but just the blow itself. Rick had never seen him so mad or felt so scared of him.

He explained. He tried to keep back the tears of cold and fright and humiliation. The explanation made things worse, made his old man madder. When he understood that Rick had hit the colt because he was scared, he said he would drive the fear out with a strap. He thought you could do that. In a million years he would not have tried it with a horse, but he thought it worked with a kid. It was the worst leathering of Rick's life, because the old man was furious at having a son who was scared. He was ashamed.

There was no permanent damage to the colt, but there was permanent damage to Rick.

He left home at seventeen, and got various jobs with horses. He could always get work, because he really had been well and thoroughly taught.

He was in Vietnam for eight months. He was scared. His old man would not have been, but he was. He had imagination. He could picture the jagged shell fragment carving into his groin. He went to pieces, and they invalided him out. He got an honourable discharge, but he didn't like the look on the faces of the army shrinks.

He came back to Virginia and to horses. He said he had a medical discharge, but he didn't say why. He went from job to job. It seemed he drifted, but he was not a drifter. He was looking for a place to stay. He married on the way, a girl out of a roadhouse, a pretty girl with a sassy, cute way of talking and a great shape for clothes and without clothes. He was nuts about her, and after the roadhouse she was nuts about a life with horses.

They found themselves in Somerset County, where Rick had

122

kin. He had two cousins, brothers, twins. They were an embarrassment, because they were crazy. Rick soon realised that their kind of gentle craziness made them better with horses and other animals than most sane people. He saw with admiration how deft and patient they were with an injured hound or a frightened horse. He got very fond of them. But they continued to be an embarrassment to his wife Janice. She held it against him.

She discovered he was sometimes scared. She held that against him, too.

When he saw Fox Hill he knew it was the place he wanted to be. It was beautiful. Mrs Phillipson was a dynamo. If she wanted a barn moved, she practically picked it up and moved it. She did a lot of the work herself. When she spread paint on a wall, her hand moved so fast it was a blur. Paint spread itself over the wall as though somebody was pouring it out of the sky. Rick knew all about the Collins and the Phillipsons, about Fox Hill in the old days and about Mr Phillipson's steeplechasing. He had never met Mrs Phillipson. He was proud to work for her.

There was a cottage went with the job. Janice, thank God, liked the cottage. She fixed it up. That kept her mind off whatever it was apt to get on.

Janice thought it was terrible that Rick was put under a coon. She held that against him. She was a country girl, with old-fashioned ideas. But Rick admired Ed Lindsey, and he was going to take over, and he could wait out the time.

Rick had had a black sergeant in Nam. That guy had driven out of Rick's mind any old Virginia ideas he might have had about one race being superior to another. Rick resented the sergeant not because he was black, or a sergeant, but because he was brave. He was killed because he was brave. He was doing his duty bravely, and he was hit.

The thing cut both ways. Rick didn't have any medals, but he had Janice, and the cottage, and a fine job doing what he loved. He worked hard. He was building his own future, and the future of Fox Hill, and they were the same thing.

Rosie discussed it with Ed: the thing to do was to get Fox Hill talked about as a modern-thinking, well-run place where the horses were really cared for. It couldn't be done by conventional publicity methods, and talk wasn't automatic. Great spreads like

Claiborne, Spendthrift, Gainesway, Rokeby, Cragrock were naturally talked about. Who'd bother to enquire about this little operation which everybody had forgotten?

The answer, a part of the answer, came to Rosie one day in the summer. She suggested to Ed they make contact with the original breeders of the mares they had bought, invite them to come to see their old friends out of curiosity or affection, see how well and happy they were and what fine foals they were throwing.

Rosie found without difficulty who the breeders were and where they were — it was all in the book — but she hesitated to write or call them direct. Sometimes her impulsiveness was qualified by a kind of shyness which masqueraded as dignity. Sometimes she got devious.

When Merivale Lucas came to Fox Hill, she saw an opportunity to be deviously dignified.

He came because he went everywhere, sniffing like an unkempt basset-hound for any hint of a deal. He was well known in Virginia, though not to Rosie. She was curious to meet him. She was not impressed. He was. He couldn't fail to be impressed. He was visibly, stutteringly impressed. He was too impressed.

Rosie was reminded of those days long before in the show-ring, when the photographers crowded round her. She was fifteen, sixteen, looked more, knew how to smile as well as ride. She sometimes influenced the judges with her smile, as though she was trying to be Miss America. She took to riding side-saddle, because a habit was more glamorous than breeches. She smiled as she rode. You could justify that by saying it showed confidence, mastery, absolute trust in a perfectly-schooled horse. So it did, and it showed her dimples and her little white teeth, and the tight habit showed her figure. She smiled at Merivale Lucas, showing her confidence in the excellence of the farm and stock, showing a warm and affectionate personality. That was in midsummer. She wore thin cotton pants and a T-shirt. They did their showing, too.

She was not cheating Lucas in any way at all. He was an expert, a professional. He came to look at the farm, and there the farm was for him to look at. Prod the stock, meet the help, nibble the grass, read the pedigrees, anything he liked. The whole thing was spread out for him. Where his eyes went additionally was his business. Rosie was there because she was the boss. She had to be there, to answer questions. If he wanted to look at her, that was his privilege.

They made him welcome in the house, too. Of course they did — a visitor all the way from England. (He never spent less than four months a year in America.) He stayed in the house. He stayed longer than anyone expected, three nights. He began to drool a little. Rosie didn't think anybody else noticed. He tried to kiss her. She didn't let him, but she was nice about it. She didn't make an enemy, as you easily could by saying 'no' the wrong way. Rosie had said 'no' the right way and the wrong way a great many times, and she was expert at it. A good 'no' carried a hint of 'maybe'. This wasn't dishonest, it was polite. It was kind. Rosie was careful to be kind to Merivale Lucas.

The result was, that Lucas went away with 'maybe' lodged in his skull. He went away promising to get in touch, casually, informally, with the breeders of the Fox Hill mares. He was going to tell them how happy and well their mares were. Urge them to go see for themselves. Start a great word-of-mouth snowball.

He had to mean what he said — his professional reputation was on the line. But the 'maybe' in the 'no' would give it a little extra.

The visitor she wanted as much as any was Matthew Carver, who had bred their Meadowsweet, Ed Lindsey's favourite. He'd see how well she was, and he'd tell people, and they'd listen. Rosie had never met Matthew Carver, but of course she knew all about him, and she knew people who knew him. Rosie wanted his voice in her snowball. She wanted him to tell everybody about Meadowsweet's yearling and weanling.

The yearling was a colt, a beauty. It would have gone to the sales, but Rosie had decided to keep it. She had decided to race it in Tim's name and colours. She thought that might be an excitement for Tim, a cheerful jolt, constructive therapy. Surely he couldn't stay plunged in that thick soup of melancholia, when a horse was running races for him? And there were months of joyful expectation, hope, before it was ready to race. She told Tim about all this, excited, trying to excite him.

He looked at her blankly, picking at the rug on his knees. His face was puffy now, with the drugs they gave him and lack of exercise; it was white, after all those years of hard brown tan. He said he didn't care to own a horse. He didn't want to hear about it. He didn't want to hear about anything. Sometimes he didn't want Rosie there, and sometimes he didn't know if she was there or not.

125

Rosie thought Matthew Carver might like to buy Meadowsweet's yearling.

Peach did not focus often. When he did, he saw with horrid clarity.

Normally, the delicacy and audacity of his thoughts were protected from distraction by an extra eyelid, a spiritual eyelid, which was made of one-way glass. People could see him, but he could not see them. Sometimes he turned the mirrors round (he was a man of remarkable gifts). Then he could see out without anybody knowing he was looking.

Thus, disguised by a unique talent, he had observed Sir Merivale Lucas. Rosie's effect on Lucas. Rosie's treatment of Lucas. The enslavement of Lucas by Rosie.

Peach was extremely shocked.

Rosie was still young and very beautiful, and moths were bound to burn their wings. But she was deliberately enticing Lucas. Her clothes were tighter than usual and she kept giving Lucas drinks. Peach grudged the drinks, though Tim actually paid for them. Peach grudged them on Tim's behalf. Tim was the reason for Peach's anger. Peach himself was loyal to Tim unto death. God knew, Tim was faithful to Rosie. And Lucas was such a grubby, dandruffy fellow.

Peach expostulated to Rosie, in their language, at dinner the second night: 'Scarlet-letter goo-eyes gyp Time-machine.'

She justified herself, saying simply, 'Busybee.'

If it *was* simply business, profit, the overman making use of the inferior, Peach understood and forgave. He was mollified. He was even pleased. He was content that Sir Merivale Lucas should be pressed, dazzled and unwitting, into the service of the Collins of Fox Hill.

And at least nothing nasty happened. Peach would never have permitted anything nasty, any of the disgusting things people were reputed to do in bedrooms. Whatever the business advantages, that would have been an unforgivable betrayal of Tim.

Ed Lindsey remembered Sir Lucas's visit and other visitors. He wondered if anything was coming of them. Had Lucas told people about Fox Hill, as he seemingly promised he would? Had the Greek gentleman? Was there a chance they'd get themselves a

126

real stallion?

All of a sudden Ed was in a hurry. He was never in a hurry with horses, but he was suddenly in a hurry with life. Fox Hill was beginning to grow and blossom. He wanted a forest of magnolia overnight.

He looked in over the half-door at Meadowsweet, contentedly waiting for her foaling in five months' time.

He wanted Mr Carver to come see her, and bring them a big stallion, and change all their lives.

Matthew Carver flew from Paris to London, his mind an ill-directed mess.

Was he suddenly old and impotent? How could he be? The Indonesian kid so lovely and so kind. So understanding. Sorry for him, and then sorrier for him. Her pity was kindly meant, but it was the most humiliating spike in a bristle of humiliations.

Matthew was frightened that next time he'd be frightened, too frightened, self-conscious, unmanned by the fear of failure to the point that failure was inevitable.

He forced his thoughts to the Mill Reef colt, that was going where it shouldn't be going, for reasons which he didn't even know. He forced his thoughts away again, as he remembered the distasteful conversation with Fred Cottle.

He tried to concentrate on the more comfortable subject of Beausoleil. Circumstances equally obscure had there produced a different kind of ending, a happy ending. He was content to think about that.

But a face clamoured at the edge of his mind, commanding his thoughts with high moral certainty, with utter lack of humour.

He thought with despair of his coming interview with Mollie, his probable failure to have an interview with Liz.

Mollie was admitted through the iron-studded door of Tibbs Hill Women's Prison, in a grim eastern suburb of London. The area had once been rural Essex; it was now swallowed by small, streaky factories and little yellow houses. There were parts of the suburb which, if not gracious, were not repulsive; there were parks, and pools, and schools with playing fields. Such things seemed improbable in the streets round the Women's Prison.

Mollie could have taken a taxi there, the enormous distance from the Cromwell Road. She could have put in a claim for the fare, each way, which the Home Office would have met without question. She subjected herself instead, weekly or twice-weekly, to a complex and interminable zigzag of tubes and buses, for reasons she could have justified to anyone who cared to listen.

She had washed her hair before leaving home. She put it in rollers, clamping the swathes of faded khaki to the plastic cylinders with pins from a china frog. There had not been time to dry it with the blower. She resembled Cio Cio San in a provincial production of *Butterfly*. She tied a grim headscarf under her chin, and so resembled a prison visitor. None of her colleagues, perhaps, would have embarked on a mission of reclamation with hair in curlers. Some notion of dignity would have prevented it — some fear that impressiveness and influence would be lost. None had her confidence that anything she did was right because she did it.

The prisoners she saw were elderly, and she saw them in a group. Some of the visitors struggled for the souls of pretty young tarts, shoplifters and pick-pockets, in murmuring tête-à-tête. Often they left the girls weeping hot tears of contrition and repentance. Mollie believed in group therapy.

'If I can help them all, they can all help one another,' she said.

She did not get a captive audience anywhere else.

She saw five women regularly, gap-toothed crones from the slums, brought up to crime and the bottle, and with no slightest capacity or wish to reform. Mollie became deeply fond of them, finding a kind of childlike simplicity in their ignorance, loyalty in the way they hung together, gaiety against all odds in their laughter, courage, family love, and in their avowals to her — in chorus, at every session — the certainty of a new life and a virtuous and tranquil twilight.

One was inside for criminal abortion, two for receiving goods knowing them to have been stolen, one for actual bodily harm (she had cut off the nose of a neighbour with a carving-knife) and the most recent recruit for the attempted murder of her common-law husband with rat-poison. Mollie knew them all by their first names. They never could remember her name. They went along with it because it made a change, it was a giggle, and she promised to find them jobs when they got out.

'My Maisie was one of you,' she told them. 'She was convicted just like you, and she had to pay her debt to society. I helped her, as I am helping you, to see where usefulness and happiness really lie — not in helping yourself to whatever you want in life, without thought for others or for God, but in *earning* what you have. You will find there is so much more satisfaction in owning something which you have *earned*. Maisie has found so, as I told her she would. "Madame," she often says to me, "the money you pay me for working feels like *gold*, compared to the money I used to nick in the bad old days." She comes and helps me clean my home. I think of her as a friend rather than as a servant. I trust her implicitly. I pay her quite generously. We have most interesting talks.'

The present gang did not expect all to be employed as scrubbies by Mrs Toffee-Nose, but they thought she might get them into somewhere where they could nick some silver.

She was let into the narrow, sweating room where they had their get-togethers. The women were waiting for her, sitting in a row on a bench with their backs to a wall. The abortionist was in the middle of a story which involved words unknown to Mollie. She stopped, sniggering. The door clanged behind Mollie, and she smiled at her good old friends.

They tittered when they saw her curlers.

'My husband is coming to see me,' she explained. 'He lives in America, so I see him very seldom. That is his choice, to live in America. I thought it right to wash my hair for his visit. Usually of course I have it done. But he is coming at short notice, so there was not time to arrange an appointment. We ought all to be able to wash our own hair. If I had taken time to dry it, I would have been late for our get-together.'

'Fuckin' shime yer wasn't, we could of 'earn ve end o' Queenie's tile,' murmured one of the receivers.

'What did you say, Muriel dear?'

Muriel belched ripely instead of replying, which threw the other old ladies into shrieks. Mollie smiled tolerantly. Not for her to judge the manners of these unfortunates by the standards of other worlds. Any of them, with a different start in life, might have been a duchess, Sister Teresa, a prison visitor.

'America. Fency,' said the attempted murderess, to keep the party going.

'I was obliged to go and live there when I married,' said Mollie, leading the group discussion which enabled and encouraged them all to open their hearts: and knowing that the lessons from her own life and experience were of value to her friends . . . were nuggets otherwise unattainable to them. 'I do not recommend it. I

129

was compelled in conscience, at last, to take my children and myself away. Americans are lax in their ways. Manners. Clothes. The men in particular. You never see a gentleman. They are materialistic. It is a dreadful place to bring up children. The Americans are dreadfully ignorant. Things everybody knows are a closed book to them. To give you a single example — simply to show you what I mean, and then we can all discuss it — they do not at all understand the significance of the style 'Honourable'. As you know I am called the Honourable Mrs Carver because my late father was a Peer of the Realm. I could not get Americans to understand that I was to be addressed in that fashion. They refer to a man as 'the Honourable John Jones' because he is the mayor of a town, or some such. Quite a bourgeois thing to be. It is absurd. Mayors of towns are not members of the aristocracy. The Lord Mayor of London, perhaps. I believe some of them have been gentlemen. You must understand that I would not have left America for that reason only. I could no longer endure my husband's conduct. It became insupportable. He was always going away, leaving me alone with my babies in a dreadful wilderness. There was nobody one could talk to at all — nobody one could admit to one's drawing-room. Not for miles and miles. It is different over here, don't you think so?'

They nodded energetically. They said England was the only country, and the Queen was wonderful, and Princess Diana was sweetly pretty. They were great loyalists.

It was not important to Mollie to have her opinion confirmed, but it was gratifying. It was encouraging to know she had the support of these grand old creatures, whose very age had given them wisdom denied the callow, who were so loyal and brave and humorous, in their funny old-fashioned way, and who were so determined to lead useful and happy lives in the future.

Matthew Carver did not expect to find any messages when he got to the Connaught, since only his family knew he was coming back to London.

But there was a message from Ottaviano di Vianello.

Matthew called the number he was given, and Ottaviano's extraordinary voice crackled out at him. Like many rich Italian children of his generation, he had had an English nanny, and spoke the language fluently. But unknown to his parents, the nanny spoke a lifelong, ineradicable Cockney, an accent which had, indeed, made work unobtainable for her in an upper-class English family. Ottaviano had acquired the accent. He never lost it. He was quite unaware of it.

'Hullo, Mush,' said Ottaviano. 'How's the boy, then? Your wife told your kid you were comin' over, your kid told my kid, my kid told me, and I want a chinwag.'

Half an hour later, Matthew was amused as always when Ottaviano came into the Connaught bar, dressed like a member of the London Stock Exchange. He was a Piemontese, Teuton rather than Latin in blood, with thinning fair hair and a thick fair moustache, prominent blue eyes, and the high colour of a fair man who gets a lot of fresh air.

Il conte Ottaviano di Vianello looked exactly like the man on the old *Esquire* covers.

He had been taken to lunch that day at White's, by Rollo Hampshire. He had seen and spoken to Ralph Hadfield and Merivale Lucas. They said there was a rumour that Matthew and George Whyte had bought Beausoleil. Were they syndicating him? Could Ottaviano have shares?

Matthew put him right. But he said Ottaviano could have nominations for the coming season. The man to get on to, immediately, was Epaminondas Makropulos, who was leasing the shares retained by the duc de Montfermainbrey. Ottaviano knew Epi, of course. Ottaviano had been, like Matthew, recipient of Epi's remarkable hospitality.

'Where will the 'orse stand, Mush?' asked Ottaviano.

'We don't know yet.'

'America?'

'Could easily be.'

'Suits me. Better for the mares I got over there than the mares I got here.'

'That's what Epi says.'

Ottaviano liked Matthew Carver and respected his judgement. But he was dubious about another member of the Carver family. The plan that Jamie Carver and his own son Mario should share lodgings in Oxford had seemed excellent. But Ottaviano, paying a flying visit to Oxford the previous day, had been a little shocked at Mario's appearance. He was listless and a bad colour. He was evasive about the reasons. If he didn't know it was utterly impossible, Ottaviano would have guessed at drugs. Torino society had been riddled with them, and he knew the effects — the sons and daughters of some of his friends had been ruined, or very expensively saved from ruin.

Ottaviano esteemed and trusted Matthew, but he deeply distrusted the influence on Mario of young Jamie Carver.

Sir Merivale Lucas telephoned. Ottaviano di Vianello had told him, at lunch-time in White's, that Matthew was rather surprisingly going back to America from Paris via London. Lucas was glad — it enabled him, without the expense of an international call, or the bother of writing a letter, to urge Matthew once again to visit Fox Hill in Virginia.

Matthew was exhausted, before the call and during it. Ottaviano, though able and decent, was an exhausting companion. Travel was exhausting, the last few days of Newmarket, Paris, le Coq, the duke and Henri de Cheminade, Tanja . . .

Tanja. Humiliation flooded back.

Curiously linked in his mind: the thought of Mollie flooded back, dread of tomorrow, despair, guilt at feeling as he felt.

Lucas talked about the buildings and the electronics and the grazing and the management, echoing Epi Makropulos. He introduced a note Epi had not struck, the excellence of Meadowsweet's yearling colt, unsold because of a change of plan. He did not introduce a note Epi had struck, the beauty of the owner's sister.

Lucas threatened to become a great bore on the subject of Fox Hill. Too tired to say no, Matthew weakly said yes, as the only way to get Lucas off the telephone without being rude to him.

Sir Merivale Lucas dialled, as he had long yearned to do, the complicated succession of digits that finished with the ringing of the Fox Hill telephone. Initiated at 11.30 p.m. in London, the call hit Fox Hill at 6.30. It was an uncharacteristic extravagance. Love twirled Lucas's finger in the dial (he wanted a push-button telephone, but not enough to pay for one). He dreamed of the 'maybe' in the 'no'.

Hazel took the call. She knew it was for her. It was one of the pesky workmen wanting a date. That kind of thing had to be nipped in the bud. A person had to be firm.

132

Before the caller had a chance to open his mouth, Hazel said, 'No. I don' plan to be cruel, but I ain't about to join *nobody* in no drinks down to no bar.'

To the yapping from the other end she said, in a kinder voice, 'I knows how yo' feels, b'lieve me, an' I's right sorry fo' yo' pains an' tohment.'

The voice on the line began to shout 'Lucas! Lucas!', which Hazel took to be a word of insult or reproach.

'I's no locus',' she said indignantly. 'I's mo' in de wild honey line.'

Minutes and much money ticked by before meaningful communication was established. Hazel said Miss Rosie was in the tub. Hazel was not about to disturb her for *anybody,* because if she did, Miss Rosie wouldn't wash properly behind her ears. Hazel promised to report that Mr Carver was coming to Fox Hill pretty soon.

The name, as she hung up, conjured pictures of long steel knives. Threats. Terror. Rape. With a man like that in the place, Hazel would not only lock her door but pile furniture against it.

Under Rosie's leadership (she was in a manic phase) prodigies of last-minute setting-to-rights were performed in house, garden and farm. Nothing could be done about the drive.

'*When* are you going to get the leather for that goddam door?' Rosie asked Peach.

'Negotiations are afoot,' said Peach, and because she was nagging put the matter at the bottom of his mental pending-tray.

Rosie had the old grass tennis-court rolled, mowed and marked, in case Mr Carver wanted to play tennis. Ancient warped rackets and squashy, greenish balls were found in a chest in a back passage.

It was important to make a good impression on this Carver. They knew — Rosie, Ed Lindsey, Rick Field — that he was influential out of all proportion to his bank-account or his personal investment in bloodstock. They'd read about him and heard about him and talked about him. Sir Merivale was a useful ambassador, and probably the Greek, but if this Carver spoke well of Fox Hill to his friends in Kentucky and California and England and Ireland and Paris, then they were on the map, and a top stallion was only a question of time, and the glory would return.

Struggling, in the midst of the hubbub, to retain concentration and to assert authority, Jefferson Dill began to audition in the library for *Circe's Island,* his allegorical reworking of the most sinister and suggestive episode in the whole of the *Odyssey.* Rosanna was elusive, but her casting as the lovely witch who turned men into swine was automatic. She could handle both the levels on which the drama functioned — she would be convincing as both the merciless priestess of ancient myth, and the madame of a New Orleans whorehouse during the Depression. Peach and Cousin Thalia Collin more than made up for Rosanna's absence by their almost over-loyal presence.

Old Miss Viola Biggs of Mount Malcolm was the first and most enthusiastic of the outside recruits.

Hazel was cast as the whorehouse washerwoman, and as a subpriestess of the Circean cult, in both roles contributing to the programme of degrading and humiliating the male.

'Men,' she said, *'stahts* bein' hogs. No call fo' de big transfo'mations.'

'That is exactly the point,' said Jefferson Dill. 'At one level.'

He wanted to use Ed Lindsey, but Rosie forbade him to involve any of the farm staff. Rick Field's wife Janice, however, was considered fine casting as one of the whorehouse girls and as a bent attendant nymph. She was promised old-fashioned garters and a chance to show them.

CHAPTER 7

Matthew Carver had paid nearly £95,000 for the lease of Mollie's new apartment. He accepted that she needed rooms for Liz and Jamie, and for Clare when she was in Britain, and that she ought to be able to have a friend to stay. Five bedrooms, at least two bathrooms. Even so he thought it a shocking price, though he only said so to himself in the middle of the night.

He was depressed by the street, and by the grimy purple building, and by the smells in the entrance hall. Mollie had a talent amounting to genius for lodging herself gloomily. But perhaps the apartment itself was light and airy, and not over-furnished or over-decorated. He indulged this hope, without much hope, as he climbed the stairs. There was an elevator, but he was not a man who used an elevator for a couple of flights. He was not old. At least, until the humiliation of Monday night he had not been old.

Clare let him in, kissed him quickly, apologised, and ran back to the telephone. She was in the middle of a call.

Trying not to eavesdrop on the call, Matthew looked round the sitting-room. There was no sign of Mollie in the flesh, but her hand was visible in everything Matthew saw. The choice of this room, this apartment. With thousands of rooms in London to choose from — and there were thousands, Mollie had sent him house agents' lists — she had established herself in this dark cavern of a room, north-facing, with a prospect of multi-story carparks. And she had decked it with massive brocade curtains with a heavy, ornate pelmet. Gloomy grandeur. Lights blazed all over the apartment, at noon. They were needed. They would not have been needed quite so badly without those ridiculous drapes.

Photographs in silver frames, drawn up like guardsmen on a shelf. To Mollie, no residence was home without photographs in silver frames. They were as necessary as a bed. More so, perhaps.

Their marriage bed had been fruitful but not very joyful.

Clare, Liz, Jamie, Mollie's parents robed for the 1953 Coronation, Mollie herself in that summer, Mollie a bride. It was not surprising he had adored her and married her, although in retrospect some aspects of the engagement were surprising. She was lovely and she was full of surprises. Her loving him was not the least of the surprises.

Clare was speaking softly to the telephone. She puckered her lips as she said goodbye. She sent a kiss down the line. Matthew saw. He looked away quickly, but Clare saw that he saw. She blushed as she hung up.

'I'll bet you a hundred million dollars,' said Matthew, 'that I know who you were talking to.'

Clare flapped her hands vaguely. She knew things were moving too fast. She had no wish to slow them down.

They heard Mollie bumping about in another room. The apartment looked indestructibly solid, but the walls between the rooms were thin. Mollie's proximity seemed to Matthew to throw a shadow into the over-stuffed sitting-room. He felt stifled. Clare looked nervous, too, as though she knew what to expect.

Matthew made conversation, which with his elder daughter was not usually necessary. He said, to lighten the atmosphere with a neutral subject, 'Your new boyfriend's involved with horses?'

'Yes.'

'In Ireland?'

'Yes.'

'He knows breeding farms? Studs? The people who own them?'

'Yes, sure. Some.'

'Does he know of one that's for sale?'

'Yes, I think so. He was talking about that. His old cousins. They still hold hands. I hope when I . . .'

She stopped, because references to enduring devotion were not tactful in this place.

'I met a very rich guy,' said Matthew, 'the day before yesterday.'

'You're always doing that.'

'Yes, it gets tedious. Non-stop envy. This one's looking for a five-star spread, the absolute tops. I should think his finance is pretty well unlimited.'

'Black?'

'Almost white.'

'Meaning Arab?'

'High-class Arab. Cream with just a dash of coffee. He's a congenial guy. I liked him.'

'I'll try to remember to tell Tom.'

Matthew gave Clare Ghalib's name and title, and the name of his Paris hotel. Clare was trying to remember the name of Tom's elderly relatives and of their estate when Mollie came in.

To Clare's relief she had taken out her curlers and brushed her hair. She had changed into a silk suit. The hem of her slip showed.

Matthew rose. Mollie crossed the room towards him. Awkwardness struck Matthew. Their relationship had been civilized since the separation; they were still husband and wife. So how did they greet each other? The question had never been definitively answered. No formula had been agreed. Matthew knew couples acrimoniously divorced, who when they met afterwards exchanged cousinly kisses. Mollie had never done this, or shown any sign of wanting it done. But the purposefulness of her advance across the room suggested something of the kind.

Matthew braced himself to respond gracefully to whatever form of greeting Mollie had in mind.

To his surprise, she handed him a piece of paper. This was the greeting. He wondered, in astonishment, if it were a note expressing feelings she was too shy or proud to voice. Prepared to be touched, he looked at the piece of paper.

It was the bill for the curtains. The cost, for materials and making, was a little over £900. Matthew struggled to keep all expression out of his face.

'It was not the most expensive material,' said Mollie, her first words to her husband for eleven months. 'It was not the stuff I really wanted. We are cheese-paring here all the time. The best silk brocade costs £25 a yard. It would have looked well in here. But I economised. This only cost £18 a yard.'

'Thank you,' said Matthew, putting the bill in his pocket.

'Your neglect of your daughter has now borne fruit.'

'Tell me what the trouble is, and what you want me to do about it.'

'I would not presume to tell you your duty. You must know it as well as I.'

'Where is Liz?'

'Living with a black communist drug-addict.'

Clare opened her mouth to speak. She closed it again.

'I'll try to see her,' said Matthew.

'You must see her and bring her home.'

'If you tell me where she's living I'll go there. I promise that, but I don't think I can promise any more.'

'Then you are betraying her as well as me,' said Mollie.

'Liz is nineteen,' said Matthew, gently, patiently, 'I can ask her to come home, if I get to see her, for your sake and for her own. If she's willing to come she'll come, and maybe stay. If I drag her back against her will, how long do you think she'd stay? One minute? Two minutes?'

'I thought that, though you choose to live 4,000 miles away from your family, you still felt some sense of responsibility for them.'

'As much as I'm allowed,' said Matthew.

Mollie looked at him without comprehension. There were signs of anger in her face, as disfiguring as rust on the bodywork of a car, or bare patches in the coat of a dog.

'I had no voice in the choice of Liz's school, or in any part of her education. I never had a chance to meet any of her friends. I would have welcomed a far greater share of responsibility for her upbringing.'

'You ran away from it.'

Mildly, Matthew said, 'I stayed put.'

'That was tantamount to running away. They call it constructive desertion. It must have been obvious even to you that our place was in England. I could not have my children brought up as barbarians.'

'Thanks,' said Clare noiselessly.

Several answers suggested themselves to Matthew. He made none of them. Scoring debating points was not the name of this game. He repeated that he would go to the house where Liz was living, and try to see her and reason with her.

It seemed to him that the ground was now covered, and the horrible interview could be terminated.

Mollie had more to say. She explored the topics of constructive desertion, the English and American educational systems, and American ignorance of social distinctions and usages, especially as regarded the proper style by which the children of Peers of the Realm should be addressed. Matthew sat patiently listening, avoiding Clare's eye, and feeling the bill for the curtains crackling in his pocket.

Clare wanted to leave the room, the apartment, the city, the country. She thought she could have slipped out, without her mother noticing. She thought a company of Grenadiers could have marched through the room, without her mother noticing. But loyalty kept her rooted — loyalty to both of them — loyalty and love. Possibly her presence might restrain her mother from the wildest extremities of injustice. She might not be too embarrassing. That would be better for them all.

He was being heroic. His face was so wretched Clare wanted to cry.

Clare crossed her fingers and her legs and called on every superstitious talisman she could think of. She prayed. She said, 'Don't let her say it.'

And her mother said it: 'It's all your fault.'

And at that her father lost his temper, which he never did. Anybody else would have lost it long before.

He said, 'You are arrogant, closed-minded, unreasonable and humourless. Predictably you've let your daughter make a mess of her life, and you're too dishonest to admit it. You're too cowardly and too stupid to accept responsibility for what you've done and for what you've failed to do.'

Clare wanted to scream. She prayed again. She said in a desperate prayer, 'Please don't let him say it.'

And he said it: 'I don't blame Liz for running away from you.'

Clare ran away from her mother, from them both. In tears she got a taxi, and it took her to Fulham and to Tom.

He was alone in the house of his friends.

She went into his arms and on to his lap, and the springs of the sofa went twang like the seats of his car. She sobbed and sobbed. He soothed her and petted her, and at last she cried herself out.

Later, when he had made her Irish coffee, she told him about an incalculably rich congenial off-white Arab who wanted to buy a breeding farm in Ireland.

Tom telephoned at once to his elderly cousins in Tipperary. She answered. She confirmed that the property was to be sold, though it was not yet in the hands of agents. They didn't care if the purchaser was brown or pale green, as long as he would look after the place, and put it to proper use.

Tom telephoned to Paris — the first time he had ever done so — and was lucky enough to speak to Prince Ghalib personally. Ghalib's perfect English surprised him, and made things easier. Tom tried to make the Tipperary property sound like a corner of Paradise, which he could do with scarcely any exaggeration, and the suppression of few facts.

Ghalib clearly knew very well what he wanted, and he knew what things cost. He expected to pay £4,500 an acre for good grazing land, and about £250,000 for a Georgian manor-house of fair size and architectural merit.

'You are earning your commission,' said Tom to Clare.

'You paid it,' said Clare, 'with Irish coffee and seats that go twang.'

Matthew went to the address Mollie had given him, his hands still shaking from the shock of the quarrel. He had said unforgivable things, and he was not going to forgive himself. The things Mollie had said were simply the sort of things Mollie said. It was horrible that he had lost control of himself, and most horrible that he had done so in front of Clare.

A man battered in soul rang the doorbell of the house in Notting Hill (it looked as battered as he felt) and then, realising that the bell did not work, pounded a big knocker.

A young man with long fair hair opened the door and greeted him with mocking courtesy. He spoke like a gentleman and looked like a failed apprentice ponce.

'I'm frightfully sorry,' he said. 'Liz does roost here, but she's out. She's working. Yes, she's got a part-time job. She's a photographic model, actually. She'll be heartbroken she missed you, I expect. Heaven knows when she'll be back. They seem to work very long hours, which wouldn't suit one. Of course the overtime is lovely. Any message? I'm practically bound to see her in the next day or two. Goodbye, then. Lovely to meet you. Do come again, now that you know your way.'

Short of camping on the doorstep, there was no more Matthew could do. A nineteen-year-old who went off with a man was not breaking any law, even if Mollie was right about the man.

At least the tattered and dingy curtains visible in the windows of the house were preferable to those things of Mollie's.

Matthew was interviewed by a sporting reporter, in the lobby of the Plaza, within minutes of checking in. He confirmed the rumour, picked up from the *Sporting Life* in London, that George Whyte, Prince Ghalib al-Jilani and he himself had acquired shares in Beausoleil, and were all looking forward to sending mares to this promising recruit to the ranks of international stallions. He would not commit himself as to the location of the stallion. He did not say that effective control of Beausoleil had passed to his group and to America. He respected the duc de Montfermainbrey's wish for secrecy on these points, although he did not understand the reason for it.

The item was printed the following morning, under a small headline. Matthew expected his telephone to ring as a result, and it did. His old friend Luis Valdes called, on a visit to New York from Venezuela. Luis arranged to meet Matthew in the Edwardian Room at eleven.

Luis wanted a nomination to Beausoleil. He was in New York to see *Simone Boccanegra* and *Lulu* at the Met, opera being the other passion of his life. Typically he was combining racing business with an operatic pilgrimage. He had mares at his magnificent Hacienda San Cristoforo which Matthew would approve without hesitation as fit mates for Beausoleil.

They had the Edwardian Room to themselves. They shared a bottle of chilled Pouilly Fumé.

Luis was an elderly nut-brown charmer in a silk suit, who spent his oil fortune with a lavishness worthy of Epi Makropulos, to whom he was predictably congenial. He talked, all at the same time, of Verdi, Berg, bloodlines, other performances he had seen of these and other operas, mating plans for his mares, the performances of Latin American horses in European races, the acoustics of various opera houses, and the pedigree of the mare he wanted to send to Beausoleil.

'*Rosenkavalier* is by Wagner out of Viennese operetta,' he said, 'so like Ribot it is better than its breeding. *Figaro* is by the music of the angels out of radical social indignation. Mozart had pure sprinting blood close up in the pedigree of almost everything he wrote, exactly as Tesio said, but *dios*! what stamina! I saw Beausoleil at Longchamp. I saw Epi Makropulos, too, with a girl with a Dutch name and an oriental face. The achievement of the Darley Arabian, in reverse. A western sire on eastern stock. Beausoleil is the overture to *Traviata*, the 'Liebestod', the great

141

choruses in *Nabucco* and *Aida*. He is by the *Flying Dutchman* storm music out of classical perfection, out of *La Fideltá Premiata*, out of *Semele*. I saw *La Fideltá* at Glyndebourne. It is bred by the royal chapel out of the garden party, not a winner of the Arc but a good handicapper. A gelding. It has bred nothing.'

Fighting to keep his head above the choppy conversational waves with which Luis Valdes was trying to drown him, Matthew undertook to secure Luis two nominations to Beausoleil, these being purchased probably one each from Epi Makropulos and George Whyte.

Matthew called Fox Hill, finding the number in the *American Racing Manual*. He spoke to a woman, obviously black, who repeatedly refused to go on a date with him, but after the entanglements of misunderstanding had been cut away promised to tell Mrs Phillipson that Mr Carver would arrive the following day.

In the Fox Hill barns everything was calm. Men and horses were calm. Ed Lindsey smiled calmly when he heard that Matthew Carver was coming. He murmured the news to Meadowsweet, who showed no visible joy.

Elsewhere on the place the effect of the news was galvanic, even though it was expected. Rosie was galvanised. After dinner, at eleven o'clock, she began hanging paper in one of the guest bedrooms. It was good paper, reproducing an authentic design only a few years younger than the house, an English design based on Venetian motifs. It deserved, perhaps, a paper-hanger who used scissors more accurately and paste more temperately; who was herself more temperate. The paper-hanging became a party. Rosie drank brandy. Peach sat himself in a chair in the middle of the bedroom; he ate candy-bars and gave advice. His advice was challenged at all points by Hazel and by Cousin Thalia Collin, who came in and out as they were intermittently required by Jefferson Dill for drama coaching. Jefferson Dill himself joined the party around midnight, bringing a bottle of bourbon. He said he got it from his own apartment, that it was his bourbon. He got it from the dining-room, and it was Tim's bourbon. He had the precedent of François Villon and Dylan Thomas.

Rosie gave up at two in the morning, utterly exhausted after an eighteen-hour day of strenuous activity. The room was one-third papered. Peach, on his way out, kicked over the bucket of paste.

Matthew Carver had intended to fly to Washington in the morning, and on to Charlottesville. He was detained by a long telephone conversation with George Whyte, and another with Luis Valdes. He wrote a letter of apology to Mollie. He wrote and tore up a letter to Clare. Through the Plaza desk he made a reservation at a hotel not inconvenient from Fox Hill. He arranged for a self-drive hire-car to meet him at Charlottesville airport. He called Fox Hill to tell them not to expect him until the following day. But Fox Hill said — Mrs Phillipson herself said — he was welcome at any time of the day or night.

It was hot, muggy, Indian summer but promising rain. He got away at lunchtime.

Expecting Matthew Carver, keyed up to greet him and impress him, Rosie found time on her hands. She considered carrying on with papering the guest bedroom. She thought of the paste spilled on the fitted carpet. Peach had promised to clean it up. Peach had not cleaned it up. The whole project filled her with boredom. Jefferson Dill was running around wanting her to read her part through. Cousin Thalia Collin was rewriting her part to make it bigger. Peach, Hazel, Janice Field and Miss Viola Biggs of Mount Malcolm were all doing the same thing.

Rosie got away from there. She went to the sanitorium to see Tim, driving herself in the half-wrecked car which somebody had lent Jefferson Dill.

It was a bad visit. It was one of the worst.

It began to rain while she was there — hard, heavy, steady vertical rain which reminded Rosie of the wet seasons in the Caribbean and Indonesia and Kenya, places she had been to with Tim in the first years of their marriage. She pointed out the rain to Tim, and reminded him of those journeys they had made. He did not want to look at the rain or talk about the journeys. He wanted to look inwards at his own misery, which had neither cause nor cure. Rosie had the sense of trying to carry Tim, lift him physically one more afternoon through life. They said she should try to interest and distract him. She tried. After an hour, she knew it was one of the days when she could not interest him in anything, when he would not be distracted from his black internal contemplation. She might have left then, but she stayed and struggled. She loved Tim deeply and sorrowfully, and her memories of their early days were bathed in golden light. Shutting her eyes, she could see a lean brown man surfing and steeple-chasing and laughing, and drinking too much, and being as polite and popular drunk as sober. Opening her eyes, she saw the pallid puffy self-pitying ruin.

She sat and talked. She made herself talk brightly, optimistically. She looked hungrily for any answering flicker. It was ten times more exhausting than paper-hanging. After three hours they brought in his supper. It was a pretty good supper. The sanitorium was very expensive, and employed a dietician and a highly trained cook. Tim picked at his supper, pushing pieces of meat back and forth on his plate. Rosie tried to persuade him to eat. He looked at her without interest, and pushed his food about on his plate.

She went out into the teeming rain. She drove home in despair. Tim was thirty-six. He had an aunt in her nineties, spry if not sane. Rosie looked greyly ahead at forty years of afternoons like that afternoon. She was thirty-two. Divorce was impossible, an obscene idea. Marriage to a real man was impossible. Add ten years to thirty-two. Add twenty, thirty years. Her body was better than it had ever been; her face too, she thought. It was wasted. She was wasted. Time was rushing by. She was married to Fox Hill. She was married to spilled buckets of wallpaper paste on the fitted carpets of bedrooms.

It was dark when she got home. It was very warm for the time of year. The warm, pelting rain felt like soup. She ran into the house, a raincoat she found in the car over her head. She stepped in puddles.

Light came from the windows of the hall, out on to the west portico. In the light Rosie saw a tree, a twelve-foot sapling with its roots in a sack. She had ordered some exotic trees, advised by the ladies of the garden club and by Miss Viola Biggs of Mount Malcolm; or she had picked them adventurously from the pages of catalogues, seduced by descriptions as marvellous as those of chicken dinners in resort hotels. Being geometrical in lay-out, the gardens had focal points, intersections, which needed special and distinctive individual specimens. Flowering trees, each in its season. Here and there a statue would be fine. Rosie intended statues. Cousin Thalia Collin promised sources of statues known only to herself. Peach volunteered to be a statue, but insisted that he perform the function seated. Rosie said that he was not President Lincoln, but he might look like President Lincoln if he adopted the role of seated statue, and statues of President Lincoln in any position had no place in a Virginia garden.

Round the sacking was a string, and on the string a label. A long Latin name was written on the label, and in large red type the words 'PLANT IMMEDIATELY ON RECEIPT'.

It was no night for gardening. Rosie went indoors.

Two dozen people were in the hall, half engaged in an orgy and half making fools of themselves in other ways. Hazel was in a big, old-fashioned laundry basket from the attics, her black head poking out like a gollywog's in a gift box. Cousin Thalia Collin was doing a kind of dance, among the couples on the floor, all of whom were known to Rosie and all of whom were fully dressed. Peach was sitting at the bottom of the stairs eating a candy-bar; it was not clear if he was part of the brothel scene from *Circe's Island*, or waiting in the wings for his entry. Miss Viola Biggs was holding a guitar as though it might go off. Jefferson Dill was bouncing to and fro like a golf-ball in a squash-court.

Rosie saw that Jefferson Dill was drunk. She realised that half those present were more or less drunk. Not Cousin Thalia Collin; not Miss Viola Biggs; not Peach. Possibly not Hazel, but that was a matter of doubt. Hazel looked drunk first thing in the morning; she looked sober when she passed out at the end of her day off.

Rosie got herself a heavy scotch on the rocks from the dining-room. She went back to the hall. She had a great need to be amused. She thought Jefferson Dill's rehearsal might be amusing, but after a few minutes she found it dull. The play was pretentious crap, and Jefferson Dill was too drunk to take the rehearsal. Most of the couples lying on the floor got uncomfortable, and rose to their feet. Jefferson Dill was unable to control them. He lost his grip. His commands were ignored. Bottles circulated. Hazel *was* drunk. Janice Field was drunk. Rosie had another two big drinks quickly, to deaden her misery about Tim. The scotch blurred the sharp edges, but did nothing about the deep ache.

'PLANT IMMEDIATELY.'

If they said that they meant it. The tree would die if it wasn't planted immediately. A beautiful, expensive, exotic tree. It was terrible to think of it dying of neglect, out there all on its own.

Rosie said, 'I want a lot of lights and a lot of shovels and a lot of people.'

They found a lot of flashlights from somewhere in back. Rosie led the way to an outhouse where there were shovels. Two men carried the tree. The warm rain still teemed like lobster bisque. A dozen of the people were drunk enough to come out into the rain. The party had taken a new turn. It was like something out of a German expressionist movie — a druidic ring of saturated people, lights glaring inwards, rain streaming through the beams of the lights, dirt-smeared figures digging a grave at the junction of two avenues.

Hazel, standing in the rain, began to sing the Baptist hymns of her childhood. Janice Field vomited behind a bush.

Miss Viola Biggs went home to Mount Malcolm in her car, not disapproving but knowing her own limitations. Cousin Thalia Collin went crossly upstairs. Jefferson Dill went to sleep on the library floor. Peach went to his thinking room, and sat eating candy in his thinking chair.

Figures came out of the house and joined the tree-planters. Bit-players, but performing a necessary function. They brought bottles. The bottles passed from hand to hand. Hazel's singing was interrupted.

Rosie had terrible trouble undoing the string round the sack which covered the roots of the tree. She found herself being helped by a stranger, a nice-looking browny-fair man of about fifty. She did not know how he got there or who he was. He had a pocket-knife. He cut the string. She smiled her thanks. They planted the tree. In the ring of lights, in the teeming rain, they began shovelling earth back into the hole round the roots of the tree.

Matthew Carver put on raincoat and hat before he got out of the car. He started towards the dark bulk of the house, then saw what looked like a burial some way off in the garden. Notions of lynch-mobs flickered through his head. That was what the scene looked like, the burial by night of a black trying to run for the state legislature, or suing a white businessman, or caught raping a schoolgirl.

Matthew approached the group warily, rain trickling down inside his collar and soaking his pants-legs. He heard a voice like a trombone singing a hymn. He heard laughter which he recognised as drunken. He saw what was really going on.

It fitted with some of the things he had heard about Fox Hill.

146

He joined the group, standing in the ring round the tree-planting between two women with flashlights. One passed him an open, half-full bottle of bourbon, wiping the neck on her sleeve.

It was certainly time for a drink. It was a funny place, but it was certainly time. He took a long pull at the bottle, wiped the neck on his sleeve, and passed it on.

Another bottle came his way almost at once, passed around behind the first one. He had another drink. Several bottles were in circulation, going clockwise around the group.

A woman, maybe a young girl, was crouched over the sacking round the roots of the tree they were planting. She was trying to undo the knot in the string which secured the sacking. But the string was soaking wet. The knot would be impossible to untie. She needed a knife. Matthew had a small clasp-knife, once his father's. He stepped forward, crouched, and cut the string.

The woman turned and smiled. He saw her face for the first time. His heart jumped. Her hair was plastered to her head. Her skirt was draggled with mud and clinging to her legs. There was a broad streak of mud across her forehead and another on one cheek. Her hands were caked with mud. She raised a hand to push back a saturated tendril of hair, leaving fresh mud on her temple and on her ear. The beams of the flashlights shone harshly on her face.

She was insanely beautiful.

They lowered the roots of the tree into the hole. He and she held it steady, his hands just above hers, while somebody shovelled dirt into the hole. She took one hand off the tree to accept a proffered bottle. She drank deep. She handed the bottle to Matthew, making no attempt to wipe it. He smiled, took it, and drank deep.

He began to laugh. It was not altogether the bourbon laughing, though the bourbon helped. He was comparing the sudden, inexplicable, surreal episode with Mollie's apartment and with her life. He was imagining Mollie's comments on the tree-planting and on the freely-circulating bourbon. He laughed so that his hands shook, as they had shaken after he talked to Mollie.

'Hey,' said the wet and dirty woman facing him across the half-filled hole, 'Hold steady, or you loosen the dirt around the roots.'

'Sorry.'

'Who are you?'

'Matthew Carver.'

'Oh, my God! You don't want to do this. Go in and get dry.'

'I do want to do this.'

'Have a drink, then.'

'Thanks, I will. Are you Mrs Phillipson?'

'What in hell will you think of us? We were hoping to make a good impression. You see, there was a card on the tree saying "Plant immediately".'

'Then of course you had to do it.'

'It did seem that way. In fairness to the tree.'

'Rosanna,' said Matthew suddenly.

'That's me.'

'Sorry, that was impertinent. I just remembered that somebody told me your name.'

Without thought, Matthew put his hands on the little tree-trunk over her wet and muddy hands.

'Your hands are cold.'

'Not really,' she said. 'The mud feels cold. Probably we should have another drink, to keep the cold out.'

The earth was replaced and stamped down. The tree was firm.

'Thank you, folks,' said Rosanna Phillipson. 'That was right neighbourly.'

Her clothes clung to her body, glued by the rain to the contours of her breasts and hips and flat belly and thighs. If she was conscious of this she was unembarrassed. Those clinging wet clothes must have been uncomfortable.

The party began to weave back towards the house, led by the black woman singing another hymn. Matthew and Rosanna Phillipson brought up the rear. They lagged a little behind.

'Let's play tennis,' said Rosanna Phillipson.

Matthew was so surprised that he stopped dead, staring at her in the darkness.

'The rackets are so terrible the rain won't hurt them,' she said, 'and the balls are so terrible the rain won't hurt them, and the night's so warm it won't hurt us, and I'm so proud of even *finding* that court I just want to play a — what's the word? — an inaugural game.'

'In the dark?'

'We'll have light. Just a little. Not a lot. That would make it too easy.'

'Oh yes.' Matthew began laughing again.

She laughed. She stopped laughing and said, 'I have things I want to forget. Just for a while.'

'So have I.'

'Terrible things?'

'Yes.'

'My things are terrible. Do your things include pity and despair?'

'Yes.'

'A game of tennis, right now this minute, is the way we're going to forget things.'

They took a single flashlight from one of the others. Rosanna Phillipson produced rackets and balls from a garage. She was right: neither would be further damaged by the wet. She led him to a grass tennis-court behind a high hedge of unclipped topiary. She put the flashlight on the grass by one of the net-posts; its beam lit brilliantly a tiny area, and produced a faint glow as far away as the baselines.

They began to knock up.

Matthew's eyes got used to the streaming darkness. The little light became more and more adequate. It was impossible to hit the ball hard with his racket, which had a warped frame and slack and incomplete strings. The balls themselves would not have travelled far or fast if fired from a gun. They bounced soggily and unpredictably on the wet grass. Matthew was laughing so much he could hardly hold his racket. He heard peals of laughter from his half-seen opponent on the other side of the net.

He discarded his raincoat, which hampered him. He lost his hat. His jacket began to cling damply. He peeled it off. He was so wet that he hardly became wetter. He saw Rosanna Phillipson, at the other end, taking off and flinging away her shoes. Slithering on urban leather, Matthew did the same. He took his socks off, she her tights. It was comforting to feel the wet grass between his bare toes, and his feet gripped better.

'These clothes are impossible,' she called through the rain. 'I'm all stuck together like a beetle.'

'I feel the same.'

'It's pretty dark.'

'Jet black.'

'Okay. On that basis.'

Dimly he saw her change shape and colour. She was pale and leggy. She hit a ball at him and he struggled to lob it back. She had stripped to her underwear. It seemed wise. Feeling crazy,

149

happy, warm, oblivious, he wriggled with difficulty out of his shirt and New York pants. His shorts clung, immediately saturated. He welcomed the caress of the warm rain on his bare chest. He knew he was a little drunk, but he thought it was only a little. He loved this unbelievable excursion into childishness, into doing something absolutely silly.

'Change ends,' called Rosanna Phillipson.

'We didn't play a game.'

'I was playing. I was scoring. I won a set.'

He laughed, and laughing met her at the net-post where the flashlight was. She was behind the flashlight, a pale blur. She dropped her racket. They were in each other's arms. Her skin was wet and warm. He felt her breasts soft and wet on his chest. She had not stripped to her underwear. She had stripped completely. He put his two hands on her small, firm, rain-wet buttocks, and pressed her body against his. He felt her hands at the waist of his shorts. She dropped suddenly to her knees. She pulled his shorts to the ground. She knelt up, against him, her arms round his hips. He felt her breasts on his loins.

'Now, now,' she whispered urgently. 'Forget, forget.'

They lay. He did not feel the coldness of the wet grass. He kissed her, all over her smooth wet body. He drank the rain on her skin. She kissed his ears and mouth and chest. They lost themselves in deep sweet kisses, their bodies touching from lips to toes.

'Now, now,' she whispered. 'Now, now, now.'

She was ready. So wet with rain was the fur of her cunt that he was not sure if the warm wetness was juice or rain. It was her aromatic juice diluted by the clean rain. His fingers slipped in, confirming, causing her to wriggle with desire.

But he?

In his excitement, in the bizarre and magic encounter, he had forgotten about himself. He felt sick with sudden anxiety.

He felt little fingers on his cock, and it was huge and hard. She steered him into herself. She was tight and hot. The sleeve grew and moistened around the entering arm. He slid and plunged. She cried out, a little wailing like an owl in the rain. A moment later the great gush of his ejaculation gave him his manhood back. She gave him his manhood back. They lay, he deep but softening inside her, her legs twined round his hips, kissing and murmuring in wonder, caressed by the warm rain.

150

Matthew awoke in a double bed. An eye on the pillow beside his was open and looking at him. Sun streamed in through two high sashed windows. The weather had changed. Everything had changed.

He said, from the depths of bottle-green slumber, 'Why? Why me?'

'I bless you,' she said in a voice husky with sleep.

'I bless you,' he said. 'But why? Why me?'

'I guess timing. You came when I needed you. You were what I needed. Not some other. I don't know why. There isn't any why, is there?'

He reached a hand to her, shyly. The weather had turned: the time had turned. This sane sunlit morning was a far cry from the delirium of the rain-soaked tennis-court.

She rolled over so that she faced him, so that she came into his arms.

She said into his cheek, 'I waited an hour for you to wake. Getting more and more crazy for you. For it. For this.'

She straddled him, and impaled herself, slowly, deep and deep. Her eyes were open and she was smiling. There was a broad excited smile on her perfect face. There was no mud anywhere on her face.

It was quick and lovely. It had morning eagerness, sunshiny shamelessness. It was a smiling fuck. Matthew felt a surge of sensation that left him laughing with happiness. There were tears of joy on Rosie's face.

Somebody had brought his cases in from the hired car. He shaved in the bright bathroom that opened off the bedroom. He put on his cotton robe, and got back into bed. Rosie had put on a robe. She was brushing her hair.

There was a knock on the door. The black nurse called Hazel, neat and demure in a print dress, came in with a breakfast tray. The smell of coffee was marvellous. Hazel winked and chuckled and mothered them.

Everybody in and around Fox Hill knew where Matthew Carver had spent the night.

Peach was shocked. The nastiness had happened. Tim was betrayed. Carver was a kind of carpetbagger, breaking in and stealing and ravishing and dishonouring.

Jefferson Dill, nursing his hangover, heard the news from Thalia when he went to the dining-room for a tuft of hairs from the dog that bit him. As always, he wondered how to turn the scandalous episode to his own account. Months at Fox Hill had given him no opportunity to do more than live and eat and drink free. The people were raffish but virtuous. There was nobody he could blackmail. But now a chance had come. Not for blackmail. Jefferson Dill was frightened of Rosanna's rage, and he was not about to threaten a man like Carver. He had heard all about Carver, *ad nauseam,* since the man's visit was first adumbrated. But Jefferson Dill had facilities denied to François Villon. He used the extension telephone, in the office by the kitchen, to call a newspaper whose editor he knew.

It was not a big item, by the standards of world news. It was not a scandal that would rock Capitol Hill or Buckingham Palace. But, as Jefferson Dill pointed out to his friend, Matthew Carver was well known, internationally known, in his special world; and the nice irony was that he was known, among other things, as a pillar of rectitude and respectability; and he had a British wife, still his wife, who had some kind of title.

Jefferson Dill thought the item was worth $100. The editor thought it was worth $50.

The item was picked up by all the papers that printed that kind of dirt, and by the Virginia and Kentucky papers to whom it was local news. Matthew Carver's links with George Whyte and Cragrock were mentioned. The New York correspondents of British newspapers and agencies Telexed the news to London. It appeared in the gossip columns of the national tabloids. It was hotter news than it would otherwise have been, because the Honourable Mrs Carver's father had been a lord; and because of the publicity about the record-breaking Mill Reef colt, and the press speculation about Beausoleil. One of the London papers got hold of an old photograph of Rosanna Phillipson, then Rosanna Collin, riding sidesaddle; one printed a recent photograph of Mollie, taken at the wedding of a relative, wearing a hat a friend would not have chosen for her.

Clare Carver was distressed for her mother's sake. She saw the anger and humiliation in that pinched face. But, herself in love as never before, she found herself in favour of love. A part of her mind deplored her father's unthinking cruelty to his lonely and vulnerable wife. A part wished him happiness.

She dimly understood that he needed some kind of therapy, after the scene in the apartment.

Mollie's own virtue had been rigid, except for the one necessary and joyless lapse which had made possible her marriage. She was angry. She was angry at her own name being dragged through the mire, and the use of her photograph with a facetious caption.

She spoke at length to her cousin Alaric, Lord Wincham, and found her anger precisely echoed. His family's dignity was important to him. He detected sniggers in his clubs. He suggested divorce, but Mollie disapproved of divorce. She had never contemplated it, and did not do so now.

The old lags in the Tibbs Hill Women's Prison agreed with her. They said the family was sacred. They were shocked that a man over there in that America should be getting his bit of fanny on the sly. Mollie was warmed and encouraged by their goodwill. She found more loyalty among them than among her own friends.

The news was discussed all over Kentucky, and nowhere more exhaustively than at Cragrock.

George Whyte was shocked. Though anxious for publicity for his farms, his horses, himself, the associations in this case were thoroughly undesirable. Sexual immorality inevitably suggested sharp dealings in other areas. A cheat was a cheat. George Whyte did not seriously suspect Matthew Carver of cheating anybody in matters of business, but he did not like the way this would look to the world.

George's secretary Doris Bernard agreed with him. She called Lee V. Lowe in New York, to get him to do what he could to kill the stories.

George was jealous of Matthew Carver. George was not a man women had ever wanted to have affairs with, except very greedy ones who smelled his money.

Jean McLean Whyte was jealous not of Matthew but of this new woman in his life. Having known Matthew for years, Jean well understood any woman wanting him. He was attractive. He was highly desirable. He was class goods. Had he not been her husband's partner, Jean would probably have made a play for Matthew herself, but the relationship was too close, the risk too great.

But the thought excited her, so that she had to go out to the barns to find Will Stevens the manager, and pull down her pants for a quick one in a feed-store.

Alice Whyte Harding was amused at these sharp differences of reaction. Living in California, she had not met Matthew Carver. She knew that she was bound to do so, imminently, now that she was home in Kentucky. She was intrigued. Jean made Matthew Carver sound worth meeting.

It seemed he did not suffer from Frank Harding's drawback.

Sir Merivale Lucas was disgusted.

He had sent Carver to Fox Hill as a favour to Rosanna, because of the 'maybe' in the 'no'. The moment the shit arrived he was screwing her. Why Carver and not himself? An uncouth Yank, rather than an English baronet?

Sir Merivale Lucas was eaten with jealousy and puzzlement. Lady Lucas observed his distress. She discovered the reason. She teased him unmercifully. It cheered her up wonderfully, which nothing else did.

Prince Ghalib al-Jilani saw the news in Paris, looking at English newspapers for the racing results.

His admiration for Matthew Carver was undiminished. A man like that took what he wanted, and gave pleasure in doing so. But it was interesting. Carver had struck Ghalib as so particularly correct, so virtuous. This lip-smacking news item was incongruous; it fitted oddly the correctly-tweeded, Duke-greeted man he knew.

The daughter. So small, graceful, bouncy, beautiful. If the father was morally lax, what about her? Memory stirred lust in Ghalib's phenomenally virile loins.

Ghalib had his things packed to go to Tipperary, to see the stud he had been told about. He made plans for meeting and seducing Clare Carver.

Epaminondas Makropulos was pleased for his old friend. Knowing Rosanna Phillipson, he was not surprised Matthew should have wanted her; knowing him, he was not surprised he should have attracted her. Tanja had wanted him the moment she met him, because he was sad but not only for that reason. It was

154

very good that, if the horrible wife had cut Matthew's balls off, Rosanna Phillipson had sewn them on again. Matthew would be a happier man and a more cheerful companion.

Tanja Dekker was puzzled. She wondered what was wrong with herself.

CHAPTER 8

Pity and despair had kept Rosie faithful. Not always prudent, in word or deed, but faithful. Now pity and despair were abolished, by a man appearing out of nowhere in the rain. Rosie was totally surprised by the turn of events. It was not in the least what she had expected, of herself or of the circumstances of her life. She thought that none of it would have happened, had not every circumstance been miraculously in the correct conjunction. Her visit to Tim; the rain; the tree; the darkness; the crazy idea about tennis; the emancipating effect of a few inches of bourbon.

And Matthew's own need, the deep unhappiness which was one of the things she saw when she watched him as he slept.

She was happy to be a help to him. She was proud. She was glad she could make some return for the huge good he was doing her.

Peach's attitude was predictable. It was annoying. Rosie had been brought up with the odd, incongruous streak of puritanism in the middle of that idle, dishonest self-indulgence. In some aspects of character they were alike. Naturally: by genetics and by environment. But Rosie could not detect a puritan streak in herself. She had searched, as a child. She thought that, if her older brother was genuinely shocked by things, she ought to be too. She pretended to be, by the divorces of family friends, by the pregnancies of maids and waitresses, by the discovery of a teacher in the back of a car with one of his pupils at the high school. But it was false puritanism, assumed in imitation of Peach. She was not the least bit shocked by pregnancies or seductions, though the divorces saddened her.

She was not shocked now, at her own behaviour or at Matthew's. She was joyful. She took and gave. She revived like a watered flower, like a man curing his hangover with a cold, hard drink at noon, like squashed velvet in steam, like a puppy being fed. She looked at herself and saw that she was beautiful again.

The newspapers bothered her only in their possible effect on Tim. It was not a serious bother. Tim had not looked at a newspaper in months, listened to a radio, watched TV. Only someone bent on inflicting misery would force Tim to hear about the affair. Nobody like that went anywhere near Tim. Certainly there was nobody like that at the sanitorium. She thought of calling them, warning them. But she was embarrassed at the prospect of that conversation.

She was angry at the treachery of whoever had betrayed them, but there was no way she could pin it on anybody.

Meanwhile Matthew had to be shown the farm. He had to love it. He was. He did.

He did.

Epi Makropulos was right; Merivale Lucas was right.

The barns were not new, but they were solid, warm, dry, airy, well-designed and in perfect repair. That they were beautiful was a bonus for man if not for horse. The foaling facilities were more than adequate. The paddocks and fences were fine. Much of the grazing was on sloping ground: a good thing for drainage, and also for giving all the stock gentle exercise which they took unconsciously all the time they were out. Hillside pasture was said to be the reason Chilean horses were so active and athletic; and Matthew had heard people in England say the same thing about hunters summered in the Cotswold Hills — they kept themselves fit just by standing on a slope.

Strongest of all the selling-points of Fox Hill Farm was Ed Lindsey. Matthew took to the old black immediately, and every meeting increased his liking and respect. Over three days they spent hours together, each as anxious to listen as to talk. They leaned over post-and-rail fences, looking at broodmares or young stock; they sat on hay-bales; they looked at photographs in Ed's office of Fox Hill stars of the old days. They talked about every aspect of bloodstock and its care, feeding, treatment of ailments, preventative medicine, clipping and shoeing, manes and tails, grass culture, fencing materials and gates, the heating and ventilation of barns, foaling, covering, stallion management, bloodlines and nicks, great races that Matthew had seen in Europe or Ed had seen when he was young.

Matthew saw the stallion-barn and the breeding-shed, and the special paddock with a fence too high to see over, where an aggressive stallion could exercise himself without trying to kill other horses. He saw where another barn was to be built to house visiting mares — against the day when they had another stallion at Fox Hill — when Mr Peter got around to having the trees felled.

Matthew found himself agreeing with remarks Ed occasionally made, about Fox Hill being a good station for a top stallion. Ed was not obtrusive in making this point. But it was funny how often the conversation veered in that direction, in the most natural fashion.

Matthew's reunion with Meadowsweet was happy. He found he remembered her vividly as foal, weanling, yearling, and two-year-old racer. He had regretted the necessity of selling her. But he had had, at the time, a full complement of mares on his own small farm, and he had needed the money.

Mollie had needed the money, for travel for herself and the children, for moving house (one of her moves) and for furniture and redecoration. All perfectly reasonable. Not to be grudged. But it was a joy to see Meadowsweet again.

Her yearling colt by Lord Primrose was usefully if not superbly bred. Matthew was sure there were races to be won with him. Ed explained why he had not gone to the sales, though the explanation left Matthew puzzled. Sir Merivale Lucas had advised them to expect around $90,000, if they did sell by auction. Matthew thought this was about right, given the colt's pedigree and conformation. He wanted to buy the colt, out of sentiment but not only out of sentiment, but he could not afford all of it, after his share of the Mill Reef and his share of Beausoleil. He said the syndicate would probably buy it, but this depended on Mr George Whyte.

Much else depended on Mr George Whyte. He was the largest individual shareholder in Beausoleil. Where Beausoleil stood depended on George Whyte. It seemed Ed Lindsey knew this, and knew that George Whyte was apt to be influenced by Matthew's opinion.

Still Ed was tactful and adroit in steering the conversation.

Life indoors at Fox Hill was in sharp contrast, Matthew found, to life on the farm. Outside, all was orderly, methodical, gentle, with Ed Lindsey and Rick Field and the rest doing things they thoroughly understood. Inside all was unpredictable, often chaotic, sometimes threatening volcanic eruption, with Jefferson Dill strenuously rehearsing his extraordinary allegorical drama (what Matthew saw of it seemed to be allegorical, and it seemed to be so bad it was funny) with varying numbers of neighbours, with Peach Collin and Miss Thalia Collin and occasionally Rosie, with the black nurse Hazel and with a formidable old lady, whom Matthew met briefly, called Miss Viola Biggs of Mount Malcolm. (It appeared that, as with certain Scottish lairds, her name was deemed incomplete without the name of her house added.)

Matthew formed only a hazy impression of Jefferson Dill and Miss Thalia. They were so preoccupied with the play that they were only visible at meals, and then talked of nothing else. Peach was preoccupied with it too, but only some of the time. Matthew found him amusing, a complete original, a genuine eccentric. There was some of Rosie's extraordinary charm in his smile, and some of her enchanting originality in the darting of his mind from one funny philosophical rabbit-hole to another. His body did not dart. The idea of him running was preposterous, although he was more than ten years younger than Matthew. There, he was profoundly unlike his sister, who in certain moods found it impossible to walk. She ran everywhere. Then her hair blew about in wild black tendrils and her cheeks were scarlet and she panted and laughed, and suddenly collapsed, into Matthew's arms if he was there, and wanted him as badly as ever, and led him upstairs without concealment, and gloriously bared herself to his eyes and hands and tongue and teeth.

Matthew had serious reasons for staying at Fox Hill so much longer than he expected. But none of them were the real reason he stayed. This was as obvious to him as it was to everybody else.

Matthew regretted the news break, but since it had happened he did not waste nervous energy in brooding about it. He did not think it would affect the opinion of him of anyone whose opinion mattered to him. People who respected his judgement of bloodstock would not respect his judgement less. People aware that he kept his word and paid his bills would not suddenly consider him a liar and defaulter.

He did not suppose the news had reached Britain. He did not suppose himself sufficiently important. He was not pleased at the probable effect on his wife and children. Clare would hear all about it eventually, without doubt. It was unfortunate. It was annoying.

Whoever leaked the item must have had absolute proof, or no editor would have touched it. Matthew thought that must have come from Hazel. But Hazel stoutly denied saying a word to any reporter. Rosie believed her. Matthew let it go.

Ed Lindsey watched Matthew's conversion with growing optimism. He arrived at Fox Hill a man not intending to stand a top syndicated stallion there. After three days he was a man with a different attitude.

Ed gave himself some of the credit for this, but he was realistic enough to give Miss Rosie some credit, too.

Rosie had not deliberately influenced Matthew's judgement in the matter of the farm or the stallion. At least, not in the way of debate, argument, plea. Nor did she regard herself as trying to influence him by those ancient and wordless techniques which brought both of them so much joy so often.

All the same, it was nice to see him happy and not brooding about his sad bitch of a wife. It was nice to know that his happiness was a part of his attitude to Fox Hill.

You couldn't think the same of a place when you were screwing there four times a day, could you? You couldn't think badly of such a place?

Miss Viola Biggs of Mount Malcolm bred horses, too. Only steeplechasers, or horses intended to be steeplechasers. It was not an easy thing to do, as there were not in America the established female families and the established sires which, in Ireland, produced unending streams of high-class jump-racers. So Miss Viola Biggs imported broodmares from Ireland. They were found for her by that specialist in Transatlantic deals, Sir Merivale Lucas. She never meant to have more than three mares, but as she never sold a horse she bred — all her ugly ducklings being swans — she was becoming overcrowded.

Of course she had heard of Matthew Carver. She was glad to meet him at Fox Hill. The circumstances were unpropitious for conversation, as it was in the middle of a rehearsal of *Circe's Island*. She was herself about to give one of her best speeches, which she had improved and increased by adding some stanzas of self-praise. She was not quite confident of having memorised the new material. She was preoccupied.

160

Accordingly she called Rosie, and asked her to bring Matthew Carver over for a drink. It was very near. It was surprising that two such imposing houses should have been built so close together, since each was originally supported by a large estate.

'They built theirs just across the fence from our land, and we built ours just across the fence from their land. Neighbourly. They were terribly, terribly neighbourly,' said Rosie.

'Were they your ancestors?' asked Matthew.

'No. Not Viola's, either. A man called Malcolm built Mount Malcolm, amazing as that may sound. A man called Fox did not build Fox Hill. Just a man who liked foxes. Running them ragged. Viola runs cottontail rabbits ragged.'

'With beagles?'

'Basset-hounds. Come see them. They slobber.'

Mount Malcolm was within walking distance. Viola Biggs always walked over, to keep in condition for hunting on foot in the winter. But Rosie was in one of her moods of collapse, and Matthew drove them over in his hired car.

The house was gaunt and gothic in character, in utter architectural contrast to Fox Hill. There was no excuse for the 'Mount' — it was in a valley, and surrounded by enormous trees. It would have reminded an Englishman of a house set in a Somerset combe, as though to avoid any possibility of a view. The stables and kennels were close to the house, and both horses and hounds were making a lot of noise. They were all just about to be fed, and they liked the idea.

Miss Viola Biggs, having been gardening, met them outside the house. She was as gaunt and gothic in appearance as her house, but exuberantly friendly. Her Virginia accent was far broader than the Collins'. She was as muddy as Rosie, the night of the tree-planting. She kissed Rosie and shook Matthew's hand, transferring to the cheek of one and the palm of the other some of the rich loam of her flowerbeds.

They went to see the hounds being fed in a part of the kennel where they could run around, and where they could be watched.

'Y'all got to look out for a poor doer,' shouted Miss Viola Biggs over the excited baying of the hounds. 'Or a dawg that gits pushed aroun' by the rest.'

Feeding them was a giant of a man, perhaps forty years old, with a gentle, vacant face. He had a shock of hair so blond it was almost white, and happy pale eyes. He was giving the hounds a

161

slabby mixture of oatmeal and pungent-smelling meat broth, ladling it into a single long trough. He crouched among the hounds, chirruping to them in the voice of a little bird. It was an extraordinary noise to come from such a huge and powerful man. Matthew could not make out any words in what he was saying.

They crossed a yard, and looked in over a half-door at a mare being given her supper. It was a big bucketful of oats, nuts, bran, maybe beet-top, linseed, vitamins. A man poured the bucket into a big stone manger, a splendid antique like its owner. The mare dropped her sweet head happily to the manger. The man who had fed her stroked her neck, and chirruped. He was another blond giant, the same age as the kennelman. He had the same manner and the same voice.

Indoors, drinking whisky, Miss Viola Biggs told Matthew about her hired men. They were twins, alike but not identical: Luke and John Field, cousins of the Rick Field who worked for Rosie.

'Their Pa jumped their sister,' said Miss Viola Biggs. 'Pearl Harbor day. He was hog drunk.'

'Patriotic fervor,' said Rosie.

'That inbreedin' was a mite too close. I reckon the whole tribe was inbred to hell already. Anyways, the boys was born lackin'. Not morons, but slow. Never did git to read an' write. Never did git to speak worth a goddam. But with dumb beasts they're marvellous.'

'Like medieval dog-boys,' suggested Matthew.

'Right, sir! Naturals. Talkin' to the dawgs in their own language. Luke an' John talk to the dawgs an' hosses. Don't have no *need* to talk to folk. I take care of that for them. I take care of ever'thing for them, an' they take care of ever'thing for me.'

Matthew thought all parties came well out of this unusual arrangement. The retarded giants had found one of the few places in the world where they could be completely happy and useful. Miss Viola Biggs had her animals tirelessly and lovingly looked after. The animals did well out of it all.

As they left, Matthew promised to come out with the Mount Malcolm Basset Hounds. They would start hunting at the end of the month.

'Bring a flask,' said Miss Viola Biggs. 'Bring two flasks.'

Miss Viola Biggs thought all parties came well out of the

current arrangement at Fox Hill. She had known Rosie, Peach and Tim Phillipson all their lives. She was happy when the lovely Rosie married the dashing and charming Tim; she was deeply sad when knocks on the head and drinks on the rocks and dubious personal bloodlines reduced Tim to an introverted vegetable.

It was obvious, from the moment that Tim moved into the sanitorium, that Rosie would one day get herself a man. It was inevitable. It was even right. That package shouldn't be wasted. What troubled Miss Biggs over the years was — what man would Rosie choose? She was capable of terrible mistakes.

It was a mercy the way things had worked out. A decent, respectable man like that.

Miss Biggs was sorry now that she had left the tree-planting party when she did. She would have witnessed the birth of a grand passion. She approved of grand passions in general, and of this one in particular. She thoroughly approved of Matthew Carver.

Prince Ghalib al-Jilani, who shared this view of Matthew Carver, finally left Paris for Shannon. He was days later than he had intended. He had business — real business — which was more important than any Irish estate. It was this scale of priorities which made the Irish estate possible.

The first person he saw at Shannon was Clare Carver, in red pants and quilted jacket and Hermès headscarf, her cheeks pink and her eyes bright and everything about her almost insanely desirable. Ghalib thought this was a miraculous intervention of Providence, an amazing stroke of luck, an omen.

Ghalib asked himself: what predictable effect would his seduction of Clare have on his future relationship with her father? He was as realistic about such things as about everything else. He was long past the epoch of his impetuous youth. At the age of twelve — precocious even for an Arab — he had taken the girls and risked the consequences. This had once included public execution, from which only his youth saved him. Now he took the girls only when there was no risk of serious consequences. He concluded that this was such an occasion. Matthew Carver was a notorious adulterer. Married, he was having a brazen affair with a married woman, reported in the newspapers of the world. He was in no posture to be priggish about other people.

A young man in a tweed coat introduced himself as Tom

Kavanagh. They had spoken at length on the telephone, several times, as other calls had of necessity followed that first call, while Ghalib's plans changed by the hour. Ghalib liked the look of Tom Kavanagh. He looked as he had sounded on the telephone.

Ghalib understood that Clare Carver was not there by coincidence. She was with them, in their party. It was she who had told Kavanagh that Ghalib wanted a property. Her father had told her, Ghalib having told him at le Coq. But there was no need for her to help them inspect the Ballycardeen Stud. She had never set eyes on the place. She was there for some other reason.

Ghalib was perfectly aware — how could he not be? — of his effect on women and his reputation among them. Allowing for an element of wish-fulfilment, of which he was also perfectly aware, his computer brain printed out the 70% probability that Clare had come because he was coming.

The probability was that Clare thought she was seducing him.

They went to Tom's car. Ghalib wanted to sit in the back with Clare, but it was impossible to impose this arrangement without a crudity distasteful to him. He had not made millions by lack of tact.

They drove the fifty lush miles by Limerick and Tipperary into the Golden Vale, beyond and behind the Galtee Mountains, the jewel in the crown of the ancient kingdom of Munster. Ghalib knew — he had informed himself thoroughly — that there the inches of ancient turf-root were bedded in limestone, and the grass was as good as any in the world for the bones and brawn of young horses.

They visited the stud before they visited the house — priorities still clear, no time to be wasted. Ghalib fell in love with it. He allowed himself to do so, because the computer between his ears had already told him that this was an excellent investment. There was more land than he needed for raising thoroughbreds. That might not be a prime investment. Land values in Ireland had peaked in 1979. But good land would never be valueless, and Ghalib foresaw putting the spare acres to profitable use with sheep and beef and dairy cattle. He might even, so far from the priesthood of his home, venture the blasphemy of pigs.

There were several sound cottages on the estate, though more might have to be built. There was a Regency dower-house, five bedrooms and a large garden, a quarter of a mile from the Court and half hidden from it. It had been occupied by the stud

164

manager. No doubt it would be again. Applicants for that job would make a line stretching to Belfast.

There was room for an airstrip. That was a priority.

Tom took them at last to the house: grey, classical, late Georgian, in better repair than many Irish houses, and much smaller than the biggest. Ghalib liked the proportions of the rooms and their outlook. He concluded that the roof needed to be reinsulated, the central heating extended, and extra bathrooms devised. He was going to entertain. He was going to make his guests comfortable. Full redecoration would be unnecessary and wrong — some of the old wallpapers were lovely enough for a few stains to be overlooked. Ghalib was too sophisticated to import Peter Jones décor into County Tipperary. The existing furniture and carpets were no more than adequate. But Ballycardeen Court was an obvious potential showcase for the antiques, pictures, tapestries and rugs which Ghalib was gradually assembling — buying shrewdly, taking the best advice, making himself by degrees expert. Some of his purchases had in two years appreciated far beyond the margin of inflation.

Ghalib was presented to Colonel and Mrs Kavanagh. He noted with amusement the nervousness which turned into almost obtrusive relief, when they saw him and talked to him. He was a well-dressed white old Harrovian. He was not robed or reeking. He had English manners and a smile that might be described as French. The neighbours would not feel betrayed. They had not the slightest objection to selling to him.

He had a slight objection to their price, which he rightly took to be a come-on. Having taken months to decide to sell, they wanted a quick sale. They came down enough so that his haggling honour was satisfied. He asked to be recommended a local lawyer. They named a well-known solicitor in Tipperary. He, immediately contacted by telephone, immediately agreed to act for Ghalib in the conveyancing. He asked for a deposit. Ghalib wrote out a cheque on his London bank for £100,000, which was cleared by telephone in five minutes.

A rich man can choose quickly and buy quickly.

Clare had come to Ireland for a mixture of reasons. She was mildly curious about Ghalib, whom her father had made sound interesting. She was more curious about Ballycardeen, which Tom had made sound beautiful. She did not want to be separated from Tom. She did want to be separated from her mother, rendered more martyred and rigid than usual by the news from Fox Hill.

Clare liked Ghalib. He was outside her experience. She had seen Arabs at Keeneland and Churchill Downs, and swarms of them in London. She had not met any of those, and none of them looked like Ghalib. She imagined none would have sounded like him, either. There was no trace of patronage or bullying in his manner to Tom, though Tom was many years his junior and had no money at all. On the contrary, he asked for information, and deferred to Tom's local and professional knowledge. Clare had become sensitive to the way people treated Tom. She might not show him respect herself, but she required other people to.

Clare saw that Ghalib was attractive. At another time, she might have been attracted. Not now. She had always been a one-man girl, though the men had changed over pretty quickly. That spin-around square dance was finished. She had set to a permanent partner. She was more and more certain of it.

She was aware that she attracted Ghalib. It was in his eye and the way he laughed at her jokes. There was nothing aggressive about his admiration. He was not about to throw her over his saddle-bow and ride off into the desert.

When hands had been shaken and the cheque written, Ghalib asked to see the dower-house. It was fair enough — he was paying about £150,000 for it. It was empty but partly furnished. They found him a key. Tom was claimed by his aging cousins who, though sweet, were possessive. They wanted family news. It was as though, in relinquishing their home, they were obliged to assert ownership of their young relative. The suggestion was made that Clare should accompany Ghalib to the dower-house. It was not clear if the suggestion came from Ghalib: perhaps from Tom, or from Mrs Kavanagh.

Clare was agreeable. Ghalib was an amusing companion. She had liked the delicate Regency lines of the dower-house, its bay windows and arched verandah; she was curious to see the interior.

The walk took five minutes. It would have been pleasant, except that Ghalib's admiration became more evident, and began to take a physical turn. He took her arm. He walked too close to her. He seemed to want their knees to brush together as they walked. That kind of thing was all right on a dance-floor, Clare thought, but inappropriate in a Tipperary driveway.

She was still not prepared for what happened.

They let themselves in. There was a high-ceilinged hall, with a delicate staircase curving up. It was all in half-darkness, as the curtains were drawn. Clare drew them back. As she did so, she heard a click. Ghalib had locked the door. She saw him pocket the key.

She wanted to say something. She could not think what to say. Anything might be misunderstood. 'No', said too soon, admitted an awareness of the potential of the situation which was itself half-way to 'yes'. 'You mustn't misunderstand my coming up here with you.' 'I'm not that kind of girl.' 'I want you to know that I'm in love with Tom Kavanagh.' None of these remarks would help the situation one bit.

Clare sped into the half-furnished sitting-room, where there was a velvet chaise-longue. It looked greasy in the curtained semi-darkness, something out of a pretentious brothel. Ghalib, moving like a great cat, was suddenly behind her as she stood irresolute and frightened. His hands were on her shoulders, and his cheek beside hers. He towered over her. He could have picked her up and put her in his pocket.

He murmured endearments into her cheek. They were flattering and terrifying. Clare cursed her folly, her innocence and rashness. She felt a stab of rage at Tom, who had let her get into this jam. He was supposed to protect her.

Ghalib lifted his hands from her shoulders. She tried to jump away from him. He was very quick. Before she could move, his hands had whipped under her arms, still from behind, and fastened over her breasts. His palms cupped over her breasts, he pulled her backwards against himself. His arms felt like iron and his chest like concrete. She was small and slim and absolutely powerless in the grip of this formidable man. He did not hurt her. He was so strong that he prevented her from struggling. Inexorably she was imprisoned in the hoop of his arms. He was still murmuring lovingly. He was taking her consent for granted. One arm now gripped her round her waist, while the other hand went under her jacket to her breast. She did struggle. She was like a butterfly in a steel vice. Screaming was no good. They were in an empty house with a locked door and nobody within a quarter of a mile. There was a greasy velvet chaise-longue by their knees.

Ghalib murmured, wetly into her cheek, that he was generous, that he was kind, that she was beautiful, that she maddened him with desire.

His right arm still gripped her like a girder. His left hand went to the hem of her sweater, and up inside it. It cupped itself over her right breast. She felt his fingertips groping under her bra.

She was sobbing and trying not to sob and trying to be reasonable and making no sense at all. Ghalib never stopped talking, soothing and amorous and completely determined.

There was a click and a bang and a shout, and Tom was swearing at Ghalib and pulling him away.

'You stinking black swine, you filthy bully.'

Ghalib released Clare. She threw herself into Tom's arms, wailing with relief. He put her aside, as inexorable as Ghalib.

Tom's face, even in the semi-darkness, was so black with rage that Clare hardly recognized him. Frightened, she looked at Ghalib. He was snarling like an animal. Tom threw a punch. Ghalib parried it easily. He hit Tom on the mouth. Tom was immediately bleeding from a cut lip, and Ghalib's knuckle from impact with Tom's teeth. Clare screamed. The two men went berserk. Sometimes they were grappling, sometimes rolling on the floor, sometimes swinging punches at each other. Tom broke a little chair over Ghalib's head, and Ghalib an embroidered fire-screen over Tom's back. Furniture splintered and pictures crashed. Clare continued to scream. There was blood everywhere. The men grunted, panted, swore.

It went on for a long time. To Clare, on the edge of hysteria, it seemed to go on for hours. They were slowing up. They were exhausted, hardly able to raise a fist, no longer capable of hurting one another. They fought crawling, directing feeble punches. They collapsed, both drawing harsh, shuddering breaths.

The fight was over. Neither had won. Neither could go on. The room was a gory wreck.

Streaming with tears, Clare fled from the room. She found the kitchen, soaked a cloth, knelt by Tom and washed the blood off his face. Apart from the cut lip, the damage was superficial, small gashes made by splintered wood and bits of broken glass. He was like a man who had shaved during a drinking bout. Clare's tears dribbled on to his face.

Ghalib hauled himself to his knees and to his feet. He lurched out of the room. Clare heard a tap running. He had had the same idea.

168

'That's the end of the deal,' said Tom painfully.

'Oh God.'

'I had a premonition. Randy Wogs. Cousin Maribell had a spare key. Thank Christ.'

'The end of the deal. My fault.'

'My fault. Here he comes.'

Here he came. He had washed the blood off his face, and wrapped a handkerchief round his knuckles. He still looked a terrible mess. One of his eyes was puffy and closing.

Tom was in about the same state.

Ghalib walked stiffly, painfully to a window. He drew back the heavy curtains, grunting with pain at the effort. Warm October sunlight flooded in over the chaos of the room, and on to the chaos of Tom.

The men stared at each other, and at the devastation they had wrought.

Suddenly, to Clare's utter astonishment, they both burst out laughing. Each, helpless with laughter, pointed at the room and at the other. It was obvious that laughter hurt their bruised ribs. They shook hands. As soon as he could speak, Ghalib apologised to Clare and to Tom. He had misunderstood. He now understood. He would not make the same mistake again.

He said to Tom, 'At least the mess we made of your drawing-room was fifty percent your doing.'

Tom frowned, then regretted the physical act of frowning. His mind was not working fluently. He said, 'My drawing-room?'

'The house goes with the job,' said Ghalib. 'Do you want the job? If you'd bitten me, I don't think I would offer it.'

'I tried everything else.'

'You succeeded. Don't call me a black again, and I won't make advances to your girl again.'

'It's a deal,' said Tom. 'I can afford to get married.'

'Who to?' said Clare: but when she kissed him he yelled with pain.

There was no need to be coy about the deal. Both parties were content that it should be announced immediately. It had moderate and rather specialised news value. Sporting writers recalled champions bred at Ballycardeen, and a few facts were turned up about Ghalib. It was remembered that he was seen at the Newmarket races and sales with Lord Goring, and that they were underbidders for the record-breaking Mill Reef yearling secured by George Whyte.

There was regret, here and there between the lines, that another Irish gem had fallen to the power of black gold.

Goring was naturally telephoned for information about his client. This was how he heard the news. His mother was frightened at his face when he put the telephone down. She was shocked by his language about Ghalib, Tom Kavanagh, Clare Carver. He mouthed obscenities about Matthew Carver, too, who no doubt had a hand in the treachery, who was now stuffing some rich bitch in Virginia and getting into all the newspapers. A fine gang.

Goring computed the money he had himself spent on the telephone, trying to find a stud for Ghalib.

Ghalib shared Miss Viola Biggs's view of Matthew Carver; Peach Collin shared Lord Goring's.

'Busybee on and on and on?' he asked Rosie at dinner.

'Rosepetal wins the five-cent seegar,' she said. 'Snail's on the thorn.'

She had won. All was right with the world. If their business with Carver was satisfactorily concluded, if they had got all they wanted out of him, Peach saw that it was time to make the fellow unwelcome.

Immediately after dinner, he drew Carver aside and led him to the thinking room. Through the candy-bar with which he followed every meal, he talked about Tim's emotional dependence on Rosie, and Rosie's financial dependence on Tim.

'In Virginia,' said Peach, 'we have opinions about the way gentlemen behave. As our guest, I gave you the benefit of the doubt. I can no longer do that. I reckon you have forfeited your claim on our hospitality. We Virginians do not lightly turn away the stranger from our gates, but neither do we tolerate caddish behaviour.'

This orotund speech, these moral sentiments, came ludicrously from the pot-bellied waster in the thinking chair. But there was no doubting his ill-will.

Rosie came in, looked at Matthew's shocked face, looked at Peach's righteous expression, and understood exactly what had happened.

'You priggish, interfering shit,' she said, dangerously reasonable, 'the day you do anything useful, anything at all, the day you do anything for anybody else in the world, you might have a little right to criticise somebody else. You don't even pay for your candy-bars, you retarded guzzler, you sponge, you crook.'

'You are forgetting how to be a lady,' said Peach, his voice thickening with anger. 'You are learning bad habits from your poodle there.'

'This poodle is worth six thousand of you,' said Rosie, raising her voice.

'One of me owns this house and decides who is allowed in it.'

'Shove your house, you pompous fraud. Shove yourself and your candy-bars.'

'Mind your tongue, you slut.'

They were screaming at each other. Rosie's language became unbridled. Matthew Carver was intensely embarrassed.

Even he and Mollie, in the worst scene in his memory, had not screamed at each other like alley-cats.

Peach yelled, 'Away, Rosamunda, and bury thy shame in the darkest grot in yonder forest!'

Rosie yelled, 'Traitor and villain, thou hast chocolate on thy chin!'

Rosie had a glass of brandy and Peach a Charleston Chew.

Matthew was unnerved by this undisciplined flamboyance, this frenzied play-acting. Leaving would be a horrible wrench. But he thought it was time he went to Kentucky.

Parting with Rosie was possible because it was temporary. He would be back, with Beausoleil.

Somehow the understanding had grown — simply grown, like a tree but quicker — that, if Matthew could swing it, Beausoleil came to Fox Hill.

There was no real future for Rosie and himself — no marriage, no permanent, semi-public thing. But neither could bear permanent separation. They clung together. Rosie wept. There was desperation in their last kisses.

Hazel wept all day. Peach sat complacently with a bag of caramels.

Jefferson Dill said, 'Now at last you'll have some time to rehearse.'

Matthew wanted to go home, but his first call had to be

Cragrock. He reported to George Whyte in greater detail the Beausoleil negotiations, and the overtures of Epi Makropulos, Ottaviano di Vianello and Luis Valdes. He described Prince Ghalib al-Jilani, with particular reference to his disposable funds.

He reported his approval of Meadowsweet's yearling colt by Lord Primrose. He urged its purchase, at a price suggested by Sir Merivale Lucas and agreed by himself.

He urged the installation of Beausoleil at Fox Hill, using arguments, in perfect honesty, which had so often been used to himself. He said Beausoleil should get there in good time to get acclimatised before the spring stallion season. He said that he himself would charge himself with the supervision and management of Beausoleil, as suggested by the duc de Montfermainbrey. He said he was willing to go to Fox Hill as often and for as long as seemed necessary.

'I'll trust your judgement about the yearling, Matthew,' said George. 'As you say, it's not expensive. But Fox Hill? Why Virginia, anyway?'

'Go look at the place, George.'

'When I have time.'

Matthew tried and failed to picture the impact of Peach, Rosie, Miss Thalia, Jefferson Dill and Hazel on George Whyte. He was happier about the effect of Ed Lindsey.

Matthew and Jean Whyte were pleased to see each other. They always had plenty to talk about. Horses seldom entered their conversation. They talked about plays, pictures, books, and the affairs of their friends. There was a low-voltage spark between them — always had been — a shared awareness that an affair would be pleasant. Also that circumstances made it a very bad idea.

Matthew met Alice Whyte Harding for the first time. He knew her history in outline, naturally, and he knew her husband. He had not expected George Whyte's sister to be so attractive. He had not expected her to be so cultured and so amusing. They made each other laugh immediately, than which nothing works so strongly to generate high-voltage sparks.

Alice had been prepared by Jean for an attractive and intelligent man. She was not prepared for someone who seemed to combine everything she admired and liked. Everything she responded to,

172

that made her tingle. She foresaw the serious disturbance of her peace of mind. She decided to buckle her seat-belt and hold on, at least for the time.

Meeting him, one thing she knew for sure, one thing the whole world knew, after those scandalous reports from Virginia. Matthew Carver was indeed beautifully free from Frank Harding's hormone problems.

Prince Ghalib could not immediately take possession of Ballycardeen.

The old Kavanaghs had to find somewhere else to live, in Ireland in the summer, in a hot dry climate in the winter. They could afford to go where they liked. They could afford to give Tom a vendor's commission on the sale. He thought this reasonable. Ghalib gave him a buyer's commission, which he thought unreasonable and refused. Clare, inwardly aghast, was obliged to support this refusal. To her relief, which she tried to hide, Ghalib overruled Tom's objections.

The existing Ballycardeen stock had to be dispersed. Ghalib bought two of the mares, but Tom in strict confidence agreed with his rejection of the rest.

The work that had to be done to the house needed supervision, but made residence a horrid prospect. Supervision would be exercised from the dower-house, by Tom. Ghalib trusted him. It was curious that such esteem derived from a fight.

Ghalib decided to go to America. It was time he renewed his contacts. Business relationships had to be kept in repair, like friendships. More than friendships. They were worth more. It was also important for Ghalib to meet George Whyte, owing to his part ownership of Beausoleil: owing to his inclination, now known to George, to consider substantial investment in the Cragrock operation.

Telexes were exchanged. Ghalib was expected at Cragrock.

Jean Whyte was dubious about entertaining an Arab. She did not quite believe Matthew's reassurances. Matthew had too large an interest to be objective. Some of her horse-breeding friends had had swarthy millionaires in their houses, in order to sell horses, and the social embarrassments almost outweighed the profits.

Her doubts almost vanished when Ghalib arrived, by chartered light aircraft, on the Cragrock strip. He reminded her of a client of her father's, of Lebanese extraction, who had earned her gratitude both by trying to seduce her when she was fifteen, and by failing.

Talking to Ghalib, showing him the house and garden, she expected the history of her involvement with the Middle East to be repeated. He would have brought out the worst in her, if they could have met in some faraway, anonymous motel. It was too fraught here. If Ghalib was coming into partnership at Cragrock, his millions replacing Frank Harding's, it was dicing with disaster. Too much comfort and importance were at stake. Jean stood reluctantly by to repel boarders.

He never attacked, even by word, even when they were out of sight of anybody and sitting side by side on a rustic seat. Jean thought Ghalib lacking in common politeness.

Ghalib was impressed by Cragrock, the first grand-scale Kentucky farm he had seen. Offices in New York, Washington, Chicago and Pittsburg were all the America he had previously seen. Cragrock was far beyond anything in Europe. It clearly represented a massive outlay. Investing here would be throwing good money after good.

He found George Whyte businesslike and courteous, a man who talked hard figures without coyness. This was a time-saver, but almost shocking to Ghalib, who had inherited a racial preference for the gradual and tactful removal of seven veils before you got to the dollar sign.

He found Jean Whyte as impressive as the farm, and in much the same way. She was expensive and classy. The materials were excellent, the construction on the best lines, the maintenance beyond reproach. The farm was avid for his money. She was avid, too, but also careful. He guessed she was almost a pushover but not quite, at least not here. She was a little old for him.

Mrs Harding, Alice, was far more to his taste. Physically she was delightful. Mentally she was diverting. She was divorced, which simplified everything morally and diplomatically.

After her loveless years, Alice was excited by Ghalib's unmistakable sexuality. She liked being admired. She was neither shocked nor frightened when, in the evening, in the small library, he put his arms around her and kissed her.

174

She was tempted to grab this exotic diversion as it flew by, knowing there was no risk of enduring complications. But the thought of Matthew Carver came between her and surrender.

George Whyte and Ghalib al-Jilani flew over the Appalachians, picked up a hired Jaguar, and arrived at Fox Hill. Ghalib being at Cragrock made sense of the trip for George. They could check the place out together.

George noted that the house was Palladian in style, reacting with well-taught accuracy and without emotion. He noted that Mrs Phillipson was exuberant in style, her brother languid, the household preoccupied and noisy. None of this was relevant, and he blocked his mind to it. He blocked his mind to what he had read in the newspapers.

The farm was as Matthew Carver had said. So accurately had he reported it that this visit was almost a waste of time. George took it that the black Ed Lindsey was assistant to the white Rick Field. The facilities were perfectly adequate for a stallion and visiting mares. Central to the viability of basing Beausoleil at Fox Hill was Matthew Carver's personal responsibility. On that basis, George approved the idea.

George had to go straight on to New York on business. Before he left, he heard Peter Collin pressing Ghalib to stay on for a while. He heard Ghalib accepting. He thought Ghalib was crazy to entrust himself to such a lunatic household. He thought Jean would be glad to be relieved of the burden of entertaining him.

Rosie understood.

She had seen Peach quiver like a gundog, pointing in response to the reek of wealth which came in with George Whyte and Ghalib. Peach loved very rich men. He loved separating them from some of it. Occasionally he succeeded. It was the nearest he had ever come to earning a living.

There was nothing to be got out of George Whyte, except approval about Beausoleil. That was secured. Rosie could give herself no credit, nor even Ed Lindsey. Rosie was relieved when George went away after three hours. He would have been as uncomfortable an intrusion in the Fox Hill household as a broken light-bulb in a gut. And Peach would have tried to con him with one of his dozen ploys, and Whyte would have seen through it and got mad, and Beausoleil would have been sent someplace else.

Peach would try to con Ghalib, too. Rosie didn't think he'd succeed. It wasn't so important. Ghalib might influence the decision, but he didn't make it.

Hazel said, 'If evuh I saw a rapist!'

Rosie thought he was a seducer rather than a rapist, although there might be a pretty fine line between them. She thought he would be good at it, and she thought he thought the same of her. But her mind was full of Matthew. This feeling of absolute fidelity surprised her. It was not what she expected of herself, in spite of her years of fidelity to Tim. You might have thought that the first cheat was the hard one, and others came easy. With her the opposite was true. The first happened miraculously, and it was the first and only. That was how it was. Her mind might say, 'Yes'. Her voice might say, 'Yes, Prince, fuck me for a laugh, and go away and we'll both forget about it.' But her cunt would say no, and rape would be the only way he'd do it.

She told Ghalib this, apologetically, as they walked back from the foaling-barn.

'It happens to me all the time,' he said. 'This is the third time in a few days.'

'Find a girl who's not in love.'

'All the girls I want are in love.'

'That's why you want them. Somebody else's candy.'

'I wonder if that can be true. What a horrible thought.'

'Do you still want to stay on?'

'If you still want me to.'

'Sure. Anyway, Peach does. He loves a new face.'

'I wish you loved my face.'

'I love your face, and I'm sure I should love your cock, which I'm sure is enormous. But it's no go. Really I'm sorry.'

'You shouldn't apologise. That's truly ridiculous.'

'I'm not apologising so much as regretting. A big hot Arab cock — talk about remedial massage! But my fanny got locked up in a chastity-belt.'

There was no constraint between Rosie and Ghalib after this. He knew that Matthew Carver was her man. The world knew. Since he knew, they could talk about it. Rosie was delighted at the admiration Ghalib felt for Matthew. They had little in common, but they had that in common.

Ghalib had been around. He knew the fleshpots of many western cities. He knew all kinds of businessmen, professional men, government officials, racing men, gamblers and pimps. He knew bewildering varieties of women. Nothing in his life had prepared him for Fox Hill.

Having changed his skin with his clothes and his soul with his skin, he accepted drinks of all kinds at all hours. The Prophet's writ did not run in Virginia. He sat bemused through stampings and shriekings in the great library, while Rosie and the rest made speeches and no sense. He sat bemused in a little secluded room while Peach droned on about how he was going to make his, Peach's, fortune by means of a coup in the off-track betting parlors.

Rosie stunned him, with her beauty and vivacity and a freedom of language he had not met among young married ladies of good family. He had not been restrained in his approach to her by his knowledge of her relationship with Matthew Carver. Rather the reverse. Her chastity was irritating. He thought it childish. He thought her childish, though bewitching.

Drink followed drink, shriek shriek, Peach monologue Peach monologue, for three days and two nights, which Ghalib enjoyed as he might have enjoyed descent into some rose-tinted underworld. He had never experimented with any drug: he felt zonked.

The third evening, after dinner, he sat drunkenly listening to Peach.

'I am not a man who wears his heart upon his sleeve,' said Peach. 'We Virginians can be orators, but we do not bare our souls in a flux of verbiage.'

Ghalib nodded owlishly, approving restraint.

'But when I like a man,' said Peach, 'I give myself the honour of telling him so.'

It seemed he liked Ghalib. He wanted to give him a token of his esteem, confer upon him a notable and unique favour. As it happened, he was in a position to do so. He could make Ghalib's fortune, as well as his own, with the mathematically certain coup in the off-track betting parlors. He explained the mathematics. Ghalib was a mathematician, but at that moment a fuzzy one. He accepted the subtlety of the formula. He agreed that it was as subtle a formula as he had ever met. Gratefully, Ghalib gave

177

Peach $20,000 in cash. He had it in a money-belt, in large bills which he carried to facilitate both his business and his sex-life. Nothing could be put in writing, since Peach's strategy was secret and irregular, though not illegal. Nothing need be put in writing, between Arab royalty and Virginia gentleman. Ghalib trusted Peach, as Peach told him he might.

Ghalib left in the morning with a hangover, half an inch off his waistline, and a feeling that he was the victim of magic. He believed in djinns. He thought Peach was a djinn, a *shaitan*, an *afrit*, a *marid*. The djinns, said the learned doctor al-Qazwini, were aerial animals with transparent bodies which could assume various forms. They were created by God 2,000 years before He created Adam, but they disappointed Him. Their Emir was Eblis, one of whose five sons was Tir, who brought about calamities, losses and injuries. There were forty troops of djinns, each troop of 600,000. They appeared to men as serpents, scorpions, dogs, cats or human beings. Some were the tutelary demons of certain places. Ghalib thought Peach was the resident djinn of Fox Hill, bringing about calamity, loss and injury. Nothing else explained the excruciating pain in his head, the lightness of his money-belt, and the way the sharpest entrepreneur on the Gulf had been conned by a (seeming) degenerate backwoodsman.

Flying from Charlottesville to Lexington, Ghalib sought to soothe his head and elevate his spirit by reciting the ninety-nine names of God, from ar-Rahman, the Merciful, to as-Sabur, the Patient. He would have used a rosary, but he had not packed a rosary for America; instead he counted on his fingers, in the manner of the puritanical Wahabis, who held that the Prophet himself had not used a rosary. The effort of memory was good for his spirit but bad for his head.

Rosie was furious with Peach, when he waved the large coarse notes at her. For a paltry sum, for a laugh, he had jeopardised the future of Fox Hill.

'Busybee,' crowed Peach. 'Game two can play.'

But Rosie was really angry, and the quarrel did not end in giggles.

Ghalib told the story at Cragrock, as a joke against himself. Reactions varied. Alice was amused and sympathetic. Life in California had accustomed her to mixed drinks and unmixed demons. Jean was amused and contemptuous, not at Ghalib's drunken gullibility but at someone going to so much trouble for an icky little wad like $20,000. George was outraged. Out of hand he vetoed Fox Hill as a safe place for Beausoleil. The case he made was pretty strong. If they were those sort of people, why, they were those sort of people.

Matthew Carver returned in time to change George's mind. Peach was nothing whatever to do with the farm — would never see Beausoleil or any business visitor. He was a harmless eccentric. No doubt his sister would see that he gave the money back. Ghalib, who was not worried about the money, surprisingly supported Matthew. But his grounds were the opposite: a place where djinns conned you was a place to have as an ally.

George's visit to New York, and to the office of Lee V. Lowe, resulted in the issue to the press of an item of high if minority interest.

Beausoleil was effectively controlled by a group headed by Mr George Whyte of Cragrock, the well-known and popular Kentucky sportsman. He was to be managed by Mr Matthew Carver, another Kentucky sportsman but not so well-known, to whom application should be made for nominations in future seasons. Beausoleil was to stand at Fox Hill Farm, Somerset, Virginia, to which he would shortly be travelling.

The appearance of this item came as no surprise to most of the people involved. It was annoying for certain French breeders who thought they had been promised nominations, and others who had shares and would have preferred the horse more conveniently in Normandy. It was a huge and horrible shock to Henri de Cheminade. He saw at once what had happened. That day at le Coq, behind his own back, the treacherous assassin Carver had wormed and toadied and bribed his way into the old duke's confidence, and contrived this abominable result.

At Longchamp, among his vast acquaintance, Henri de Cheminade went to and fro, spreading a version of events which he had almost come to believe. Carver was blackmailing the old duke. As to the power he had over him, one knew what one knew but of course one's lips were sealed. Charity demanded so much. One could not forbid speculation, though one might deplore it. Delicious speculation followed Henri about like the tail of an overweight comet.

CHAPTER 9

Matthew's home was known as the Carver Place. It had had another name, long forgotten. It was an inconvenient distance from Lexington, which was, however, since its rapid, recent and unbeautiful growth, the place to fly to and the place to buy things. It was quite outside the Bluegrass, that compact, elliptical tract of unspectacular country lying mostly between Lexington and Paris. Matthew's 200 acres were worth less than the going Bluegrass rate of $7,500 an acre. They were not much different. It was good grazing land. The difference in price reflected convenience and snobbery rather than climate or chemistry. Matthew could van a mare to Cragrock and back in a day, but he preferred not to do so. His special position at Cragrock permitted him the rare privilege of boarding a mare there, for foaling and breeding.

His house was the oldest in its area, 1800, quaint rather than beautiful, something like a chapel in effect, something Scottish in its solid angularity. It was a little dark inside, the rooms a little small. The barns were brighter. There was no garden — just grass and trees, then barns and paddocks and fields. Matthew's mother had cultivated a flower garden. Mollie had not cared to do so.

Fay Candy, the colour of a Havana cigar, had kept the place clean as a young girl in Matthew's father's time. She lived in the house then. She married and moved out just before Matthew married and moved in. She continued to come in most days, and one bride welcomed another.

To Fay, Mollie was the most precious and glamorous creature in the world. Her pale Anglo-Saxon beauty, her apparent fragility, her gravity were exactly what Fay thought proper in the daughter of an English lord. It was almost cruel of Mr Matthew to have brought so delicate an orchid so far, to have transplanted her from her London hothouse into the coarse Kentucky pastures. Fay did everything she could to shield Mollie from all harshness, from any labour that might roughen her slim white fingers. She was priestess of the cult of Mollieolatry.

When Mollie went away with her two younger children, she left Fay heartbroken and unforgiving. It was Matthew she refused to forgive. Mollie could have done no wrong. Still she came in, and swept and scrubbed, in memory of Mollie, in honour of Mollie, keeping bright the shrine sacred to Mollie. She cooked for Matthew when he was home, but not with the infinite pains of the days when her hands were honoured to set dishes in front of Mollie.

She always spoke of 'Our Lady', without intention of blasphemy.

There were just three mares of Matthew's own at home. All the stock in which he shared an interest was at Cragrock, because in all of it George Whyte had a much larger interest. Two of the mares were in foal, one barren. All three had nominations for the spring. By far the most valuable was Dame Ninette, by Northern Dancer, due to go to Beausoleil. She would foal at Fox Hill, and be covered almost at once. The foal that she was carrying would be early. She would be among Beausoleil's first mares — perhaps his very first. This was good, because she was experienced and placid. He was no horse for a maiden mare, and certainly not in his first season. Matthew would be there at Fox Hill. It was a moment of great importance, that cover, and great promise. The two other mares would go to Cragrock, to foal and be bred to Cragrock stallions.

The outdoor staff consisted of Patti and Chuck Mungo, who lived in a cottage behind the barn. Patti was about fifty, Chuck approaching thirty. Both had lived on the place and worked for the Carvers all their lives. They looked as though they had been carved out of wood and left to weather. If they ever needed help, they had kin scattered around the neighbourhood, and they had Brothers and Sisters in Christ in the Tabernacle in town.

A Brother Ezra had founded the Tabernacle about 1890, in disgust at the laxity of conventional Primitive Baptists. The people never smoked or drank. The men wore black serge, the women black dresses from chin to wrist and boot-toe. They forbade all but sacred music. Though rigid Sabbatarians, they allowed themselves to work on Sundays if they were responsible for the welfare of animals. The Mungos put God first in their lives, and horses a close second. They had never been to the races or had a bet. They read only the Bible and the sermons of Brother Ezra. No member of the sect had a radio or TV, and none read any polluting newspaper. None had any but the barest necessary contact with any outsider. Matthew disagreed with them profoundly, and thanked God for them. They were tireless and incorruptible. He could leave them in charge with an easy mind.

He never knew what they made of Mollie's departure. Unlike Fay, who spoke of Mollie constantly, they never mentioned her. They never discussed any aspect of Matthew's private life, or permitted discussion of their own. They knew nothing about Matthew's affair with Rosie Phillipson, although everybody else who had any contact with him knew all about it. They never would know, because they insulated themselves against all news except the Good News from Heaven and Brother Ezra.

Matthew had always loved his own place, his castle, but it depressed him terribly. The rooms had been full of running feet and shouts and Mollie, in the days of her beauty, with the sun on her hair, Clare practising scales on the piano and Jamie with a train going clear round his bedroom. Fay made it worse, asking about Liz and Jamie and Our Lady. She was ominously quiet about Rosie, though she certainly knew what had happened.

The Mill Reef colt arrived by air from Newmarket. He looked round Cragrock with friendly interest. He had his sire's equable temperament. Alice was much more excited than her horse was. He was a lovely animal, a perfect little specimen. Alice's eye was pretty well trained, and she thought he looked every inch a champion.

She kissed George in gratitude for the kindness of the thought and the prodigal generosity of the gift.

Bert Duffy the trainer began at once breaking the colt, patiently and cheerfully, with the assistance of marvellously gentle black grooms. At this stage of the baby's life, any crudeness or cruelty or impatience could have permanent and incalculable effects. Just occasionally, a young horse's spirit was broken by a heavy-handed breaker, and he was condemned to listlessness and cowardice. More often — still mercifully rarely — a rebellious streak was developed, sometimes vicious and violent. A horse like that could be dangerous to man and beast; he could be virtually untrainable, and therefore valueless.

One step had already been taken, before the yearling left England. He had learned to accept the bit. He took it placidly, as he did everything, without clamping his teeth or tossing his head. The next thing was to accustom him to the feel of a girth round his chest. A surcingle was used, a simple strap with nothing attached. In no sense was it painful, but horses are often ticklish. The experience of constriction all round their ribs is new and alarming. Even the Mill Reef did a small rodeo performance the first time the surcingle was tightened. A padded saddle with a normal girth was not tried on him until he had thoroughly adjusted to the surcingle.

Tacked up, the colt was ready to be lunged. This point was reached quickly and smoothly, thanks in equal measure to Bert Duffy and to the horse himself. Soon, but not too soon, a groom would be riding him. Again, his initial surprise would give way to enjoyment. One problem remained, to which there was no infallible solution. The colt had been used to freedom, to rushing round a paddock with others. Now he spent nearly all his time in a stable, with nothing to do and nowhere to go. If he became seriously bored, he could pick up all kinds of bad habits, like eating his straw bedding or gnawing at the woodwork of the stall. An eye had to be kept on him, and he had to have company and distraction as often as possible.

Bert thought the colt was great, marvellous, though he was unfamiliar with some of the European names on the dam's side of the pedigree. Like a lot of other people, Bert had heard that Mill Reef had been sent to England to be trained because his slightly long pasterns might not stand up to cuppy dirt and ceaseless sharp bends. The yearling had long pasterns. Bert thought they'd do well to keep him to grass tracks, though this limited his opportunities.

Before Bert had a chance to say this, he heard George Whyte telling Mrs Harding and some others that this was their Kentucky Derby horse for the year after next. He kept quiet about grass. He was not about to disagree with Mr Whyte in public or in private. It couldn't be smart to disagree with that many million dollars, with that tremendous empire of bloodstock.

The Mill Reef colt had travelled well. He seemed to enjoy the attention, and gave no trouble, in spite of his inexperience.

Not so Beausoleil, in spite of his experience. He baulked at the foot of the coir-netted ramp, then went up to it with a rush, men hanging round him like tassels. There had been one or two episodes of stallions going berserk at twenty thousand feet. It seemed a serious possibility. In the event the journey passed safely, though with never an easy moment for the grooms who travelled with the horses. Beausoleil resented his companions. Though he disliked the hold of the aircraft, and all the fittings designed for his comfort, he thought he owned it because he was there. He would certainly have bitten and probably kicked, if his handlers had given him the chance.

The transit company was responsible for bringing Beausoleil to Fox Hill. They could be trusted to do so. All the same, Matthew Carver drove to Dulles to see the disembarkation of the treasure.

He was not surprised to find Ed Lindsey there too. Ed had driven the fifty miles north-east in his diesel Rabbit.

Nor was Ed surprised to see Matthew Carver.

They greeted each other as older friends than the hours they had spent together actually warranted: but their friendship had grown with unusual speed and depth.

Beausoleil came down the ramp like a train. He was full of himself — far too full. His eyes rolled and his ears were flat back.

Ed whistled. Matthew correctly interpreted the whistle. It expressed admiration for the splendid, arrogant athlete he was seeing for the first time; and it said they were going to have problems. No one was ever going to be able to relax with Beausoleil around. But in symmetry and in majesty he was more than all Ed had dared to hope, even after the stories he had heard and the pictures he had seen.

Rick Field kept well clear when Beausoleil came down out of the box. His line was that the transit contractor's men were handling it. Interference would be tactless and officious. Ed would take over, and he with Ed, when delivery was complete and the documents signed.

Looking at the newcomer, Rick felt the familiar, humiliating sickness in his gut. Against all that his commonsense told him, his experience, his pride of manhood, his imagination galloped. He saw the bright battering steel of shod feet lashing back to break his hip and spine and skull, and then pounding at his rib-cage

184

and his balls. Every instinct except one sent him towards the horse, confident and competent. One tugged him away from it. Only one, but it was stronger than all the others.

Rick was scared of Beausoleil, and the horse would know it, and Janice his wife would know it. He prayed that no one else would find out. He thanked God that Ed Lindsey would have personal care of this prodigious money-earner.

Peach Collin had been dimly aware — as of boring gossip on a telephone with a bad connection — that some important horse was arriving. Rosie was excited, which made her look very beautiful. Peach cultivated his aloofness, which gave him the opportunity for meditation and candy-bars.

He found to his chagrin that man as well as horse had arrived. Expected, though not by him. In his refusal to be interested in Beausoleil's coming, he had not taken in that Matthew Carver was coming. He was shocked and angry. He had made himself clear to Carver and to Rosie. He had made it clear that he was arbiter, he and no other, of invitations to Fox Hill.

'Whittlepants ick,' he said to Rosie. 'Supreme Court rules unconstitutional.'

Whittlepants was no better for Carver than Pickle for Dill, but Peach's mind had been too full of higher matters, and of *Circe's Island*, to find a more cryptic and witty code-name.

'Nine old men can take nine running fucks at nine rolling doughnuts,' said Rosie, dismissing the Supreme Court. 'Geegee busybee. El Dorado.'

In private she said, 'He has to be here. Don't you want to be rich and famous?'

'No,' said Peach after a moment's thought. Tim Phillipson's money did very well. He had no need for much of his own.

'Oh God, I've missed you,' said Rosie.

'It's not long.'

'It seemed long. Do horrible things to me. Every beautiful thing there is. I want to be beautifully defiled. Now! More! More! There! Clever! Oh God, I can't live without it. I could when I didn't have it. But now I need it. You. More. In. Push. Deep. Slow . . .'

'We ought to wait for rain, and go back to the tennis-court,' said Matthew later.

'Yes, but let's don't. Let's don't go to the tennis-court and for Christ's sake let's don't wait.'

Hazel was thrilled.

Peach sulked. He refused to offer Matthew a drink, though he had not paid for the drink.

Matthew and Ed Lindsey discussed the immediate routine of Beausoleil. Both had seen stallions of widely varying temperaments handled in widely varying ways, some running with mares and foals, some kept close in boxes. Ed thought Beausoleil should run two or three hours a day, maybe an hour each morning and afternoon, in a paddock with high post-and-rail but not planking he couldn't see through. He should have a view of young stock, but not a close view. He would neigh to them. He would tell them he was king. It would settle him temperamentally. He would run about wildly when he found himself at liberty — buck, kick, rear, paw the ground and the air as though fighting a rival — and this would keep him supple and well-muscled for the very considerable physical ordeal he faced in the spring. It was all very different from the demure caperings of broodmares. Yet sometimes colt-foals, in the first few days of their lives, totteringly imitated the awesome cavortings of stallions.

Matthew accepted Ed's view. He was sure Beausoleil's feet would pound grooves into the paddock, because of a stallion's strange way of following the same route, even at full gallop, time after time and day after day. He would probably etch a figure of eight in the turf, and maybe a small circle also, going round and round as though defining the plot for some special, mystical purpose, until suddenly losing interest and wandering off to graze.

They brought him out, keeping all other horses well away and out of sight, this first morning, until he was released in the paddock. Old Corporal the grey was especially kept well away; he was as gentle as a baby, but he was another stallion.

It would not have been wise for anyone to have interrupted Beausoleil's first plunging and screaming. He had had a long day's journey, and a night in a strange stable. He had a powerful head of steam to let off. He still looked fit to race, with a summer bloom to his coat; but already he was taking on the massiveness and manner of a stallion. Ed Lindsey, Matthew and Rosie watched him, awed.

Rick Field watched him, from a distance.

Miss Viola Biggs stumped over from Mount Malcolm. She was wearing a man's hat, carrying a heavy cudgel, and leading two elderly basset-hound bitches long retired from running with the pack.

She wanted to see Beausoleil, she wanted to see Matthew, and she wanted Matthew and Rosie to come out with her hounds the next day. It was her opening Meet, one of the high spots of her year.

'Ah don' trust yo', chile,' she said to Rosie, in the accent that seemed to Matthew a deliberate parody of the old Deep South. 'Distractions come along, an' yuh ain't whar yo' bid. Ah'll be beholden, Matthew Cahvah, ef yo'll kin'ly swear tuh bring this wayward chile tuh ma house at noon tomorrow.'

Matthew promised to do so. He swore to do so. In the face of such goodwill, it would have been impossible to refuse. He did not want to refuse. He liked Miss Viola Biggs very much, and Rosie promised him an amusing day.

Late in the afternoon, a large flat truck bumped painfully up the drive. It was loaded with prefabricated timber sections. Men started to unload them. A boy ran to report: these were the makings of the new barn, justified by Beausoleil, made necessary by him. There was urgency about this. The weather was all right for building work, but it could not be expected to remain so. Everybody remembered the freak snowfall of October 1979, which brought down trees all over Virginia, and left Washington in darkness for two days. A gang of men was coming from the building contractors to sink the foundations, then bolt the sections together. Electricians and plumbers were following. The whole thing was immediate; it was happening at once; it had to. If the work was postponed, the men might not be free for months.

This was all according to plan, but one hitch had occurred in the plan. Peach had undertaken to have trees felled, by a local lumber company, to make room for the barn. The trees were old and dangerous anyway, and where they stood was by far the best place for the barn. Rosie and Ed had picked it months before, after conferences with dozens of officials.

Peach looked mildly regretful. He said the lumber company had let him down. He said there were all kinds of difficulties, complexities beyond the understanding of those present, which had inhibited the removal of the trees.

Rosie ran indoors and called the lumber company. They had had no communication of any kind from Mr Peter Collin, from anybody at Fox Hill. They would do the job, but not for several weeks. There was a heavy demand for firewood, naturally in October, and the lumber company had contracts to fill. They could get to the Fox Hill trees near Christmas. They hated to be disobliging, but if only somebody had said something in June or July . . .

Rosie was really angry. Peach's face was blank. He withdrew to his thinking-room with a candy-bar.

Ed Lindsey said they had three big power-saws on the place, and enough ropes and wires for safe felling. He had done plenty of forestry, in the years when he was taking care of the farm.

It had to be the answer. A damned nuisance, hard work, wholly avoidable, but the necessary answer.

It was too late to start that evening. Felling big trees in the twilight appealed to nobody.

'We *have* to go to Mount Malcolm tomorrow,' Rosie said to Matthew.

'We'll be here, Miss Rosie,' said Ed. 'No problem.'

'I will be here,' said Peach, reappearing refreshed by meditation and chocolate. He dropped a Baby Ruth wrapper on the grass and said, 'I will take personal charge of the operation.'

Rosie opened her mouth to forbid this. She remembered a lesson from her childhood — a good rule about not saying certain things in front of the help. She waited until they were out of earshot of Ed Lindsey. Then she said, 'The farm is mine. Keep out of it. I won't have you taking charge of the men or doing a single goddam thing to those trees. I mean it, Peach. You caused enough trouble. Just let somebody sane pick up the pieces. Wait until the day after tomorrow. Don't even start those saws until the day after tomorrow. Promise me.'

Peach waddled away, munching stickily.

Miss Viola Biggs, Master and Huntsman, her Field Master, the four amateur Whippers-in, were dressed as resplendently as the Beaufort. They wore green hunting coats with old-gold collars and scarlet piping, stocks with winking gold pins, and white breeches. The remainder of the field of two dozen were more casually dressed. Seven couple of endearing basset-hounds were sniffing the legs of the people, sterns waving, excited at the prospect of hunting, under the gentle control of the giants Luke and John Field, who were dressed in the one-gallus tradition.

The Meet was on the small lawn among the trees standing sombre sentry round Mount Malcolm. Some tables had been put on the lawn, and enough drinks on the tables for a crowd ten times the size. As though to compensate for their small number, the field attacked the drinks as though they *were* a crowd ten times the size. Miss Viola Biggs and her Hunt staff felt an evident obligation to show a lead. Only the giant twins were not drinking.

Matthew carried a flask of scotch (not two, as instructed), Rosie a flask of brandy.

Rosie tried to allow the time-honoured booze-up to push out of her mind the infuriating negligence of Peach. Brandy helped also, and Matthew's smiling presence.

Rosie had on a ridiculous hat, by Sherlock Holmes out of Tugboat Annie. Utter and blissful self-abandonment to love, night and morning, had given her face a remembering softness. The chilly, fitful breeze and bright sunshine gave her cheeks colour, and anger with Peach her eyes a hard hot sparkle.

Field and Hunt staff whispered to one another that Rosie looked more beautiful than ever. Their lubricated whispers rang among the trees. They all knew why she looked as she did. They stared at Matthew with interest, respect, envy and disapproval. They all knew Tim Phillipson.

At twelve-forty-five Miss Viola Biggs tooted her horn in a call unconventional in form but unmistakable in content. As the field began to move off, bottles disappeared magically from the tables, and there were strange lumps in the pockets of breeches. Some of the field also disappeared, having done all that they came to do, and drove hazardously home. One of the amateur Whippers-in, a heavy-set woman, sprained her ankle after a hundred yards, and withdrew from the chase. The Field Master tried to quiet the rest. They proceeded to look for cottontails.

Peach was not the man to be given orders in his own house, or in the purlieus or policies of his house. He was the owner of Fox Hill Farm. The deeds were clear on the point. Rosie's attempt to exclude him was impertinent and improper.

In her repeated charges to him, to stay right away from those trees, there was also a hint — more than a hint — of an accusation of incompetence. She pretty well said, right out in front of witnesses, that he was incapable of directing the felling of a few sticks of lumber.

She said it in front of the man Carver, a guest uninvited by himself and disapproved of by himself on grounds of morality and courtesy.

Rosie needed to be shown who was head of the family. They all needed to be shown.

Ed Lindsey had not heard Rosie telling Peach to stay away. If either Cousin Thalia Collin or Jefferson Dill had heard, they had paid no attention. They agreed to come help cut the trees down. It was an occasion, one of hundreds, when Cousin Thalia Collin knew her advice would be needed. Not asked for, but generously given. Jefferson Dill had been to Oregon. He had not actually worked as a lumberjack but he had seen logs coming down rivers.

Ed called his men, and got out the power saws. If he was surprised at Peach arriving, he was too polite to show it.

Peach, Thalia Collin and Jefferson Dill did not handle power saw, handsaw, axe, hook, rope or wire. Their role was advisory. Their advice conflicted. Their voices were raised in continual antiphony. Peach snowed candy-wrappers. Ed, Rick Field and the men got on with the tree-felling.

They all agreed it would be a fine surprise for Miss Rosie, when she came home from the Hunt, to find the trees abolished and the roots hauled out with the tractor.

There were too many cottontails. The small pack divided into several minipacks of a couple or so, each gleefully and musically following its chosen scent. 'Turning and turning in the widening gyre,' thought Matthew, 'The falcon cannot hear the falconer.' The basset-hounds couldn't hear Miss Viola Biggs, because she had lost the power of blowing her horn, and her shrieks were whisked away by the blustering wind. She stood precariously on a tree-stump, purpled with attempts at horn-blowing, and trying to discipline the Whippers-in. They were trying to discipline the hounds, but one had stumbled, and lay at full length, giggling weakly, one had inexplicably burst into tears, one vainly tried to crack her whip, standing alone and forlorn in the middle of a pasture, and one had already retired with that early, fraudulent sprained ankle.

Rosie had trotted cheerfully along with the rest. Now she sat down and took a pull from her brandy-flask. Matthew felt a surge of love for her, love and gratitude, love and lust. This happy travesty of hunting was typical of the surreal delights she led him into: like the tree-planting; like the tennis-court.

'We did our duty,' said Rosie. She wiped her mouth with the back of her hand, leaving a smear of mud like an off-centre moustache.

Matthew laughed and nodded. They walked hand in hand back to Mount Malcolm and the car.

No one knew exactly how it happened. Afterwards it seemed like a simple disaster, an act of God.

Rick Field had been called away to the telephone. He took the call in Ed Lindsey's office. It was his wife Janice, calling from the diner where she worked, telling him to switch on the electric cooker in the cottage, not later than three o'clock, setting it at 250. He missed the whole thing. By the time he got back it had happened. He could probably have prevented it, by being alert, by having some sense and some experience.

It was the last of the six big trees to be felled. The trunk was two foot in diameter. They had picked the line of its fall. The ropes were rigged to commit it to this line, and another to stop it going too soon. Probably the ropes were not fixed as a professional would have done it. The men had done this kind of thing, but they had not been taught how to do it. There was a lot of discussion about just where the ropes should go. Jefferson Dill had clear ideas about this, differing from those of Miss Thalia Collin.

Ed Lindsey with a power saw, Rick Field with an axe, between them cut out the big melon-slice on one side and the smaller one on the other. Peach stood close, instructing them in the use of their tools. Thalia Collin was urging the lopping of more branches, and Jefferson Dill comparing these methods with those of Oregon. The man controlling one of the ropes was out of sight of Ed, behind a little hummock in the ground. This was okay as long as he could hear Ed's voice. He could exert tension or slacken it as Ed told him. The gusty wind made things a little more difficult, but only a little. Rick was called away to the telephone, by Ed's wife. He put the axe down and went off. Thalia Collin said the axe should be moved, or the tree would fall on it. Peach picked up the axe. There was a loud crack from the wood, the noise timber makes when a few straining fibres are holding it together.

'Let her go,' said Peach.

'No, sir, she'll split, spoil the wood,' said Ed.

Peach turned away, not hearing what Ed said, not interested in anything that Ed said. He dropped the axe.

Ed crouched to deepen slightly the cut in the larger melon-slice, the side the tree was supposed to come down, confident that the tree would be held safely vertical by the tension of the three balancing ropes.

Another power saw ripped into life, then another, trimming the trees already felled. They drowned the noise of Ed's saw.

'Pick up the axe,' shouted Thalia Collin.

'Timber!' bellowed Jefferson Dill, in tribute to Oregon.

'Let her go!' called Peach, taking command, as was his privilege and duty.

'Hold it,' called Ed to the unsighted man with the crucial rope.

His voice was drowned by the other shouts. The man let go. He blamed himself afterwards but nobody blamed him. Ed jumped clear. He fell over the handle of the axe, lying where Peach had dropped it. He was caught across the chest by a big branch, and on the head and shoulder and hip by smaller ones. He looked like a frail black doll pinned down by the nightmare network of branches.

Miss Thalia Collin screamed.

A man ran to the telephone, the nearest, in Ed's office. Rick was still on the line to his wife. She did not want to hang up. She had more to say. Rick hung up on her. They called the ambulance. They ran out to help the others cut away the branches which were crushing the life out of Ed. Ed was unconscious, maybe dead. He was bleeding from a hole in the head dug by the broken end of a branch.

Thalia Collin tried to reach Ed, to give him first aid. The branches stopped her even touching him. Jefferson Dill stood stunned, silenced. Peach turned and walked away.

They were still cutting away the timber when the ambulance arrived, and they were still doing it when Rosie and Matthew arrived.

The paramedic said Ed was alive, but only just.

They loaded him on to a stretcher, and the stretcher into the back of the ambulance. His wife got in with him. She was calm. She was praying. Rosie and Matthew followed the ambulance to the hospital.

He was still alive when they got there. He was rushed into an emergency theatre. They waited miserably, the three of them, for a time none measured. They were given no news, because there was no news, until Ed's rib-cage had been pulled out of his lungs, his bones set, his skull X-rayed. His wife prayed. Rosie prayed. Matthew wanted to pray, but he thought God would find his prayers impertinent after so many prayerless years.

At seven p.m. they were told Ed was a mess but over the worst. He was still on the critical list. Rosie staggered and almost fainted. Matthew held her up. Ed's wife's face was a miracle of strength and happiness. She was to stay, to be near Ed when he regained consciousness. There was no more to keep the others.

'Responsibility?' said Peach. 'I? I should think not. I am conscious of regret but not guilt. If I say I am sorry that it happened, that is what I express. I am sad but not contrite. I was holding no rope, wielding no tool. No act of mine brought the tree down, just as no act of mine could have prevented it coming down. Let us have no more of your nonsense.'

'All this fuss about a nigra,' said Janice Field. 'Nobody hangs up on me. Anyway, now's yo' chance. Pass it up an' yo' lose mo' than a job. A gentleman from Richmond propositioned me today. He had six cups o' cawffee, but what he *wanted* was me.'

'I don't know, Rick,' said Rosie. 'Of course I don't have anything against you. If I did, you wouldn't be here anyway. It's just . . .'

'Well, *what* is it, Miss Rosie?'

Well, *what* was it?

'It's only 'til Ed's better,' said Rick. 'Naturally. I'd just be keepin' the job warm for him. It ain't a secret I hope to take over one day. Ed always knew that, an' I guess you did too. Anything I didn't know when I came here, why, Ed bin teachin' me just so I *can* take over.'

'That's true.'

It was true.

'The horses know me,' said Rick. 'See the way the mares an' weanlings come to me?'

They did. Rosie had seen it, and been pleased and impressed. 'The men know me. They'd lief not have a stranger.'
The men themselves had said the same.

Miss Viola Biggs said, 'Give him the job, honey. Yo'll do it one day anyways. Why not now, 'till Ed's fixed? An' listen heah — the twins, his kin, he can call on them any minute he needs mo' hands. Like with that stallion. *Any* minute yo' needs 'em, ah guess ah can spare 'em.'

Convinced — ninety-nine percent convinced — Rosie consulted Matthew.
He had been consulting himself, and he was unconvinced. He had made himself personally responsible for Beausoleil. There was no escaping the implications of this. He had recommended Fox Hill in large part because of Ed Lindsey. Now what? One solution was to move Beausoleil to another farm, to be handled by a manager of Ed's calibre. That would be a shocking blow for Rosie, a betrayal. It was to be avoided if possible. Another solution was to find a highly qualified manager with proved stallion experience, to fill in for Ed until Ed was back.
Rosie urged a third course. She was bound to, out of loyalty to her own man. Beausoleil was already beginning to acclimatise at Fox Hill. It would surely be folly to move him, upset him and annoy him again. Matthew had seen Rick with the horses. Had he ever seen more skill, patience, gentleness? He had the help, on call, any time, of those strangely impressive retarded giants, his cousins. He had the recommendation of Miss Viola Biggs, who was nobody's fool and who wished the best for Fox Hill. The other men liked Rick, and wanted to work under him rather than any high-talking overbearing stranger.
'I have nothing against Rick,' said Matthew. 'I just don't think I know him well enough to recommend to my friends that we entrust —'
'If that's all, then *get* to know him,' said Rosie.
Matthew made a deliberate effort to do so, at once. He had not the immediate rapport with Rick that he had found with Ed Lindsey, even though they had plenty to talk about. But you didn't turn a man down, for a job like this, because he was shy, reserved.
Miss Viola Biggs's recommendation was a strong point.

194

Matthew assumed Rick had worked for her — that she was in a position to give a testimonial.

He was still undecided at bedtime.

Night-time, morning (so shameless in full sunlight, the nakedness more naked, the same acts more audacious and beguiling) drowned doubt and logic.

Black arts, white arts, pink arts had influenced Matthew in the choice of Fox Hill. Now they influenced him to accept Rick Field. Somehow the arrangement was made, the consent given.

Rosie's sustained championship of Rick — her determination that Matthew should consent to his looking after Beausoleil — was no more logical. It was founded on obstinacy. Once she had said 'Yes', 'Yes' must be the answer. Pride was involved, which she mis-defined to herself as loyalty.

In Rosie there was a large hidden element of Peach.

'I'll stay, for a spell,' said Janice Field.

Matthew stayed for a spell. He could argue a clear duty to do so. It was useless using this argument to mollify Peach, though Rosie tried. She said the accident to Ed Lindsey, itself Peach's fault, made Matthew's presence the more necessary. This was a good debating point, but Peach let it pass him by. He went away to think. His hostility to Matthew soured the atmosphere a little, but still Matthew stayed. He had done all that was needed at home — answered all the mail, paid all the bills, checked up, needlessly, on the stewardship of the Mungos outdoors and Fay Candy indoors.

Matthew wondered how grossly he was lying to himself. Rosie bewitched him. He felt young and strong. Now that he knew her whole history, her whole heart, he knew she needed him as much as he her. Nobody except Clare had needed him for years, and she not much. Now he was responsible for Rosie's happiness. She said so, and he knew it was true. The therapy was altogether mutual. He welcomed the responsibility. He could argue that Rosie needed him at Fox Hill, even if Beausoleil no longer did. She argued that way, but not to Peach. Hazel purred lubricious approval. The weather grew cooler.

The arrival of Sir Merivale Lucas surprised nobody, though he was unexpected. He said he had both written and rung. Nobody disbelieved him. It was a house where messages were mislaid.

Matthew was moderately pleased to see Merivale Lucas, to whom he felt a clear debt of gratitude. Lucas had sent Matthew to Fox Hill. Without Lucas at the races, Lucas boringly on the telephone, there would have been no midnight tennis in the rain. Matthew was not more than moderately pleased.

What was surprising was the open delight with which Peach welcomed Lucas. One would not have supposed them congenial. Lucas could talk only horses, or gossip about people concerned with horses. One would have expected this conversation to send Peach away to his thinking room and his candy-bars. He did go away, and he took Lucas with him. They spent hours together. Nobody knew what they discussed. Rosie speculated, but without deep interest.

Lucas said he had come to look at the weanlings which would be going to the sales the following summer. He wanted to look at Beausoleil. He wanted to secure nominations to Beausoleil on behalf of various clients. He wanted another try at Rosie. This was almost immediately obvious. Matthew felt slight anger, not because there was the slightest chance of Lucas succeeding, but because there was something obscene in his even trying. It was unpleasant for Rosie to be pestered by a man with dandruff on his collar.

Hazel said he was a British rapist, the worst kind, come to mess around with her. She pushed a table against her bedroom door.

Lucas was himself surprised to be given such a welcome by Peach, who on his previous visit had seemed to regard him with a sort of apathetic hatred. Hours of boredom threatened when Peach talked about himself. But the conversation, though too long, contained matter of interest.

Peach was just as angry as Lucas was. He considered Carver's behaviour devious, immoral, ungentlemanly and treacherous. He thought Carver was betraying Tim Phillipson, while Lucas thought he was betraying Lucas, but the disapproval was just as bitter.

There was no longer any 'maybe' in Rosie's 'no'. Nobody could doubt that this was Carver's doing.

Lucas would have been prepared to share Rosie with Carver. He was not a selfish man. Tarts are liberal with their favours. Clearly Rosie was a tart, continually drilled by Carver and making

196

no secret of it. Carver was paying her by standing Beausoleil at Fox Hill, and by buying a yearling for $90,000. Lucas could pay her, too. Lucas *had* paid her. His good offices had been massively at her service.

Lucas found that he did not believe the disappearance of the 'maybe' from Rosie's 'no'. It was a trick of the acoustics. He found that he was entitled to take delivery of that for which he had already paid. He found that he was specifically encouraged (in a flux of stately words), by Peach, to cut Matthew Carver out.

Had he worn a twirlable moustache, Lucas would have twirled it.

Matthew went before dinner to the little room where Rosie sometimes wrote letters (she sometimes even mailed them), which had a chesterfield and an extension telephone and a tray of drinks. He had a great desire to see and touch Rosie. He had not seen or touched her for an hour, and the deprivation was becoming intolerable.

Rosie was there, on the battered little chesterfield, telephoning. She was talking to the sanitorium, to one of the doctors. She was tied to the telephone. She could not escape. She could not escape from the telephone or from Merivale Lucas, who was sitting beside her with one hand on her knee and the other arm round her shoulders. Rosie was trying to get rid of Lucas's hands with her free hand, but as soon as she removed a hand it returned. Her face was distressed, by the telephone conversation rather than by Lucas. Her voice was distressed when she talked to the telephone. Lucas wore a roguish look. His face said that he knew he was being a bad boy. When Matthew came into the room he looked embarrassed and angry. He took his hands away from Rosie's shoulder and knee.

'I have to leave it to you to do whatever you think best,' said Rosie in misery to the telephone. 'Just so you don't hurt him or frighten him.'

Matthew crossed the room to the chesterfield without any clear idea of what he was going to do. Lucas stood up, probably with no clear idea of what he was going to do. Matthew found his mind made up for him, by the fact of Lucas standing up.

'I hate you shooting all those drugs into him,' said Rosie to the telephone, 'but if you have to you have to.'

Matthew put his hands on Lucas's shoulders and ejected him

197

from the room. Lucas went meekly. There was no unseemly fracas. No punches were swung, or insults spat. Matthew shut the door behind Lucas. He sat on the chesterfield beside Rosie. She smiled at him brilliantly, then frowned as she listened to the telephone.

Business took Lucas away immediately. It took him to Cragrock, to look at weanlings and discuss nominations. He had rung; the message had not been lost, because Doris Bernard had never in her life lost a message; he was expected. Jean Whyte and Alice Harding were interested in his account of Fox Hill. The other accounts they had heard — from George, from Ghalib, from Matthew — were in various ways unsatisfactory. Lucas was a little waspish about Rosie Phillipson, but he had enough sense not to be waspish about Matthew Carver, in this house, to these women.

Lucas saw everything on the farms and everything in the stable. With George Whyte he saw the yearling by Lord Primrose out of Meadowsweet, being gently broken by Bert Duffy and his grooms.

'What do you think of him?' said George Whyte, not because he cared but because it was what you said.

Lucas was directly responsible for Matthew Carver having seen this yearling, indirectly for George Whyte having bought it. The taste of gall filled his mouth. He had been thrown out of a room.

He said, 'Matt's choice, I believe.'

'He found him, yes.'

'And he made the deal? Ninety *grand*?'

'Too much, do you think?'

'It depends what you're buying,' said Lucas. 'Matt Carver was buying Virginia cunt, not horseflesh. But it beats me why you should be paying for that.'

That sort of family, thought George Whyte. The brother got Ghalib drunk and cheated him. The sister got Carver infatuated and cheated him. Cheated George. Carver got his kicks. All George got was the bill, and the note of amused astonishment in Lucas's voice.

George went back to the house, leaving Lucas with Bert Duffy. He found that his son Hal was home for the Christmas vacation, unexpectedly, two days early for some disciplinary reason. George was angry about that. He saw Hal through the door of the library, laughing with Jean and Alice. It was amazing that they could bear to look at him, talk to him. He looked terrible. He had shoulder-length hair and bare feet. Hal was nearly seventeen. To go around with bare feet was ridiculous, demeaning, a pose. Hal was working hard at being something horrible. George slipped away before any of them saw him. He'd have to face Hal and he'd have to say something, but he was too angry with Carver and Mrs Phillipson. You had to keep cool, talking to Hal, or he twisted what you said and made it funny.

'Mr Whyte thinks he's a little overpriced,' said Lucas to Bert Duffy as they looked at Meadowsweet's yearling.

'I guess maybe, a little,' said Bert, agreeing with his employer even in his employer's absence.

Of course Lucas should have been paid commission, by Rosie, on the sale of the yearling to Cragrock. Nine grand. It was one more infuriating aspect.

He was not a vengeful man. There was no malice in his character. But he reverenced justice. Justice required exposure, punishment.

He borrowed the telephone in Bert Duffy's office. He spoke to a newspaperman with whom he had a long-standing and fruitful relationship based neither on friendship nor on mutual trust.

The item was hardly newsworthy in itself, but it was a nice follow-up to some real news — hard international news which was also hot local news. Beausoleil. The Mill Reef and the record. The idyll of Fox Hill, and the British noble family. Now a yearling costing twice what it was worth. Sin at $45,000.

The reporter rang George Whyte.

George was fairly well used to talking to the press, though it had not come easily to him. In a case like this he knew what to say, with or without Lee V. Lowe. He would make no comment beyond expressing complete confidence in the judgement and probity of his partner. Anyone who thought the yearling overpriced was entitled to that opinion. When it ran they would all see who was right.

George opened his mouth to make this dignified reply, when Hal went past the window outside. Sent home from school two days early. Still barefooted, out there in the cold, not an authentic rebel but conforming to some disgusting archetype. Hair blowing around like a girl, like a dirty slut of a girl, like a whore, like Rosanna Phillipson.

'An expert independent valuation does suggest we were taken for something of a ride,' he said to the telephone. 'I consented sight unseen, you know. I won't make that mistake again.'

This confirmation by George Whyte was beyond the reporter's wildest dreams. He taped the words, to make the paper legally safe. He requested and secured permission to quote verbatim, taping the permission. He heard the anger at the other end. He heard references to long hair which puzzled him, and which he later wiped from the tape. He heard what was tantamount to an accusation that Matthew Carver was gullible or dishonest or both.

George gave Bert Duffy permission to speak to the newspaper. George's remarks, transcribed and edited, were read back to Bert. He agreed with them. The yearling was very overpriced.

It was like *The Village that Voted the Earth was Flat*: it was a matter of chance, negative chance. A war, the assassination of a pop-star, even the boring double-talk of a Middle Eastern summit or a meeting of the Organization of African Unity would have forced the titbit out of the columns and into the waste-basket.

But it was a nice follow-up. Sub-editors had fun with headlines: *Colt jolt, Moxie for Doxy, Cider with Rosie*. Somebody discovered that a name had been registered, neatly derived from the breeding: Primrose Path. This was a bonanza. Jocular paragraphs followed up again. Still there were no royal weddings, bribery scandals at the Pentagon, or flying disasters. It was the season of jocoseness.

Mollie in London was very angry indeed.

CHAPTER 10

'It is inconceivable that my husband could have been hoodwinked,' said Mollie. 'His judgement is internationally respected. His probity. He is a man of honour. His behaviour to me may have been unsatisfactory, but never his behaviour to his colleagues. Of course that is a thing one often sees. I expect you have all seen it. Men who are paragons in their business and sporting dealings, but far from satisfactory in the home.'

The old lags looked at her apathetically from their bench. The prison wall sweated above them. They did not know what 'paragon' meant. The men in their lives were drunken criminals.

'This George Whyte they talk about,' said Mollie, 'the one they quote in the newspapers. Of course I knew him well. He is not what I call a gentleman. I never liked him. He is too rich. He thinks his money entitles him to make these scandalous imputations. But he has left something out of account. In slandering my husband he is slandering me. We are still married. Badly as he has treated me, I stand his loyal friend in times of crisis. I will not have him accused of incompetence or dishonesty. I will not permit it. Mr Whyte is in for a surprise.'

'Bash 'im,' said the abortionist.

The others belched agreement. They had no idea what Mrs Toffeenose was on about. It passed the morning.

Mollie was warmed by the support of her wonderful old friends. They were the stuff of Old England, staunch and plucky, real characters, seeing straight through pretence into the bones of things.

'Tell 'im where 'e gets orf,' said the attempted murderess.

''E 'ad no right.'

'Bash 'im.'

The swelling chorus encouraged Mollie to action. Someone should tell George Whyte where he got off, in the colourful language of her friends. They used language yet more colourful, but unfamiliar to her.

'We live in a free country with a free press,' said Mollie. 'If we are traduced we have the right to reply. In this case I have a duty to reply. I shall write letters to all the newspapers which have printed this poisonous rubbish.'

She composed the letters aloud, to her fine old friends, and they leered and scratched.

Mollie bought an evening paper outside the prison. She read it on the bus home. She read that the leader of a trade union had given a press conference, in which he replied to criticisms made of him. Carrying the war to the enemy camp, he attacked the Director General of the Confederation of British Industry, the government's economic policy, and the employers. On another page, Mollie saw that someone in the City had given a press conference, someone involved in a take-over and in trouble with the Monopolies Commission. He refuted criticisms made of him. A boxer's manager refuted criticisms, the management of a Manchester casino in which eight persons had died in a fire, and the owner of a pornographic bookshop.

Mollie realised that, in planning a lot of letters, she was thinking too small. She was giving herself unnecessary trouble. She did not shrink from trouble, but she wanted to refute in the most effective way the criticisms of Matthew which were by implication criticisms of her too. She had chosen him, married him, borne his children. It was intolerable that a purse-proud colonial should say these things unchallenged. He needed a sharp lesson.

Clare came back to the flat to find her mother telephoning.

'I wish to speak to the editor. Very well, someone else in a position of authority. This is the Honourable Mrs Carver. I am calling a press conference. I wish to refute criticisms. I insist on my right to do so, to be heard and correctly quoted. I intend to deliver some home truths. They may not be palatable to certain persons. I cannot help that. If the cap fits let them wear it. The truth must out. Eleven o'clock tomorrow morning. I shall serve coffee. Men are coming from several newspapers. You will not wish to be left out. You may send a photographer. He thinks that because he is rich he can libel his betters with impunity. He must be taught a sharp lesson.'

Clare was aghast. She wondered if it would have been possible to dissuade her mother from this disastrous project. Probably not. Anyway it was too late now. Journalists would already be giggling in El Vino's, looking forward to larks in the morning.

'He is very interested,' said Clare's mother, hanging up. 'He will send an important reporter, and a photographer. You can be here if you wish, although there is really no need.'

'I wonder if Dad would appreciate —' Clare began.

But her mother was already dialling again, asking for another editor, announcing her press conference.

Mollie looked critically round the flat, anxious that she and all that was hers should make a good impression on Fleet Street.

She saw cobwebs, high, grey, like tattered banners in a cathedral but not very like. If one looked for them they were obtrusive, horribly visible. The gentlemen of the press noticed everything. They were trained to do so. Mollie was aware of the concept of 'image', and her image in the morning should not be festooned with cobwebs. She saw herself as a bright blade, tempered steel, sunlit, aflash to defend and avenge.

Maisie should have removed the cobwebs with the pretty instrument provided by Mollie for the purpose, a bouquet of bright false feathers on the end of a bamboo pole. With a martyred sigh, Mollie got the jumbo feather-duster from the housemaid's cupboard in the kitchen. She strained upwards at the cobwebs, dabbing. The thing did not reach. The bamboo was too short, or the cobwebs too high. She was betrayed by artefact or nature, man or spider.

There were steps, tall steps, in a yawning cupboard outside the kitchen. They were awkward to move, aiming blows at the ankles. Mollie struggled, alone as always. Clare had gone out, though she might have foreseen that she would be needed. Mollie placed the steps below the cobwebs and grimly began to climb. She had a bad head for heights. The steps wobbled. She remembered that the handyman, the elusive Mr Curtis employed by the landlord, had blown on his moustache and recommended abolition of the steps. He said they were unsafe. Men who came to do things refused to use them, window-cleaners, paper-hangers, then men who came to put up the pelmet. They preferred their own steps and climbed them jauntily. Mollie would have bought new steps but for the price of steps. Meanwhile they were usable if you were careful. The lower classes were cowardly, pampered. They wanted everything done for them. Mollie wobbled perilously halfway up the steps, and waved the feathers at the cobwebs. Afterwards she put the steps away, barking her ankles and shins. The steps were perfectly all right to use if you had character and background.

Maisie the ex-convict tried to get round the room with a tray of coffee. The room was too crowded. She bumped into the men from the newspapers, spilling the coffee into the saucers. She spilled anything she carried, because she was either drunk or recovering from drink, but today it was hardly her fault. There were not nearly enough cups for the number of visitors. They were of different patterns, and most were chipped. Maisie was heavy-handed at the sink. Men who secured cups of coffee drank little, because it was cold. They extinguished their cigarettes in cold half-cups of coffee.

Clare was watching and listening but hiding, suffocating with vicarious embarrassment.

Mollie was dressed up as though for a wedding.

She called for silence by beating on a little gong. Silence immediately fell. If there were sniggers they were muted. The men were polite, and listened to Mollie attentively. Mollie read a prepared statement which she had written on many sheets of her engraved writing-paper from Harrods. The statement was one part a proclamation of her husband's skill and integrity, and the universal esteem in which he was held; it was two parts an exposé of George Whyte's ignorance, arrogance and malice.

Departing from her script, Mollie said, 'After all, Mr Whyte has never bought a horse on his own, never in his life. He has never trusted his own judgement. He has never dared to do so. He has not got the knowledge. Of course it is largely a matter of background.'

This, if true, was an interesting point, adding spice to a situation already amusing. A reporter picked Mollie up, asking if she were quite sure of her facts. She became annoyed. She was not accustomed to being accused of lying, exaggeration, or speaking without full knowledge and careful thought. She repeated with emphasis the fact, known to all, that George Whyte had never trusted his own judgement because he had no judgement.

'And this is the man,' said Mollie, 'who has the effrontery to make the kind of disgusting remark you people have been printing.

You can all see that he needs a rap over the knuckles.'

Pencils flew happily over notebooks.

Mollie spoke of loyalty, of her own to her husband in spite of the way he had treated her, of George Whyte's lack of it. She said it was a matter of background. She said she herself worked in harness with Maisie to keep the flat nice for her friends and children, and she felt in consequence an obligation of loyalty to Maisie. Maisie felt one to her, too. Maisie had been a criminal, but had paid her debt to society. She understood now that anything honestly earned was sweeter than anything stolen. The reporters looked at Maisie, who smirked. She was a greasy old woman with wrinkled stockings. Nobody would eat soup into which she had stuck a thumb. She smoked a cigarette in a loyal way.

The reporters asked Mollie a great many questions about herself, about her marriage and circumstances and children, her prison-visiting and her aristocratic relatives. They drew her out about George Whyte, his arrogance, his wealth, his ignorance of horseflesh, his utter reliance on Matthew Carver.

Clare found herself thinking that, although what her mother was doing was calamitous, she was doing it rather well. She was dignified. She was loyal. She was doing battle for her husband, although they had been separated for years. Although their last meeting had ended almost in murder by words: the murder of each other and of Clare. It was lucky no one had taped that scene and given it to the newspapers.

Photographs were taken of Mollie and of Maisie and of Mollie and Maisie together. They were photographed with brooms, sharing the task of keeping the flat nice. They looked loyal to each other.

The press reports were brief but numerous. They fell into three categories. The regular dailies reported the press-conference as a follow-up to the other items — now a considerable series — about Matthew Carver and his woman and his partners and their purchases. *PEER'S DAUGHTER SLAMS TURF TYCOON. The Honourable 'Mollie' Carver reacted angrily today to suggestions that her husband . . .* The specialised sporting press focussed not on Mollie and her *vie intime* but on George Whyte and Matthew Carver and the signs of a rift between these long-established partners. There was speculation about the future of a bloodstock empire largely financed by George Whyte but effectively managed, so rumour had it, by Matthew Carver. This was serious stuff, with implications for breeders and bloodstock agents all over the world. A third category of report was distressingly facetious. The photographs of Mollie and Maisie with their brooms. Maisie's loyalty to Mollie ascribed by Mollie to Maisie's background.

All three categories quoted Mollie's raps over George Whyte's knuckles. He had never bought a horse on his own judgement, was incapable of doing so, depended wholly on his partner.

George Whyte was as angry, reading Mollie's remarks about him, as Mollie had been reading his remarks about Matthew.

Jean said, 'You brought this on yourself, George. Maybe they put words into your mouth, but they *quoted* you as saying Matt was conned by that lady in Virginia.'

'Lady.'

'She is a lady, yes.'

'They're a bunch of degenerates.'

'Not necessarily a contradiction.'

As so often before, George found his wife incomprehensible. He had expected her to share his anger with Mollie. He had expected every right-thinking person to do so. Now he found himself blamed. He had the feeling, not for the first time, that he was the only person in the world with a logical mind.

He called Lee V. Lowe in New York, who urgently counselled a dignified silence.

'Don't mix it, Squire,' said Lee V. Lowe. 'Don't descend to their level.'

Doris Bernard did not presume to offer advice, but her fluttering and twittering communicated that she agreed with Lee V. Lowe.

Indeed she did. Lee V. Lowe might have been summoned to Cragrock. He would have come like a shot. Press releases dictated, typed, amended, retyped, photo-copied, mailed, messages on the Telex, sporting journalists personally telephoned — Doris would have had seventy-two hours of hell. Not normally hell. Normally one more chance to be indispensable, cool under the twittering, unflappable under the fluttering, ever more central, ever more powerful, her fingers ever nearer to the jackpot. But Alicia, pink kitten, was bringing her boobs and her ass and her pussy back to

206

Cragrock, back for the vacation from college, and Doris wanted to be free.

Matthew Carver arrived at Cragrock only hours after the first newspaper cuttings. Jean met him with them, a little reproachful. It all came as a complete surprise.

'What triggered this?' said Matthew, mystified. 'A press-conference? What could have been in her mind?'

'You can't guess?'

'Absolutely not.'

'But you saw the stuff they quoted George as saying,' said Jean.

'Did I? What stuff?'

'Where have you been, Matt? Don't they have newspapers in that place?'

Did they? Yes, probably papers arrived. Maybe Hazel lit fires with them, or Peach took them away to his study.

'I guess it's days since I saw a paper,' Matthew said, himself surprised that this was so.

'It sounds like the land of the lotus eaters,' said Jean.

'Yes,' said Matthew, part of him aching to be back there, wondering why it had suddenly seemed necessary to his sanity to leave.

'Mollie has been a little — unguarded.'

'Hm,' said Matthew, looking through the cuttings.

He felt sick, picturing his poor Mollie grimly, loyally, courageously, making a monstrous fool of herself, in that awful sitting-room, in front of a crowd of reporters. The brooms. The ex-convict. 'It is all a matter of background.' He felt a knot of guilt in his gut, for losing his temper in that room, for having said terrible things to Mollie in front of Clare.

'And you really don't know,' said Jean, half amused, wholly amazed, deeply sorry for Matthew, 'what brought this on?'

'No.'

She showed him the earlier cuttings. George quoted at length, Bert Duffy briefly.

'My God,' said Matthew. 'Did George say this?'

'I wasn't there,' said Jean. 'I can't understand why nobody called you. Or Mrs Phillipson. They knew where you were. I assume there's a 'phone.'

'Sure there is,' said Matthew. He pictured Hazel taking calls from the press, imagining attempts to lure her into dark bars; he imagined Thalia Collin or Jefferson Dill or Peach taking the calls. 'They probably called. They must have. None of it percolated through to me.'

He turned back to the cuttings. Jean watched his frown deepen as he read that he had paid an inflated price for Meadowsweet's yearling because he was romantically involved with its owner. She watched him turn from these cuttings to Mollie's defence of himself against George Whyte. He looked sick. He looked mad. He was entitled to be mad with George and Mollie both.

It came to Jean that, in all the years she had known Matthew, she had never heard him say, so much as hint, a disloyal word about Mollie. He would not permit criticism of her, sympathy for himself. His rule in the matter was absolute. It was admirable, of course. A bit silly, but admirable. Almost any other man would have let himself go occasionally, after a drink, with old friends, congenial women friends. He was not likely to break his rule now.

George came into the library with an almost ingratiating face. He was going to make peace, because he had sound commercial reasons for doing so. He began to talk about over-reaction, as a phenomenon to be observed among women of a certain age. He mentioned the menopause, deprecatingly. It became clear, though not immediately, that he was inviting Matthew to agree that Mollie had over-reacted, with potentially mischievous results.

'If my wife gets up and says I'm an honest man,' said Matthew, 'you can't expect me to disagree, George.'

'That's not all she said.'

'I don't disagree with anything she said.'

'I think, on reflection, you may wish to reconsider that remark. After you have studied this material.'

'Even if I disagreed with some of the things she said, I'd sure as hell understand her saying them.'

'When,' said Jean, '*did* you ever buy a horse on your own judgement, George?'

George turned and left the room. Jean shrugged at Matthew, making a face. Her rules were not the same as his.

'I don't think I'll stop here, Jean,' said Matthew. 'Somebody's liable to say something regrettable. Probably me. If I may, I'll come back when the dust has settled.'

'I'm sorry you won't visit,' said Jean. 'I guess you're right, but I'm sorry. Why actually did you come? That sounds unwelcoming, but you know it isn't meant that way.'

'I came by on my way home. I came to see you all. I came to agree the final line-up of Beausoleil's nominations. I came to see Ghalib.'

'Is Ghalib coming here? Yes, that's right. He called from Washington. But he's hung up there, making another few billion. If you want to see him, I'll call you when he gets here. Where will you be? Home?'

'Could be.'

'Or Fox Hill?'

'It's possible.'

'Lotus land. Always afternoon. No newspapers. It sounds like heaven, in some ways.'

'It is, in some ways.'

Alice heard that Matthew had come, only after he had gone. She was very sorry to have missed him. She had been thinking about him, and trying to exclude thoughts of Mrs Phillipson. She was astonished that he could have been insulated against the press of the world, or even the press of Virginia. Of the accounts of Fox Hill that she had heard, Ghalib's now seemed the most credible — a place of djinns and sorcery.

She was distressed to hear from Jean that George and Matthew had come close to an open quarrel. George could have said he had been misquoted, his words taken out of context, his meaning twisted. It happened so often. It had happened to her, when she divorced Frank Harding. George could have said all that without precisely retracting, apologising, putting himself in the wrong. And Matthew simply had to point out that he couldn't be held responsible for what a crazy woman said on the other side of the world. All it took was sense, maturity. Surely both men had both of those. They'd be crazy to let a thing like this blow up between them.

Alice wanted Matthew to come back. She was miserable to have missed him. There had to be peace between him and George.

Prince Ghalib al-Jilani was thoroughly disturbed by the pieces he read in the newspapers.

He considered it entirely possible that Matthew Carver had paid too much for the yearling at Fox Hill. He, Ghalib, never paid a penny over the odds for anything. He always got value for money. Matthew Carver had had value for money. If the yearling were worth only $45,000, if he had paid $45,000 for Rosie Phillipson, that was value for money as Ghalib understood value, and money, and Rosie. But George Whyte could not be expected to see things in this light. He was not a man as Carver and Ghalib were men. It was amazing he had conceived children. Probably he had not done so. Perhaps they were Carver's children. The point was unimportant. What was important was that Carver should continue to be the directing intelligence at Cragrock. It was convenient having George Whyte's limitless finance. To it Ghalib was prepared to add his finance. But not if George Whyte were left to direct operations. He, Ghalib, could have directed them, but he was far too busy. He had to travel the world. He had a home and family on the Gulf. He was delegating management of his investment at Ballycardeen to Tom Kavanagh. He was delegating management of his investment at Cragrock and Fox Hill to Matt Carver, to him and no other.

There was another aspect, less clearly verbalised in Ghalib's thoughts but hardly less important to him. Matt Carver's position at Cragrock made him Ghalib's colleague, confederate. Friendship sprang. It was a great deal more than being a racetrack acquaintance. Ghalib had plenty of those, and they had not changed his life. A friend and colleague would: one who was slapped on the shoulder by English dukes, who was asked to luncheon by French dukes.

Ghalib's instinct was to drop his business in Washington and rush to Cragrock, or Fox Hill, or both, and labour to repair the breach between Carver and Whyte. But the business held him, day following day, meetings that could not be ducked, big meetings and very much more important little meetings. Ghalib never lost his sense of priorities, but he was in an agony to get to Kentucky.

Matthew, at home, discovered in himself a tiny, nagging burr of self-doubt. How much had Rosie, his feeling about Rosie, influenced him in buying Meadowsweet's yearling? In agreeing the price without a haggle?

Was George right?

Doris Bernard met Alicia at the Blue Grass Field. This was achieved by the kind of strategem she enjoyed, which made her

210

feel cleverer than anybody else. She ran out of carbon paper in the American Quarto size, by dint of hiding four boxes of 500 sheets each. She needed it, by dint of choosing American Quarto for certain categories of business letter. It was clearly convenient that she went into Lexington in the early afternoon. Somebody else — not she — remarked that Alicia's flight was due in from New York just about the time Doris would finish her shopping. Thus it was none of Doris's doing, as far as anybody knew, that an exhausted Alicia was welcomed with flutters and twitters and feminine attentions. And they had a nice ride and a nice gossip, two girls together and the rest of the world shut out, and Doris heard that Alicia was tired from studying and parties, and fed up with all the boys she knew, and looking forward to a rest.

Alicia started grumpy, because she was tired. She thawed, grateful for Doris's interest, trusting Doris as she always had, amused by the twittering as everybody was. Doris made her laugh. The car was warm. They had sexy music softly on the radio.

Alicia wanted to seem adult to the adult Doris. She had been a child; she was a child no longer. Doris had always thought of her as a child, and that must be put right. Alicia consequently dropped mentions of her three most recent involvements. Rod was a bullyboy, Kit was a half-gay, Ralphie was always zonked. All three were macho, even Kit. None of them had any real poetry.

Gleeful, Doris realised that Alicia was exactly in the predictable, the optimum state. She was in the state of a great majority of not-too-bright nineteen-year-olds who got away from home but not far. She wanted it but it hadn't worked. Her girls friends sold it to her, and she didn't want to be chicken, but the stars hadn't blazed. Those boys had used her but they hadn't satisfied her. She hadn't come, not with them, that was obvious. Doris was ready to swear that Alicia's only orgasms had come from her own fingers. Successful hetero sex would have made things hard for Doris. Doris thanked God for the uncouth selfishness of young men.

It was probably lucky, thought Doris, that she needed both hands for driving. She couldn't otherwise have kept them to herself. It would have been premature: a day or two premature.

Ghalib was man of the world enough to meet Alice Harding

without embarrassment. Alice was woman of the world enough to meet him without embarrassment: even though their brief relationship had included a sexual encounter of a preliminary kind, which often gives rise to an enduring social hang-up, and had ended with that parent of embarrassment a rejection. Alice *had* rejected Ghalib, but she liked him. He *had* been rejected (second of three consecutive, unprecedented rejections) but he liked her.

She met him at the Blue Grass Field as Doris Bernard had the previous day met Alicia: with the difference that this time the coincidence was genuine. It just happened that Alice had to be in Lexington with a car at the hour when Ghalib flew in from Washington. It really did just happen.

'It just happened,' she said to him. 'I'm not that kind of a teaser, not yet. I don't think I need to be, yet.'

He laughed, understanding that it was a coincidence, understanding that the conclusions he might have drawn — might quite legitimately have drawn, with maybe seventy women in a hundred — were quite wrong.

Ghalib had a great deal of sexual vanity, and he was a howling snob. But he had not become a multi-millionaire by any lack of realism.

Realism had sent him on a scheduled commercial flight to Lexington, rather than a charter flight to the Cragrock airstrip. The extra expense of the latter was not justified by the small extra convenience, the small saving of time. He was a man prepared to carry a suitcase a few hundred yards, and to read a newspaper without boredom while he waited for half an hour. He did not understand why George Whyte had an airstrip at Cragrock. Ballycardeen was different. It was seventy miles from Shannon. Realism called for an airstrip, at whatever cost.

'What brings you to Cragrock?' asked Alice, as they started up the Paris Pike from Lexington.

What did? There was a book answer and a real answer. The book answer talked about investment, selection of bloodlines for long-range planning, purchase of yearlings in July, possible bids for broodmares and fillies in training. The real answer was about having the right management at Cragrock, and introductions to the right dukes.

Both halves of the real answer contained implied criticism of George Whyte. He was not to be trusted with management; he was not the intimate of dukes. It was not appropriate to say these things to George Whyte's sister. Ghalib's present role was diplomatic. He was a peacemaker. He wanted the confidence of all parties. Consequently there were things not to say, however true, and there might be things to say, however untrue. Especially in the way of deferring to George Whyte's judgement, of going on record (perhaps not in front of Carver) as disagreeing with the quoted remarks of Mrs Carver.

Resolving to be very, very careful, Ghalib astonished himself by saying, 'I came hoping to make peace between your brother and Matthew Carver.'

Alice glanced at him quickly. Her eyes on the road again, she nodded. She seemed to expect him to go on.

He went on, in his perfect Old Harrovian English, 'It is not good business to join a fragile partnership. Unless you intend to replace one partner or another. I do not so intend. That is not at all what I want. The present partners seem to me, ah, to complement one another. That is as it should be and as it should remain. My hope is to, ah, provide cement. Additional cement, to perpetuate the present excellent arrangement.'

'What cement? Sweet words? Or money?'

'Both.'

'I'll join you in the sweet words. I really will. I quite agree with you. From all I hear . . .'

'Yes?'

Alice stopped herself saying that Jean had told her, quoting much expert opinion, that George relied heavily on Matthew's judgement, and would be unwise ever to stop doing so.

Emending a remark which threatened disloyalty to her brother, she said, 'Matthew Carver likes being around here, with our horses. Since I like him, I'd be sorry if he lost that.'

'We are in partnership, then,' said Ghalib. 'Doves of peace.'

Nobody, thought Alice, had ever looked less like a dove than the hawklike royalty beside her. But, short of billing and cooing, she was happy to play dove to his dove. She wanted Matthew Carver back at Cragrock.

Rosie continued insulated from the news, by the circumstances of life at Fox Hill. When Matthew was there, she thought of little except him. When he was not there, she still thought of little except him. She thought a little about the horses and the wallpapers and Tim. She had no time for newspapers, and anyway such papers as came to the house never came as far as her.

Other people knew what had been happening — Rick Field, Miss Viola Biggs of Mount Malcolm — but when they were talking to Rosie other subjects came up. Talking to Rosie, you seldom picked topics. She did that, and you followed as best you could. Jefferson Dill knew what had been happening, but he kept his knowledge until he was in a mood to use it.

Cousin Thalia Collin became incensed with Rosie, because of Rosie's rejection, couched in unseemly language, of Thalia's views on the redecoration of a room. Ill-temper induced Thalia to quote to Jefferson Dill, because she had to get back at *somebody,* what she had heard Janice Field say to Miss Viola Biggs, during a rehearsal of *Circe's Island.* Janice was herself quoting Matthew Carver, quoting a remark made by Matthew to Rosie, itself overheard by Janice. Matthew allegedly said that *Circe's Island* was bad enough to be funny, but too boring to be very funny.

That did it. Jefferson Dill took a stack of newspapers to Rosie, the relevant passages ringed in red ballpoint.

Rosie found herself accused, at least by implication, of screwing Matthew Carver in order to sell him a yearling for twice its value. She over-reacted, as Mollie was said to have done. She rang Cragrock, demanded George Whyte, spoke instead to a chintzy-voiced secretary; her tongue, never rusty from disuse, was lubricated by medicinal brandy, taken for the shock of reading the newspapers. When at last she hung up, Jefferson Dill derisively applauded her invective. Peach heard clapping as he had not heard voices. He raised his eyes from contemplation of the zip in the front of his pants, rendered visible by the distension of his paunch, and asked why Jefferson was beating his hands together. Rosie called Matthew at home, and told him to come to Fox Hill immediately.

It was not absolutely convenient for Matthew to leave home immediately.

Rosie said, 'Beausoleil's running a temperature.'

Matthew said he would come at once.

Hanging up, Rosie was a little aghast. She glanced at Peach. She was not interested in the opinions of the others. But mention of Beausoleil had returned Peach to contemplation of his zipper, and lesser matters were excluded from the awesome deliberations of his brain.

214

Matthew's relief, finding Beausoleil in perfect health, almost dissolved his annoyance.

He had asked friends to stay, people not rich or important but ancient friends of his family. He had put them off, almost at the moment of their starting, with an excuse which he now knew to be false. It was a disagreeable thing to have done, and for them a great disappointment. They were people who seldom got away, seldom saw the country, never had a servant making their beds or waiting at table.

Matthew should have been angry with Rosie. But Beausoleil was fine. Rosie was fine. Rosie, night and shameless morning, was a wriggling miracle of joy.

Rosie planned revenges. She planned the punishment of George Whyte.

'This Whyte has slandered me, and you, and the farm, and Ed Lindsey, and Meadowsweet, and Lord Primrose, and the yearling. Why is he called Whyte? I call him black. He is dirty grey. He is a vulgar yellow, a sickening puce. He is the colour of shit. I sentence him to be drowned in the shit that he talks. I sentence him to eat his own words. I sentence him to sit through *Circe's Island*. I sentence him to discuss modern painting with Cousin Thalia the whole of a hot week, in a subway station. I sentence him to go hunting barefoot with Viola's bassets. I sentence him to go to bed with Scruffy Lucas. I sentence him to be driven in a car by Peach along the Skyline Drive in a snowstorm. I sentence him to buy Jefferson Dill's drinks for the rest of his life. I sentence you to sharing my bath.'

'It was crazy, real funny, something *else*,' said Doris Bernard to Alicia.

Alicia was changing for dinner. Doris had come in to borrow a belt. George, Jean, Alice and Ghalib had gone for drinks with a neighbour.

Doris imitated the slurred Virginia voice on the telephone, exaggerating the accent but not the language. Alicia, grown up, laughed at the four-letter words. Doris, helpless with laughter too, clutched at the girl, who was wearing only a silk robe after her tub. Doris contrived that they collapsed together, laughing, on to Alicia's bed. Doris herself was wearing only a robe. Nobody could be frightening who was laughing so much; nobody could be frightened.

'Oh God,' said Alicia, 'it's horrible. It's disgusting. Stop. Please stop.'

She was crying. She was shuddering from the strength of her sensation.

'More?' whispered Doris.

'Yes.'

Hal Whyte took a different car and went to a different party. His was on the southern edge of Lexington, near the University. He was a little young for the party, and for the drinks they served. On the way home he went off a bridge into a creek. Some people brought him home with a crack on the head but nothing broken. There was no point in bringing the car home, after it had been winched out of the creek. Twittering, tactful, discreet, forgetting nothing, saying all the right things to all the right people, Doris Bernard dealt with the wreck of the car and the damage to the bridge, and got medical certificates comparing the effects of concussion with drunkenness. Jean was truly grateful. Doris was a treasure.

After his first fright, George Whyte was angry. The wrecked car was imported and expensive, and the insurance did not cover Hal. Worse, much worse: a wild teenager wrecking cars was publicity of the very worst kind — quite as bad in its way as Mollie Carver's mouthings. People might picture Hal screeching around Cragrock in a Jaguar, hitting horse-vans, hitting broodmares; they'd picture a raffish kind of establishment, ill-disciplined, casual, a bad risk. There was nothing Lee V. Lowe could do.

'Is that all you can say?' said Jean. 'Is that the sum of your reaction to an accident, to your own son, which could have been fatal?'

'It is not the *sum* of my reaction,' said George. 'It is simply an aspect which I am bound to consider."

This reply so angered Jean that she went into Lexington herself, and bought a gold, imported, perpetual, wafer-thin, everything-proof wristwatch as a Christmas gift for Will Stevens. She gave it to him, saying, 'Now. Anyplace. Standing up, if you like.'

Will hid the watch, but Mary Jane his wife found it.

'I get it,' she said, without absolute certainty. 'Finally I get it.'

Will was frightened of the mischief Mary Jane could make. She herself was not getting her rations. She'd be mad as a bee if she knew somebody else was getting her share of prick. If she really knew that. She thought she owned his prick. She said so. She'd ruin him, and Jean, just out of spite, out of jealousy.

Will said the watch was a gift from some of the owners of mares which had visited Cragrock, last breeding season. The mares were in foal, they were grateful to Will, they showed it this way. It was a normal thing, to give a farm manager a nice gift when your mare was tested in foal. Will was hiding the watch from himself, not from Mary Jane. He was hiding it so as to surprise himself at Christmas. He said he didn't know exactly which owners, which mares; he said the card had dropped out of the package.

'You find out which owners,' said Mary Jane. 'Find out and tell me. I want to thank them.'

She didn't want to thank them. She wanted to check up on Will's story. It was a pretty good story. It could have happened just the way he said. He'd been given a lot of things, pens, gold chains, a silver cream pitcher, by the grateful owners of mares. Mary Jane couldn't disbelieve him out of hand, but she didn't believe him either.

Will promised to find out which owners had sent the watch, so that Mary Jane could thank them next time they came to Cragrock.

'Or else,' said Mary Jane, 'the bomb will go up, but good.'

The approach of Christmas: of the night of the Fox Hill Theatricals. Matthew had to stay for the performance. It would have been unfriendly in the last degree, to his new friends, not to do so. He was begged to do so, by Rosie, by Miss Viola Biggs, by Hazel. Peach did not forbid his staying, or openly deplore his presence. It was possible that the ham was in conflict with the Virginian castellan.

Voices called Matthew home, but they were not as strong as Rosie's arms around him.

Voices called him to Cragrock, too — Jean's voice, Alice's, and Ghalib's, attempting the telephone. In the bedlam preceding the performance, messages were more certainly undelivered than usual. Hazel, on a sustained dramatic high, was in no mood to be bothered with messages. Rosie took one of the calls. Usually she let the telephone ring itself to sleep, unless Hazel answered it. But expecting a call from the sanitorium, from Tim's doctor, she picked it up. A cool voice said it was Jean Whyte, from Kentucky, from Cragrock, making a fifth attempt to contact Mr Matthew Carver. Scenting danger, Rosie became an ultra-Hazel, crooning the patois of some remote antebellum plantation. The message was that Mr Carver should come at once to Cragrock, as Prince Ghalib was there and anxious for a meeting. Rosie said that she would tell Mistuh Cahvuh dat de Pinch Gah wuz tuh Cabrank yonduh tuh Kaintuck. She did not do so, though she had liked Ghalib.

All could perhaps have been well, on the night of the performance. An audience arrived in adequate numbers, full of curiosity and goodwill. This was the reward of sedulous advance publicity. Many Virginia newspapers had carried stories, given to them by Jefferson Dill, about his historical researches and his happy discovery; some had quoted verbatim the affable paragraphs in the hunt history. All welcomed the rebirth of the Fox Hill Theatricals. A national news-magazine, alert to the desire of America to rediscover its roots, to celebrate its traditions, actually sent a reporter and a photographer to a rehearsal. They were made very welcome, but their story was killed. The editor thought it was cruel. It would have forewarned the audience, some of whom would have been less eager to see the performance, some more so.

There was no stage. A stage had been designed and commissioned, but not built. The carpenter said he was owed too much money already, to give Mr Collin hundreds of dollars worth of timber. His pick-up had also been run into. This circumstance was not, of itself, fatal. People could see. This circumstance was, perhaps, fatal.

A semicircle arranged itself, seventy-odd people, variously dressed, uncomfortably close together in little chairs hired from far away. Those in the centre of the semicircle had their backs to the great front door. They faced the arc of tall doors which led into the principal rooms, the lovely doors which should have been covered in leather, the sad doors with their festoons of perished hide hanging like election posters weeks after an election. Props dotted the area in front of the doors, incongruous, their purpose no doubt to be explained as the action developed — a laundry basket, old as a tree and big as a cabin-trunk, a kitchen chair with a broken wickerwork seat, a camp cot, an Indian canoe, a chaise-longue with a fur thrown over it, a ruined top hat.

The audience studied its programmes. It had plenty of time to do so. The programmes were very smart, booklets with stiff covers, embossed on the front with the golden emblem of the Fox Hill Hunt, a monogram over crossed whips; inside was reprinted the account of the original Theatricals; followed by a historical essay, from the pen of Jefferson Dill, on Virginian social life at the beginning of the previous century, an extract from his forthcoming book; a preface to the play, pleading the precedent of Bernard Shaw but in manner obscure and mystical, from the same hand; a note on the nature of allegory, which associated the work of Jefferson Dill with that of Jean Genêt and Ionesco; and at last the characters and cast. The cast-list should have been substantially amended, but the printers had not received the changes in time. A number of the players had dropped out, during the weeks of rehearsal, giving a variety of reasons. Several parts were in consequence doubled; the author himself was playing five minor characters as well as the role of Odysseus and the latter's alter ego, the skipper of a coaster from Algiers.

Two local reporters, comparing notes, compiled a list of those present. Rank and fashion were well represented. Initials and the like would be carefully checked before the names were printed. Matthew Carver was identified, and his name added to the list. He was sitting with Rick Field, the Fox Hill farm manager. Both looked attentive, apprehensive. Rick Field had a drink from a flask.

The audience waited, rumps shifting in the hard little chairs. Conversation swelled from hum to babble. People stood and stretched. People wondered what to do with cigarette-ends.

Raised voices could be heard beyond one of the tattered doors. A scream could be heard, cutting through the hubbub of the audience. It was a womanish scream, but the voice was male. Some of those present recognized it as that rare sound, Peach's scream. A second scream really was a woman's. It was Rosie's scream, unmistakable, a scream not of terror but of rage. There were other screams. Matthew thought one of them came from Miss Viola Biggs of Mount Malcolm. Rick Field thought one of them was Janice's. They might have been screams of laughter or excitement. Janice's scream sounded to Rick like one of hysterical excitement. It was a drunken scream. She was not a girl who held her liquor.

The dining-room door opened and closed quickly. The volume of screaming rose, then fell. It was a stage entry. Someone had appeared. The action had begun. Few of the audience were aware of this, since people were facing in other directions, many standing up, some strolling. The person on stage was classically robed, bearded. From the programme he could be identified as Odysseus. He stood uncertainly in the midst of the props, looking at the backs of the audience's heads, listening to the noise they were making. People who had noticed his entrance nudged others who had not; people resumed their seats; silence almost fell.

Odysseus got into the canoe, and mimed the action of paddling. Anybody could see he was a voyager, travelling somewhere.

Another door opened, from the library. Conversation could be heard through the open door, voices raised in dispute, but not screams. The noise was that of a drunken altercation which stopped just short of screaming. Two persons entered, robed. They were Chorus. Members of the audience looked at their programmes, and murmured the word 'Chorus'. Some recognized the newcomers, and told others that the man was Joe Cummings, the woman Marcia Ladbroke. People told other people that Joe's younger boy had a glue-sniffing problem, and that Marcia and Barty Ladbroke were on the verge again. The Chorus said, antiphonally, that Odysseus was nearing an unknown island, that he hungered and thirsted and needed sleep. They were pretty clear in their diction. Everybody could hear them and understand them, though the language was fancy. Odysseus passed the back of his hand across his brow, and groaned. You could tell he was hungry and thirsty and tired. Everything was straightforward so far. It was dull, but there were no problems.

Odysseus got out of his canoe. It was to be assumed that he had landed. The assumption was generally made by the audience, and remarked upon. A lot of the audience had had a few drinks before they came, and some had brought flasks.

Odysseus searched around. He shaded his eyes with his hand and looked this way and that. He seemed not to see the Chorus, or the chaise-longue.

The dining-room door opened. A figure backed through it, leaving it open. This was considered a curious stage entry (many people said so) and concealed the actor's identity.

Not from Matthew. His heart lurched with love and with undiminishing lust as Rosie backed on to the stage, draped in a bed-sheet and wearing a wreath of laurel askew on her head.

She was going backwards because, though making her entry into the drama, she was continuing an offstage conversation. She said, 'You fat toad, you pompous incompetent, you're not fit to pick up his shit.'

She glanced over her shoulder, saw Odysseus, and said, 'Hi.'

To the open door she said, 'If you don't like my house-guests, go live in the hog-house. Eat candy till you vomit.'

Over her shoulder she said, 'Wayfarer, welcome. Who and how are you?'

Peach stood in the open door, though the programme suggested that his appearance was premature. He was dressed in pyjamas, with a lampshade on his head. He screamed, simply screamed, wordlessly.

'I have ploughed a puzzle-furrow through the wine-dark sea,' said Odysseus, 'Zig and zag, hither and yon, until the arching stars spell weariness.'

'Slut! Catamite!' screamed Peach.

Hands, several hands, tried to pull him backwards through the door. He lurched forward, pulling with him Hazel and Janice Field. Hazel was wearing a lace cap, Janice a satin dress split to the waist and revealing a black garter. Peach screamed at Rosie and she screamed back. Odysseus said something, but his voice was drowned. Peach shook off Janice, but Hazel still clung to the jacket of his pyjamas. Hazel screamed at Peach to go lie down. Peach turned and slapped her. He tried to slap Rosie. Odysseus took his arm. Jefferson Dill was tiny beside Peach, tiny and stringy beside that height and that paunch. Peach hit Dill in the midriff and sent him sprawling. Rosie dodged a blow from Peach, tripped over the top hat, and fell backwards. She was a little drunk. Peach was drunk. Hazel and Janice Field were drunk.

Peach screamed down at Rosie, unintelligibly, garbled filth. He picked up the kitchen chair. He raised it, as though to smash it down on her head. She crawled out of the way. Twenty people, thirty, crowded forward from the audience to restrain Peach. He battled with them, screaming, flailing the chair. He was buried under people.

Jefferson Dill struggled to his hands and knees. He knelt,

sobbing and retching. Rosie was sobbing, and screaming between sobs. That was the last Matthew saw. He could take no more. There were people laughing.

CHAPTER 11

Clare longed to go to Tipperary. Tom was camping in the half-furnished dower house, cooking most of his own meals, probably starving, probably poisoning himself, sleeping in damp sheets and wearing socks with holes. Clare was needed there, but she couldn't go there. He had to think of his family. So, now, did she. And there was the question of local public opinion. He must be respected in the community.

Beside and beyond all that, Clare had to be with her mother for Christmas. Jamie was going away, going with a friend to Italy. Liz continued to be unreachable. Somebody had to be with their mother on Christmas morning. It would be terrible for a mother of three children to wake up all alone in a flat, have solitary meals all day, go to bed without anybody to say goodnight to.

Clare's London friends did not tell her what was being said about her father. She was bound to hear in the end, and she did. Nearly all that was being said was being said by Cousin Alaric Wincham, the present Viscount, in defence of his family. Clare scarcely knew Lord Wincham. He scarcely knew her father. That did not stop him saying that Carver was a sponge, a millionaire's hanger-on, a blatant adulterer, and a man so cowardly that he let his wife fight his battles for him. Many people in England knew Clare's father well enough to dismiss all of this (except the adultery), but obviously there were far more who did not, even among the relevant group, the world of racing and horsebreeding, even among people who had heard of Matthew Carver, read about him, seen him interviewed on television. There was no reason for such people to disbelieve what Wincham said, to question it for a second. Carver was married to Wincham's cousin. It was stable information, bound to be reliable. It was all repeated as fact by people who had never met Carver.

Clare was very angry, but there was nothing she could do about it. It was not the occasion for another press conference.

Jamie came home for a day, to pick up his passport and some clothes. He apologised for not having presents for his mother and Clare. He said he would get them something in Italy. Clare thought he looked tired and sick, but her mother saw nothing wrong.

Jamie was shown all the horses at the Razza della Stellazura. He nearly died of fatigue and boredom, looking at mares and foals and yearlings. It was a necessary courtesy to his host, to Ottaviano di Vianello, who would not have believed that Matt Carver's son could fail to be interested in horses. Jamie failed in many ways, but not in politeness. He used good manners as a lubricant, sliding through life. He admired and imitated his father's manners, having observed their effect on people. In this spirit he suffered himself to be led from loose-box to loose-box, paddock to paddock; and in this spirit he listened with a straight face to the conte's accent and diction, though Mario his son was embarrassed by them.

'This is the Marie Lloyd of the whole bleedin' cast,' said Ottaviano, pointing to a mare heavily in foal, in a paddock for an hour's sunshine. 'She crosses the ocean in the spring.'

'Oh yes,' said Jamie. He was beginning to catch Mario's eye and read there the message he was sure was in his own. Fix time neared.

'She goes to Beausoleil,' said Ottaviano. 'You know all about that, in course.'

'In course,' said Jamie gravely, having never heard of Beausoleil and thinking it was a place.

Mario told him later what Ottaviano was paying to have his mare covered by Beausoleil. Jamie was shocked. He turned the dollars into pounds and calculated the number of fixes they would buy. A lifetime of happiness: and it was all being spent on one horse fucking another. Jamie thought the adult scale of values ridiculous.

The Happy Valley Commune was successfully evicted from Notting Hill Gate by the owner of the property. Liz and her friends found a derelict house in Camberwell, south of the river, an area into which Liz had never set a foot. It seemed all right to

224

her. It wasn't her mother's flat. Nearby were the heavy West Indian and Asian settlements of Brixton, a place of unemployment, despair and frequent violence, into which the National Front and its skinheads made murderous raids. Liz made money when she or the mothers and babies needed it. She bought a Christmas card for her sister Clare whom, though a creature from another planet, she rather liked. She gave it to her boyfriend Ali to post. He dropped it somewhere in Peckham High Street.

They draped paper streamers through some of the rooms of the house, over the politico-religious objections of the Wykehamist, and Liz bought a turkey.

Fay Candy draped paper streamers through the downstairs rooms of the Carver Place, because Mrs Mollie had done so when the children were small. No tradition founded by Mrs Mollie was ever allowed to lapse.

The dusty, tatty paper decorations depressed Matthew. They increased his loneliness. He understood that Clare had to stay in London, but he missed her very much.

He missed Rosie very much. Years of sleeping alone had adjusted him to sleeping alone, but nights with Rosie had torpedoed all stoicism. It was miserable to wake up and find an empty pillow beside his pillow.

In his mind's ear rang the derisive laughter of the audience at the Fox Hill Theatricals.

Dame Ninette, Matthew's own mare by the great Northern Dancer, was due to have a very early foal. It was lucky that she lived where she did. She might have been in England. A January foal was a bad idea in the bitter east winds of Newmarket, but it was all right in the gentler Kentucky winter. Earlier foals made possible the July sales at Keeneland; European yearlings waited until the fall to be led out in front of buyers. This was one of the advantages of breeding horses in America; one of the arguments for bringing Beausoleil across the Atlantic.

Dame Ninette could foal at home, and go at once to Fox Hill to breed; or go there to foal, and go to Beausoleil as soon as she came in use. Either way she would be one of his first mares; probably his very first. This was a fortunate chance. She was exceptionally placid, taking everything as it came with flapping ears and a tranquil eye. She was experienced, at stud since she was four, used to breeding with all kinds of stallions. She was an ideal personality for Beausoleil's first experience in the breeding-shed. It would not be a good idea to face an aggressive young stallion with a frightened maiden mare. But Dame Ninette would make it easy for him, and make the whole breeding season easier for everybody.

At Fox Hill some of the hangovers lasted until Christmas Eve. Not Rosie's. She took a lot of exercise and breathed a lot of fresh air. She saddled up old Corporal and went for long rides. She ran after the Mount Malcolm Basset Hounds. Her skin was as clear as a petal and she was bursting with energy. She felt reborn. Love was good for her. She missed Matthew terribly. She was joyful that Beausoleil would bring him back in the spring.

Peach's jags were infrequent and disastrous. The after-effects were like a lingering death. He took no exercise and breathed no fresh air; he had no golden memories and no blazing hopes. Oblivion covered for him the night of the Theatricals, the hours preceding the performance, the lurching hours afterwards, the delirium and the collapse into coma. He was aware of headache and nausea. He ascribed them to disease, virus, brought into his home by strangers, probably ill-bred bugs from Kentucky brought by the man Carver. He denied having drunk anything, since it was generally known that he never did drink anything. Stories to the contrary were the fabrications of the malicious, of Rosie turned shrew, of Rosie turned against him, her brother, her lord, by the execrable Carver, the swine who cheated poor sick Tim.

Poor sick Tim was fetched out of the sanitorium to spend Christmas at Fox Hill. A nurse came with him, a woman called Beth of uncertain age and remorseless jollity. Before their arrival, all drinks had to be hidden away. Liquor was the one thing that lit in Tim the spark of animation. But the spark did not stop there. It became a bush-fire. Beside his mindless violence then, the efforts of Peach at violence were feeble, spinsterish. Peach might raise a chair, but he was unlikely to hit anybody with it. Tim was apt to run at you with a carving knife. Rosie locked up all the liquor, and hid the key. It was annoying for Jefferson Dill, whose own post-Theatricals hangover had been a thing of epic proportions, an experience to wring the heart of a statue with pity and terror.

Without drink, Tim sat as apathetically at Fox Hill as in his

226

bright room in the sanitorium.

'You're home with your folks,' cried Beth, who had changed from her uniform into what she called mufti, a caramel woollen dress and a garnet brooch. 'Look lively, sailor! Crack a yarn and a smile! I always say there's no cloud so dark but a person can see a silver lining.'

'I am sick, nurse,' said Peach, 'of a virulent distemper. What physic has the pharmacopoeia to minister to the throbbing of my temples?'

'Alka-Seltzer,' said Beth, with an indulgent laugh that went through Peach's head like a hacksaw.

He groped his way angrily out of the room, and went to his thinking chair in his thinking room. He peeled a bar of chocolate-covered caramel; but even as he raised it to his lips his nausea returned. He dropped the candy. It rolled, stickily gathering fluff. He disdained to stoop for it. He let it lie. He blamed Rosie for the way he felt, for the pitiable condition of Tim, for the reported fiasco of *Circe's Island* which he himself had been too sick to prevent, even to remember. He blamed Rosie for Beth's laugh.

He told her so, at what would have been the cocktail hour.

Rosie had been taking a nap, earned by hours of cutting back undergrowth in the artificial dell in the wild-garden: a nap she would have shared with Matthew. The sharpness of her desire sharpened her temper. Guilt, too. To long for her lover with her husband in the house gave her a twisted feeling, a sick feeling. Peach's pompous maunderings were more than she could bear.

The argument began at six-thirty on Christmas Eve, and continued throughout dinner. The nub, to which Peach again and again returned with the infuriating pertinacity of a mosquito, was Matthew Carver. Tim sat up there at the table with them, pushing his food about on his plate. He took no part in the argument. Beth misunderstood the argument, which was conducted in allusive terms because Tim was there. She thought Peach and Rosie were disputing about some game in which each accused the other of cheating.

'Least said soonest mended,' cried Beth, always one for doing her bit. 'Kiss and make up, you two! It's Christmas Eve, you know! Don't you agree, Mr Dill? I say it's the season of goodwill.'

'Kiss and muck up,' said Jefferson Dill, who had not forgiven anybody for his theatrical failure, but who was not leaving. 'Kiss and fuck up. Piss and cock up. The season of ill-will. The season of ill Dill.'

'Somebody ought to be writing this down,' said Rosie.

'Somebody will,' said Cousin Thalia.

'Ill-will,' said Jefferson Dill.

'You folks are all too clever for me,' said Beth.

'Yes,' said Peach.

At nine-forty-five a man arrived at the door, a little old man in blue work-clothes.

'Come to do the doors,' he said.

'Not now,' said Rosie.

'As you say, ma'am, as you say. Eff'n I doan do you now, I woan fit you in for a year. All my leather out yonder in the truck. Give me a hand, you-all. Tacks in the barr'l. I'll need my shears an' my ladder an' I'll thank *you*, ma'am, for a little mo' light.'

He had a tool which removed the old tacks from the doors. With them came the tattered festoons of leather. The tacks fell out of the perished leather, and presently hundreds littered the floor of the hall. Rosie, Peach, Cousin Thalia, Jefferson Dill, Hazel and Beth stood at the expert's shoulder or at the foot of his ladder, two or three or more at a time. The soles of their shoes filled up with brass-headed tacks, so that they clacked over the floorboards like tap-dancers. They advised the workman. Jefferson Dill, in witty vein, talked of tacks, tax, taxis, doors, boars, bores, boors. Beth said he was too clever for her. Peach and Rosie continued to quarrel about Matthew Carver, which they could do more explicitly once Beth had put Tim to bed.

By midnight all the doors had been purged of old tacks and leather. By one a.m. the new pieces of leather had been cut to size and hung in position. It was now time for the new tacks to go in, in their geometrical patterns, in their thousands. The banging of the hammer was magnified by the resonant acoustics of the hall. Tock-tock: bam-bam-bam-bam-*bam*, that was the cadence of each tack, two light blows to position it, five heavy ones to drive it home through the leather and firmly into the wood. Throughout the small hours of Christmas morning, the merry hammer-blows rang through Fox Hill, echoing up the stairs and along the passages, and into all the bedrooms of the mansion.

Epaminondas Makropulos, that Christmas morning, ate fruit and drank coffee on his private Aegean island, a place of rocks and aromatic herbs. His villa was simple, and his life there. He tried to use the place for a few weeks every year. He often lent villa and island and servants to friends, but he seldom asked friends when he himself was there. The solitude was what he wanted, the time to sit and think.

Epi had been amused, at Fox Hill, to see Peach sitting and thinking. He was amused to find he had anything in common with that eccentric gorger of candy-bars. Epi did not have Peach's almost unlimited time for sitting and thinking, because he was very busy; but he made *some* time, and used it. He thought about God, art, nature, politics, his friends, his business and his horses. His extraordinary memory made reference books unnecessary. If he wanted information to assist thought, or had decisions to communicate to his staff, he used the radio-telephone. The island was only 250 kilometres from Athens, almost all sea. Reception was good.

Among subjects for thought on Christmas morning were the mating plans for his mares. Many decisions had been taken but few finalised, because of shortage of time for thinking. Thought finalised them, subject to the sending of messages and the signing of cheques.

Epi decided to send two of his mares, already in Virginia, to Beausoleil. He could see the pedigrees, unrolling back through the generations like a scroll; he could see the inbreeding and outbreeding and nicks. He was pleased to patronise Beausoleil, unproved though he was, and pleased the horse was in Virginia. He would sell his remaining nominations, though the sales would be subject to approval of the mares by Matthew Carver. Epi was glad this hurdle existed: it would have the effect, with reasonable luck and over a period, of enhancing Beausoleil's value. From all points of view Epi was glad Matt was managing Beausoleil.

One of the nominations would go to Ralph Hadfield at Newmarket. Epi knew which mare was involved. He knew Matt knew. Approval was automatic, and not because Hadfield was who he was. Epi thought that, having sent the mare to Virginia, Ralph Hadfield might leave her there for a few seasons. Ralph did not *have* to worry about the cost of transport, but he *did* worry about it. He called it being careful, but Epi called it being silly. Epi pitied any man who allowed himself to worry needlessly. It did not make for happiness. It inhibited passionless, purposeful thought.

For lunch Epi ate a red mullet and drank mineral water. As he ate he pondered a metaphysical problem, not new but not solved either: how could the foreknowledge of events by God, a basic tenet in any serious theistic position, be reconciled with human free will, a basic tenet in any respectable philosophical position whatever? Epi thought about the point in relation to his own life and to the fate of empires. He concluded that free will was usually a delusion, as coincidence was almost always a delusion, but that he himself had made *some* decisions which God could not have foreseen except in terms of overwhelming mathematical probability.

This started a further line of thought, with which Epi occupied part of Christmas afternoon: foreknowledge forbids surprise. Was it possible to believe that God was never surprised? Would life, even an eternal and divine life, even an omnipotent and all-loving life, be tolerable without surprise?

Meditating about the quality of surprise, Epi concluded that he had not given enough people enough nice surprises for Christmas. He listed beneficiaries in his mind, confident of remembering the list until his office opened after the break.

Christmas and the days after Christmas, in many parts of the world, were full of thoughts like the Christmas morning thoughts of Epaminondas Makropulos on his island: though horse-breeders were rare who thought along the lines on which, at lunch and in the afternoon, he had indulged a taste for vague and useless speculation about the capacity of the Divinity to be astonished.

Luis Valdes chose two mares to be sent to Fox Hill to mate with Beausoleil. They were called Papagena and Leonore, after two of his favourite characters in opera. Luis amused himself (aware that he was counting chickens, tempting Providence) by considering names. Beausoleil out of Papagena, if a colt, must surely be Sarastro, high-priest of the cult of sunlit enlightenment, ally of Papagena in the salvation of her bird-catcher. It was possible the name could be registered, at least in Venezuela. Firebird would do for a filly, ballet instead of opera but nicely derived from the breeding, most unlikely to be available anywhere. Fidelio had to be the first choice for a colt Beausoleil x Leonore. For a filly he might better look at that other Leonora, the one in *Forza del Destino*. Even Forza *tout simple*, perhaps. Only it sounded as though bred by Forli . . .

Ghalib al-Jilani spent Christmas in a Lexington hotel, not wishing to observe unbelievers celebrating the birth of One whom they believed God and he knew to be only one among many preliminary prophets, with a message of pacificism and humility emphatically denied by the Prophet. Nor did he wish to intrude on a family party at what he knew, though he had never seen it, to be a significant occasion.

He went then to visit Matthew Carver, who had declined with what appeared to be regret an invitation to Cragrock. Was it regret? Did he have to stay at home? Was he still angry with George Whyte, for those incautious remarks about the Lord Primrose yearling? Was the collaboration seriously threatened, and Cragrock to be denied the value of Matthew's judgement? Ghalib was anxious to know how things stood; Alice Harding, in his confidence to a qualified extent, was anxious to know.

Ghalib did not really find out, although the men got on well enough, and had plenty to talk about. Matthew Carver was guarded. He would not be drawn to comment on what George Whyte was said to have said, or on what his own wife had said. He was noncommittal when Ghalib suggested that George Whyte did *not* trust his own judgement of horseflesh — was right not to trust it.

In order to use his shares in Beausoleil, Ghalib intended buying mares privately in time for the breeding. This seemed to him a better idea than selling nominations, although his decision plainly surprised Matthew Carver. Matthew was sure he could arrange for Ghalib's mares to board at Fox Hill. He agreed to help find suitable mares, but declined to go into partnership with Ghalib in buying them. There was nothing personal in this; simply, he had already invested in bloodstock up to and even beyond a sensible limit. He had to keep some capital in stocks in order to provide an income to pay the bills.

Ghalib did not press the matter — he was too adroit a negotiator to make himself a bore by chasing the impossible — but he was disappointed. Inspection of Matthew Carver's unpretentious house and farm made him no less anxious to be the man's confederate. He pictured the response of the Duke of Hampshire, of the duc de Montfermainbrey, to Matthew's rooms and furniture, and to his barns and paddocks. Without effort he modelled his reaction on what he supposed theirs would be; he did not make the mistake that Henri de Cheminade, or Lord Goring, or even George Whyte might have made.

Ghalib went to Louisville, thence to Washington, thence to Shannon. He called Tom Kavanagh, and picked up a Hertz. He looked forward to the opening of the Ballycardeen airstrip, but that day was still far off. He drove through January weather as mild as Kentucky's. He remembered reading, as he went, that the Irish had never been good at skating: ice was rare and brief, thanks to the gulf stream. He could breed early foals in Tipperary.

Work at Ballycardeen was getting back into gear, after what Ghalib considered a Christmas break of preposterous length; but he depended on these people, and he was not about to try to rewrite their traditional calendar. The later stages of Ramadan, especially if it fell in midsummer, did awful things to productivity in his own country. That, of course, was the result of too little fluid, instead of too much.

Satisfied with progress as soon as progress was resumed, satisfied with Tom Kavanagh, Ghalib flew to London. He did business in London for two days. He called Clare Carver, not with invitation or proposition but to report on her father's well-being. His conversation with Mollie Carver, before she fetched Clare, was baffling. He thought she thought he was a reporter.

Clare would have been glad to see him, even to dine with him in some place sufficiently public; she would have liked more news of her father; she would have liked Ghalib's impression of how Tom was doing at Ballycardeen. But Ghalib had no time.

He had no time to see Lord Goring, either, nor at this moment anything particular to discuss with him. He was not yet buying more broodmares for Ballycardeen, and when he did he wanted Tom Kavanagh fully involved.

In Paris he had neither time to see, nor anything particular to discuss with, Henri de Cheminade.

Henri knew Ghalib was in Paris. He called Robert Goring. Goring did not know Ghalib had been in London. His intelligence was not as good as Henri's. It was obvious to the gentlemen of the Fille de l'Aire agency that their business was being cut out from under them, and that Matthew Carver was doing the cutting.

Ghalib was reunited with his private jet. He underwent an air-change. As an embassy is the territory of the nation it represents, as a ship is the territory of the nation whose flag it flies, so Ghalib's jet was Arabia. Whatever electrical implements cleaned it, whatever aerosols drenched its air, it smelled of the streets and suqs and shuttered palaces. No alcohol was carried. Women were veiled. If the stewards were not slaves, the line was a fine one. The passenger cabins — male and female — were luxurious to a degree Ghalib knew to be absurd. He neither liked nor disliked it; both as a mode of travel and as an instrument of public relations, the jet was simply a tool of business.

It was a tool pickled in the spices of the Gulf, and Ghalib changed out of his English tweeds and his French silk underwear. Nothing he put on instead — drawers, long shirt, caftan and girdle — was of silk. 'Whoever wears a silken garment in this world shall not wear it in the next.' The Sultan of Oman was said to have bought several hundred silk shirts in one morning, and to wear them at home. The Omanis were lax. Their women went unveiled. No wonder God had not rewarded them with oil.

The hour was *zuhr,* the beginning of the decline of the sun at midday, second of the five times appointed for prayer. 'Oh believers,' says the Koran, 'when you prepare yourselves for prayer, wash your faces and hands up to the elbow, and wipe your heads and your feet to the ankles.' Ghalib went a good deal further, obeying the exact traditional rules for the ablution before prayer: he washed his hands three times; rinsed his mouth three times, by throwing water into it with his right hand; three times threw water up his nostrils, snuffing it up and then blowing it out with his nose held ritually between the thumb and forefinger of his left hand; washed his face three times, throwing up water with both hands; three times washed each forearm; wetted his head with his right hand; twiddled his forefingers into his ears, wiping the backs of his ears with his thumbs; wiped his neck; washed his feet, prodding meticulously between the toes. He intoned the traditional prayers while washing. As he rinsed his nostrils he said, as best he could while inhaling and expelling water, 'Oh my God, if I am pleasing in Thy sight, perfume me with the odours of Paradise.'

Through long practice, Ghalib performed the whole ceremony of his ablutions in less than three minutes.

He stood for the first part of his prayers, facing the nose of the aircraft, facing Mecca. He repeated the obligatory and several discretionary chapters of the Koran. He dropped to his knees to say, 'God is great,' he touched his nose, then his forehead, to the carpet of the cabin while extolling the holiness of God. He remained on his knees, in various prescribed positions, during the rest of his prayers, which ended in a protracted supplication quoted from the Koran.

Now that he had re-assumed his central, his Arab identity, nothing would have seduced Ghalib from his duty of prayer, one of the three central rites of Islam, with the observance of the fast of Ramadan and the pilgrimage to Mecca.

When he had finished his prayers he washed again, hands and mouth and nose, because it was time to eat. He sat on a small carpet, and they placed bowls of spiced meat and pieces of bread on a cloth in front of him: for Qatadah said that Anas said that the Prophet did not eat off a table, as was the manner of proud men, who did it to avoid bending their backs. He ate barefooted, as he had prayed, using only three fingers of his right hand, careful neither to swallow too rapidly nor masticate too long, careful to drink without unseemly noise. He licked his fingers when he had finished, as commanded in the scriptures, and then again washed his hands, mouth and nostrils.

Halat al Bhudi had existed over unrecorded centuries on pearl fishing and nomadic herding, with a little trade in slaves from Africa and qat from the Yemen. When pearls became harder to find and harder to sell, about 1930, the country became poor beyond any western imagining. Some years five inches of rain fell; five or ten years could go by with no rain at all.

Maps showed a frontier with Saudi Arabia.

Ghalib's grandfather succeeded in 1931, one of ninety-three male members of a royal family which had established itself at an uncertain date by means of violence and fraud. The royal revenue was derived entirely from harbour and customs charges, and was less than £40,000 a year. Attempts by British and American companies to prospect for oil were forbidden; so were most visitors and all journalists. The Emir had over 300 black African slaves. There was no school. The one small hospital was run by American Baptist missionaries.

The old Emir died under unexplained circumstances in 1950, to be succeeded by one of his fifty-three legitimate sons (those sired on slave-girls were thought to number 500). The new ruler consented to exploration. Oil was immediately found and almost immediately exported. The unimaginable wealth which then poured into the country came just in time for Ghalib's education; and he was adult just in time to take advantage of it. His first major entrepreneurial coup was the placing of the contract for the first desalinisation plant, which made possible market-gardening in the countryside behind the capital. He did well out of that, too. The capital itself was transformed at dizzy speed from a mud-walled village into a concrete city with twelve-lane highways, skyscrapers, huge schools and hospitals and laboratories, a university, art galleries, parks, an international airport, all so far beyond the needs of the tiny indigenous population that only the armies of immigrant Pakistani workers made sense of them. Ghalib was the man in the middle when many of the contracts were placed.

Some of the Pakistanis were given citizenship of Halat al Bhudi, in order to raise the population to the minimum which qualified the country for membership of the United Nations. Ghalib contrived to be offered the post of Permanent Representative, because his wife wanted to try life in New York. But in the event he declined the appointment. It meant a dramatic drop in his income, and he did not want his wife in New York.

So gigantic was the oil revenue that even the scale of public works left a lot over. It was invested abroad, all over the world, in real property and in shareholdings in heavy industry, aerospace, arms, electronics, insurance, banking, shipping, gambling and other fields. Ghalib was crucial in the selection of many of the investments. The royal family owned a majority shareholding in hundreds of companies by 1980. They did not as a rule attempt to exert control or influence management; they would probably do so when the oil ran out about 1995 and the country became a rentier.

Sophisticated methods of budgeting, accountancy and communications were adopted by the Emir and his cabinet. No faintest whiff of democracy entered. The country became modern and remained medieval. In the Bedouin tradition, the Emir was readily approachable by any of his subjects. Not even Ghalib would have considered trying to make a profit from anyone exercising the right to make petition to the Emir; unless he was a foreign businessman. The law was as unchanged as the system: the Islamic code, exactly interpreted and exactly enforced. Larceny was, with certain prescribed exceptions, punished by the public striking off of the culprit's right hand at the wrist; highway robbery by the loss of hands and feet; robbery with murder by crucifixion; adultery by lapidation; fornication by a hundred lashes, alcohol by eighty. All these crimes were extremely rare.

Like nearly all his brothers and cousins, Ghalib built a marble palace, electronic as an automated factory. Like nearly all of them he imposed within it a régime of the strictest traditional orthodoxy. The harem faced on to an inner court, and had no windows on the world. In it were Ghalib's wife (his one wife) the lovely Fatima, her younger children and their servants. She was a woman of education, a product of the wealth and adventurousness which had produced Ghalib himself; but she was content, after the first disappointment of not going to New York. Ghalib's daughters would be content, too, although they had been sent to Heathfield or Benenden.

Viewed from that inner court, after evening prayer at the hour of *maghrib*, life in the west seemed infinitely distant and barely credible. It was difficult for Ghalib to accept that he had himself made an unambiguous sexual approach to Rosie Phillipson; that Matthew Carver had conducted a flagrant affair with her under her own brother's roof. They were both married. They were committing a capital crime. Here they would be identically punished, except that she would be stoned to death having been buried up to her waist. Here, or in Saudi Arabia, or any other orthodox Arab country, her husband or her brother could without crime, without fear of the slightest disapproval, kill both man and woman. Could, and should. The laws of the Americans would, after such an act of honour, make life uncomfortable for the executioner; but Paradise would reward him.

Dame Ninette, Matthew's mare by Northern Dancer, was due to foal in the first week in February. Had Beausoleil been within an afternoon's van ride to and fro, she could have been separated from her foal for that length of time, visited the stallion, and returned from sex to motherhood. But 300 miles divided her from Fox Hill. Mare and foal could be vanned there together, but not when the foal was only three or four days old. It meant waiting one month or nearly two months, until her second or third heats after foaling, by which time her foal would be sturdy enough for the ordeal of the van ride. That would have been satisfactory — still a mid-March or early April cover, with time enough for a second visit if necessary — but Matthew decided to adhere to his original plan. Dame Ninette would go to Fox Hill long enough before she foaled to get used to the place and people, foal under the excellent new conditions and in the care of excellent people, and go to Beausoleil immediately, when she first came into season, after nine days. It was still a good idea that a sensible, docile, experienced mare should be his first bride. It was still a good idea that Matthew should put his horse where his mouth had been: he was urging a lot of other people to trust those facilities and those folks, and he ought to be seen to be trusting them himself. The Fox Hill boarding charges were reasonable. It seemed odd to outsiders that a mare should be treated as a foal-making machine — no sooner one out than another started — but the mares themselves were usually agreeable. Breeding and foaling were much more natural to them than racing.

Always a quiet lady, Dame Ninette became quieter, slower, more thoughtful as her eleven-month pregnancy reached its final stages. Undoubtedly she could feel her foal kicking and wriggling in her womb, but she showed no signs of minding. Some young first-time mares were puzzled or alarmed by the strange activity inside them, but Dame Ninette had been through it all before, season after season, and she stood cowlike in stall or paddock with a dreamy, inward-looking eye.

In mid-January she chugged over the mountains into Virginia. Chuck Mungo drove her. Matthew wondered what the Mungos, fanatical mother and son, would have made of Peach and the Fox Hill menagerie. Chuck would not make contact with any of that. He would judge Rosie, Rick Field and the rest by their handling of the mare. He would come back the same day, not because he was needed but to share his mother's prayers.

Most mares foal at night: perhaps because, when they were members of wild herds, they had at night the protection of their gathered fellows against predators. Rick Field was on duty. He thought tonight was the night. Dame Ninette, usually a slow but thorough feeder, ate only half her evening meal. She was unusually restless. She shifted about her stall, sometimes snatching a wisp of hay from the overhead rack, but strewing it about her straw bedding instead of eating it. It had become awkward for her to lie down and stand up again; she made no effort to do so. Rick watched her on the closed-circuit television screen in the grooms' room. He would be with her when she needed him; meanwhile she was best undisturbed. She turned her head to stare with a kind of impatient wonder at her distended flank. She pawed at her bedding. She was sweating lightly on her neck and between her forelegs.

She lay. Sometimes mares foal standing up, a bad idea and dangerous for the foal. But Dame Ninette lay sensibly, and the first membrane began to protrude. Rick was with her now, not interfering, a comforting presence. Inside the inflated membrane he saw the first tiny hoof, covered with the fungus-like sock which had protected the walls of Dame Ninette's womb against little sharp feet.

Dame Ninette struggled to her feet, which was illogical but normal. Like a dog she wanted a different place to lie, somehow better, more suitable, more comfortable. As she lay down again, in a place mysteriously chosen, the first membrane ruptured. Within the second Rick saw the other forefoot, more clearly, just behind the first. The serious labour began, and her muscles worked strenuously, slowly, rhythmically, and she grunted with effort and total concentration. The nose appeared, tight to the forefeet, and then the rest of the head, life, an expression, an independent personality. The thickest part of the foal had now to be pushed out, the shoulders and withers. Suddenly the entire foal, all but the hind feet, slid clear and lay glistening in the lamplight. Dame Ninette lay still for a moment, contented, recovering from the huge muscular effort of the birth, her nose buried in straw. She raised her head and turned to the little wet bundle behind her. She made a small, doting noise. The foal was a colt. He shook his head, seeming surprised that he had a head, that he could shake it, that he was alive. He gave a tiny cry, as though complaining that he had not asked to be born, to lie wet and bewildered on a bed of straw.

Mother and foal remained still. The foal's hind feet were still imprisoned. Rick was quiet, tactful, not wanting to disturb the mare, not wanting to get her on to her feet until she felt ready to stand. She was best judge of that. The foal was best judge of when he was ready to stand. The foal twitched his forefeet and tried to flap his ears. Presently Dame Ninette shifted, finally releasing her foal's feet. Slowly, tired, happy, she rose to her feet. She turned to the foal and licked it. She fondled it with her nose.

Fifty-seven minutes after the birth, the foal began to try to stand up. It looked impossible. His legs were grotesquely disproportionate to the rest of his body, and he had no idea how to use them. Suddenly he was up. The time was normal enough. He looked about, as though for ideas about what to do next. Seventy-one minutes after the birth, the mare delivered the afterbirth of placenta and membranes which had sustained the foal during pregnancy. Six minutes after that, instinct drew the foal's muzzle to the nipple, and he was feeding.

Rick Field had seen it all hundreds of times before, but he was still moved by the emergence of new life, by the tenderness of the mare and the clumsy, trusting gesture of the foal.

For two or three days the foal would be feeding on colostrum, the first milk after parturition. Dame Ninette might give him four or five gallons of it, richly nutritious and transferring to him her natural immunities to disease.

The foal dropped the nipple, staggered a stride or two, and lay down to sleep. Dame Ninette nuzzled him adoringly. Within half an hour he was up again, thrusting his nose under her belly. He was learning. He went confidently to the small nipple and seized it and sucked.

Rosie was down at the foaling barn at seven. She called Matthew at eight. He said he would come over for the breeding, Beausoleil's first, an event of crucial importance to the future of scores of millions of dollars. He raised a cup of coffee as he held the telephone, a temperate toast in celebration of Dame Ninette's foal.

Business and love jumbled on the line.

'Ninette has to wait nine days, but I can't, said Rosie.

'I have to leave everything here in a state to manage itself all spring,' said Matthew. 'But I'll come as quick as I can.'

'Quick as a bat, quicker than that,' said Rosie. 'I can't live without you.'

The weather was mild. After three days Dame Ninette and her foal were put out in a field, under Rick's eye. It was a brief outing, a bit of necessary education for the newcomer. The foal's instinct was to stay close to his dam, but he could become confused and attach himself to another mare. If he did that he risked being bitten or kicked by a mare at least as protective of her own foal as Dame Ninette was. Dame Ninette followed him when he was not following her. She covered far more ground than he did, placing herself between him and the other mares and foals, hovering protectively.

There was always a risk that a mare, having been kept immobile for days, could be desperate for freedom and exercise. They sometimes forgot their foals and roared off, bucking and screaming, their foals stumbling piteously after them. The foals' own dams, momentarily wild, sometimes kicked them because they tried to follow so close: sometimes fatally. Not Dame Ninette.

The foal tried to graze. His neck was too short and his legs far too long. He contrived to get his teeth to the grass by bending his forelegs, at knee and ankle, into something like a letter C, so that his back sloped at forty-five degress from rump to withers, and his nose decended to the turf between his forefeet. He continued to suckle with peremptory energy, beginning to demand as a right what he had groped for as a mysterious blessing, tickling Dame Ninette with his whiskery nose until she gave little screams. He grew almost visibly.

The veterinarian passed Dame Ninette fit for immediate breeding: there had been no complications at the birth and no infection after it.

Matthew came.

Rick Fields was sick. It was something he ate, or some virus he picked up. Rosie went to see him. He was in bed. He did look sick. Janice his wife had gone out to work, because he said that all he needed was rest and starvation. He couldn't keep down anything he ate or drank, he said, so no medication was any good to him. When Rosie said Beausoleil was about to breed, now this minute for the first time, Rick struggled out of bed. But he looked terrible and he was shaking. He was sweating, and his skin was a bad colour. He seemed to have a bad smell, although the Fields were respectable people who took a pride in cleanliness. Rosie ordered Rick back to bed and told him to stay there.

There was no problem. Matthew had been his own farm manager. He could be stallion man or groom. His father had brought him up to do anything on a horse farm. Rick would take over when he was well.

Old Corporal was used as the teaser. His job was to get Dame Ninette to show if she was in season, by exciting her sexually if she was in a state to be excited. She would show her readiness probably — not certainly, but probably — which would show that she was ovulating and could conceive. If the physical moment were not right, she would not only not conceive but also violently resist the whole process.

Corporal leaned in towards Dame Ninette, over a solid wooden barrier. He nuzzled her neck and shoulder. This was a moment to watch her closely. She might be as aggressively defensive as a militant spinster, if Corporal arrived too soon. She might kick men behind her and bite the old horse in front of her. She might be physically ready and hide the fact, out of what in a human could be prudery or embarrassment or bloody-mindedness.

Dame Ninette pricked her ears and responded swoonily to Corporal. She acted like a proper old whore. Just nine days after the birth of her foal, she was more than ready to start another. She seemed to go into a sort of erotic trance.

Her tail was bandaged. Luke Field, borrowed for the afternoon from Mount Malcolm, led her to the breeding shed. He twittered to her in an incongruous soprano, a little song that meant more to her than to any human listener. Her tail was held aside and she was swabbed down, to remove any risk of infection to what had become the most valuable part of Beausoleil. The twitch was put on her upper lip, a loop of leather on the end of a stick. Use of this was invariable, though by no means always necessary. Matthew fitted a leg-strap to the pastern of her near-fore — a half-inch webbing band on a brass D. With this she could be made to stand on three legs as the stallion mounted her, which stopped her kicking him. Dame Ninette had never kicked in her life, and the leg-strap had not been used on her for years; but this was not the time to omit any normal precaution. A kick in the testicles would not enhance Beausoleil's value. Boots to cover Dame Ninette's hind feet, and hobbles to strap her hind legs to her forelegs, were available, but Matthew decided against them. She might also have been bitted and bridled, but twitch and halter-rope would hold her.

Luke's brother John led Beausoleil from his barn to the breeding shed. Beausoleil's eye rolled and he arched his neck. He had no idea what he was there for. He was bitted. An eighteen-inch chain was clipped to the offside ring of the bit, and ran under his chin and through the near-side ring, like a curb-chain. Attached to it was a long strap of heavy leather, by which John held him. The end of the strap could be used as a whip. John led Beausoleil to Dame Ninette, who stood placidly. Matthew had bent her fetlock joint, raised her foot, and by tightening the leg-strap had tied the pastern back to the leg. She trembled a little. Beausoleil sniffed her, puzzled.

Sometimes stallions came roaring and prancing into the shed, leaped within seconds, and were finished before you could believe it. Sometimes even experienced horses sniffed and pondered for a long time before the penis stiffened.

A man on Dame Ninette's offside held her bandaged tail across her quarter. Beausoleil sniffed. After a long time her eagerness communicated itself to him. He became visibly excited. He pawed at the sand of the floor. At last he reared, enormous on his hind legs. He held Dame Ninette with his forelegs. She was held by twitch and halter, and her tail was held up and away. The moment Beausoleil's weight was on her, Matthew dropped the leg-strap, so that she had the use of all four legs. At the same moment he took the stallion's rein from John Field. John was free to whip or push Beausoleil, or to guide the inexperienced penis. He did all these things. Beausoleil roared. He clutched Dame Ninette and slobbered copiously over her neck and mane. He slipped backwards and off her. The cover had not worked. Dame Ninette's near fore was strapped up again and Beausoleil's strap returned to John Field. Beausoleil was hauled, pushed, urged. And at last, roaring and slobbering, he impregnated Dame Ninette. He had become awesomely noisy, aggressive, excited. He was a stallion. Dame Ninette's mane was full of froth from his mouth, and there were moon-shaped marks on her neck where he had bitten her.

His penis was swabbed clean and the swab thrown into a pail. John Field threw away his gloves. Dame Ninette's tail bandage was taken off and thrown away. John led Beausoleil away, back towards his stall. Beausoleil was relaxed. Luke took Dame Ninette back to her foal.

'He'll be a-rarin' t'go, nex' time,' said the man who had held Dame Ninette's tail.

He was already raking smooth the sand in the breeding shed, then brushing back from the concrete apron outside the sand which Beausoleil had kicked out. The trash was disposed of. Almost before the two horses had disappeared into their barns, the breeding shed was immaculate. Matthew was pleased. He had known to expect love and understanding of horses, but he had not expected this brisk efficiency and tidiness. It was good stablemanship and good public relations. The gigantic, childlike Field twins were perhaps not the best public relations, but they would be invaluable all spring. Matthew felt happier than ever before about the whole arrangement. After unnerving moments of doubt about his own motives, he was positive now that he had done the right thing by Beausoleil, by George Whyte and the other shareholders.

Beausoleil was normal. He might not turn out to be fertile, but at least he was not one of those occasional, heartbreaking stallions who never became interested in mares. If he had been, he might have gone back into training: perhaps to win more good races, but with his value reduced in minutes from $20,000,000 to $10,000.

Rick Field had crept out of bed to watch the breeding from a distance. He was disgusted with himself. He cursed and despised himself. He blamed his father and Viet Nam and Janice. He was not really yellow in most ways, about most things, with most horses. He was scared of Beausoleil. He thought Beausoleil knew it.

He could hide his fear if he kept clear of Beausoleil. He could walk tall with all other animals, with all men. But face him with that one, that killer, and it would show. Rick's imagination showed him technicolor close-ups of his head and his groin kicked or stomped by those iron-bound feet.

Janice came back full of the sassy remarks a gentleman from Richmond had made to her.

Matthew went with Rosie to the house, to lovely Fox Hill where the work was almost complete. Rosie looked very beautiful but tired. She had lost weight. They kissed and clung passionately when they were out of sight. Then she told him about papers and drapes he had not seen. She said that for dinner there were Maryland crab cakes and fried chicken, and a new Californian wine she had discovered in a Charlottesville market, a dry white for under five dollars.

At the door they were met by Peach, who was whimsically dressed in some ancestor's black frock coat, with a string tie, a cane, and a pistol in a holster. Behind him stood two of the painters or paperhangers whom Matthew remembered. They

243

stood either side of Peach, at his shoulders, so that the three of them blocked the door.

Peach refused Matthew entry to Fox Hill.

'Any attempt at unlicensed and unwarranted intrusion, suh, will be prevented bah force, bah mahself and mah honourable friends heah.'

Peach's accent had become antiquely Southern. It was possible that he was play-acting, but the pistol looked real. It was a target pistol, a long-barrelled .22 which could not make a large hole in Matthew but a perfectly lethal small hole. The workmen looked glum. One was carrying a monkey wrench and one a claw hammer.

'Stand aside, fatso,' said Rosie.

'You are, of course, welcome undah mah roof,' said Peach. 'Alone.'

Rosie began to scream at Peach, that she was tired and needed a tub, that Matthew was tired and needed a tub, and they both needed dinner, and the joke was a bore.

Peach closed the door in her face. They heard the old key turn in the lock.

Rosie picked up a rock. She was about to pitch it through the glass of one of the huge windows which flanked the door, under the portico.

'We can't get through a hole you make with that,' said Matthew.

'No, but I can get a little satisfaction.'

'I can think of better ways to get satisfaction.'

'Yes. Let's go away.'

'I can't go away.'

'I can't not. I need you.'

'So does Beausoleil.'

'For Christ's sake, why? Who ever heard of a man like you playing nursemaid to a stallion all season? What do I pay a manager for, those other guys, the Mount Malcolm twins? Can't you see everything is *running,* darling, it's all *working*? This place *goes*. It's ridiculous you should be tied here.'

Well, it was.

'I'll have to talk to Rick Field,' said Matthew uncertainly.

'All you want. He's sick but not deaf. In the meantime go visit with Viola Biggs. I'll go with you, then come back and eat that crab. Not crow, crab. And pack. I want a change, my darling

Matt. Oh God, I do need a change. I really do. I exhausted myself in this place, and I couldn't get away, and now it's done and I can and I must and I will. Can you imagine what it's like, to come to the end of an eighteen-month *marathon*? I want a change from Peach and Thalia and Dill and Hazel. I have to see Tim before I go and I have to see Ed Lindsey before I go, but *I want to go*.'

'Where?'

'Well, where?'

'I'd like to take you home, but I can't.'

'Ashamed?'

'Proud. But people I depend on wouldn't understand.'

'They'd understand all too well,' said Rosie. 'No, you can't take me to your place. I'm not sure I'd want to go. I might feel ghosts. You might feel ghosts. How are you for money?'

'Okay.'

'Then let's go to Europe. Or California. Or the Far East. Be back in April if you want for Keeneland and the Derby.'

'Europe,' said Matthew uncertainly, thinking of Clare's involvement, Liz's disappearance, Jamie's health, Mollie's problems which were no less intransigent for being self-created.

'*Banco*,' said Rosie.

'I'm not sure about any of this.'

'Not sure if you want to go someplace with me?'

'Oh yes. I'm sure of that.'

'Then come to Mount Malcolm with me, and we'll face the next step when we get to it.'

Miss Viola Biggs made Matthew lavishly welcome, winking like an ogre and pouring bourbon. She confirmed that Luke and John Field would be available to assist their cousin Rick all spring; she had not nearly enough to keep them busy, and kept them on her payroll for other reasons than her needs; and Matthew knew how good they were with the horses, and could leave things at Fox Hill with a clear mind; and Rosie needed a real vacation and a change, and he should take her at least as far as Europe for at least a month.

'I have to go because I have to pack,' said Rosie. 'I'm not going for crab cake or fried crow. Shall I come back for the night?'

'No,' said Matthew, thinking of local opinion.

But at the same moment Miss Viola Biggs said, 'Yes,' more loudly.

Matthew called his home, because he had given Fay Candy the Fox Hill number for messages. Fay said Mr Cottle had called from Britain; would Mr Carver call back; it was urgent.

At six o'clock Matthew called Fred Cottle in Newmarket, hoping that at eleven Fred would still be up.

He was up, and grumpy.

Like half a dozen other English trainers, Fred was taking some horses to Cagnes-sur-Mer, the opening meeting of serious European flat-racing. Unnecessarily justifying this ploy, Fred explained that the French government betting monopoly paid generous travelling expenses, and the same source provided far bigger prizes than the British system. Matthew knew all this, and assented patiently. He already knew what Fred was going on to say, and waited with a song in his heart. He had a ticker on the cost of the call. It made a discordant sound, but not one to drown the song. The yearling of which Matthew had bought a half-share at Newmarket in October, the sprint-bred sort, had been a February foal and was now a sturdy, precocious two-year-old. He was called Dandy Dinmont. Fred said Dandy Dinmont was bursting out of his breeches with fitness. His sire had been a stone better on the soft. He was a perfect type for Cagnes. Did Matthew agree? Would Matthew come?

'It usually rains like hell,' said Matthew. 'Horrible. The Riviera in March in streaming rain.'

'Horrible,' said Rosie. 'I already packed a raincoat and binoculars.'

CHAPTER 12

Travelling with Rosie was a delight, though never simple. She reacted immediately to almost everything, even if she had seen it before. She reacted with total honesty. She never said what she thought she ought to say. It was possible to suspect her of saying what she thought she ought not to say, but after a few days Matthew acquitted her of deliberately shocking him. Sometimes she deliberately shocked other people.

She was bad at packing for herself, and being places on time. She was good at finding devious ways of saving money. She was rapturously good in bed, everywhere they went. Need fed on fulfilment. Neither was ever sated. Wonder was daily renewed. Matthew was astonished at his own virility.

Matthew went to London, briefly, alone. His tact was needless. Mollie was away with cousins in the country, Clare in Ireland with Tom Kavanagh's family, Jamie in Italy with the Vianellos, Liz God knew where. Matthew reported to Ralph Hadfield that Beausoleil showed enthusiasm for his new career, and that Hadfield's mare would be beautifully looked after at Fox Hill. Hadfield seemed surprised that Matthew was in Europe. Matthew continued to be a little surprised, himself, that he was in Europe.

He rejoined Rosie in Paris. There were places in Paris she would not visit, owing to memories of Tim.

Matthew called Epi Makropulos's Paris office, wanting advice about where to stay for the races at Cagnes. He guessed Epi would know somewhere unusual, special, more discreet than the obvious palaces of Nice or Antibes. Epi was on his island, but his Paris secretary recommended a small hotel between Vence and Gattières, inland, in the hills, with five bedrooms, one star in *Michelin,* and the extreme improbability of the sight of anybody they knew. The secretary made the reservation for them, organized a hire car, and said that wet weather was forecast.

Fred Cottle sent two four-year-olds, two three-year-olds and Dandy Dinmont by road to Cagnes. He flew down in time to see them into the racecourse stables and to work them on the track. Of course the owners had all been consulted. Two others besides Matthew Carver were coming, making their horses the excuse for a wet Riviera holiday. Fred had been obliged to consult Matthew Carver. He had thought the man would stay away. It had seemed odds on, with the stud season just getting into full swing, with 4,000 miles to travel. Fred's certainty that Carver wouldn't come had been a factor in bringing Dandy Dinmont to Cagnes. But the bastard was on his way. Fred had not forgotten, would never forget, the sickening shock of his disappointment about the Mill Reef colt. Or the drunken disgrace which that shock had caused. Properly considered, that episode was Carver's fault. There might have been trouble, ruin, prison. That would have been Carver's fault.

Fred was a professional. He would train and place Carver's horses as well as he knew how, as well as for any other owner. His reputation and his income depended on that. His personal honour depended on it — he couldn't take the fee and not do his best to deliver. He didn't have to like the man. It wasn't so much the fact of the horse going to America that stuck in Fred's craw. It was the way it was done. A telephone call at midnight. No real explanation. Nothing you could call an apology. And, worst of all, the whole thing on top of all the publicity, on top of public declarations that the horse would be trained in England, at Newmarket, by Fred.

Fred should have said, at the time, there on the telephone, 'If you take that one you can take the others too.' Many a trainer had said that, under similar circumstances. It had been said to owners much more important than Matthew Carver. Some trainers regretted saying it, of course. Fred regretted not having said it, and now it was too late.

The French government monopoly of pari-mutuel betting generated far more money to be ploughed back into the industry than the British system, where the Tote was a poor relation of the bookies and betting-shops. Prize money, breeders' premiums, travelling subsidies; and also such expensive facilities as full race-course watering. Of course the major British tracks had watering systems, paid for mostly by the Levy Board out of their percentage of betting turnover, but the French were equipped to put much more water on much more grass, and seemed to do so regardless of season or sense.

So thought Fred Cottle, walking the course at Cagnes-sur-Mer with his jockey, two days before racing started. The ground was very soft. There had been a lot of rain. It was drizzling as they plodded round. More rain was coming, the radio said. Fat black clouds were marching in from the sea with unbroken grey above them. It was impossible to believe that even the Frogs would be such nits as to water artificially when God was doing it for them, overdoing it for them, but you never knew. Minor racing officials were capable of amazing idiocies, in France and everywhere else. They thought they had to use facilities because they existed, like a man having free drinks when he didn't want a drink, because he couldn't bear to pass up the chance. The ground felt as though it had been watered. It squelched and printed in deeply. Fred's heavy brogues were saturated; he could feel the wet mud between his toes. He wished he had brought his Wellingtons, but you don't expect to want gumboots on a racecourse.

There was policy in this French over-watering, thought Fred. Their horses were used to running on a bog. English horses were used to decent ground. So the French started with an unfair advantage. They were fed up with their best races, their biggest prizes, going to English raiders, better horses, better trained, better ridden.

In part of his mind Fred knew that this was rubbish. But he felt sour. He didn't like it at Cagnes; he didn't like it in France. He didn't like French cooking or the price of whisky. He hated being surrounded by jibber-jabber he couldn't understand. Ivy his wife had insisted on coming, saying he needed her to chat up the owners. She caught a chill, naturally, from sitting about in wet stockings, and now she had a bad case of the trots and a worse case of the moans.

And the bastard American was coming, the bastard Carver. Fred would have to touch his hat-brim and even sort of smile, because you just had to, there in public with everybody watching.

For the first time in his life, Fred suddenly began to think about retiring.

Epi Makropulos went back to Athens, glad to see his friends, sorry to leave his island. He talked from there to his Chantilly trainer, and agreed that two of his horses should go to Cagnes. He called Tanja Dekker in Paris; she was not his only girl but she had been for nearly a year his favourite girl. They arranged to meet in Antibes and to go to the races. A suite was reserved for them somewhere. The hotel of Epi's choice — the little one, remote in the hills, with only five bedrooms, between Vence and Gattières — was full; Epi trusted his staff to find him something he would like. He was not immoderately fussy, but Tanja hated vulgarity. She liked her comforts. She liked a lot of things she had only learned about since she met him. She was very intelligent, a quick study.

Before he left Athens, Epi heard from the manager of the farm near Middleburg where his American mares were boarded. One had foaled and had already visited Beausoleil. If not in foal she would return. The other due to visit Beausoleil had not yet foaled. Everything was under control. Epi was comforted to know that Matt Carver was responsible for the successful impregnation of his mares.

The first person Epi saw, on the opening day of the races, in horrible teeming rain, was the last person he expected to see: Rosie Phillipson. She looked insanely beautiful. He remembered her as beautiful, but with a sad and vulnerable beauty, tragic, doomed, Greek. He admitted to himself, remembering, that he had perhaps supplied the injections of Phaedra and Electra, that they had not really been evident at Fox Hill. But sadness had.

The sadness had vanished. Rosie, laughing in the rain, looked younger, lighter, more beautiful, higher in colour and lither in movement; she looked like a happy panther on a diet of vitamin pills; she looked like a lady with a satisfactory love life.

Epi was sorry for Matthew, over there in Virginia, while Rosie laughed in the rain at Cagnes with a new lover.

They had a cheerful reunion. Epi kissed Rosie on both cheeks, though he had not done so before, though they had not been on kissing terms after his one visit to Fox Hill. This unexpected meeting in the South of France, on a racecourse, made kisses on the cheek inevitable. Tanja had already twice been kissed by friends of Epi who were no more than acquaintances of herself.

Rosie's cheeks were wet in the rain. Raindrops clung in the black curtain of her hair. You might have supposed her weeping except that she looked so happy. You might have supposed her crying with joy.

Epi asked after Peach, Miss Viola Biggs, and other Virginia friends. He did not ask after Tim, whom he had not met and about whose condition he was vague.

'Peach?' said Rosie, her smile not disappearing but shrinking. 'No nearer sanity than when you saw him. He still has a hangover from Christmas. Is that a record? *Before* Christmas. He was acting but he rewrote his part. It threw the play a little out of shape. He was a smash hit, but not in the ordinary sense.'

'And Beausoleil?'

'He likes eating and fucking and running around. He's fine.'

Epi concealed the distaste which he felt at the use of four-letter words by women. He reflected that Rosie was not swearing, but referring to a natural function in economical terms. He would still have preferred a euphemism; both literary and colloquial English offered a generous selection.

'My God,' said Epi suddenly, looking over Rosie's shoulder, utterly astonished.

Rosie looked round. Matthew was walking from somewhere to somewhere, briskly, rain dripping off his hat-brim.

Looking back at Epi, Rosie saw annoyance as well as astonishment. Epi looked shocked. She was herself astonished. Sophisticated Epi, himself a celebrated international womaniser, shocked that she and Matthew were together? What had come over everybody? Was Peach's disease catching?

She said, 'Don't you know any other fallen women? Or fallen men? Everybody's falling these days, like the dollar, like this rain. Don't *look* at me like that.'

'Oh, you entirely misunderstand,' said Epi.

'I was hoping one of us did.'

'I always hoped that you and my old friend would be friends. That is not what caused whatever expression on my face you disliked. It is that all the arrangements concerning Beausoleil have been conditional on the fact of Matthew's management. I have sold nominations myself on that basis, giving that guarantee. I know this was not precisely contractual, it was not in writing. But it seems to me that it was very clearly understood by everybody.'

'Oh,' said Rosie. 'But look, you don't expect a top manager to be staring at guys in the machine-shop all day? Your own business functions along without you in the office all the time. If not, what are you doing here? Your business must be a lot more complicated than steering a prick into a cunt once a day, which is what they call stallion management. You delegate to a reliable staff. Don't you do that? You must do. To get here, you must do. Well, so does Matthew.'

'A reliable staff —'

'A *very, very, very* reliable staff.'

'Well, that is true. Your man Ed Lindsey impressed me very much. I imagine that he and Matt developed a good relationship immediately.'

'Yes, they did,' said Rosie. 'Matthew thinks very highly of Ed.'

'Of course. Well, on *that* basis, I suppose my surprise was unnecessary and my disapproval even impertinent. Forgive my moment of shock, and the discourteous expression on my face.'

To Matthew Rosie said, 'Don't mention Ed Lindsey's accident to your Greek friend.'

'Why not? Epi will probably send Ed a terrific gift, or ask him to convalesce on that private island of his.'

'Because I beg you not. That ought to be enough. If it's not, the reason is that Epi's very happy at the moment, and it's nicer when people are happy, and he's nicer when he's happy, so don't make him sad with something he can't actually do anything about. Promise.'

She made him promise. She knew he would keep his promise because he was a man who kept his promises.

The moment Tanja saw Matthew, she knew something good had happened to him. The haggardness had cleared. There was no misery behind his eyes. He looked ten years younger.

The moment Tanja saw Rosie, she understood what it was that had happened to him. She knew, as an objective and reported fact, that they had had an affair. Report had credited Rosanna Phillipson with charm and beauty. Tanja, a good judge, saw magic, witchcraft. She saw need. Matthew and this woman needed one another. Tanja thought that the woman needed Matthew even more than he needed her, even though her magic had given him his manhood back. Tanja thought that, as a rule, women did need men more than men needed women, because love and sex and that kind of need bulked larger in women's lives. Men had money and so forth to concern them, battles, buildings, big male preoccupations, and women waited for them on sofas or in beds

252

or at bus-stops. This was not a full picture of life or of the sexes, but it was a true part of the picture. To Tanja, the sort of women who did not need men were lesser women, not greater, than the others.

This Rosanna Phillipson, thought Tanja, needed Matthew too much. He was so necessary to her that she would end by eating him. Perhaps that was what he wanted, to be gobbled. He looked at her as though gobbling or being gobbled were on his mind. They both drooled. Their feelings were very visible. Tanja hoped there would be a happy ending, but she thought not. She distrusted Rosanna Phillipson. Anybody who neded anything so badly would commit atrocities to get it.

Henri de Cheminade's flamboyance was muted by the weather. His *panache* was ratty and sodden. It is hard to cut a dash in a raincoat that makes you look like an elephant. He was splendid in Nice in the evening.

He was in Cagnes to represent certain owners whose commitments prevented them coming. Perhaps they did not want to get wet in the Midi in early spring. Their trainers would have represented them adequately, but Henri felt obliged to be present. Reporting back gave him an excuse for contact. He could claim credit for success, blame others for failure. He wanted to get away from his wife and his mistress. He blossomed in the Negresco.

The second day's racing gave him an opportunity to show himself at his best. Dignity was an aspect of his character not always obvious to the ignorant. He exhibited it by means of a stately rebuff. His manner of turning away, silent, of staring past a man as though he were a wooden post, of staring through him as though he were glass with matters of interest beyond — these were the gestures of a greater age, of the *belle époque* to which in spirit Henri de Cheminade belonged.

He cut Matthew Carver dead, in front of dozens of people who knew who they both were.

Some of the people knew why he did it, because he had not been coy about the betrayal. They told the others. Those not informed by their friends were informed by Henri. Visiting English owners, trainers and bloodstock agents were among the witnesses.

Matthew saw Henri's gesture, with surprise but little curiosity.

He put it down to jealousy, but tentatively, because he knew very little about Henri. Jealousy of Matthew for having a companion like Rosie, who lit the sodden race-course like a domesticated comet; jealousy, possibly, of his having been asked to luncheon by the duc de Montfermainbrey. In the latter hypothetical reaction, Matthew recognized a touch of Mollie. She had refused to speak to people, for similar reasons. It was odd to find common ground between Henri de Cheminade and Mollie. Introspectively, resentment of this kind was not within Matthew's experience. It was not something he remembered feeling. But observation established that it was possible.

Matthew could think of few things that mattered to him less than the opinion of Henri de Cheminade, but anyone dislikes being disliked, and he was uneasy to think that he had somehow, inadvertently, given such offence.

In the hotel they had a bedroom and a little sitting-room and a bathroom made out of another room which was bigger than the sitting-room and had the best view. You could not see out of the window from the bath, which caused Rosie to plan surrealistic methods of enjoying at once the view and her bath. She made Matthew laugh so that his ribs hurt where he had long ago cracked them hunting with the Bicester in Oxfordshire.

The smaller the room, the more intimate the contact, the tidier you have to be. Rosie was not accustomed to looking after herself, and she was not instinctively orderly. Like Peach, when she dropped things she let them lie, confident that someone would come along behind her. Matthew knew that this was not ill-will or selfishness. It was the way she had always lived. Hazel or somebody else had picked up the things she dropped. He worked hard at not getting irritated at something Rosie could not help. He picked up things she dropped, except the jar of face-powder, and the tube of toothpaste she trod on, and the perfume bottle which broke on the corner of a chair.

She found it more difficult to suppress her irritation at his tidiness, which was perhaps an inherent aspect of character, perhaps the result of a different early training. She was, by the same token, less well schooled than he in suppressing irritation. It had not been a part of her marriage. She did try not to get mad, impatient, contemptuous, when he hung his pants carefully on a hanger and put trees in his shoes, when she was already in bed and waiting for him. She did try. It was sweet to see her trying. Matthew loved her for trying. He loved her for being naked there in the bed, responding to him with ever-renewed passion and wonderment, and making him laugh with plans for raising the bath to the ceiling.

Long before, Mollie had induced Matthew to read some books on psychology. Some woman, some heavy-minded Kentucky neighbour, had introduced her to them. A new duty was born, from which she did not flinch, to understand the souls of everybody around her. The books appealed to her solemn view of life, to her conviction that there was a great deal wrong with nearly everybody. She searched for the leaden lining in every cloud. They were very humourless books. Matthew read some of them dutifully. If Mollie could not share his interests, it the more behoved him to share hers.

There was a tidy distinction made between two types of human personality — or had been, when the books were written — between the obsessive and the hysteroid types. They might have written it 'hysteric'. Matthew's lack of interest had not helped to fix the words in his mind. Obsessives were tidy, and upset by the slapdash. Hysteroids were untidy, and didn't give a damn. Aristocrats were hysteroids, and so were the lowest classes. The middle class was obsessive. It made a kind of sense, as a vast generalisation. Aristocrats had things picked up for them, the dregs lived in slums; middle class persons lived in neat houses in neat streets, or in apartments sufficiently cramped to make tidiness important; they worked at tidy desks in tidy offices, while aristocrats were striding their estates and peasants were dropping beer-cans in the street. Rosie was a duchess and a slut, and Matthew was a middle-class man with a modest house and a modest inherited competence. Matthew was tidy and upset by the slapdash. He saw it as impractical and uneconomic, as well as inconsiderate. If you dropped things and didn't pick them up, you gave yourself trouble rather than saved yourself trouble: yourself and other people. Rosie could not be made to see that. So utterly was she incapable of seeing it that it was pointless to say anything about it.

She continued to try not to be irritated when he took time to hang up his pants. That large effort, made out of love and loving-kindness, compensated for the toothpaste squeezed out of the tube and trodden into the carpet by her foot. Oh yes, oh yes, the effort and those breasts and the plan to raise the bath so that she could see out of the window while she was soaping between her toes and his.

Before leaving Kentucky, Matthew had sought and found three mares he thought Ghalib al-Jilani would like, three that ought to go to Beausoleil. One was barren, two due to foal. None was purchasable with an existing nomination to any stallion, which would normally have been a disadvantage and was now an advantage. All were for sale, at an odd time for buying and selling broodmares, only because Ghalib was offering prices over the odds. He was agreeable to doing so because of the special circumstances: because of his mixed motives. Everything was ready to be finalised, but nothing was finalised, when Matthew left home for Fox Hill, Fox Hill for home, and home for Paris. He sent messages at all points to Ghalib, urging immediate action. He left the American end in the hands of a fully-briefed Lexington bloodstock agent. He had done all that friendship required. He had not asked for, and was not expecting, any commission from Ghalib. Commission from the vendors would go to the agent.

Ghalib called the hilltop hotel from Halat al Bhudi, announcing his arrival. He had never been racing at Cagnes, and wanted to see it. He wanted to see Matthew, to discuss the mares.

'Old home week,' said Rosie. 'All we need is Jefferson Dill.'

They watched Dandy Dinmont working, in the drizzle of dawn. He seemed to handle the ground. He was a big, precocious two-year-old. He was entered in several races. He faced a lot of French two-year-olds of similar stamp and comparable breeding; he probably faced several that had already run, and he might face a winner.

'Why doesn't somebody put a clock on him?' said Rosie. 'These people are amateurs.'

Matthew explained the irrelevance of American methods in conditions so totally different. Rosie was unconvinced. She had been brought up to all this. She knew how you used the clock to assess a horse's chance in a race. You timed it against the opposition and against the average and record times for the track. She understood that old Fred Cottle had been taught in a different school, that he was a survivor, a backwoodsman, too old to learn what was commonplace among the tough young professionals of America. She could not understand Matthew's bland acceptance of Fred's rigid, self-defeating conservatism.

How good a chance did Dandy Dinmont really have? Nobody knew. Nobody took the trouble to find out. He looked good galloping, okay, and he was a well-made colt. They hadn't tried him with a three-year-old with exactly known two-year-old form. They hadn't clocked him. How did they expect to have a bet?

Rosie discovered that Matthew didn't expect to have any but a very small bet. He was not a gambler. Dearly and deeply as she loved him, she recognized that that in his character which made him so maddeningly deliberate, so ridiculously tidy — that which, almost with rudeness, kept him out of her bed while he hung up his pants — ran all the way through. Slice him where you liked, and he was a man who never cut loose. Slice a toe and there was prudence; slice an earlobe and you saw the colour of pussyfoot. You might as well not come to the races, you might as well not fool around with horses at all, if you never formed an opinion and acted on it.

Rosie wanted money. She had little of her own, and spending Tim's under the circumstances would have been distinctly sick. Matthew seemed to have enough and to spend it ungrudgingly, but it was a bore for them both if she had to go to him all the time. Rosie wanted clothes for the spring. Here she was in France, with the best clothes in the world hanging in racks all around her, and she wanted double or treble or ten times the money she had.

She tried to clock Dandy Dinmont's gallops against those of the other two-year-olds being worked. It was impossible, with a wristwatch. Nobody had a stop-watch she could borrow. She bought a stopwatch in Nice, before meeting Epi Makropulos and his girl for drinks. It was expensive, with a lot of sophisticated gadgets. She carried it around all day, protected in her bag by a scarf. In the evening, back in the hotel, tired, longing for her tub, she pulled the scarf out of her bag forgetting for a moment about the stopwatch. It fell and bounced on the tiles of the bathroom floor. It was smashed, shattered beyond repair. Rosie clutched the ruins of her lovely new stopwatch. She burst into tears of fatigue and frustration, with anger at her carelessness and with fate that was blocking her chance of a good bet. She fought not to vent her rage on Matthew, who had no idea she had spent a lot of money on any stopwatch. She crooned stupidly over the broken dial of the stopwatch, while her bath ran, and hid it under her towel when Matthew came in.

Confidence was growing behind Dandy Dinmont, though. Fred Cottle's, the jockey's, Matthew's, her own. They picked the race and declared the horse to run. Still the rain fell. When beaten jockeys came in, their faces were masked with mud.

Rosie cashed a traveller's cheque. She went to the races on the day of their race with her handbag distended by banknotes. She said she was going to the john, and she went to the pari-mutuel. Her intention was to bet 2,500 francs. Peanuts. She stood in line. She heard Frenchmen buying tickets on two, three, four, six, seven, eight. Dandy Dinmont was number five. Nobody was backing it because it was unknown, a foreigner. English horses were usually at a falsely long price in France, as Irish horses were in England. Not prejudice but ignorance. It was a coup, a snip, the chance of a lifetime.

Yes, well. Five hundred dollars already made a large hole in the money she had with her.

Omens, omens. Omens?

Matthew had made love to her after they had eaten breakfast in bed. Having swept out some of the crumbs from their croissants. Sweet, utter abandonment. As good as the best ever. No day that began like that could be other than blessed.

Little Tanja Dekker had wished them luck; a girl Rosie mistrusted. Rosie hated enigmatic people. She was not fond of beautiful girls, ten years younger than herself, who were not so enigmatic that they didn't reveal admiration for Matthew. One of Epi's horses had been beaten the previous day. Elegance required that Rosie's man's horse should win where Tanja's man's horse had been beaten.

Fate had broken her stopwatch. Okay, then fate owed her the price of a stopwatch.

Rosie was a Collin of Fox Hill, carrying the banner of the Old Dominion among a lot of overweight Frenchmen.

In the distance she saw Henri de Cheminade, fattest of Frenchmen. He had been introduced to her. He had been desperately gallant, until realising she was with Matthew, after which he trembled with affront, pursed up his little wet mouth, and rolled away. Show him.

258

She wanted to buy Matthew a gift. Any gift.

She had 5,000 francs on Dandy Dinmont. Really too much. Not *really* too much, but a lot for her, as she was just then placed.

She felt a little aghast until she joined the others. Matthew was calm outside but visibly excited inside. He looked like a man who knew his horse was going to win. Fred Cottle was grumpy, almost insolent, but there was no doubt in Rosie's mind that he was sure they were going to win. The jockey showed a little more than Fred — only a little: he came from Yorkshire — but Rosie was sure he was sure Dandy Dinmont would win. She forgot her doubts. She marvelled at her cowardice, in having so little on their horse.

Dandy Dinmont ran pretty well. He ran a creditable third. The first and the second had both run before at the meeting, and the second was carrying a penalty earned by his previous win. Experience told. This race would bring Dandy Dinmont on many pounds. He would be better on ground not quite so bottomlessly soft. The jockey dropped his hands when he saw he couldn't win. To give a two-year-old a really hard race, in heavy ground, when he couldn't win, first time out, was a good way to break his heart. The jockey did right. So they all said.

Rosie felt sick. She couldn't understand why they made these excuses, for a flagrant breach of the rules of racing, for a betrayal of owner and trainer and better. She felt sick at the money she had lost, at her doubled bet.

'Don't take it hard,' said Matthew, glancing, troubled, at whatever her face was showing. 'We do this for fun. Don't blame Dandy for not being good enough.'

'I don't,' said Rosie, a little louder than she meant. 'I blame that dummy you had riding. Who paid him to take a dive?'

It was not obvious that many people heard this or, hearing, understood. 'Dive', to a listener with less than perfect colloquial American English, might be supposed a reference to the wet weather, or to the jockey's having had a morning swim in some heated indoor pool.

Rosie heard Matthew saying, softly, in a soft voice full of anger, 'You must not speak like that.'

In part of her mind Rosie knew that she must not, that it was contemptible to be a bad loser, that these were racing conditions and personalities unknown to her, that she was wailing through the hole she herself had made in her pocket.

'The little son of a bitch threw it away,' said Rosie, stridently, to her own horror.

Reconciliation was accomplished without words; by actions only; before and during and after a bath in the bath from which the view could not quite be seen.

Rosie lay awake at three in the morning, Matthew deeply asleep beside her. His breathing was untroubled, hardly audible. He was a restful man to sleep with.

Rosie prayed: please God, don't let me do anything like that again. God, let me grow up. Please God, make me grow up.

Flying over Saudia Arabia, Ghalib was Imam of his family and of the crew of his jet. A little relaxation entered, as though through pores in the metal, from the tolerant air of Egypt. Over the Mediterranean Ghalib changed his clothes and his soul, so that when they landed at Nice he was ready for a drink.

He had hoped to be in the same hotel as Matthew Carver.

The first person he saw at the races, unobtrusive, obliging, conducting his business illegally, was Trevor Plimsoll, the bookmaker known to Lord Goring, one of whose favourite clients Ghalib had instantly become. One large losing bet at Newmarket had raised Ghalib to this gratifying eminence.

Trevor Plimsoll told Prince Ghalib that he would be happy to accommodate him to any sum, betting at pari-mutuel odds.

Trevor Plimsoll reported seeing Mr Matthew Carver with one very beautiful young lady and Mr Epaminandos Makropulos with another very beautiful young lady, but that they had not done business with him.

'Not sporting gentlemen like you an' me, your Highness.'

'But they have the beautiful young ladies.'

Ghalib had been surprised that Matthew Carver was in Europe. He was surprised Matthew had a beautiful young lady, since there was no secret about his heavy involvement with Rosie Phillipson. His surprise on the second count disappeared when he saw Rosie. He and Rosie had a friendly reunion, then he and Matthew. He met Epi and Tanja. He and Epi knew about each other, the connexion between them being Matthew.

Aside, Ghalib said to Epi that Matthew should surely be in America.

'You know Fox Hill?' said Epi.

'Yes.'

'Then you know Ed Lindsey, the manager, the old black man?'

'Yes.'

'He is the reason it is okay for Matt to be here. Ed Lindsey is the best man with horses I have ever seen.'

Ghalib accepted this. What Epi said carried weight, not only because he said it but also because it made obvious sense. Matthew delegated because he felt absolutely safe in doing so. It was true that Ed Lindsey had a magic touch with horses. He was another Fox Hill djinn, a beneficent immortal who hid his gull wings under a plaid shirt.

Ghalib tried to proposition Tanja. She turned him down politely, not displeased to be asked.

Ghalib arranged to discuss with Matthew, immediately after the races, all that had to be discussed concerning his new American broodmares.

Ghalib propositioned Rosie, more out of habit — more as an immediate, unthinking reaction to the fact of meeting a beautiful woman — than with any hope of success.

'You'd be insanely generous,' said Rosie, 'and I do need the money. But it wouldn't do. I couldn't deliver. Even if I wanted to. It's just like it was before. I don't change because I cross an ocean.'

'I can lend you money, if you want money.'

'I don't know. Thank you. I still couldn't deliver anything. I think if you hadn't started the way you did, I could borrow money off you. But now I can't. I didn't think I had any morality, but I guess I'm getting old.'

'No. You are with Matthew. Why do you need money?'

'The only betting here is like with us. Cash. I cleaned myself out. I want to climb back, but they took away my ladder.'

'Bet on credit.'

'How?'

'Nothing easier.'

So Ghalib introduced Rosie to Trevor Plimsoll. Introducing people to people was a major part of his working life; he thought very little of conferring this favour on both of them. He knew that a lot of American women were extremely rich in their own right. He knew how Rosie lived, how she spent money at home.

Trevor Plimsoll understood privately from Ghalib that Mrs

Phillipson was the owner of the Fox Hill Farm, where the great Beausoleil now stood. That was quite good enough. Anybody placed like that was certainly obliged to pay debts of honour, and certainly capable of doing so.

Rosie was 1,200 francs up with Trevor Plimsoll at the end of the first afternoon of their association.

'Don't mention any of this to Mr Carver, please,' said Rosie to Trevor Plimsoll.

'Dealings between a bookmaker and 'is clients are in strict confidence, ma'am. Besides, I don't know Mr Carver. Much as I'd like 'is business.'

'Not a word of this to Matthew, please,' Rosie said to Ghalib.

'What do you take me for?' said Ghalib, becoming very Old Harrovian.

Ghalib agreed to buy the broodmares recommended by Matthew. He examined the pedigrees, but many of the American names were unfamiliar. He heard about the three mares' racing form, the previous offspring of two of them, the winners bred by their female relatives, the records of their sires. He agreed to board the mares at Fox Hill for the spring; he would move them to Cragrock or to Ballycardeen after they were tested in foal to Beausoleil.

These arrangements seemed to Ghalib to cement his friendship with Matthew. Matthew continued visibly surprised that Ghalib was sending three expensive mares he had never seen to an untried first-season stallion. But Ghalib knew what he was doing. Having done it he left, for meetings in Zürich and Düsseldorf.

They decided not to run Dandy Dinmont again at Cagnes. Fred Cottle had scored twice with his other runners, and had sent two of them home. There was no more for them there. The party was breaking up.

Rosie had backed both Fred's winners massively with Trevor Plimsoll. They ran with stable confidence; she knew about them. She did not know much about other horses she backed. Her winnings were swallowed up in a deepening pit. She did what she had been taught all her life not to do: she tried to get out by having double-or-quits bets, ever larger as her losses mounted.

She owed 45,000 francs to Trevor Plimsoll on the day before the day they were leaving.

She was sick at her folly. She was sick at the thought of Matthew's face when she told him.

Ghalib would have lent her the money, but Ghalib had gone. It was not a request you could make by long-distance telephone or Telex or cable.

Tim could pay and not notice. At home, Rosie could pay and not notice. The cheque would disappear among farm expenses or bills to electricians and plumbers.

'Are you goin' straight 'ome, ma'am?' asked Trevor Plimsoll.

'No. Sure. I don't know. We might go to Greece. Somebody lent us an island.'

'Ooh, lovely this time o' year, I imagine. Well, let's approach from another angle. Is there the name of a lawyer or a banker you could give me? With a note from you, see, that the indebtedness is genuine? You mus' see how I'm placed, ma'am. This goes on my overdraft. If you'd finished in credit, you'd of 'ad my cheque before we all kissed goodbye. I don't insist on that, though it *was* my understandin' from 'is Highness that there'd be no trouble about the account. Beausoleil an' all. Never mind, you tell me where to write an' we'll fix it all up regular.'

'Oh, no. No, no. Don't write anybody. I can't give you the kind of note you'd want.'

'What *am* I to do, ma'am? There's the newspapers. There's Mr Carver. I must an' I will talk to somebody. I can't keep this to meself. Flesh an' blood won't stand it. Disappearin' to a Greek island, eh? I got to think o' the kids.'

'Yes. Oh, Christ. Give me twenty-four hours.'

Matthew was surprised when Rosie said she would meet him later, in the evening, in Nice. She said something about an appointment. She was mysterious without being secretive, a trick she had. She looked wrong. He was worried about the drawn, sick look on her face, but she was brusque about it, dismissive. He thought she was seeing a doctor, and not telling him in case it worried him. He wondered for a moment if she were pregnant. He wondered about the implications. He would have preferred frankness from her, but he knew better than to insist. He knew that even people intimately close to one another, even after years, must have secrets. Not everything should be gushed out and not everything should be pried into.

He said that he would go to dinner at the Périgord, expecting her to join him by nine.

'Don't wait,' said Rosie. 'Eat at nine. Eat *foie de canard*. I had it when we dined there with Epi. I'll join you when I can. I'm not terribly hungry. I'll be there in time to eat something.'

They had never made an arrangement like this before, insecure, open-ended, all maybes and if-I-cans. It was not very terrible. It was normal between couples, even though it was new to them. Married couples often made arrangements like this, thought nothing about it. Matthew wondered if they were moving into what some of his friends called a new time-cube. He hoped not. With certain unimportant qualifications (concerning toothpaste in the carpet and ashtrays upset on the pillow) he liked the time-cube they were in.

Bankers are used to people coming to see them. People in trouble. Coming in confidence. Epi was used to privy visits from very important people, wanting enormous loans to tide them over a cash-flow crisis, to avert or achieve a take-over, to buy time or treasure.

Epi was used to women coming to see him, because he was seen to be handsome and said to be generous.

He might thus have been less surprised than he was by Rosie's urgent and muttered telephone call, and by her appearance in his hotel room. Rosie was Matthew's. She did not belong to Matthew, because to Epi nobody belonged to anybody else: their souls were their own and probably God's. On this point Epi was uncertain, because of the variety of gods in which men of high intelligence and undoubted sanctity devoutly believed — had seen and spoken with, in religious ecstasy. If it had been a moment for metaphysical speculation, Epi would have wondered about Rosie's soul. Her soul was not Matthew's. She did not look as though it were in her own charge; she did not look as though any god had responsibility for it. It was extraordinary that anyone could look at once so beautiful and so haggard.

But the trouble was only money, after all. Not a thing to look so sick about, to make the voice hoarse and the eyes haunted. Epi was very far from despising money, but he regarded it as he regarded gasoline. That it was necessary did not make it interesting. If you had no gas you stayed put; if you had no money you postponed buying things. There were other things to do than travel or spend. Rosie had plenty of things to do. She had

Matthew.

Rosie did not all at once raise the subject of money. There was nothing in what she said to suggest that she wanted money. But Epi, banker and man, did sums in his head of a thoroughly familiar kind that had become easy with familiarity. There might be all kinds of things Rosie wanted, and for most of them she would go to Matthew.

She fiddled with a bracelet. She began to talk about herself. She said, 'Women are not supposed to be like men, but I am. In some ways I am. Do you know what I mean?'

'No,' said Epi. 'This is scotch, or there is champagne on the ice.'

'Nobody thinks worse of a man who has more than one woman. A man can be *essentially* faithful, and kind, and the rest of it, and still need variety, and all it takes is discretion, and you don't necessarily torpedo a good relationship by reading a different book once in a while. I mean, I wouldn't expect total one hundred percent lifelong eternal fidelity from you, but I don't think you're a tomcat.'

She rambled on in this vein. She drank the scotch he poured her, and drank a second stiff drink without seeming to notice it. What she was saying made sense to Epi, insofar as coherent sense could be extracted from it.

And Epi experienced an emotion rare to him. He felt embarrassed. He felt deep sympathetic embarrassment for what Rosie was making herself do.

'Do you find me attractive, at all?' asked Rosie, looking at him and at the window and her glass.

She might have sat so that she showed more of her legs, which were lovely, or leaned back so as to show the contour of her lovely bosom. She might have smiled or taken off her coat. But she sat solemn, a little hunched, and she kept her coat on.

'All you have to do is say no,' said Rosie, aiming at brightness and sounding abject.

Epi was at a loss, for the first time for a very long time.

He said, choosing his words, finding the English he spoke so fluently more foreign and intractable than usual: 'Any man would have to be made of stone or plastic not to find you attractive, Rosie. Of course you are very beautiful and desirable. I agree with you that absolute fidelity is not always necessary to a valid relationship. But . . .'

'I find you attractive, if you want to know,' said Rosie. 'If you can say it to me, I can say it to you. I'm a big girl. I can choose. I do choose. You're far too smart not to know that you're very attractive to women. There's no reason to feel surprised. My reaction is perfectly normal. You must have met it a lot of times. It's just that for me a moment just happens to have come when . . And so why the hell wait for a chance that may never come again? I mean I hate to waste chances. I mean, Providence may never . . . I mean, I truly believe you regret the things you don't do much more than you regret the things you do do. Oh Christ, I'm talking too much.'

'How much, Rosie?'

'Far too much. I always do when I'm a little scared . . . Oh. Oh, my God. Do you think that's why I came here?'

'If I don't make love to you now,' said Epi, 'it will maybe seem rude. If I do make love to you now, I think it would be ugly. Probably all my life I shall regret this, regret not doing it more than I would regret doing it. A thousand million men would give their eyes and all their teeth to be honoured as you are honouring me . . .' Epi sought for better words, and found some he hoped were good: 'I will tell you. You will take a cheque and I will take a rain-check. For many reasons this moment is not good. I am proud and flattered and moved and unable for many reasons to take advantage of this incredible good fortune. But still I will be proud to help you in any way that you need help. To give a return, you understand, for the honour you have done me.'

Rosie burst into tears. When Epi extracted from her what she wanted, he made out a cheque to Vernon Plimsoll Ltd, on his French bank, for 45,000 francs.

When she went down in the elevator, a thought obtruded from the jumble of Rosie's thoughts: he could have had me and he didn't want me. I'm getting old.

Matthew was still ordering his dinner, at 8.45, when Rosie joined him. She was quiet. She was very hungry. Her appetite had returned and she drank a lot of wine. She did not say where she had been, whom she had seen. Whatever it was had done her good but left her thoughtful and humble.

Tanja was shocked. She was careful with her own money and

266

with Epi's. She liked the excitement of betting on the races, but she bet only what she could comfortably afford to lose, especially in a strange place and at the very beginning of the season and after heavy rain. She was incredulous at the folly of Rosie's betting, contemptuous of what seemed to her the selfish, the childish irresponsibility of the whole episode.

She thought Matthew Carver would pay dear for the return of his youth and his balls.

Andílitos was one of the smallest inhabited islands in the Cyclades. Litos, its larger neighbour, was no great size. There was not really enough for Rosie to do. A weight had been lifted off her head, leaving her bursting with energy. The sea was still too cold for any but the briefest swims. The sun at midday was hot enough to sunbathe, but Rosie said she had no wish to turn her skin into suède. She was not someone who could lie in a long chair with foil over her nose, content to relax, thinking or not thinking. You could walk the length of the island in a few minutes. Matthew loved the thymy smell and the sense of extreme antiquity, the clear sea and the absence of clutter. He liked Epi's villa and found many books to interest him. Rosie read five books in the first two days, then tired of reading.

The idea had seemed such a very good one. Matthew's house was barred to Rosie and Rosie's to Matthew. Bumming across Europe was horribly expensive. There were other houses where they could stay — Ottaviano di Vianello's, Ralph Hadfield's — but not where they could share a room. Ottaviano's mother, the aged contessa madre, lived in a wing of his castle. She knew everything that went on. She attended mass every morning of her life. Ottaviano's inadvertently lurid English was misleading. The Hadfields talked as though they were more tolerant, but it was only talk. They would not have permitted a bad example being set to their servants. But to Epi's servants Matthew and Rosie were utter strangers, welcome strangers, accepted at face value as a couple, an audience, a diversion. Epi had said it would be so. It was a standing invitation to Matthew, issued years before.

Rosie almost cried with delight at the silence. After the press of the Riviera, she embraced the solitude. After cramped hotel rooms, a little overstuffed in the French fashion, she revelled in the cool spaces of the villa.

They said they were staying for ten days, until the end of the first week of April. Epi's inconspicuous yacht would then take them both back to Athens. A change of plan would be possible, thanks to the radio telephone. Rosie said there was no question of any change of plan. There were a million things to do on the island, and she would like to stay much longer than ten days.

When she was done with reading, on the morning of their third day, Rosie took to walking. She walked up and down for half an hour and then she had seen every rock on Andílitos. She had a swim. She came out and got dried and dressed and warm again, and that was another half-hour gone. There was still an hour to lunch and it was still only the third day.

Prowling, she found a globe. She spent a little time spinning it, pleased with the humming noise it made when it spun, but not so pleased that she went on doing it long. She looked for the Cyclades, and for Virginia. She found that Andílitos was just south of the 37th parallel, and Somerset County was just south of the 37th parallel. She said the 37th parallel was a rope, a big wire hawser, stretched right across the globe joining Andílitos to Somerset, to Fox Hill.

Rosie wanted a flat green field to run across, a horse to ride, a ladder to climb. She found a ladder and climbed it, and then climbed down again.

Next day they took a boat out, a clinker-built wooden boat, about fifteen feet, with an outboard. Rosie found a use for her bubbling surplus energy in getting the boat all ready, a spare can of gas under the thwart, two bottles of red wine and a corkscrew, oars in case of emergency. She got fishing-lines and hooks, and they gave her scraps of meat from the kitchen to use as bait. She put cushions in the boat. She decided against the awning that could be stretched over most of the boat. That was something for pitiless midsummer, not for this soft, classical spring.

Rosie was proud of thinking it all out and doing all the work. It proved she didn't need Hazel or anybody.

Matthew started the outboard with difficulty, because it had not been used for months. Once it was going it worked well enough.

There was no breath of wind. The sea was as flat as a tin tray. It glared like a tray under a light. It was the hottest day they had had. It was an amazing day for the end of March, after the drizzling miseries of Cagnes.

'Which way?' said Matthew. 'Towards the big island? Explore

that coast?'

'No. Villas and people. Trash in the sea. Go the other way, that way. South, is it? Go to the little rocks you can just see, just poking out of the water. Fish like a place like that.'

They chugged for a long time over the glassy sea. The boat was heavy for the little outboard. The outboard was smelly, with a smell of rubber and hot oil. Rosie wore shorts and a cotton shirt over a bikini. She put a towel over her legs to stop them burning. There was a little oil on the gunwale of the boat. Rosie got oil on her bare leg. She tried to rub it off with the towel, but she smeared the towel with oil without cleaning her leg.

Matthew cut the motor and they drifted.

The rocks were chunks of rubbish and driftwood, something dumped off the deck of a freighter. There were Coke cans and fruit-skins mixed up in it.

'Phoney rocks,' said Rosie, 'put here by one of those gods to lure Whosis to his doom.'

'With cans of Coke?'

'Updated gods. Pepsi on Olympus.'

'I'll get away from the garbage.'

'No, this is where to catch fish. Damn, there goes the bait.'

'Where?'

'Some on my leg and some on this pillow.'

'Those are smart pillows for a boat. Where did they come from?'

'I don't know. A closet. They're boat pillows. Anybody can see that. Will you bait my hook? Look, there's a fish. There's sixteen million fish. Those are the little ones. We'll catch some of them and use them as bait for bigger ones, and use them as bait for bigger ones, and . . . Open a bottle?'

'Why red wine?'

'Why not? Don't grouch. Can't you do something about the smell of that motor? The sun's terrific. I was crazy not to bring a hat. Did you bring sunglasses? Can I borrow them?'

They caught no fish. The sun was as high as it would get and it glared on the sea. The metal of the outboard was almost too hot to touch. Because it was hot it continued to smell, long after it had been switched off. The scraps of meat had stained Rosie's candy-striped pillow with blood, and there was an oil-stain on it.

'I'd be glad of that awning,' said Matthew.

'Don't be a grouch. My wine, my arrangements. You're the one who's supposed to be able to relax. I wish you would kindly please stop rocking this boat. For God's sake sit still.'

'Queasy?'

'Who wouldn't be queasy, with that stinking engine and the boat rolling around and the blood from this meat. I think they gave us bad meat. I think the meat's stinking, too. The hell with the bait. I don't like fish anyway.'

Rosie threw the scraps of meat overboard. Hundreds of tiny fish nuzzled the fragments which, slowly sinking, oozed a thin cloud of blood into the water. Rosie rubbed the blood off her hands onto the pillow and the towel.

'You might have washed them,' said Matthew.

'How?'

'That stuff is an ocean.'

'Ocean full of garbage. What's wrong with you today?'

'Do you have a headache?'

'Yes, a splitting headache, if you want to know. Thanks for enquiring.'

Matthew was getting one too, owing to the glare of the overhead sun on the sea. He would have liked his sunglasses, but Rosie needed them.

Peace fell. Rosie's mood improved. She seemed content to sit looking at the distant lump of Andílitos, or down into the bottle-green water. She drank most of a bottle of red wine, from the bottle. Matthew opened a book. Rosie glanced at it, but said nothing.

She began to shift about on the thwart where she was sitting. It was hard, even with the candy-striped pillow. There was nothing to lean back on. The sun was merciless.

Suddenly Matthew said, 'These pillows came out of the other guestroom. They were on the window-seat there.'

'So?'

'So you made them filthy.'

'We made them filthy. I didn't get that oil on the one you're sitting on.'

'Oil and blood. Pillows out of a bedroom. God Almighty, Rosie, is that a way to return hospitality?'

'Pillows can be cleaned. You take the covers off and clean them.'

'These don't have covers.'

'They should have. It's ridiculous to have pillows without

covers, in a vacation house, a place by the sea. They're bound to get dirty.'

'Epi would hardly expect anybody, any guest of his, to do anything so utterly inconsiderate —'

'Oh, shove it. I have a blinding headache and I'm seasick and I'm sick of being preached at. Don't be so middle-class. I suppose you cover everything with cellophane. I suppose you put a cellophane cover over your hat, in case it gets wet in the rain.'

'You know I don't.'

'How do I know what you do when I'm not looking? I suppose you were screwing that Indonesian hooker when I wasn't looking.'

'I wouldn't call Tanja a hooker.'

'I wouldn't call her the Virgin Mary. What was she whispering to you when we left?'

'I don't want to talk about that.'

'I'll bet you don't. Middle class Eagle Scout, my ass. I challenge you to tell me what she was saying.'

'Very well. She told me Epi gave you 45,000 francs which you owed to that illegal British bookie.'

Rosie stared at him blankly. She said, 'You knew that for five days and you never said anything? Let me go on thinking you didn't know anything about it? Are you truly evil or just crazy? You held it over my head, waiting for a moment. When were you going to drop it?'

'That was not my intention.'

'That was not my intention,' Rosie crudely mimicked.

Red wine, queasiness, glare, headache, guilt, boredom, knowledge that she was in the wrong about the ruined candy-striped pillows, that she was deeply and dreadfully in the wrong about her bets, combined to give stridency to her voice and bitterness to her tongue.

Without answering, Matthew opened the gas-cock on the outboard, opened the choke and throttle, and pulled the cord. The outboard roared. He closed the choke and eased the throttle so that the outboard gurgled in neutral, exhaust drifting in over the stern. He swung the tiller, let in the clutch, and opened the throttle. The boat surged ponderously forward. The outboard coughed and died. Matthew checked the gas-tank. It was empty. He reached for the spare tank, under the thwart where Rosie was sitting. She moved her legs so he could get at it, not looking at him or speaking. It felt light when he lifted it into the stern. He twisted the filler-cap and hinged it back. The spare can was empty. Rosie had put it into the boat without looking inside it, without the lightness of the can conveying any message to her.

Matthew got the two heavy, long-bladed oars out of the bottom of the boat. There were no rowlocks: only wooden pins. He moved to the centre thwart and began to row. It was thoroughly awkward. When he pulled the oar-handles towards him, pressure kept the oars snug to the pins, but when he leaned and reached for the next stroke they slid along the gunwale away from the pins, until he learned the trick of keeping them in place.

He had a very long way to row and it took a very long time. His back was not used to rowing, nor his hands to the scarred wood. The sun was hotter than ever and it glared on the water. Rosie squatted in the bow, her back to him. She said nothing. He looked over his shoulder to steer. Doing so, he saw his sunglasses, too big for her, slip off her nose into the ocean.

Rosie jumped ashore. She looked back. Matthew was purple. Sweat was pouring down his face and neck and forearms. He looked at his hands, straightening them slowly.

It was the moment to end the madness. All he had to do was look at her, come ashore, take her hand.

He did not look at her, but picked up one of the oil-smeared, blood-smeared pillows. He turned it over, and looked at the other side. It was torn. He looked not at Rosie but at the tear.

Rosie said, 'I'm glad I forgot the gas,' and turned and went away into the house.

272

CHAPTER 13

The humiliation was that Rosie had to let him buy her airline ticket home. He did it with his American Express card. She had had one when she started for Europe, but it was one of the casualties of packing and unpacking.

He bought himself a ticket for a different flight. She did not know which, when or whither. It had been impossible for her to break the silence between them. It could have been done in the first minute, the first five minutes, the first hour. After an hour it was impossible. Rosie remembered occasions when she had met people without catching their names, and then finding that, a few meetings later, it had become impossible to ask their names. The question had become a bus which she had missed. She went all kinds of devious ways about discovering names she should have known, was assumed to have known — the names of people who called her 'Rosie' and legitimately thought of her as a friend. In the first minute the question could be asked: 'What did you say your name was?' But every minute after that it became more difficult. Breaking the silence with Matthew was like that. It was like facing a bogy jump on a pony when you were young — the longer you left it unjumped the more hairy it seemed, until it became impossible.

Life was full of things you did all at once or not at all. Having an affair with Matthew was one of them. Others were better, like jumping a hairy fence or asking somebody's name.

Rosie had been airborne for an hour before she suddenly realised that Matthew would pay Epi the 45,000 francs. He had probably already done so, the moment the Dekker girl told him about it: either slipping Epi a cheque when they were saying goodbye, or leaving it under an ashtray in the villa on Andílitos, or giving it to the skipper of the yacht, or mailing it in Athens. It would make him feel marvellously macho, generous, superior, godlike. You could buy a lot of self-satisfaction with $9,000.

A man like that could get self-satisfaction free, a barrel of smugness, just by putting his pants on a hanger, as though having your pants on a hanger was more important than politeness or tenderness or love. She should have stuck to her own kind. Tim had been her kind. She wept for what Tim had been and what he had become. They were whisky tears because by this time they had been airborne for seventy minutes.

Rosie expected to be met at Dulles, the only beautiful airport in the world. Her cable had been undelivered, misunderstood, or ignored; or Hazel had read into it a threat to her virtue. Rosie had no credit cards, cheques or cash. She could not buy a ticket to Charlottesville. She scraped together small change for the telephone. Nobody answered the telephone. She took a cab all the way to Fox Hill, for which the man wanted $75.

Peach glanced outwards, having been looking inwards. He did not get up out of his thinking chair.

He said, 'You are alone?'

Rosie said, 'You were right. For the wrong reasons.'

Hazel was inconsolable. Nothing would stop her talking about Mr Carver. When Peach tried to silence her by threatening to fire her, when he actually did fire her, ordering her out of his presence and out of his house, she ignored him.

Jefferson Dill said, 'Carver. Lava. Lava and leave her.'

Cousin Thalia Collin was deep in a video about expressionist painting, Peach having recently bought a video attachment to the TV with Tim's money.

There was no change in Tim. They looked at Rosie a little oddly at the sanitorium, because she had never before, ever since he went in there, failed to visit him at least twice a week. Tim looked at the wallpaper of his room, and picked at the rug on his knees.

Ed Lindsey, in a different hospital, was definitely better. But he was still there and still in bed. He was fretting about the farm and about Beausoleil. He said it was a load off his mind, knowing that Mr Carver was around and making himself responsible.

Beausoleil looked fit to jump out of his skin. Rosie was sure he had put on a lot of condition since she saw him. Breeding suited

274

him. Often a stallion after a full season of breeding looks drawn, tired, tucked up. Owners are reluctant to have their stallions photographed in the late spring. But Beausoleil had thrived. He was just finished. The mares obliged to revisit him had done so. It seemed his fertility was exceptionally high, which would be an enormous relief to the shareholders.

Rick Field deserved a lot of credit, and Rosie gave it to him.

'We found the trick, Miss Rosie,' said Rick. 'It's havin' folks around that gets to the Beau. It's like he demands his privacy. I never heard of it before, but horses are all different, an' this one is bugged an' spooked an' mean when folks are watchin'. So we shut the big doors, an' just the three of us handled it.'

'You and the twins from Mount Malcolm?'

'That's so, ma'am.'

'I guess we owe those two a lot of money.'

'They don't have no use for money, Miss Rosie. Miss Viola, she gives them ever'thing they needs. They're happy guys.'

'That makes the whole lot of us. Thanks, Rick.'

'My great pleasure, ma'am.'

Matthew found everything at home precisely as he expected it. Fay Candy had the house spotless and his dinner ready. Patti and Chuck Mungo had the farm tidy as a suburban garden and the stock blooming with well-being. Dame Ninette, the Northern Dancer mare, was placidly carrying her foal by Beausoleil.

Fay Candy talked about Miss Mollie, or Mrs Mollie, or Lady Mollie, or the Mistress, following Matthew around with questions and memories. It was ironic that to this fixation Matthew owed Fay's loyalty to himself.

Matthew was not given to introspection but he was given to making plans. He found himself unable to make any plan about his own future, except that, he supposed, he would go on as he was going on. A certain amount of income had to be generated to pay for Mollie and the younger children. His own domestic expenses were trivial. The farm showed a profit. The small quantity of tobacco he had sent to the local auction in January fetched $1.75 a pound, probably ten cents less than it would have made in a bigger warehouse like Lexington's. The new season's seedlings were already being forced under plastic; when they were six inches tall they would be planted out mechanically. The Mungos would get in extra help for that, and for the spraying and hoeing of the young plants, and for the harvest. There were a few Aberdeen Angus bullocks being fattened for the butcher. George Whyte was trying Charollais at Cragrock; it was a possibility for the future. Another possibility was to grow his own hay; Matthew had tried it, and concluded that it was more economical to buy the few tons he needed, but he liked the idea of self-sufficiency and kept the question under permanent review. There were two yearling colts to go to the sales. They were the farm's cash crop, with tobacco an important second. It was all very small beer, and it was his life and it chugged along.

The European adventure had been horribly expensive, in spite of Epi's hospitality. That crazy gambling debt. Epi had torn up a cheque. But Matthew had paid another directly into Epi's account in Athens. The $9,000 had not been sitting to his credit in his own bank. He had to cover the cheque by selling stocks. His broker said it was a bad moment.

A sense of liberation, of uncomplicated relief, lit the days. A sense of loss sometimes hit him in the night so that the muscles of his abdomen knotted like wet string.

Matthew went to Cragrock for the Keeneland races, which had started in the first week of April. He went a little reluctantly, not sure how things stood between himself and George Whyte. Meeting George made him little the wiser. There was no doubt how things stood between himself and Jean: she gave him the kind of welcome that makes walking through a door into a festival. From Alice, from George's sister, his welcome was a little more restrained, but it was a welcome all right. He was happy to see Alice again. She was looking very well and very attractive, having spent an active winter often on horseback, her skin having been lightly bronzed by the spring sunshine. She was soothing and orderly and she made him laugh.

Confirmation was coming in from all around that Beausoleil had got nearly all his forty mares in foal: including those of Ghalib al-Jilani, Epi Makropulos, Luis Valdes, Ralph Hadfield and George Whyte.

Floss, Alice's two-year-old by Mill Reef, was pleasing the trainer Bert Duffy in his fast work on the half-mile dirt training-track. Primrose Path, the two-year-old out of Meadowsweet, was an attractive individual and a good mover, maybe not in the same class but still a potential winner of nice stakes. They were both entered at Keeneland and in the bigger meeting at Louisville.

The Bluegrass Stakes, the principal Derby trial and the most important race of the month, was not run until the penultimate day of the meeting, April 23. The Cragrock Stable's best horse Master Mariner was expected to win it, and to go on to win the Derby. Bert Duffy thought he would do it. Matthew thought he would do it. George Whyte listened to them gravely, and did calculations in his head about the syndication of Master Mariner.

Keeneland was Matthew's favourite track in America, and one of his favourites anywhere. He liked the polished furniture and the great bowls of flowers in the clubhouse. He liked the trees and ornamental shrubs, the grass and sculptured hedges. He liked the seat with his name on it, in the front of the grandstand, among seats bearing names far more celebrated than his. He liked above all the deliberate traditionalism (and he knew how hard they worked to maintain it) and the unobtrusive, sophisticated technology which made the racing more fun for the public and more profitable for the Association. There was no loudspeaker commentary, which would have struck a jarring note, redolent of airports and racing cars; mechanical walkers were forbidden because the horses would have dug trenches in the grass. On the other hand, if there was any episode in a race which resulted in an objection or an enquiry or a disqualification, the videotape was put on a loop and played over and over on the big monitors all over the grandstand. And the pari-mutuel was organized on the most modern lines: every window was both play and pay, to save you standing in two lines; a man with his winnings in his hand, able to have another bet immediately, is more apt to do so, and apt to do so for more money, thus increasing the day's handle and everybody's profit.

The third race on the eighth day was the one chosen for Primrose Path. Maiden colts and geldings, 118 pounds, on the Headley Course of four and a half furlongs. The purse was $10,000, plus $2,300 from the Kentucky Thoroughbred Development Fund if the winner was a Kentucky-sired Kentucky-bred. Primrose Path was not eligible for this bonus. If he won, the premium would revert to the Fund. The race was called the Cragrock; the significance of this was that Mr and Mrs George Whyte had the privilege of presenting a silver julep cup to the winner, as did the owners of all the other farms for which most of

277

the meeting's races were named.

The race was Tuesday. Bert Duffy made the entry by 9.30 a.m. the previous Saturday, the usual forty-eight hour entry rule extended because of the intervening weekend. Primrose Path was inspected by the Starter, who approved him as properly schooled at the gate. Bert Duffy galloped him on the training track — pure sand, so that it was a real all-weather surface — and next day on the main track, which had to be vacated by 9.00 a.m. for maintenance. It cost the stable $2.50 a day per horse to use this facility. Bert used it not because the Keeneland tracks were any better than the one he had at home, but to familiarise his horses, especially the two-year-olds, with Keeneland and with the people and bustle and excitement. Like the other trainers, Bert brought a groom per four horses, a work-rider per half-dozen, and some enthusiastic kids to work as hot-walkers. They brought collapsible cots and bedding, and slept in the tack room. They ate in the 'Keeneland Kitchen', the canteen where Matthew himself had often had excellent meals but to which he had never tempted George Whyte. Bert Duffy's men did not require what some fellows did — the free soup handed out by the Association to grooms whose money had not arrived.

Just before the hour of his race, Primrose Path was led up the two-minute walk from the barn where Bert had his horses. The groom was neatly dressed, as the rules sternly required. Matthew, George Whyte and Bert Duffy were waiting under one of the big trees in the paddock, the one which carried Primrose Path's programme number. The groom led Primrose Path round and round their particular tree. The other nine horses were going round their trees. The crowd, unrestrained and perfectly restrained, pressed all round them. Primrose Path was saddled out there, by his tree; there were stalls the trainers could use, but they only used them in heavy rain, and often not then.

The groom led Primrose Path into the main ring, a tiny area innocent of any stand, surrounded by a hedge like the one in the paddock at Longchamp. The jockey mounted, circled the ring once, then went out by the tunnel on to the track. The field paraded in front of the grandstand, in programme order, policed by three outriders in hunting scarlet. A pony boy in a uniform jacket accompanied each horse. A two-year-old race in the spring meeting was the occasion most likely to call for rodeo riding by outriders and pony boys, if a nervous débutant got rid of his rider and bolted.

The track was in perfect condition, lightly watered by the sprinklers to bind the sandy loam and prevent the meteor-like displacement of dry powder which produces 'cuppiness'. Excess water rolled down the 3½-degree camber to the infield side, and was if necessary squeezed by tractors through the weepholes into the drainage ditch under the inside rim. Nobody connected with a place like Keeneland could understand the blind European loyalty to grass.

Primrose Path, impeccably schooled, behaved well at the gate. He went in like a lamb and came out like a lion. Too like: he punished himself for three-and-a-half, then ran out of gas. He was fifth, beaten three lengths.

'He'll win,' said Matthew to Jean Whyte and Alice Whyte Harding.

'He'll win,' said the jockey to Bert Duffy.

He needed the race, he needed the experience. There were similar races on the tenth, twelfth and fourteenth days of the meeting: same distance, same purse, mostly the same runners except the previous winners.

'You see?' said Sir Merivale Lucas, dandruff on his collar, among the oil paintings and silver salvers of the club house. 'Matt Carver's judgement slipped a bit that time. Of course I'm not implying anything. He bought what he bought, and it wasn't all horseflesh. At least that's the way it seems to me, but you must remember I'm only a poor professional horse-coper doing this sort of thing to live, not a jet-setting bloke taking other blokes' wives to the French Riviera.'

On the thirteenth day, April 22, the Lafayette Stakes was run, the big two-year-old race of the meeting. But Duffy had entered Floss on the closing day, April 8, subscribing the required $25. They considered but rejected the idea of getting a preliminary race into the tough little Mill Reef colt. It cost another $200 to start. The purse had $20,000 added to the tiny sum subscribed by the owners of the entered horses. The $2,000 provided by the Kentucky Thoroughbred Development Fund was, of course, irrelevant to an English-bred. The julep cup presented to the winning owner was gold instead of silver, as with the other six stakes races of the meeting.

Rain fell torrentially all that third week of April, bringing welcome green to the over-dry pasture of the Blue Grass country. Though heavy machinery squeezed and squeezed at the five-inch layer of mixed sand and loam above the two-inch layer of clay, forcing the water out of the surface into the infield ditch, still more rain fell, sopping into the track as fast as the rollers pushed it out. The effect was a kind of cuppiness opposite to that of a dry and powdery surface. The sandy loam slopped away from the impact of a horse's hoof, too liquid to bind. The foot slipped backwards an inch or two or three every time it hit the ground. The strain on pasterns and tendons was doubled.

With hindsight, Bert Duffy thought they should have taken one of the minor races of the previous two weeks, have a bird in the hand while the track was perfect. He had an idea Matthew Carver shared this view, but neither of them voiced it. It was nice to see Mrs Harding so excited, after the rough time she'd had in California. It would be a shame to say anything to spoil her pleasure.

The rain eased to a drizzle when the horses came up from the barns. They saddled in the open. Nobody used the stalls. Some of the runners were fretful in the wet.

A few minutes before post time. Horses met jockeys in the main ring. With six minutes to go they went out on to the track, parading in the drizzle. They reached the gate and began to load. Men and horses had trouble. The assistant starters were physically manhandling some of the nervous two-year-olds into their slots. It was difficult through the thick air to see from the grandstand what was going on. Drizzle steamed the lenses of binoculars.

Hands trembled, trying to hold binoculars steady — Alice's, Jean's, Matthew's, Bert Duffy's.

The dash through the mud was over almost before it had started. Floss won, on three legs. It was a performance of the utmost merit and the utmost courage. Travelled racegoers were reminded of Henbit's victory in the 1980 Epsom Derby. Nobody could guess what pain Floss suffered in the last few strides, or while he was pulling up. Maybe the adrenalin pumped by the battle hid the pain for a moment.

All the gilt was rubbed off the gingerbread, and off the gold julep cup presented to Alice by the Keeneland Association.

A sour, sick thought came into Matthew's mind, as they loaded a hobbling Floss into the van with the vet hovering and Alice close to tears: Fred Cottle would be pleased. Ashamed of being pleased, but nobody could help feeling a bit viciously pleased.

The next day, Blue Grass day, saw a notable triumph for the Cragrock Stable. Primrose Path won the two-year-old maiden race, $6,500 to the winner and a silver julep cup. Master Mariner won the Blue Grass Stakes, $97,500, $15,000 from the K.T.D.F., another gold julep cup. He was confirmed automatically as one of the favourites for the Derby, nine days later at Louisville.

By this time it was known that Floss would not run again as a two-year-old and probably not ever.

'Ironic, isn't it?' said Sir Merivale Lucas. 'The horses Matthew Carver picks break down or win piddling little maidens. The horses George Whyte breeds are favourites for the classics.'

'Matt Carver bred Master Mariner,' said someone who knew Cragrock. 'At least, I believe he planned the mating.'

'Of course you believe that, dear trusting soul. Because that's what he's been telling everybody for years. If Carver's so much cleverer, why is Whyte so much richer?'

There were indications that George Whyte shared this view, though he never said so to his family or to Matthew. He did not mention Matthew's contribution to the breeding of Master Mariner, in his evening call to Lee V. Lowe in New York. 'Popular Kentucky sportsman acclaimed for local victory in Blue Grass.'

'Antony had a sort of hex on Caesar,' said Jean to Alice. 'Every time they played any kind of game, Antony won.'

'In the end, Caesar had a hex on Antony,' said Alice. 'Every battle they fought, Caesar won.'

'They do need each other.'

'I know it.'

'Part of the time George knows it, too, and it irritates the hell out of him. And it shows and it gets to Matthew. There's a limit to how much needle Matthew can be expected to take.'

'We have to glue them together, for everybody's sake,' said Alice. 'As I said to Ghalib, or maybe Ghalib to me.'

'What about his kids?'

'Ghalib's?'

'Matthew's, dummy. Suppose we got them out from under the Prison Visitor? Asked them here for the summer vacation? Would that be glue?'

'I guess that depends on what the kids are like.'

'The older girl is great. The others I don't know anything about. They fit perfectly with Hal and Alicia, age-wise. I'll see what Matthew thinks.'

Matthew thought the idea completely excellent, for reasons unconnected with his relationship with George. He was not certain Liz would be prised out of her commune, or even contacted; he was not certain Clare would want to be 4,000 miles away from Tom Kavanagh; he was very certain Jamie would benefit from country air, Kentucky cooking, supervision, and an ocean between himself and his mother. He wrote to each of the children immediately, quick affectionate letters, promising to pay for the tickets. He wrote with extraordinary care to Mollie.

Lee V. Lowe made all that he possibly could out of Master Mariner's victory in the Kentucky Derby, which was achieved on May 2 with the authority of a really good horse. Potted biographies of Mr George Whyte. Accounts of Cragrock, interior and exterior. Pictures, dozens of pictures. Mr George Whyte with mares and foals, giving rides to handicapped children, among his books. Mrs George Whyte among her roses, her antiques. Notes of her Baltimore background. Tradition of public service, charitable work. Rewrite men did ruthless things to Lee V. Lowe's more lyrical handouts, but some of the pictures got printed.

Two weeks later Master Mariner went to Pimlico and won the Preakness. Baltimore people gave a great welcome to Jean McLean Whyte, of which Lee V. Lowe was able to make further use.

Matthew saw Rosie in the distance. He maintained that distance. He imagined she was taking the same evasive action. A number of horses were running at the meeting in the colours of Tim Phillipson, of which a two-year-old and a four-year-old won. Matthew's fleeting and distant impression was that Rosie looked less than her best, even in victory. He thought her face was thinner but the rest of her less thin. He did not know the people she was with.

The Cragrock Stable picked up more prizes to add to the tally from Keeneland and Churchill Downs.

At the beginning of the Pimlico meeting, Matthew heard from Fred Cottle that Dandy Dinmont was entered in a good-class maiden at Newbury; on Preakness day he heard that his colt had won, on good ground, in a good time. The news stirred complex memories.

At Louisville and at Baltimore Matthew's most constant companion was Alice Whyte Harding. This was to an extent the result of manoeuvres by Jean, which were neither crassly obvious nor quite invisible; it seemed to accord with Alice's wishes; it accorded with his. Summer suited Alice. Her petals opened in the sun like a periwinkle. She laughed more. Thin silk and cotton clothes revealed the suppleness of her figure. She looked an athlete, a swimmer and tennis player.

Tennis not drunken. Tennis not in the dark, in the rain.

Alice was excellent company, rational, well-informed, excited by the races, moved by the beauty of thoroughbred horses. She was friendly to old friends and new friends. She was punctual. When she dropped anything she picked it up. She was sometimes pensive but never sour. She was unmoody. She was at once stimulating and restful.

Matthew remembered a remark made by a man friend about a woman friend: 'She would be my favourite person to sit next to in a long chair on a lawn in the sun.'

Many of the horsemen who came to Pimlico had heard by now about Beausoleil's exceptional fertility. A number had actually been to Fox Hill to see him. There was heavy demand for nominations for the following season, for which Matthew was able to ask, on behalf of the members of the syndicate, prices which already went far to covering the original investment. If any shares had been for sale, they could have fetched twice the original price. This was still eight months before Beausoleil's first foal would be born; nineteen months before the first foals were yearlings; twenty-six months before the first yearlings came into the sale-ring; and almost three full years before the first two-year-olds saw a race-track.

Everybody knew that Matthew Carver was acting as an agent in the management of the stallion. Many people knew that, in this capacity, he had somehow supplanted Henri de Cheminade and the Agence Fille de l'Aire. An increasing number of people knew, as day followed gossipy day, that Matthew had treacherously seduced the owners of the horse from an absolute moral commitment.

Clare was spending more money than she could afford, commuting between London and Tipperary. During April, with Jamie at home with his mother from the Oxford crammer, she had felt able to spend most of her time with Tom at Ballycardeen or with his family in County Meath. May was more difficult and more expensive.

Her father's letter to Liz had been enclosed with hers. She managed to deliver it. She did not see Liz.

Her engagement to Tom was entirely settled between them, and had been for months. There were problems about making it official. Dr Kavanagh and his wife were careful, old-fashioned people who thought six months was a dangerously short time for a couple to have known each other; in their world engagements were 'an understood thing' for years before they were announced, and lasted years after they were announced. They grew very fond of Clare, but as a wife for their adored only son they viewed her with a certain alarm. Her accent was so strange, though like most of the rest of Ireland they had American connections. She adapted herself cheerfully to their busy, unglamorous way of life, and made herself much loved by Tom's younger sisters, but she gave his parents the impression of a bomb with an unpredictable detonator. They were dubious about a father living with and off horses in Kentucky, in spite of their son's own choice of career. They were dubious about a titled English mother, and dismayed at the separation of Clare's parents.

Mollie was an obstacle which, ultimately, Clare foresaw having to ignore. She did not want to hurt and enrage her mother by marrying in defiance of her wishes, of her most passionate convictions, but she faced doing so. Mollie hated Catholics. She referred to bog-Irish, hedge-priests, and sometimes even to the Scarlet Woman. Clare had great difficulty keeping her temper, when she heard Tom's serious and deeply humane father called a Mick quack. It was a problem to which there was no ultimate solution, and a temporary one only of silence.

Tom's parents were in favour of her going to America in the summer. A separation would make them more certain of their feelings. Tom and Clare were perfectly certain of their feelings, and did not at all want the separation: but putting all factors together (including a free ticket) they agreed that Clare should go.

There was a possibility that, at Ghalib's expense, Tom would go to the Saratoga sales in August.

Mollie was violently against any of her children going to America. The dear old friends she visited in prison warmly supported this view. America was full of gangsters and blacks and materialistic values and martini cocktails. Mollie returned from each visit to her grand old friends confirmed in her determination to protect her younger children from the contagion of their father's country.

She tried to make Liz and Jamie wards of court. The family solicitors advised her that the attempt was misconceived. At her insistence, there had been neither divorce nor legal separation. The children were not children. They were of an age to choose where they went, and with whom. The father was well-known and respected. Persons of the highest standing vouched for him. There was no way he could be debarred from giving them a summer vacation in America. They both still had the option of choosing American nationality. Mollie took her grievances to the Tibbs Hill Women's Prison, where the view was generally held that all lawyers made a good thing out of the troubles of the underdog.

Mario di Vianello warned Jamie that smuggling drugs into America was a bad idea. Uncertain of supplies when he got there, Jamie nevertheless made plans involving waterproof sachets inside bottles of hair-oil.

Liz pictured swimming pools, gardens, unlimited hot water, sheets changed every few days, food paid for and prepared by somebody else, and her mother 4,000 miles away. The commune had become less attractive in hot weather, the people rancid and the babies fretful. Ali regretted her departure, but he was too lazy and too tolerant to do anything about it. She went with the apathetic goodwill of her friends.

Matthew was in New York. It seemed a pointless additional expense for Clare to go there, with nothing particular to do, in weather already uncomfortably hot. She flew to Chicago and on to Lexington, and went straight to Cragrock in a Blue Grass Limousine, one of the fleet of misnamed minibuses operating from the airfield. Her father would join her there, when he had finished with his bankers and brokers. There was more for her to do at Cragrock than at home; more for him, too. He had to be in Lexington for the Fasig-Tipton and Keeneland Select yearling sales in July.

Clare had been to Cragrock many times, though not recently. She had known the family all her life. George had not changed within her memory. He remained aloof and alarming, with little to say, with interests above anything anybody young could talk about. Jean had changed a little, growing cooler and more formidable, more certain even than before to wear the right clothes, do and say the right things. It would be easy to incur her disgust. But she was most welcoming to Clare. The ice queen showed her sunniest face. The stranger to Clare was Alice, the divorcée, the ex-Californian, the hardly credible sister to George. Clare liked her very much, and immediately. She understood that her father had been at Cragrock a good deal, and with the Cragrock party at the races; that he and Alice were great friends. Alice herself made this clear. Clare understood that her father and Alice would be congenial. She did not understand why her father had never mentioned Alice, in his letters or on the telephone. Was he so little interested in this charming, amusing, highly attractive lady?

Clare deduced that her father had never mentioned Alice for the opposite reason.

This naturally set her speculating. Her mind recoiled from what seemed the probabilities, not because she was a prig but because he was her father. There was no future in it. It was consequently furtive and squalid. Not for anybody else, necessarily, but for her father. Clare knew her mother's views. She would have to have been autistic not to have been mistress in detail of Mollie's views on a thousand subjects: most notably marriage, sanctity of.

It was thoroughly unseemly, thoroughly distasteful, for Clare to compare Alice to Mollie. It was impossible not to. Clare imagined her father refusing to make the same comparison, and making it.

It appeared that the woman in Virginia was out of her father's life.

Doris Bernard had never seen anybody who attracted her as strongly as Clare Carver did. The bouncy walk, the coiled-spring look, the perfect skin and wide-apart eyes, the little tilted nose, the tiny wrists and ankles, the small high breasts jutting joyously . . .

'Jutting joyously': that was the phrase Doris used to herself, aware that it was mawkish but rolling it around her tongue. She fluttered and twittered about Clare, and showed her which guest-room she was in. She pictured a fleece black and richly curly, little buttocks pink after a bath, avid acquiescence, tremulous gratitude.

Doris watched Clare on the tennis court, in very short shorts, her legs slim and lovely. She watched her by the pool, in a one-piece and then in a bikini, a tiny European bikini. She made friends with Clare, talking to her about books and horses and the new places to go in New York. She talked about a bar where only girls went, where only girls were welcome except for a few known gays who were their friends. It was like a singles bar for girls only. You never saw so many beautiful girls under one roof, said Doris. It was moving, touching, impressive, to see so much beauty, so much kindness and affection. More trust than with men. More gentleness. Less risk.

Clare seemed interested, curious. She smiled at Doris. Doris saw complicity, invitation in the smile.

Doris went softly to Clare's room when she knew Clare was having a tub after tennis. It was the best moment. It had worked times without number. Clare came naked and dripping out of the bath into the bedroom. She squeaked when she saw Doris. She did not seem much embarrassed. Of course she had been to boarding-school and college. Doris gurgled with joy at the clear translucent pink of Clare's nipples. She fluttered forward, offering to dry Clare.

Clare heaved her out of the room and slammed the door on her.

Doris was angry and humiliated. She had a gut-ache from frustration. Clare hurt her wrists, heaving her out of the room. She was stronger than she looked, stronger than Doris, stronger than she had any business to be. She was a snob and a cold fish and a bully. She had not even taken time to cover herself up before laying violent hands on Doris. She was that contemptuous. She was arrogant and cruel and unfeeling, and she needed taking down a lot of pegs.

Clare had been amused by the secretary's ultra-girlish birdlike act. She responded to friendliness with friendliness, and Doris could be pretty interesting. The ineptness of the overture, when it came, startled her more than the fact of it: she had attracted dykes before. She assumed Doris would now leave her alone, since she had made her position clear. She wondered whether to say something to Jean, not by way of complaint (because nothing had happened) or in the way of outrage (she was irritated but not greatly shocked) but because it might be more of an abuse of hospitality to keep quiet than to tell. A little uneasily she decided it was none of her business. But she would keep an eye on Liz, if Liz did ever turn up.

Alicia came home from school, a big girl, almost unrecognisable to Clare who remembered her as an unformed child. She seemed genuinely pleased to see Clare again, and to be a genuine and responsive person. She was lazy. The heat got to her. She lay around, in sharp contrast to the aunt from whom her name had been derived, in sharp contrast to Clare herself, who went riding — usually with Alice — very early every morning.

Clare wondered a little about Alicia and Doris Bernard. But there was nothing visible between them. They seemed to have no common ground — nothing to say to each other. Short of a horrible kind of snooping, Clare could learn nothing. It was still none of her business. She was a guest in the house. It was not only Jean's responsibility to interfere, if there was anything to interfere with, it was also her privilege.

Doris and Alicia liked it best in the dawn. Doris would wait until she heard the horses being brought round to the front door. Voices below. The horses clattering away. Then she crept into Alicia's room and slipped into bed beside her.

Hal came home from his school, a surprise to Clare but only for a moment. Shoulder-length hair, jagged-ended jeans and bare feet looked strange at Cragrock, but Hal was not much different from a million others. He was incongruous, set against the rest of his family: but anywhere except Cragrock they would have looked as much oddities as he, survivals, too good to be true, People of Distinction in a full-page colour advertisement in a *New Yorker* of thirty years earlier.

Hal had plenty to say to his mother, his aunt, his sister, and Clare. He suffered from excess of communication, rather than lack of it. He was into world affairs, politics, whaling and other conservationist causes, self-help in the third world, and various New Sounds from Detroit and London for which Clare already felt herself too old.

As far as Clare saw, Hal and his father never exchanged a word.

Matthew arrived from New York with Jamie and Liz. Thereafter, the adults practically never saw any of the kids again. Jean had been right: they fitted age-wise and in all other wise. It was curious to see them, which the adults occasionally did, fleetingly, at a distance. Liz and Alicia, Jamie and Hal. The girls might have been sisters, both describable as juicy, wholesome. The boys were in amusing contrast, Hal so hippy, Jamie comparatively square, neatly dressed and with his hair brushed. It was possible to forget completely about all of them, confident that they were amusing themselves and each other, confident that they could come to no possible harm.

'Of course I know I look grotesque to you,' said Jamie to Hal. 'And sound like a caricature of somebody with buck teeth and a top hat. Camouflage. Invaluable. Anyone looking at me would assume I knew the latest cricket score. Anyone looking at you would assume you smoked pot.'

'I do.'

'Is that all?'

'A guy gave me some tablets at school. I threw up.'

'How lucky for you that Jamie the genie has come into your life.'

'Jesus, I don't know.'

'Chicken. Try it once. Good boy.'

And Hal had his first injection of heroin.

'It's the sweetest thing,' said Doris. 'You won't believe what you feel. It's the cosiest thing, three of us together. Ah, my God, I could eat you, darling. I'm gonna eat you. And Alicia's gonna eat you. Doesn't that feel something else?'

Under the expert caresses of Doris, the eager tyro fingers of Alicia, Liz presently exploded into an orgasm more powerful and prolonged than any she had experienced with Ali.

There was no declaration. There was no moment at which Matthew said anything unequivocal. Friendship grew, subtly changing, putting out leaves of a different shape and texture, as though radioactive isotopes had secretly bombarded it. Hands touched and stayed touching, clasped and stayed clasped, out of sight of anybody, below table-tops, in cars. He put one evening, in the dark of the porch, a hand on her knee. That was the nearest he came to a speech. She put a hand on his hand. That was the nearest she came.

When he went to her room she was expecting him. They had the bonus of a moon. She had wanted it very badly, for a long time. He was astonished at her passion, at her storm of silent tears. She was a lovely, sobbing animal in the moonlight. She was the more exciting because of her daytime self-possession, her cool friendliness, her affable correctness.

Her smile transfigured her, outshining the moon, and, when he left her, the red peep of the rind of the rising sun.

'She's too gabby,' said Alicia to Liz. 'The lovey crap. All that *talk*. It's kind of embarrassing, actually.'

'It's a bore,' said Liz.

'It's a *baw*. I do love your accent.'

'As long as I don't use it too much.'

'Yeah. That qualification. What a long word for this time of night. You want it?'

'Yes.'

'Me too.'

So, silently, together in the dark of the garden, they did some of the things to each other Doris had taught them.

There were suddenly voices near them, very near, the other side of a hedge. They had not heard footsteps on the thick sward of daily-sprinkled grass. Fingers froze. Tongues withdrew. They lay like logs.

A couple were making love on the grass on the other side of the hedge. Perhaps not literally. The preliminaries. A woman's uneven breathing, unmistakable though voiceless. The tiny clearing of a man's throat.

The girls stole away, fixing their clothes.

'You know who that was?' said Alicia.

'Yes.'

'I don't blame either of them. If you go for the hetero bit.'

'Yes, but my papa is married.'

'That didn't stop him before.'

'I know. Everybody was talking about that. Even I heard about it. I read about it.'

'What do you want to do about it?'

'Nothing. I like your aunt.'

'So do I. She's nice. But what a bomb. What a *grenade* we have.'

'To make a bang if we want one.'

'Kind of a distraction, to take the enemy's eye off something else, like maybe for example us.'

'That kind of thing. Silence in the meantime.'

'I promise. Come to my room.'

'Doris is too close.'

'I'll come to yours.'

'No,' said Liz. 'Not now. Not tonight. I'm suddenly not in the mood.'

Matthew had been relieved to meet in New York a Liz looking clean and conventional. Jamie had always looked clean and conventional; he looked reasonably healthy too. Clare at Cragrock looked marvellous. No doubt love helped. Matthew gave his blessing to her union with Tom Kavanagh, but that depended on the resolution of problems which existed in areas he could not influence. He was glad Clare and Alice got on so well, and Clare and Jean, and Liz and Alicia, and Jamie and Hal. He himself got on moderately well with George, who was mellowed by the two classic victories of Master Mariner, and by the much-publicised purchase of two million-dollar yearlings at the sales.

Matthew suggested taking his children to his own home, but Jean was very anxious they should all stay at Cragrock. And really it was a much better idea. He could not offer pool or tennis court, or nearly as much social life for the kids as there was round Lexington. Jean was quite frank that she was thinking of her own children as much as of Matthew's.

Matthew found a happiness, a kind of tranquil and ordered happiness relieved from all banality by passion, that he had stopped believing in. It was wonderful to believe in it again: the optimum relationship; the best of all worlds; except that it led nowhere beyond her bed or his. She knew that as well as he did. They settled for a second best with gratitude.

CHAPTER 14

Miss Viola Biggs of Mount Malcolm seldom went to the races in Kentucky or Maryland and never on Long Island, but she always made Saratoga in August. It had simply become, over the years, a thing she was in the habit of doing. She always stayed at the same motel near Hudson Falls, hiring a car from the same man when she got there. She always took her distant kinsman Fairfax J. Creevey. This year Fairfax wrote to say he'd slipped on the steps of a hotel in Richmond and broken his pelvis. Miss Viola Biggs had no wish to go to Saratoga alone, no intention of forgoing her annual outing. Reservations were already made for two cabins at the motel, and the car was fixed. Her choice of a substitute companion was automatic: Rosie. Rosie had been worrying Miss Viola Biggs. She had been in a state of apathy not for minutes or hours at a time but for weeks at a time. Fox Hill was full of unfinished projects — doors half-painted, holes half-dug — because apathy had overtaken the only person there who ever got anything done.

Rosie immediately accepted. Peach forbade her to go. She had already been away for weeks in the spring. She was needed at home. He needed her. Tim needed her. She would meet the man Carver at the track or at the sales.

'I'll avoid him like I did at Pimlico,' Rosie said. 'He'll avoid me too.'

'He is a snake.'

'I'll put my foot on his neck.'

'He will turn and bite you, injecting the venom of his treachery.'

'I'll bite him back. I wouldn't mind a confrontation, actually. I didn't scream at anybody in weeks. I think it would be — what's the word?'

'Unseemly? Repulsive?'

'Cathartic. Now there's a word I didn't know I knew.'

'I form the view that you do not know it. How can screaming be purgative? How can forcible emission of air from the lungs, by way of the larynx, scour the bowels? The idea has only to be examined to be dismissed. You may not go to Saratoga. That is my last word on the subject.'

'I don't believe you,' said Rosie.

She decided to take Hazel. This was Miss Viola Biggs's suggestion. Hazel could look after them both. Rosie was indignant at the inference that she could not look after herself, but memories of the spring returned to silence her. Hazel was excited. She had never been north of the Mason-Dixon line. All the Yankees would try to defile her virtue, by blandishment or violence, but she'd be steadfast, stand like a rock.

Ghalib al-Jilani told Tom Kavanagh to be ready to go to Saratoga at the beginning of August. Business had prevented Ghalib from going to Keeneland, or from sharing as he might have some of the glory of Master Mariner's victories. He wanted to increase the scale of his involvement at Cragrock. He wanted Matthew's advice about yearlings and about another European trainer. He wanted to give Tom Kavanagh a vacation after the hard work of the previous ten months. He wanted Tom to feel important, involved with the selection of stock for the future, because he believed this would make Tom a more efficient and committed manager at Ballycardeen.

Tom wrote to Clare at Cragrock . . .

. . . a letter which she read 130 times, and then put under her handkerchiefs in a drawer with his other letters. She got to work on her father immediately. Matthew was dubious. Bert Duffy was taking a few horses to Saratoga, but they were not important ones and they were not entered in stakes races. Cragrock was not selling yearlings, and had no plans to buy. George was not going. Jean and Alice had social commitments. None of the kids wanted to go. Matthew was on the point of letting Clare go to Saratoga on her own, if she could find anywhere to stay, when he heard from Ghalib. Ghalib's invitation was pressing, and he offered, in the most tactful way, to pay all Matthew's expenses.

Saratoga was full of horses, under the sunny elm trees, crossing busy streets, led or ridden or both. For three and a half weeks a small town with medicinal mud became a seething pudding of wealth, chicanery, drink and outrageous overcharging.

Matthew steered Clare towards the track and then towards the clubhouse, where they were meeting people for lunch. Clare stopped dead. Her face went pink. Matthew laughed. He went on ahead, to tell their friends that Clare might be a little late for lunch — might even miss it completely. He glanced back as he went into the clubhouse from the paddock. Tom Kavanagh was holding both Clare's hands in his. Their grins looked so broad as to be painful.

At the Lake View Motor Inn, Hazel was washing some underclothes for Miss Viola Biggs.

'Saw that Matthew Carver today,' said Miss Viola.

'Man,' said Hazel. 'I'd like to *resurrect* that scene.'

'So would I. He was good for Rosie.'

'Sho was. She bin pinin'. Say she hate him, but she don't, not deep.'

'Well, here they both are.'

'What we gon' do 'bout *resurrectin'* the scene?'

'Plant a tree in the rain, in the dark.'

'Ain't got no tree, no rain. Gotten us a heap o' *dark*.'

'An' bourbon.'

'They ain't *no* harm,' said Hazel, 'in assistin' resurrection night by the means o' lubricatin' juice. We-all gotta set an' *plan*, Miss Viola.'

'I'll set,' said Miss Viola. 'You-all keep right on with the laundry.'

Matthew was surprised to be called by Miss Viola Biggs. She said she had found out from friends where he was stopping. She said she was calling rather than taking the chance of meeting him at the track or the sales. She said that, in any case, she wanted a talk with him a little more leisured and confidential than they could have in those places. There were a few things she wanted to ask him about. Advice she needed. Help she needed. Could he make time to drop by for a drink, next day, after the evening session at the sales?

'That's *good,* Miss Viola,' said Hazel. 'Muss Matthew not a man evah gon' turn down a S.O.S. fum a lady.'

'A helpless ol' lady,' said Miss Viola Biggs. 'A mischievous, meddlin' ol' fraud.'

Rosie was asked, by a foreign-sounding voice on the telephone, to be in her room at 10.30 to take a transatlantic call, a call from Paris.

She thought it must be horse business, a breeder or a dealer. Conceivably Epi Makropulos, with conceivably a query about Beausoleil. Whoever it was would have called Fox Hill, and been given the number of the motel. This was a lot more probable with Hazel out of the house. Evidently the call from Paris had been reserved. This was odd. Three-thirty a.m., Paris time. And why not just dial? Anyway it was perfectly convenient for Rosie, however late the party in Paris was staying up.

It was a hot night. Rosie undressed and showered, and lay on her bed in a short terry wrap provided by the management of the motel. She drank bourbon on the rocks and smoked cigarettes and waited for the call.

'God almighty,' said Rosie. 'What are you doing here?'

'I came to see Viola Biggs. This is the number she gave me.'

'I get it. You know what you are? You're a call from Paris.'

'The old snake.'

'Hazel's in it too, I guess. She spent the evening looking roguish. Ever seen Hazel looking roguish? Repulsive spectacle.'

Rosie was talking quickly and foolishly, in her intense embarrassment.

Matthew looked extraordinarily well and very handsome. He was not an obviously, a flashily or conventionally handsome man, but to her he was beautiful. His face was kind and puzzled and he looked as embarrassed as she felt. She wanted him badly and immediately.

If she had ever had any pride about anything she forgot it. Pride was supremely unimportant compared to what was important, which was having Matthew back. If she had ever felt rage or impatience with him she forgot them, too.

'I was wrong and stupid in the spring,' she said.

'I wasn't very charming.'

'You were horrible. You were wonderful. Ah God, we're talking. I thought we never would. Have a drink.'

She saw him hesitate.

He could at that moment have turned around and walked out, politely, saying something polite. It was another of those moments. Every second that he didn't walk out made it more difficult for him to do so.

Rosie watched him, wanting him, suffocated by suspense. His hesitation seemed endless.

'There's a bottle of what they call branch-water, in the ice-box,' Rosie said in a voice that sounded silly to herself. 'But I think it comes out of the faucet. They fill the bottles out of the faucet. That's what I think. The *label* is genuine. You can drink bourbon and branch-water with a genuine label. I can offer that much hospitality.'

Rosie was talking to hold him in the doorway. He couldn't decently turn and walk away, not while she was talking. He had perfect manners. If a lady was talking to him he would hold still and listen, even if she was talking aimless crap. She continued talking aimless crap in order to prolong his moment of indecision, in order to make it more difficult for him to go, in order to get him back into her life and into her bed.

'I didn't mean one single one of those things I said in the spring, even at the time,' Rosie lied.

She thought her bare legs looked good in the shaded golden light. Her hair was a mess and her face was creamed clear of make-up.

'You don't have to forgive me,' said Rosie, 'but you do have to have a drink.'

As though handling the detonator of a large bomb, Matthew took a drink.

Rosie burst into tears. She had not expected to do so, and did not want to do so, but the tears came beautifully on cue. She sobbed into his shoulder, which was suddenly and inevitably there to be sobbed into. Good manners, again — good manners, of course. Surely to God, thought Rosie as she sobbed, I have him back now?

He comforted her, and she had him back.

She felt more of a whore than when she had offered herself to Epi Makropulos.

After the sales Clare was with Tom Kavanagh. Ghalib was due in Saratoga the following day; Tom's time would no longer be his own. This factor, and the joy of reunion, caused things to get quite out of hand. It was dawn when Tom dropped Clare back at her hotel. She went in self-consciously, avoiding the eye of a cleaning-lady. She went to get her key from the night clerk at the desk. She found her father doing the same thing.

They both put a bravely casual face on it. She was more surprised than he was.

Matthew came face to face with Rosie in the paddock. They nodded to each other, and after a moment shook hands. This much-discussed pantomime was observed by many persons who knew one or both, who knew about the fall and about the spring.

Rosie tried to keep a straight, cool face; her smile escaped like a bird bursting out of a paper bag. Matthew had to grin too.

'My, what a lovely couple they do make,' said Miss Viola Biggs sentimentally.

Miss Biggs was overheard by a bloodstock agent, a jockey's agent and a journalist, none of whom misunderstood and none of whom kept quiet.

Sir Merivale Lucas was one of the first to hear, and one of the first to see Matthew Carver and Rosie standing grinning at each other like dummies in a rose-coloured window. The sight turned spades in his stomach. Rosie was suddenly insanely beautiful, after a summer in which she had not been at her best, in which Sir Merivale had persuaded himself that she was not worth powder and shot. Now his desire was increased by the fact of somebody else desiring her, of only too evidently having her. Sir Merivale felt ill with jealousy.

Henri de Cheminade was one of the first to hear. He immediately told Prince Ghalib al-Jilani, who had just arrived by helicopter from a manufacturer in Albany. Henri used the conjunction of events to discredit Matthew Carver, with the ultimate object of recovering the position (which he had never quite officially occupied) of Ghalib's racing manager.

Ghalib looked like a well-dressed hawk, an Old Harrovian predator. He looked as though he would have carried a dagger in his belt, but that his pants were too well cut to require a belt. Ghalib pointed out Rosie to Tom Kavanagh as the owner of the farm where Beausoleil stood. Aware from Clare, from racecourse gossip and from newspapers, of Rosie's reputation and recent history, Tom looked at her with interest. He was captivated. He wanted to meet Rosie, but Ghalib seemed reluctant to go over and introduce him.

Clare joined them to find Tom goggling and Ghalib uncharacteristically embarrassed. She saw her father talking, talking with a very broad smile, to a beautiful woman about ten years older than herself.

The woman turned, saw Ghalib, and waved. Matthew nodded to Ghalib, Tom, and his daughter. Politeness obliged Ghalib to cross the grass to Rosie, to shake hands with her and Matthew, to introduce Tom and Clare. Clare saw his reluctance with a surprise that disappeared when she heard Rosie's name.

That was where he had been all night. It was supposed to be all over.

No wonder Ghalib was embarrassed, introducing herself to her father's mistress. Her father should have been embarrassed too, but he looked like the cat that had got at the cream.

Clare scrutinised Rosie with suspicion, and responded ungraciously to Rosie's greeting. Loyalty to her mother and affection for Alice Harding fought an illogical battle in Clare's head. Rosie was caught in the crossfire, neutral in the war between Mollie and Alice but deadly enemy to both. Rosie tried to be charming to Clare. Objectively Clare understood that Rosie had charm as well as great beauty, that she was not only a man's woman, but she resisted the charm.

Tom did not, made no attempt to. Later he was tactlessly extravagant in his praise of Rosie to Clare. Clare bit his head off.

'Your father's grown up,' said Tom. 'She is smashing. You can't be jealous unless you've got an Elektra complex, which I don't think you have, or you wouldn't be marrying me.'

'I don't know if I am,' said Clare.

'You don't mean that.'

'No. But shut up about that woman.'

Matthew and Clare pretended to each other that both had been behaving, Clare with her fiancé and Matthew with various old friends. They pretended that Rosie was a casual acquaintance, even referring to her, to each other, as 'Mrs Phillipson': even after the gossip was published, the testimony of a maid at the motel eliminating any risk of libel.

Ghalib had long conferences with Matthew about the future of his new American mares and their produce. Profiting by Matthew's advice, consulting Tom Kavanagh also, he bought two yearling fillies whose breeding made them potential broodmares. He was able to feel that he was now in intimate collaboration with Matthew; the next time he went to Newmarket he would be on different terms with Lord Hadfield and the Duke of Hampshire.

Unless the bundle of dynamite labelled Rosie Phillipson blew Matthew out of Cragrock and out of the eminence in racing Cragrock helped to give him. Ghalib hoped this Saratoga reunion was a romp or lark such as people enjoy on shipboard. But he detected a depressing stench of permanence in the way Matthew and Rosie looked at each other.

Clare took a passionate farewell of Tom, saying that she would come almost at once to Ireland, that his parents could now be sure they were sure of their feelings.

'As long,' said Clare, 'as you keep quiet about that woman.'

She went back by herself to Cragrock, to pack her things and say goodbye to them all.

They knew all about it at Cragrock.

Jean kept quiet about it, in deference to what she knew were Alice's feelings. Alice kept quiet about it because she had dignity and courage. Liz and Jamie refused to discuss it or hear about it, which Clare thought right. Alicia and Hal were not interested. Hal was not much interested in anything. Doris Bernard twittered something about it, with the evident intention of enraging Clare. She succeeded, but Clare did her best to deny Doris the satisfaction of seeing this.

George had been away. He came back full of bitterness against Matthew, whom he suspected of having trifled with Alice. He, most taciturn of the household, was the only one who talked about the Saratoga scandal.

'Don't be mad on my account,' said Alice. 'I never owned Matthew or any bit of him. How could I, ever? He has a wife.'

'I wish he'd remember that,' said George.

Alice was glad he'd forgotten it. At the same time she wished she had never met Matthew. It was hard luck to have your heart broken twice.

From the moment of Rosie's tears in the motel bedroom, Matthew knew he was hooked, caught, netted, gaffed, imprisoned, a lifer, not by anything Rosie did or said but by his own passion for her, by the way his spirits lifted when she came into a room so that he nearly did a song-and-dance, or turned cartwheels.

He felt badly about Alice Harding. He wondered whether he should write, or call, or visit. He decided good manners would be counter-productive, inflict more pain. He remained dubious about this. The best thing would be if Alice turned against him, decided he was worthless. He could not bring himself to want Alice to hate him, because he liked and admired her very much, but for her peace of mind it was best.

It was difficult now for him to go back to Cragrock. Probably he would have to meet George Whyte in somebody's office in Lexington.

He went to Washington to see Liz and Jamie off, back to London. Clare had already gone to Shannon. The kids seemed oddly cold. They were shocked by him. He was shocked by himself, but he thought they came from an unshockable generation.

Their flight was delayed. They told him not to wait, but he waited. Then he was pulled down into Virginia by a hawser. He went by arrangement to Mount Malcolm. Rosie was there.

'As we go through life, we help one another,' said Mollie. 'No lady is an island. I expect you have all found that.'

The old women stared at her apathetically. If they understood her they showed no sign of it. The abortionist scratched her crotch. It was very hot in London that August.

'I am helping you, as you know,' said Mollie. 'But you may be surprised to learn how much you have been helping me, through a very difficult time when I have been faced by ingratitude and loneliness. It is the same with my friend Maisie. I have told you about Maisie. She is only a servant but I think of her as a friend. She used to be one of you, imprisoned here for an offence of which she is now ashamed. She has paid her debt to society and is now a useful member of it. She helps me in my home. I feel quite safe in leaving her alone there, although I have some valuable things, some jewellery and excellent Georgian silver. She has a latchkey to my flat, so that she can come in and Hoover and scrub even though I am out. That will show you how completely I trust her. You can understand that she and I are helping each other. She gives me the kind of simple assistance in the house of which she is capable, while I have given her back her dignity as a self-respecting and useful member of the community.'

Two of Mollie's listeners were asleep. The combined odour of the five was indescribable. Even Mollie began to feel that she was losing the attention of her listeners. She embroidered briefly the theme of ingratitude, and left early with a headache.

Liz and Jamie were due home the next day, from an escapade from which Mollie had been unable to protect them. Mollie remembered with bitterness their willingness to fall in with their father's plans. Their callous acceptance of his bribes had hurt her deeply. But she was not one to bear grudges. She would welcome them home as though their behaviour to her had been considerate.

She stopped at a Sainsbury's on her way back to buy them a welcome-home lunch. She remembered what they liked, not as tinies in America but when they were restored to civilization. Jamie had had a gigantic appetite, a real schoolboy's appetite. Liz liked sweet things. All afternoon Mollie laboured in her stuffy kitchen. She made a steak-and-kidney pudding, not with the lazy evasion of frozen pastry but with good old-fashioned suet. She made a treacle roll for dessert. Some mothers, she knew, might have pretended to be influenced by the oppressive weather, and saved trouble with cold meat and salad and fresh fruit. That was not her way. She exhausted herself in the cause of feeding up her babies. Her headache moved from her left temple to her right, intensifying. The telephone rang many times, but she was too busy to answer it.

She scrubbed the pans, though not the floor. Maisie was coming at ten in the morning. She would scrub the kitchen floor and Hoover the other rooms. Maisie was not always quite scrupulous about the pans. Mollie had to stand over her to make sure she really scoured them. It was easier to do it oneself. Mollie blamed lack of education. She tried to remedy this disability, for which Maisie's background was responsible, but it was uphill work.

Mollie was up at seven in the morning, to continue preparations for welcoming her children. She made a cup of tea and glanced at the papers.

What she saw so shocked and enraged her that she knocked over her cup of tea. The kitchen table was a lake of khaki tea. That did not improve her temper.

Matthew Carver the Kentucky sportsman, well known in this country as a sprightly and socialising turfite, part-owner of the colt by Mill Reef which last October broke the yearling price record, part-owner of the middle-distance champion Beausoleil, a kind of collateral member of the British aristocracy through his marriage to the Honourable 'Mollie' Bardsley, daughter of the late Viscount Wincham and cousin of the present Viscount, had, at Saratoga Springs, that summer Mecca of the transatlantic sporting set, resumed the romance of which we gave you many earlier bulletins, each more sizzling than the last, but which we thought — as you probably thought — was a thing of the past. Perhaps the celebrated medicinal qualities of the mineral springs or the mud-baths have rekindled the flame? Mrs Carver has been unavailable for comment, but Viscount Wincham told our reporter, 'Americans don't know the rules, do they?' Watch this space for further bulletins, which will be relayed by jungle drum from Kentucky and Virginia.

With his children in the same country. Under their very eyes.

When the telephone rang Mollie did answer it, and spoke of betrayal, lust, irresponsibility.

As she hung up after the third call she found herself staring at the drawing-room curtains. Matthew's curtains. She thought of them as his. They were a reminder of him, a hateful reminder. They symbolised Matthew so that he was present in the room. Mollie could not endure for another moment to have those great florid symbols of the adulterer cutting the sunlight out of the room. She would not welcome the children home to a place degraded by such objects.

To think was to act with Mollie. She considered waiting for Maisie, who would arrive in an hour. She could not endure the curtains for an hour. Maisie had the floor to scrub. The curtains were all wrong for the room, too opulent, too grand. It was typical of an American to spend so much money so stupidly, so ostentatiously, as though a London flat could be turned into a gentleman's house just by getting overpriced brocade curtains.

Mollie went to get the step-ladder from the passage outside the kitchen. She barked her shins as she carried it into the drawing-room. She set it up by the window. It wobbled. The floor was uneven. She climbed, indomitable. Mr Curtis, the caretaker and odd-job-man allegedly employed by the landlord, was supposed to do this kind of thing. He was never to be found. He was an idle coward. He refused to use the step-ladder, and wasted time fetching his own metal contraption. All the other workmen were the same. It was the fault of the parents, who indulged them and gave them too many sweets and taught them neither manners nor morality.

Mollie began to unhook the gigantic curtains from the runners on the metal track above the window, under the pelmet-board. It was easy. There was no need to have waited for Maisie or any other assistance. The left hand curtain subsided into a dusty heap on the foot of the step-ladder. In no time there were two heaps. Mollie dragged them away. She would sell them and use the money for something sensible.

The pelmet was backed with heavy buckram. A half-inch flap of the buckram, behind the top of the pelmet, was tacked to the edge of the pelmet-board. The tacks were hammered firmly into the pine. It was difficult to drive the end of a screwdriver under the head of a tack, to lever it out of the wood. The pelmet-board was almost too high for the step-ladder. Mollie had to stand on the top step. She tried to lever out the tacks one-handed, so that she could use the other hand to hold on to the board. Sometimes she had to use both hands for the screwdriver. She was angry with the workmen who had driven in the tacks so hard. It was typical of modern thoughtlessness. She successfully extracted two dozen tacks, not much tearing the buckram. The heavy pelmet began to sag away from the board, getting in her way, making it difficult for her to see what she was doing, making it difficult to fold the top of the pelmet away from the board so that she could get at the tacks. She had to use one hand to fold the stiff brocade away from the backing, while she struggled to force the screwdriver under the tacks. The stepladder wobbled. She clutched the pelmet-board, steadying herself. She was hot and dusty and furious. She had to reach a long way to operate on the next tack. For the one after she would have to climb down and move the stepladder. She reached far to her left, from the top of the stepladder, with her left hand holding the top of the pelmet away from the flap, with her right punching angrily at the tack with her screwdriver. It was an obdurate tack, driven deep into the wood. The buckram made it impossible to ease the blade of the screwdriver under the head. Mollie jabbed violently. The blade of the screwdriver skidded across the head of the tack, and drove into her other hand. She cried out, and let go of the pelmet. The stepladder rocked. She grabbed at the pelmet. The pelmet came away from the board, the buckram tearing. The stepladder collapsed. Mollie fell sideways, with an armful of ornate brocade pelmet. She and the ladder fell together, slowly and then fast. Her head hit the pink marble kerbstone which surrounded the imitation fireplace. She fell a long way, from the top of a tall stepladder, and the impact was considerable. It cracked her skull. She died instantly.

Maisie arrived a little unpunctually. She had seen nobody in the street or in the building. She let herself in with her latchkey. She found her mistress dead, with her head in the fireplace and a broken stepladder lying across her.

Maisie went to Mollie's bedroom. She pulled from under the bed the small suitcase Mollie kept there. She filled the suitcase with all the jewellery in the drawers of Mollie's dressing-table, and with the silver in the sideboard in the dining-room. She crept away, seeing nobody.

Liz and Jamie got out of a taxi at 12.30, grubby and exhausted after travelling for twenty-four hours. They went up to the flat. Jamie let them in with his latchkey.

They thought at first that their mother had forgotten: that the flat was empty.

Beausoleil's condition delighted Matthew, and that of the several mares at Fox Hill in foal to him. His visit was surreptitious. He saw Rick Field, but not Peach or any member of the household.

He went back to Mount Malcolm with Rosie, in the middle of the morning, to a winking welcome from Miss Viola Biggs. Rosie was wearing jeans as tattered as Hal Whyte's, dirty sneakers, one of Matthew's shirts, and a cotton hat of unguessable provenance. She looked like an urchin and like an angel. Matthew was fleetingly reminded of Paulette Goddard in *Modern Times*. Rosie's manner was gentle and pliant, trusting, almost submissive.

Matthew was moved to be the object of a love so unconcealed.

'There's a call for you, boy,' said Miss Viola Biggs, 'from London.'

Lee V. Lowe saw the news in the airmail edition of *The Times*. He could see no obvious publicity value for his client, though he explored all the angles. He reported by telephone to Doris Bernard at Cragrock.

Doris hoped it was a put-down for Clare the Snob, was otherwise indifferent to the accidental and tragic death of somebody unknown to her, and reported to George Whyte.

George looked solemn and felt pleased. Mollie had been a pain in the ass with her press conferences and her defences of Matthew, who should have kept her under control. He told Jean.

Jean had always detested Mollie, because of the way she had exploited and bad-mouthed Matthew. Jean herself lied and cheated in order to stay sane and also stay rich, and she had no illusions about herself, but she had always been able to feel authentic moral indignation about the Prison Visitor. She told Will Stevens, who liked and respected Matthew, after they had enjoyed the rare luxury of a leisurely roll in the hay — literally, a ton of unbaled timothy in the roof of an empty barn. Afterwards, having combed the hay out of her hair, she told Alice.

Alice thought: poor woman, but where does this leave me? Matthew was free. But it seemed he was not free. Matthew had never discussed his wife with her, even in their most dreamy and confiding post-coital chats. He had never discussed the Fox Hill woman. Clare, whose opinion Alice valued, had never discussed Mrs Phillipson and seldom her mother: and the latter only in regard to where she bought her shoes, and how she was related to Lord So-and-so. Nobody else around Alice knew anything relevant about anything.

She had the feeling that her hand was poised over the thing she wanted, open and ready to grab, and somebody had whisked the thing away with a piece of nylon fishing-line.

Many of the Bardsley family were buried in the churchyard of All Saints, in the straggling village of Cottingham, in the Vale of Pewsey, on the northern side of Salisbury Plain, exactly in the middle of Wiltshire. It was not an ancient custom because they were not an ancient family. Like many new-rich Victorians they created tradition. Their association with the village was authentic: they had bought it, and two others neighbouring, from older and poorer families. The title came from one of the other villages, because Cottingham was too like Cottenham, an earldom created somewhat earlier.

The family's association with the church was authentic, too — they had restored it in 1882 and again in 1911. Woodworm had been detected in the oak linenfold panelling of the choir. It was stripped away. Decontaminated, it looked well in the hall of the Manor House, giving that raw building an air of antiquity reassuring to the family. The old pew-ends, hiding the worshippers, were odious to late Victorian opinion, which liked its piety visible; oak was throughout replaced by varnished pitch-pine. The nave was remodelled, and given a ceiling which reminded the irreverent of the barber-shop at Waterloo Station. Encaustic tiles gleamed from floor and walls in hectic colours undimmed by time, and needing only a wipe with a damp cloth. There were new stained-glass windows over the altar and in the transept, predominantly mauve and lime, and memorial windows sacred to the memory of Bardsleys in the nave. The pulpit, of veined caramel marble, was the gift of the 2nd Viscount Wincham, and the pulpit, a ton of brass, of the 3rd.

There was a good turn-out for Molly's funeral, considering the filthy weather. The fine spell had broken. The yews in the churchyard dripped on humble mounds and Bardsley marble. Molly's grave had been dug next to that of her father. The sexton had bailed it out with a bucket before the people began to arrive for the funeral, but there were soon two inches of water in it, pitted by drops from the over-arching trees, red from the red mud.

Most people had come by car. A long line of cars leaned on the muddy verge of the road by the church. Lord Wincham had laid on a bus to bring people to the church from Devizes station, seven miles away. Four passengers had occupied the huge bus, prison visitor colleagues of the deceased, who were making an outing of it together. Lord Wincham had done everything else, too. Matthew arrived in London to find the undertaker engaged, the church fixed, the parson booked, many of the probable congregation telephoned, the gravestone designed though not yet executed, the memorial plaque commissioned.

The funeral was at three. Matthew drove Liz and Jamie down,

lunching on the way, arriving at 2.30. The kids were subdued. Liz wore a black dress and a black hat, both belonging to her mother but more or less fitting her; it was impossible to imagine her living in a squat in a slum. Jamie wore a dark grey suit and a black tie. He excused himself during lunch, at a pub outside Newbury, reappearing from the Gents looking a little better. He said he had an upset tummy.

Matthew felt numb. He felt a huge regret at waste and error; pity; horror at the way it had happened, the stupid and avoidable way. He felt a generalised burden of guilt, though he could not, honestly, accuse himself of blame for the events of the immediate past or the events of the previous fifteen years.

They all got wet feet, walking from the car to the church door. Matthew had an umbrella, under which Liz partly sheltered. Jamie had neither hat nor coat. The shoulders of his dark suit were darker with the wet, and his hair was plastered to his head. He looked young and innocent and ill. They thought they were early. They were early, but the church was already a-hum with Bardsleys. When Matthew shook out his umbrella, in the church porch, fifty heads turned, most old, white and yellow and purple faces. A silence fell in the church. Many of the faces were completely unknown to Matthew, but they all knew who he was. He went slowly up the aisle with his children. A youth showed them to the front pew on the right, where there were cards on the seat with their names. Alaric Wincham and his family were in the pew immediately behind. Matthew nodded to him and his wife. The wife gave a slight smile but immediately, as though remembering orders, looked down and away.

An army of Bardsleys and Bardsley connections was ranged behind the chief of their clan. Everyone was staring at him, even those who, having arrived just ahead of the Carvers, were on their knees. Matthew looked back for a moment, before he sat, glancing up and down the rows of faces, wondering if eyesight or telepathy would communicate to him any message of sympathy. Neither did.

They all three sat, and knelt. Liz and Jamie adopted the conventional position of prayer. Matthew wondered if they were praying, if they knew how to. He wished he knew how to. He wished he knew what to pray for.

From Ralph Hadfield, Matthew knew what Wincham had been saying about him. He had been saying it, without doubt, to every single person in the congregation, the Bardsley battalion behind him implacable in their internecine strife but united in detestation of the interloper who had become a traitor and deserter. Matthew felt hatred burning into the back of his neck. The hum of an elderly congregation before a service recommenced, with what was certainly a new and a single topic.

Clare arrived, in black, alone. She looked shattered. She whispered that Tom Kavanagh had brought her. He was at the back of the church. Matthew was thankful that Clare had Tom's support, and would go on having it. He had felt himself trying to support Liz and Jamie, but finding that they did not need support: at least not his. They supported one another, perhaps. They had grown a long way away from him, and the summer in Kentucky had increased the distance rather than shrunk it. Matthew wished Clare was beside him, but she was the other side of Jamie. They all obeyed Alaric Wincham's orders, and sat where the cards told them to. Nobody would join them in the front pew.

More people could be heard coming in. Footsteps clumped on the hideous tiles of the aisle. The hum became at once shriller and deeper, as persons who had been in the place for twenty-five minutes relaxed, grew bored, and felt that the passage of time had given them licence. There might by now be other topics, but Matthew was sure he remained the main one. He felt paranoid. Liz glanced back quite often to see who was arriving. Of course she knew many more of her mother's relations than he did. Clare glanced back once or twice. Matthew felt unable to do so. He did not want to do so. He did not want to find himself eyeball to eyeball with Wincham.

Two men came in who wore black coats and blackish striped trousers, like fashionable doctors. They carried wooden trestles like those of picnic tables. Matthew, allowing himself to glance, was baffled until he realised that they were for the coffin. The men put the trestles by the sanctuary steps, and withdrew in a pious way.

The choir began to file in from the vestry door by the altar: a dozen men and women in puce vestments; no choirboys. They were followed by the parson, a bald man who blew his nose as he advanced to the sanctuary steps. The parson announced a hymn. It was immediately obvious that he had a heavy cold. Matthew was sorry for him, a cold in the head being more disagreeable in summer, but regretted it also from the point of view of the congregation and the dignity of the service. The hymn was presumably of Wincham's choice:

> 'Now the labourer's task is o'er;
> Now the battle day is past;
> Now upon the farther shore
> Lands the voyager at last.
> Father, in Thy gracious keeping
> Leave we now Thy servant sleeping.'

During the many lugubrious stanzas of the hymn, the fashionable doctors reappeared, with colleagues, carrying the coffin on their shoulders. They deposited it on the trestles. The trestles did their job of supporting Mollie better than her stepladder. There were many flowers on the coffin. Matthew's were roses, because Mollie had always said she liked them. Blue roses, because one of the first things he knew about her was that blue was her favourite colour. They were not really blue. Matthew regretted the colour of his wreath, but there was nothing he could do about that.

'I ab the resurregtion add the life, saith the Lord; she that believeth in be, though she were dead, yet shall she live.'

The parson's cold was really very bad. He should have been home in bed, especially on such a wet day as this.

'We brought dothing indo this world, add id is certaid we gan garry dothing oud. The Lord gave, add the Lord hath dagen away; blessed be the Dabe of the Lord.'

Liz was crying.

There were prayers, a lesson read by an elderly man with a tremendous voice, a psalm. Matthew could hear Clare's voice clear and sweet in the psalm. He was incapable of singing.

Alaric Wincham gave an Address, from his ancestor's pulpit. Mollie's sense of duty, of service. Her selflessness and devotion. Example of practical Christianity. If more like her in the world today, problems of the world would disappear. It was very correct stuff, containing an element of truth. Matthew waited for the phrase 'salt of the earth'. It came.

Not fortunate in all aspects of her life. Not always the luck she deserved. Not treated kindly by fate. But a brave and joyful face in adversity, a high and shining courage.

Liz had stopped crying, and was listening with an expression of disbelief.

Wincham did not say that Mollie had made a disastrous marriage to a cruel and conscienceless man. He did not, in fairness, come near to doing so. He said that Mollie had weathered storms and come safe to port.

Matthew thought this was a strange way to describe falling off a ladder.

Wincham went on far too long.

Another hymn. Prayers. The parson's cold even cloggier in his nasal passages. Frequent recourse to handkerchief. One questionably sufficient.

The coffin followed the choir down the aisle and out. Matthew followed the coffin, with Clare. Liz and Jamie next. A serpentine army, in black twos and threes, slowly progressing among the weeping yew-trees. It was still raining. Umbrellas were tacitly permitted to the congregation, but not to the principal mourners. Elderly and infirm people were better not coming to the graveside, but many did.

'Bad thad is bord of wobad hath bud a shord dibe do live add is full of bisery.'

It was truly gallant of the parson to stand bareheaded in the pouring rain, when he should have been in bed.

They lowered Mollie into inches of red water.

'Foreasbuch as id hath bleased Albighdy God of his great bercy —'

There was a commotion at the gate into the churchyard.

A woman, hatted and veiled, in black, had got out of a taxi. She stood looking at the scene at the graveside, the silent crowd in the rain, the pallbearers withdrawing their cords from under the coffin and tactfully edging backwards. Matthew could see the newcomer by moving only his eyes. Others had to turn their heads, and did.

'Ashes do ashes, dust do dust.'

The woman was unsteady on her feet. She was ill or drunk. One of the undertaker's men hurried across the saturated grass of the churchyard to deal with this potentially embarrassing situation. The young usher from the church, doubtless a Bardsley, darted forward also.

The newcomer's hat was getting very wet. It was not intended to be worn in the rain. It was smart but frail. The brim drooped.

It was impossible to see the face behind the veil.

The choir, wetter by the second, sang an anthem with plummy Victorian harmonies: 'From henceforth blessed are the dead which die in the Lord.'

The undertaker's man and the usher seemed to be remonstrating with the newcomer. The undertaker's man took her arm. She pulled free. He took it again. He was standing immediately in front of a lichened and leaning gravestone, the top of which was level with the back of his knees. Perhaps seeing this, perhaps fortuitously, the newcomer put the palm of her hand on his chest and pushed. Caught at the critical point by the gravestone, he went over backwards so that he sprawled on the grave. She turned to the youth and said something through her veil which caused him to recoil. She advanced unsteadily towards Mollie's grave.

Matthew knew who she was, and he was aghast. He did not understand how he had not recognized her immediately, veil or no veil. It was inconceivable that she should be here.

Rosie was twenty yards from the open grave, and still coming. All faces, scandalised, were turned towards her. It was imperative that she be stopped. Matthew, widower and principal mourner, had to leave the graveside to stop whatever outrage was imminent.

'Even so saith the Spirit,' sang the choir, 'for they rest from their labours.'

Matthew had to push his way between two choir-ladies, who stopped singing and looked at him with wet, shocked faces.

Matthew met Rosie. He blocked her way up the path between acres of wet grass which needed mowing.

'Amen,' sang the choir, and fell silent.

Rosie pushed her veil up and over the sodden brim of her hat. Her face was wet. Matthew wondered numbly how rain had got in under hat-brim and veil, and realised that the drops he saw were tears.

'Lord, have bercy ubon us,' said the parson.

Matthew glanced back. Everybody, including the parson and the choir and Clare and Liz and Jamie and all Mollie's relations, was looking at him.

'Christ, have mercy upon us,' mumbled the people, still looking at Matthew and Rosie.

'You wept no tears for your wife when you heard she was dead,'

311

said Rosie, her speech a little slurred. She spoke loudly enough so that everybody by the grave could hear. 'Somebody has to. I'll do that for you. I'll do anything for you. I thought you'd need me, so I came. Peach tried to stop me, but I decided to come and I came.'

The parson led the people in the Lord's Prayer. Rosie joined in, loud and a little late.

Matthew wondered if he dared leave Rosie, to return to his place by the grave. He glanced back again. The parson was reading a prayer. A wall of blank wet faces met Matthew's eyes. He saw Clare whispering to Liz. Clare was telling Liz who Rosie was. Clare looked furious. Liz suddenly left the graveside, pushing between people, and crossed the grass.

Liz said coldly to Rosie, 'You came to grab him the moment my mother was killed. The moment she was in her grave. Before they even covered her up. You can't have him.'

Matthew tried to silence Liz. Liz was too angry to be silenced. She was almost hysterical. Against the adenoidal incantations of the parson she said, 'You're too late. My father is not your property. He's somebody else's property.'

Rosie looked at her in drunken astonishment. She was still weeping.

Liz exploded the grenade she had been carrying for a month. She said, 'My father was having an affair with Alice Harding all summer. He loves her. I heard him say so, when they were on their way to bed together.'

'Amen,' said the people, the parson having concluded his prayer. He embarked on another.

'Amen,' said Rosie unexpectedly.

The parson said the Grace which ended the burial service. The people began to drift away from the grave. They were going in their cars to the Manor for tea. Wincham had made this arrangement with everybody, on the telephone. The gigantic bus took the four prison visitors to tea with Wincham. Nobody looked at or spoke to Matthew. Clare went away with Tom Kavanagh, not speaking to her father. An aunt of Mollie's, dimly remembered by Matthew, took Liz and Jamie away. Matthew and Rosie were left alone in the churchyard. The rain came down harder.

'Is there no end to your folly?' said Matthew.

Rosie sat down suddenly on a grave.

'Oh God, I'm tired,' she said. 'I'm too tired to stand up.'

She looked bedraggled and exhausted and beautiful.

Matthew turned and left the churchyard. He went to his car. He started it, and drove away towards London. The legs of his trousers were wet.

Rosie sat for a long time, until she became aware of the wetness of the grassy mound she was sitting on. She rose awkwardly. She was bottomlessly tired. The quarrel with Peach preceeding the journey, the long and complicated journey, had utterly exhausted her. She had eaten nothing for twenty-four hours. Perhaps the miniatures of brandy on the train had been a mistake.

She went to find her taxi. Somebody had taken the taxi, to go to have tea with Lord Wincham. The lane was empty. Rosie walked slowly into the middle of the village. There was nobody about. There were no cars. She began to walk the seven miles to Devizes, rain and tears mingling on her cheeks.

CHAPTER 15

Matthew had to stay in England, to talk to Mollie's lawyers and executors and trustees, to dispose of the flat, to help the police and the insurance company with lists of the stolen silver and jewellery, to make arrangements, as far as they would let him, about Liz and Jamie.

He was aware that Wincham's tongue was wagging its hardest.

There was a moment when it seemed that the undertaker's man was going to sue for injuries received, to person and suiting, as a result of assault; but a cheque for £250 replaced the damaged garments and kissed the place to make it well.

The newspapers reported George Whyte buying on an heroic scale at the Keeneland September sales.

The catalogue was full of yearlings whose breeders had not tried, or who had tried and failed, to get them into the Select July sales. Average quality and average prices were lower, though in neither regard low. It was possible to get a bargain. It was possible to buy a bad horse cheaply, and a good one expensively. It was possible to buy a bad horse expensively, and there were those who thought George Whyte had done so. He was relying on his own judgement, supported by that of Bert Duffy his trainer and Will Stevens his farm manager. Both forebore, for different reasons, to come right out and disagree with their boss.

George Whyte assumed that Epi Makropulos, Luis Valdes, Ghalib al-Jilani and others would come in with him, as all the colts he bought were potential stallions and all the fillies potential brood mares.

Ghalib spent part of September in Halat al Bhudi, teaching his eldest son the elements of falconry. He went straight from his home to Ballycardeen, not pausing as he usually did in Rome or

Paris or London. There was still sand on his Lobb shoes when he shook hands with Tom Kavanagh at Shannon. He heard Tom's account of the scene in the churchyard with ears still shockable.

Tom was a champion of Rosie who had changed his mind. So was Ghalib.

Ghalib did not want less to be Matthew's partner. He wanted to protect Matthew against himself and against Rosie.

Clare arrived, well chaperoned, from Tom's family. She knew no more than Tom the weird magic of Fox Hill, place of djinns. Less than either Tom or Ghalib could she appreciate the magic of Rosie. She saw eye to eye with Ghalib about Alice. They discussed it all, at great length. It struck both of them as odd that a man's partner and his daughter should discuss his affair with a divorcee, and canvas the possibility of his marriage to her, both as a defence against his doxy and as a guarantee of his professional future.

Lord Wincham decided against a memorial service for Mollie in London. He said that Carver's drunken friends would turn it into a beargarden.

This decision finally released Matthew from London.

He was happy about Clare. He was happier about Liz than he had been: she was sharing a big flat in Bayswater with another girl and three men, all apparently respectable as respectability went in the early 1980s. She was working in a cake shop in Chelsea, but was probably not content to do so for ever. She seemed to have no wish to go back to her squat and no curiosity about its personnel. Rebellion had been rendered needless by the falling of a ladder. Matthew was not very happy about Jamie, but the boy was back in Oxford, sharing digs with Mario di Vianello and facing his imminent Oxbridge entrance. Matthew fixed a small allowance for Liz and Jamie, to replace the unpredictable handouts they had had from Mollie. They seemed as indifferent to his departure as to his presence.

Matthew thought that the residual solidity he might have represented in their lives had been washed away in the rain and tears of the churchyard.

At home he was lonely and bored. He felt sick when he thought of the graveside. He felt sick at himself for his weakness, at the dog returning to his vomit in Saratoga. He felt sick with embarrassment when he remembered barring Rosie's way to the grave, and Liz's furious revelation, all within sight and sound of

God and this congregation.

His mind turned more and more to Alice, by whom he knew himself loved.

He remembered a story of Kipling's: one of the best. Mulvaney a young, sober, up-and-coming Non-Commissioned Officer; Mulvaney deeply in love with and about to marry his Dinah. Mulvaney, somehow *because* he loved Dinah so dearly, making unmeant advances to a slut with a witch for a mother. The slut jilted. The witch's curse. Dinah loses her baby and Mulvaney takes to the bottle. Matthew wondered if Cousin Thalia Collin would curse him, now that he had done with Rosie for ever.

He was done for ever with that kind of preposterousness, that extravagant impulsive folly, that grotesque tactlessness which no generosity of motive could excuse. There could be passion in sanity and sanity in passion: Alice and he had proved so, night after magic night. But it was impossible for him to approach her. He had put himself out of court.

Ghalib went from Ballycardeen to New York, Washington, Detroit, Chicago and Cincinnati. From there he called Cragrock. He was immediately invited to stay. George Whyte wanted him to buy legs or halves of his new yearlings.

George was almost effusive, because he wanted two million dollars. Ghalib was not surprised at the yearlings George had bought, considered as horseflesh without reference to price; he was not surprised at the prices George had paid, because many people had paid more; he was surprised that George had paid those prices for those yearlings. He was not instantly inclined to buy legs for what those legs cost. Neither Bert Duffy nor Will Stevens was prepared to commit himself to any view, even in private.

Ghalib wanted Matthew. He trusted his own judgement to a point, but not to two million dollars' worth. He was able, on this basis, to ask Jean Whyte to invite Matthew to Cragrock. He thought this accorded with Alice's wish, although they were not such close friends as to discuss her feelings for Matthew.

Jean had to pretend to George that Matthew was being invited not to advise Ghalib, but for personal and social reasons. She had to pretend the opposite to Matthew. She worded the invitation, on the telephone, as though business was the single excuse for disturbing him. He accepted on that basis. He did not know if the basis was genuine, a face-saver, or what. He did not know if he would even see Alice. He thought it possible that, since he was coming on business, she would go to other people in another place.

He came. He saw the yearlings before he saw any of the people. Privately he advised Ghalib to buy one half of one of them. George was kept in ignorance of advice given and taken. He sold a half share in a yearling filly to Ghalib for $300,000.

Matthew himself said he would not come in on any of the yearlings, because he was already over-invested in bloodstock. George thought it a mistake to do business with a man who was not really rich enough for the game.

Sedulous matchmaking began. Jean and Ghalib, a new and formidable alliance, worked to recreate the mood and opportunity of the early summer. Alice was shy with Matthew, and thoroughly distrustful. He was shy with her. Things hung fire. George was heard to wonder audibly how long Carver was stopping. Ghalib had to leave, to talk to a man in San Diego.

Jean recognized that hang-ups were inevitable, what with Matthew's behaviour and Alice's scar-tissue. She thought grown, experienced people, who loved and needed each other, should have overcome them without help. It seemed they were not doing so. She helped all she could.

But the nudge, when it came, was fortuitous, maybe providential: a litter of kittens in an empty stall. Somebody told Matthew about the litter. Sentimental about new-born animals, he went into the stall to see. It was dark after the glare outside. He was unsighted. He did not realise that he was not alone, that somebody had told Alice about the kittens. They were alone together for the first time in the week of his visit, in spite of efforts coyly made by the others. Even then shyness, guilt, mistrust could have chilled and killed the moment. But Matthew, his eyes still unadjusted to the dark, watched so carefully where he put his feet down in order not to tread on kittens, that he hit his forehead on the hay-rack. There was a sharp pain, a cut, a little blood. Alice had to wet a handkerchief to clean the cut. Nobody civilised could have withheld that service. Alice was not an East German frontier guard on the Berlin Wall, but a woman nervously in love seeing blood on the forehead of her love.

The only mention either made of Rosie was a remark of Matthew's, pillow to pillow: 'It's very hard to kick an addiction without help. Help me.'

She nodded, horizontally, uselessly in the dark.

A formal engagement was possible but premature. They were both well-known. Matthew had to consider the reactions of his children. He was sure they would be all for it. But Clare, reacting, would have to consider the rigidly conventional Kavanagh family. Liz and Jamie had shown an equivalent, an astonishing rigidity of conventional Bardsley morality. April was the very earliest that anything could be made public.

'Darling, I'm happy,' said Alice to George. 'Do you think you could manage a little happiness for me?'

George could. By far the most human and creditable thing about him was his love for Alice. With her he was gentle, generous and protective. He would have given his right arm for her. He would have lent it, at interest, for his wife or children or friends. He could see that Alice was a foot off the ground. He gave the secret engagement his blessing. He reflected that Matthew, married to Alice, would become something like his own financial equal.

Jean accepted the need for secrecy. It came naturally to her; her secret life had made her secretive, except with one person. Orgasm unblocked all tubes, including the windpipe.

Will Stevens genuinely shared Jean's pleasure in the news. He promised to keep quiet about it, but from his angle all the discretion was a little overdone. He knew nothing about Matthew Carver's children, although he had met them in the summer; he assumed, if he ever thought about it, that Matthew and his wife had been divorced for years.

Doris Bernard knew about the engagement, because she knew everything that went on in the house. She was family. Knowledge might be power, but she had never used it. No leak of anything had ever been traced to her.

Sir Merivale Lucas came to Lexington, soup on his tie, to look at weanlings and shop for stallion nominations. He had business with many farms, and stopped at a Lexington hotel. He was asked to lunch at Cragrock, but the business he had to do could be done almost wholly with Will Stevens and Doris Bernard.

His pride still hurt, his jealousy rekindled by Saratoga, Lucas made snide reference to Doris about Matthew Carver's judgement.

Doris was still sore at the brutality of her put-down by Clare. She suspected that Clare's sister had treacherously carried on with Alicia behind her own back. She spat in the eye of the whole family. She twittered agreement with Sir Merivale. She said it was dreadful to think of all Mrs Harding's money being spent on horses that broke down.

She clammed up when Lucas tried to get more out of her. But a bulb came on in his head. He watched Carver and Mrs Harding at lunch.

Looking at weanlings with Will Stevens, Lucas floated in a remark about Matthew Carver and Alice Harding.

'But I don't suppose they'd tell you anything about that,' he said.

Will Stevens would have been conscientiously boot-faced if asked a direct question by somebody ignorant of the facts. It was different to be accused of ignorance by someone already in possession of the facts. Status was involved.

Will said he knew what was going on around Cragrock, and as long as Sir Merivale knew there was no point in playing dummy. Lucas thus had the confirmation he wanted. Operation Rosie came alive again.

Sir Merivale Lucas found excuses to go to Middleburg and from there to Somerset, and to ask himself to Fox Hill.

It was to Peach, not Rosie, that he mentioned ever so casually the forthcoming union at Cragrock. He asked Peach particularly not to tell Rosie, and, as he expected, heard Peach greet Rosie with the news when she came back from seeing Tim in the sanitorium. With every sort of gruff reluctance, Lucas, appealed to, confirmed the report.

'That kind of man,' said Peach. 'An unusual specimen. A venomous butterfly.'

'A bonhomous flutterby,' said Jefferson Dill, 'a polygamous phoney-boy.'

Rosie had believed Matthew's daughter, there in the churchyard. She knew Alice Harding by sight; she knew something of her history and her bank-balance.

The expedition to England had been an expensive mistake, no doubt about that, although it had all seemed in advance a supremely right thing to do.

It had given her a cold in the head as bad as that of the Reverend burying Matthew's wife.

Rosie's mind had been in a paralysis of muddle for a month. First hangover and blisters had stopped her thinking straight, then the cold, then Peach and Cousin Thalia and Jefferson Dill and Miss Viola Biggs and Hazel, singly or in combination.

Rosie believed Lucas, and left the room and went and lay on her bed. She felt battered by misery. She reached out, across the bed, imagining Matthew there. Day turned into night. Hazel and others banged on the door. Lucas apparently went away. Rosie faced at last the central truth about herself, to which everything else was subsidiary and relative. All factors of incompatibility notwithstanding, Tim notwithstanding, Alice Harding notwithstanding, she could not live without Matthew. She might die of having him. She would surely die of not having him.

The moon rose, and she made a plan.

In the morning she took somebody's car, and drove a long way to a city where nobody knew her. In the local yellow pages she found a veterinarian. She gave him a false name and a false address, and described to him a horse, an unimportant but well-loved old horse, with a deep cut on a fetlock joint. The cut was refusing to heal because the horse was restless. He wouldn't hold still. The local vet had an obsessive and illogical hatred of depressant drugs, of tranquillisers of any kind. He said that if animals needed tranquillising they tranquillised themselves.

The strange vet made untold objections. He could not prescribe for an animal he had not seen. He could not ethically prescribe for an animal in the care of a professional confrère. Rosie wept. The vet sold Rosie a cannister of white powder, tasteless, marketed under the brand-name Sonodox.

Rosie mixed a measure of Sonodox with Beausoleil's feed. He lapped it up. She could not give him a dose every time he was fed, but she could do it most times.

Rick Field became concerned about Beausoleil's listlessness

320

and lack of appetite. Normally he was energetic to a fault, and ate everything put in front of him. The vet came. There was nothing obviously organically wrong with Beausoleil. It could be something he had eaten. The vet took blood and urine samples and sent them away for analysis.

Before Rosie herself suggested it, Rick felt obliged to report Beausoleil's condition to Matthew Carver at Cragrock.

George Whyte was worried and angry. He suspected negligence. He regretted having been persuaded to stand Beausoleil in Virginia. He blamed Matthew. He told Matthew to go at once to Fox Hill: to see that Beausoleil was cured; to stay there until he could come back and say, with his hand on his heart, that $20,000,000 was safe.

Nobody could disagree with the line George took in the matter. George spoke for the other interested parties — the duc de Montfermainbrey, Ghalib al-Jilani, Epi Makropulos, Luis Valdes, Ottaviano de Vianello.

Matthew was worried about Beausoleil but he was not worried about himself.

Alice was not worried. She was in love as never before, because what had gone wrong had come right.

'I'm prophylactic,' she said to Jean. 'I'm antibiotic. I'm vaccination and antitetanus. I'm one of those movies that make you give up smoking.'

'He left the theatre,' said Jean, worried.

Jean understood *nostalgie de la boue*.

Matthew reserved a room in an hotel. His dealings with Fox Hill were with the farm. He did not expect to go near the house or see any of its inhabitants. He found a message at the hotel from Miss Viola Biggs, asserting an old woman's right to entertain him at Mount Malcolm. He tore up the message. Then he thought that although Miss Viola was the cause of what happened, it was not her fault that everything had happened. She meant well and she deserved courtesy. He called, and explained that under no circumstances was he prepared to meet or deal with Mrs Phillipson. He put it like that — 'Mrs Phillipson' — to show he meant what he said. Miss Viola said he could meet or not meet whom he pleased, but *she* wanted to see *him*. He said he would try to call in, but he would not stay in the house. She sounded cross and disappointed. He hung up sorry to have disobliged her, but knowing he was doing the right thing.

He called Rick Field at the farm, and arranged to look at Beausoleil first thing in the morning with Rick and the vet. Nobody else was to be there. Rick seemed surprised by this instruction, but agreed.

Beausoleil had no temperature, never had had. His nose was dry and his coat looked good. Faeces were normal. He ate faddily and seemed half-asleep. All fire had gone out of him. He seemed not so much sick as changed. Even old Corporal was friskier than this magnificent, all-conquering four-year-old. He had had no medication of any kind for months.

'He's been doped,' said Matthew.

'Not by me,' said the vet.

'Not by anybody,' said Rick. 'Nobody been near him, 'cept the guys here, the twins from Mount Malcolm, an' me.'

'Then we just have to wait for the analysis.'

Rosie was not doing Beausoleil the smallest harm. She had read with the utmost care the small print on the leaflet wrapped around the Sonodox container. The stuff was meant for just such a case as the one she had invented — it kept a horse quiet so a wound had a chance to knit.

It was natural for her to come to watch Beausoleil in his paddock, or feeding, out of concern. She had continued dosing him, every chance she had. She kept out of Matthew's way. A casual meeting in the stables was not what she had in mind.

She had thought of a new way back into Matthew's heart, based on what she knew about him, on what he had loved about her, on the differences she guessed at between herself and Alice Harding.

It was an old, old gag. It came out of Hollywood comedies of the 1930s, lots of them, now only known as late late movies with forgotten stars, with scripts by people who preferred stealing a good idea to inventing a bad one.

In a huge closet in the cellar, nine months before, the costumes and props of *Circe's Island* had been stacked. Rosie burrowed in there like a terrier.

She put on respectable clothes, and packed a duffle-bag. She checked that Matthew was on the farm. She saw him in the distance with Rick. Something jumped inside her, like a fish, and caught in her throat.

The way clear, she drove to his hotel eight miles away. It was one of very few in the area, and she and Miss Viola Biggs had had no trouble finding that Matthew had a reservation there. Rosie knew the place and some of the staff, naturally. She had used it off and on when they started moving into Fox Hill. The same girl was on the switchboard behind the desk. Rosie got Matthew's room number. She gave the switchboard girl ten dollars, and said that no call must go out from Room 33 to any number with a Lexington area code. She said it was part of a joke. It took another ten dollars to get the switchboard girl to see the joke.

She went to see the housekeeper on the third floor. She paid out some more money, and explained about her joke. They let her use a staff washroom to get ready. The housekeeper laughed when she saw Rosie half an hour later. That was a good omen. It seemed to be a pretty good joke. Rosie sat waiting in the housekeeper's room, which had a smell of fresh laundry.

Matthew punched the buttons that gave him Cragrock. He had to report to George that he had nothing to report. He wanted to talk to Alice, for strength to kick his addiction.

The hotel operator interrupted, because it was a long-distance call. He gave her the number. After a clicking pause she said it was inoperative, not a wrong number but a fault. She would report the fault.

Matthew took off his coat, tie and shoes. He put his coat on a hanger. He remembered with a feeling of sudden agony how Rosie had complained about the time he took, putting his clothes on hangers. He called room service for ice.

A boy came into the room with a bucket of ice and two glasses on a tray. Matthew looked at the boy with amazement. He was small and slight, black but with delicate features as far as they could be seen under a heavy moustache. He wore a uniform cap far too big for him, a kind of naval cap with braid on the brim. He wore a kind of naval uniform, the cuffs of jacket and pants turned up six inches.

Matthew recognised the hat and uniform. They were one of the costumes Jefferson Dill would have worn in the Fox Hill play, had the performance proceeded to that point.

'It's no good, Rosie,' said Matthew.

Rosie dropped the tray with the ice-bucket and glasses. It made a terrific crash. She stood looking at him dumbly. Her moustache came partly unshipped, so that it hung at forty-five degrees from cheek to chin. She smelled of shoe-polish. Her face, neck, ears and hands were shining and pleasantly reeking with black shoe-polish. Her hair was all pulled up inside the naval hat. Her black neck looked fragile.

She said, 'You were supposed to laugh.'

He shook his head.

She turned and went out of the room. She collided with the doorpost as she went out. Matthew realised that she was blinded by tears.

She started to try to scrub the shoe-polish off, in the staff washroom. It came off, but gradually and painfully. She was doing her skin no good, scrubbing at it with a stiff nylon brush and cheap soap. It no longer mattered, not at all. There was no longer any need to be beautiful.

The washroom door opened. Matthew came in, shoeless, in shirtsleeves.

He said, 'You took all that trouble.'

Piebald, her face covered in soapsuds, she went into his arms.

Epi Makropulos had business with the International Monetary Fund in Washington. Tanja Dekker joined him there, from Los Angeles. She was not his only girl or he her only man, but they continued fond of each other. She was the cleverest of his girls, and he was far the cleverest of her men.

Epi had written to Matthew about the death of his wife, a difficult letter. Matthew had replied. Epi thought that must have been a difficult letter, too.

Epi and Tanja went south into Virginia, to see Epi's mares. Epi called Fox Hill. To his surprise they tried to put him off, both Rosie and Rick Field. They did not want him to see Beausoleil. This determined him to see Beausoleil.

They found Matthew, Rosie and Rick Field looking at Beausoleil. The horse looked well but he was all wrong. He seemed to Epi to be drugged, but they said he could not have been drugged.

Matthew and Rosie treated each other with distant politeness.

Epi understood. He had heard from Ralph Hadfield, who had heard from Alaric Wincham, about the battle of the graveyard.

There was something peculiar about Rosie's colouring, as though she needed a scrub. Epi wondered if she had caught a disease from Beausoleil, or he from her.

Tanja looked away from the too-placid horse, because his torpor distressed her. Stallions breathed fire. This one breathed a cloud of apathy.

Glancing from Matthew to Rosie, she saw a glance between them. There was a twitch in Rosie's face and a twitch in Matthew's, as though they both wanted to burst out laughing. The aloofness was an act. They were embracing, making love, with their eyes. Their eyes undressed and caressed each other, in an eighth of a second.

The vet arrived. He had the analyst's report. He wanted to talk to Matthew privately, but Matthew said the others were involved and had a right to hear.

Beausoleil had been given, over a period of a week or more, large doses of something with a long chemical name which could not conceivably be a constituent, even by accident, of his normal feed nor present in the grass of any paddock. The drug was the active ingredient of several commercial veterinary products and could in some areas be bought without prescription.

Rick Field and his men were as shocked and astonished as anybody. They passionately denied doping Beausoleil. It was impossible to disbelieve them. It was impossible to suspect the Mount Malcolm twins. It was barely possible that an outsider could have got at Beausoleil's feed, but it was wildly unlikely that any outsider could have visited the barn regularly, unobserved. It was impossible to guess at motive, for outsider or insider. It was possible that the drug might have undesirable long-term side-effects, for example to a stallion's fertility. It had been rigorously tested, but not in that regard. Nobody would prescribe it for a stallion at stud. It was a useful product, but the profession used it with extreme caution.

A twenty-four-hour guard was put over Beausoleil, and Rick Field mixed his feed with his own hands.

'That woman did it,' said Tanja.
'Impossible,' said Epi.

'Yes. To get him here. I never heard of anything so ruthless. I never saw anything so awful as that drugged horse, like a zombie. She is a Borgia.'

'This is all nonsense.'

'Believe me, Epi. Trust me.'

'I trust neither your intuition nor your discretion.'

'Discretion! That woman must be crucified. Everybody must know about this.'

'No. Even if you are right, it would be very difficult to prove. You would be in bad trouble if you said something you could not prove.'

'I am sure I can prove it.'

'I forbid you to try. The publicity.'

'But, darling, I want publicity. This must not be buried. Imagine what she'll do next. She'll poison Matthew so as to keep him.'

'It must be buried deep, little one. I have a lot of money invested in Beausoleil, and I don't want everybody telling everybody that he's been drugged and may be infertile.'

Tanja looked rebellious.

Matthew felt not like a drug-addict but like a schoolboy. He felt a nonstop surge of vivid happiness. He could no longer fool himself, about sanity and compatibility, about taste and culture, about shared interests, about punctuality and tidiness, about the opinion of his children. He felt guilt not about what he was doing but about what he had done.

It was necessary to be discreet as never before, because of Mollie's death. Rosie was. She behaved responsibly. Miss Viola Biggs was discreet, and everybody at Mount Malcolm. Nobody knew that Matthew went there, or that Rosie went there. None of the Fox Hill household knew anything about it, nobody on the farm, nobody at the hotel. The blackface joke they knew about was only that, a typical prank by the wild Mrs Phillipson on a business colleague.

It was a huge relief that Beausoleil's ailment was diagnosed. Off the drug, he picked up quickly. He breathed fire again. Meanwhile he remained a reason for Matthew to stay in Virginia.

At lunch at the River Club in New York, Tanja listened to

praise of Rosie from a Virginian who remembered her at horse-shows.

'A silken thread to the bit. A seat like an angel.'

'A seat in hot pants,' said Tanja.

'Pardon me, dear one?'

'She is a piranha fish,' said Tanja, goaded beyond bearing by the old man's rhapsody. 'She eats people.'

'I have known her all my life. She never tried to eat me, alas.'

'She is eating Matthew Carver.'

'Ah, that old story. It is true that she behaved with impropriety. They both saw the error of their ways, as I understand it, and severed unsanctified relations.'

'They unsevered them. They're having an affair this minute.'

Tanja was overheard. She knew it. She raised her voice to make sure that no mistake would be made. She felt like Justice, with a sword but without a blindfold.

It should never have been news, but once again it was. It was not printable without something a little nearer proof. Newspapers peppered Fox Hill with calls. Peach trembled with anger and screamed at Rosie. Cousin Thalia Collin, snooping at Mount Malcolm, confirmed that the two of them were going at it like little dogs. Peach forbade her to say so. Making one of the only sensible decisions of his life, he forbade any member of the household to say anything to any reporter about anything.

Miss Viola Biggs vehemently denied that things were going on under her roof. She threatened libel. The press got nothing out of the hotel, either. Matthew denied the affair. Rosie was unreachable.

The press looked for other matters of large public concern. One reporter made one final attempt, crawling into the Fox Hill shrubberies hoping to interview somebody. He found Miss Thalia Collin sketching a tree.

If Cousin Thalia had inherited Fox Hill, there would have been gracious revelry but nothing nasty. Rosie had disgraced her name and home. Cousin Thalia had been observing Rosie all year with alternate satisfaction and resentment. She was losing her looks. She recovered them. She had lost them when she came back from Britain, and sat around looking at once puffy and haggard. Now she had got them back. It was supremely obvious what made the difference. It was a sickening irony that the fruits of nastiness were a bright eye, a high colour, a clear skin. Cousin Thalia told the newspaperman in the garden about Rosie's yo-yo appearance and about the reason. Yes, she was absolutely sure. Yes, she had proof.

'Putting the love into loveliness' was the headline they used. The piece was amusing. It was only a little scoop. It was only a little newspaper. It made a few lines in many other papers. On women's pages there were articles about the effect of sex on complexion, bustline and digestion.

This time Alice was incapable of pride. Her misery was naked, shameless. Jean was deeply sorry for her. She felt, but tried to fight down, a touch of impatience. These Levantine excesses of clamorous grief were embarrassing, unseemly. Jean had never felt as deeply about anybody as Alice showed she felt.

George had, about Alice. His attitude to Carver went past anger, past murderousness. He wanted to do more to Carver than hurt him. He wanted to disgrace and humiliate him. He wanted to make him repulsive to the whole world. He wanted to make him despised, shunned, a leper.

Peach Collin indulged sticky-candy daydreams of running Carver through, after a deceptively casual display of gentlemanly swordplay.

He almost went and saw Tim.

Lord Wincham and the Bardsley regiment saw mention of the renewed scandal in the 'Letters from America' in the newspapers they pretended they took for their servants. It surprised none of them. It was exactly what you expected from an outsider, an adventurer, a notorious cad, an oik without breeding or background. A woman who had behaved as that woman had behaved, brawling and staggering on the very lip of Mollie's grave.

Clare was puzzled and angry. She thought the scene in the churchyard must have killed anything her father felt. She was embarrassed. She tried to keep the story from the Kavanaghs.

Tom knew better than to talk about it. But he knew that

Cragrock was important to Ghalib, and Clare's father to Cragrock. In his regular report to Ghalib from Ballycardeen he felt bound to mention the matter.

Liz had taken up with an actor, a serious young man who insisted on tidiness and taught her to cook. She decided her Lesbian experiments had been childish. She was no more tempted to repeat them than to regress to a squat. She was against sex without love. She lost weight, washed her hair twice a week, and made new friends who read the *Guardian*. She took a view of the news about her father which was astonishingly close to Wincham's.

Lord Hadfield had occasion to telephone the duc de Montfermainbrey, with whom he hoped to stay in Paris for the Prix de l'Arc de Triomphe. They chuckled about Matthew. Neither thought either worse or better of him. Fidelity had never seemed to either necessary or even desirable. They would have hated it. They were both good husbands, quite considerate, and kind to any animals they were not killing.

George Whyte worked at his plan. He discussed it with a few people, in a roundabout way, citing hypothetical cases. It was no good simply saying the man was treacherous and cruel. George knew it was a matter of fact but people thought it was a matter of opinion. It was no good saying he was notoriously immoral. George had been resistant to Rosie's magic, as he was resistant to all magic, but he was aware that Rosie was considered highly desirable. This aspect had often been mentioned in connection with Beausoleil. Carver was therefore doing what many people would like to have done. To point out that he was enviable was not the object of the exercise.

Carver was a swine and a crook, but he was not a *crook*. His probity was well known, on the turf and off.

George broke his own rule, and discussed the matter obliquely with Doris Bernard. She suggested getting in touch with bloodstock agents, who knew more different people in racing than anybody else, and were involved in various countries, and heard all the gossip, and spread much of it.

There were several agents in Lexington. None had anything

but good to say of Matthew Carver, whom they respected and trusted.

Sir Merivale Lucas, yet again in Kentucky and busy as a bee, was much more helpful. He repeated his earlier suggestions: the two-year-old out of Meadowsweet had *not* been selected by Carver for sound professional reasons; the siting of Beausoleil had *not* been determined on sound professional grounds. Lucas put it to George that any doubts he might have had on these points had surely been resolved by recent events. The fellow was infatuated with the bird. Turn your back for a second, and he pops up at Fox Hill, pops up in the woman's bed screwing like a ferret. The bitterness in Lucas's voice came musically down the wire. George was gratified by the intensity of his dislike for Carver.

George covered half a sheet with notes.

Lucas suggested contact with Henri de Cheminade, whom Carver had double-crossed.

Had he, indeed?

He had, indeed.

Corruptly, and with lies, Carver had cheated Henri out of management of Beausoleil and of Prince Ghalib's racing interests, and he was cheating other people all the time in ways of which Henri was not empowered to speak. He *was* empowered to speak of Carver's treachery to himself, conducted under a mask of smiling friendship, and he did so at length.

George covered a full page with notes, in very neat handwriting, arranged under heads, and with key words underlined.

Henri de Cheminade suggested contact with his own colleague Lord Goring, whom Carver had double-crossed.

Had he, though?

By God, he had!

Carver was part of a conspiracy which had cheated Goring in the matter of finding a stud-farm for Ghalib and of the commission payable thereon. A clear moral commitment had been thrown aside. Ghalib, an innocent abroad, was clearly blameless. Wogs knew no better, but Carver should have known better. Obviously he was not the loser financially.

It all looked a little thin, perhaps, when typed up by Doris Bernard and sent off to Lee V. Lowe. He made what use of it he could. One or two items were printed, riding on earlier news. It made a kind of groundwork. The stuff would be remembered, because everything in racing was remembered.

Events had made Matthew a kind of celebrity in central and northern Virginia, and newspapers consequently carried some of the handout snippets.

Jefferson Dill saw them. His memory of small-time, small-town newspaper work convinced him that the reportorial and editorial staffs had not originated the items. From old acquaintances on newspapers he got the name of Lee V. Lowe Associates, with a reassuring midtown New York address.

He called Lee V. Lowe, at Peach's expense (at Tim Phillipson's expense), and made a suggestion for which, he hinted, he expected substantial rewards. He was sure François Villon would have done the same.

Lee V. Lowe passed the suggestion to his client in Kentucky. The suggestion now masqueraded as his own. George liked it. He called Peach Collin at Fox Hill. He expected a hymn of hate against Matthew Carver, and he got it. Their meeting of minds was gratifying. Had they been vis-à-vis, and Frenchmen or footballers, they would have embraced.

Matthew went home, in response to a call from Patti Mungo that he was needed immediately. He could leave Beausoleil.

He was needed. The moment he arrived, Patti and Chuck Mungo left, with faces of stone. They simply walked out of the place where they had spent their lives. They went away with all their belongings in a cousin's truck. They returned the balance of the wages he had paid them in advance. News had finally got through to them, penetrating the insulation of their creed. They would not work for an immoral man.

Fay Candy had already quit. She was loyal to Mollie's memory. The house was clean. There was no food in the larder, but some in the freezer.

Matthew had difficulty recruiting other help locally, because a West Coast electronics corporation had opened a factory nearby. He found a man for the farm but nobody for the house. He had a lot of heavy work to do with the horses, and with vacuum and polisher and scrubbing-brush. Too tired to go out, he cooked meals with a cookbook propped open on the kitchen table.

He tried to call Rosie. There was no reason now for her to stay away. He was unable to get her to the telephone. He was sure no message got through to her.

George said to Jean and Alice, in terms as oblique as those he had used to Doris Bernard, that he was preparing a bomb to place under Matthew Carver. He was astonished at their reaction. Neither would have anything to do with anything he was doing. He found this impossible to understand.

Lee V. Lowe enlisted a photographer, and borrowed a sophisticated battery-powered tape recorder. He flew to Charlottesville with this baggage, and there met his client. George Whyte arrived with an attorney, an officer of the court whose signature to any affidavit carried massive and neutral weight.

The party made a precautionary telephone call. Reassured, it proceeded to Fox Hill. Mrs Phillipson was out, having made an appointment to see the head shrink at the sanitorium.

They were greeted by Jefferson Dill. George Whyte had met him but forgotten him. Lee V. Lowe had not met him but remembered him vividly. Jefferson Dill drew Lee V. Lowe into a corner of the library. He explained his needs. Lee V. Lowe said he had influence with some of the little magazines, in which he bought advertising space. He was sure he could place some of Jefferson Dill's poems.

The photographer shot pictures of Fox Hill and its courtly master, and George Whyte was photographed with Beausoleil looking over the door of his stall.

Peach read a prepared statement, to which he did not adhere, critical of Matthew Carver's seduction of his sister while her husband lay chronically sick in hospital. Lee V. Lowe taped the speech.

Lee V. Lowe taped a statement from Jefferson Dill that all the money spent on the house and farm was Mr Tim Phillipson's. When Matthew Carver was entertained at Fox Hill by Mrs Phillipson, it was Mr Phillipson who paid for everything he ate and drank. Jefferson Dill was quite certain of this; he could and did swear to it.

Photographs were taken of Jefferson Dill in the library, but there was no serious intention of trying to place them in the press.

Jefferson Dill called the sanitorium, and confirmed that Mrs Phillipson had left. Peach and Jefferson Dill joined the others in the hired car from Charlottesville. It was a tight squeeze, because Peach insisted on sitting in the front beside the driver. He ate a candy-bar and dropped the wrapper on the floor. They went a back way to the sanitorium, in order not to meet Rosie in whatever car she had taken.

It was Peach's first visit to the sanitorium. Jefferson Dill had not been there either. They were as lost as the others. Peach was distressed by the atmosphere.

Tim Phillipson was apathetic, neither pleased nor sorry to see them. A nurse said it was good for him to have visitors, to be encouraged to talk, to be taken out of himself. If the visit did him good he showed no sign of it. He did not want to talk, but stared at the wall and picked at the rug on his knees. His face was grey and puffy from lack of exercise.

George, who remembered him from long before, from the races he had ridden, from his win in the Maryland Hunt Cup, would not have recognised him.

Peach and Lee V. Lowe led their witness into saying how much he loved and depended on Rosie. It had been a very bad and lonely time for him, when she was away for weeks in Europe in the spring. Her visits, which were terribly important to him, had been less frequent and shorter. Tim did not want to say any of this, or anything else, but they induced him to do so. He repeated after them what they told him to say. He was not interested in what he was saying, and did not understand it. The lawyer was present throughout, so that there should be no doubt that he did actually say those actual words.

The photographer took dozens of pictures of Tim, lit to look as sick as possible.

The tape was edited to remove the voices of Peach and Lee V. Lowe. It was transcribed. Peach's and Jefferson Dill's statements were edited and transcribed. The photographs gave Tim a look of pathos, for the force of which no retouching was necessary.

CHAPTER 16

'Orchestrate it,' twittered Doris Bernard. 'If I might suggest. Those delinquent kids.'

'Are they delinquent?' asked George, who had not taken any notice of Carver's kids when they were in his house.

'I should say.'

'Theft? Forgery? What?'

Doris was unable to be specific, but George saw merit in the suggestion.

He was still thinking about it when Hal came home for a three-day break from school.

Hal looked terrible to both George and Jean, but they were used to him looking terrible. Alice, who had been preoccupied in the summer, looked at him properly for what seemed the first time. She was appalled. She dragged him to a doctor, though he fought not to go.

The doctor needed only three seconds to confirm Alice's horrified guess. He examined Hal. He put the fear of God into the boy.

'Well, young man,' he said, 'how long has this suicidal folly been going on?'

'Since summer. Middle of the summer.'

The doctor called Alice in.

'Midsummer,' she said blankly. 'My God. Jamie Carver.'

'You can kick this if you want,' said the doctor. 'But you have to want to and you do need help.'

Everybody in Alice's life seemed to need her help to kick addictions. In spite of the very best she could do, some of them failed.

Hal was immediately put in one of the seventeen detox centres in Kentucky. Their main function was to dry out some of the state's 214,000 alcoholics, but in some of them there were facilities and skills for rehabilitating mainliners.

Jean was distraught. She blamed herself for not noticing, not thinking, not caring, for being preoccupied with flowers, functions, money, Will Stevens. She accused herself with horror of being an unnatural mother.

It was probably good for Alice to find herself comforting somebody. Anyway it made a change.

George reacted in front of his family as any father would, with indignation and disgust. In private he remembered Doris Bernard's twitter about orchestration.

He called a New York lawyer with contacts in London. He was able to make his motives sound generous, responsible. He gave himself grounds for requiring, for the time being, absolute secrecy. His point was taken; also his cheque.

The New York lawyers Telexed London lawyers, a large and recently established firm with a commercial emphasis. Two of the partners did divorce business, and had in this connection employed the Cornhill Detective Agency.

The Managing Director of Cornhill sent for Gareth Rhys.

Gareth Rhys had name, age and description. He knew James Carver was studying at Oxford, but not at what school or college. The American principal in the investigation knew astonishingly little about a boy he was supposed to know well. Gareth Rhys thought the subject was too young to be at the university. He tried the public school, the best-known of the various crammers and then — using an educational directory for the first time — the less celebrated. Something called the Longwall Intensive College admitted the enrolment of Carver, James. Gareth Rhys drove down from London in his office Metro. He went to the Longwall College office. He showed the receptionist a card which confirmed his statement that he was Dr Gareth Rhys, of Brecon.

He might have been a doctor — evidently he was in truth a doctor — but he looked more like a shopkeeper in a genteel way of business: soft furnishings, stationery, china, books and prints. He was a little fat man of fifty, over the bald dome of whose head were glued a few long surviving hairs. He wore a dark suit wrinkled by his shape and by sitting in his car. His little black shoes were dusty. His fingernails were extremely clean. He carried a scuffed black bag, a doctor's bag. When he took his card from his wallet, he pulled out with it a sheaf of passport-sized photographs of children. They were dog-eared. They looked as though they were constantly taken out and shown to strangers. He looked a man who would do that.

'My business with the lad is private, you understand, family business, it may be said to be concerned with the lad's sister, the younger of his two sisters. I would not be troubling him, but his mother is most unfortunately and tragically no longer with us, and his father is in America. More than that I am not in a position to say.' Nevertheless he went on talking, almost chanting, in a rapid and heavily inflected tenor, beaming at the receptionist, the happiest of all doctors, a music-hall parody of a voluble Welshman, a harmless, good-natured and extremely boring little man.

The receptionist was thankful to get him out of the office so that she could return to *Photo-Love*. All he wanted, in the end, was the address of Carver J.'s digs.

They were in Walton Street, half of one of a row of shabby little houses. Gareth Rhys parked his car a little way away. He sat in it, filling in forms, making entries on pads with interleaved carbon paper. He was a travelling salesman recording his calls for head office; he might have been engaged in market research or a political opinion poll; he might have been employed by the city council in connection with drains or street lighting. To look at him was to dismiss him from the mind.

It began to get dark.

Lights came on in the house he was apparently not watching, on the ground floor. He put away his pieces of paper. After a long time the lights went out. A young man, a boy, came out of the house. He slammed the door against the spring lock, and used another key in the transom. He went under a street lamp. Gareth Rhys recognised young Carver from the description; five-eleven, slightly built, light brown hair of moderate length, unusually neat in the classless clothes of his generation.

Gareth Rhys felt a surge of anger. He was a strict Methodist and a loving father. He was angry that that degenerate half-Yank had seduced a decent lad into addiction. His own children and millions like them had to be protected against the Carvers of the world.

He understood that scandal was to be avoided, for the sake of an important father. There was no question of going to the police, whatever he found.

He got into the house with tools from his doctor's bag. A skilled eye would see marks of his entry on the window-frame, but he did not expect any skilled eyes to be looking. He searched, using a pencil flash. One of the two ground-floor bed-sitting-rooms was not being slept in at the moment, though evidently occupied by a young man. The other was in use. It was clean and tidy. Gareth Rhys had a battle getting even his own well-behaved children to hang up their clothes. They seemed to think the floor of their rooms was where you kept your clothes. He was interested to note that young Carver used pegs, hangers and drawers, like an adult. It made everything all the sadder, all the more shocking.

He found what he was looking for. It was hidden, in the sort of place amateurs think is a hiding-place, the back of a shelf at the top of a wardrobe behind a pile of books. The stuff was in a cardboard shoe-box — disposable and other syringes, pills, sachets of white powder which Gareth Rhys tasted and spat out.

Gareth Rhys put all the contents of the box into his doctor's bag. He returned the box to the shelf and hid it behind the books. He put a chair by the door so that it was hidden when the door was opened. He put the bag under the chair and himself on the chair. He waited in the dark for another two hours.

He heard a key in the front door. He saw light under the door of the room. Somebody was in a hurry. The door burst open, cracking against Gareth Rhys's chair. Young Carver blundered into the room, switching on the light as he came. He went straight to the wardrobe, opened it, and pulled the shoebox from behind the pile of books on the shelf.

Gareth Rhys moved his chair a yard to the right, so that he blocked the door. The doctor's bag slid along the floor under the chair. Carver was too anxious to get to his shoe-box to notice the movement behind him. He opened the box. He spun round with an expression of almost comical astonishment. He saw Gareth Rhys for the first time.

'Who the hell . . .?' said Carver. 'What . . .? Please . . .'

'I see you take a mixture,' said Gareth Rhys. 'It must increase the expense and inconvenience, I imagine it must do that, but I have read that many people do as you do. A mixture, just so.'

Carver and Gareth Rhys stared at one another, under the glaring overhead light of the room. The boy looked underfed, unhealthy, a bad colour, not so obviously sick as to attract notice in the street or even in a classroom, but a worrying sight in the merciless overhead light.

'I have read,' Gareth Rhys went on with a cheerfulness he was far from feeling, 'that the cocaine alleviates the constipating effects of the heroin. Have you found that to be so? I should be interested to hear your experience of the matter. Not for my personal guidance, you understand, but in a spirit of professional enquiry. I hate being constipated, myself, and I can tell you I take pretty good care to keep the movements regular and satisfactory. An infusion of senna pods does the trick for me. Cheaper than your coke, boyo.'

'What have you done with it?'

'I am sitting on it. There you are. All safe and serene.'

'Give it to me.'

'No, boyo. This is cold turkey time for you.'

For a time Carver tried to be reasonable, persuasive. It became harder for him to control himself, to keep his voice down. Pride stopped him being abject, kept him from weeping, kept him off his knees. Gareth Rhys made a deliberate effort to exclude pity from his mind. He felt a glimmering of respect for the boy's desperate attempt at dignity. He excluded that, too, by stoking the fire of moral outrage.

Carver darted forward to the chair. He tried to pin Gareth Rhys down with one hand while he pulled the doctor's bag out from under the chair. Gareth Rhys was stronger than he looked, and much stronger than an overgrown boy who had not had a good appetite for months, who had taken no exercise, whose digestion was in a mess. He threw Carver off and pushed him away across the room. Carver tripped over his own feet and fell. He hurt himself. He did cry, angry tears he tried to control. As he sobbed he began to gag.

Time was passing, a long time.

Gareth Rhys struggled to keep his mind cold and objective. He called on reserves of indignation. He noted the onset of withdrawal symptoms: nausea, physical weakness, streaming eyes. He saw hands and features beginning to twitch.

338

Need grew larger and pride ran away. The boy was abject. He was blubbering at Gareth Rhys's feet. He wet himself. He was a ghastly yellowish grey, sweating, twitching, his nose running, his voice a thin incoherent whine.

'Right, boyo,' said Gareth Rhys. 'Who started you on this? Where do you get it? How do you pay for it? Who do you push it to?'

Carver made a visible effort to speak coherently, in a pathetic attempt to please his torturer.

'Can't tell you,' he said. 'Can't grass.'

This attempt at loyalty was a vestige of decency. It showed guts. It had to be admired. But it was a great nuisance. It prolonged a scene which Gareth Rhys disliked very much.

Carver made further efforts to grab the bag by force. By this time his limbs and hands were unco-ordinated, almost powerless. Gareth Rhys pushed him away with a foot. There was a new stench in the room. Awful minutes dragged. Carver was no longer capable of coherent speech and certainly incapable of mixing, dissolving and injecting his fix.

With distaste, with compassion, Gareth Rhys dissolved one sixth-grain tablet of heroin and a few milligrammes of the bitter-tasting white cocaine salts in a tumbler, heating the water with a succession of matches. He half-filled a disposable syringe. He had to help Carver with his sleeve. He tied his own handkerchief round Carver's forearm, waited a few seconds until a vein inside the elbow rose blue from the skinny and pallid arm. He mainlined the horrible mixture into the vein, to get this all over with as quickly as possible. The change in Carver was speedy and startling, and in a way the most awful part of the whole business. He became human. He became rational and able to communicate. He also became brave and unwilling to communicate.

He badly wanted to change his fouled clothes. Gareth Rhys prevented this, prevented anything, until he had talked.

He talked about Mario di Vianello, now in Italy. Gareth Rhys got the message of an older, richer, more sophisticated youth precociously involved with a bad set in Turin, and of this Anglo-American boy with parents who were or had been, for different reasons, grossly unsatisfactory.

Carver was able to give Gareth Rhys the address of his own father in Kentucky, and of Mario's father in Italy.

Gareth Rhys showed Carver the photographs of all his own

children, and talked about damnation as described in the chapel of his youth. They were at it most of the night, until the boy collapsed into a sleep that was like a coma.

Gareth Rhys let himself quietly out of the house. It was just beginning to get light. He looked at himself in the driving mirror of his car. He was greasy and scruffy, his chin blue with heavy Welsh stubble, his hair unglued from his pate. He was very tired.

He went home, cleaned up, and clocked in at the office. He reported verbally to the Managing Director before dictating his formal report. He went home early to catch up on his rest; he was the wrong shape for sleeplessness. He had been asleep for twenty minutes when he found himself wide awake and aware of a duty.

Technically, as he was vividly aware, he was stepping out of line. But he brought morality to his profession and made it a way of life to be proud of. He was clearly bound not to tell the police or any doctor about Carver, but what he was obliged to do was only a technical breach of confidence. Nobody's security was threatened and two souls might be saved. He telephoned il conte Ottaviano di Vianello in Italy, said he was Dr Gareth Rhys from Brecon, said he had reliable but confidential information that the count's eldest son Mario was a heroin addict. He hung up on outraged gobblings at the other end, and telephoned Mr Matthew Carver in Kentucky.

Ottaviano dismissed the long-distance rantings of a crazy Welsh doctor as a joke in bad taste, a case of mistaken identity, or an attempt to manufacture scandal for purposes of blackmail. But one of Mario's sisters, herself given premature glimpses of smart life in Turin, had observed him with a less idolatrous eye. She told Papa to make sure, and she told him how to do it. Mario was apologetically locked in a room, until his screams declared the truth of the lie.

He was in a clinic in the foothills of the Alps, at murderous expense, within hours. He had by this time named Jamie Carver as his mentor and supplier. Very angry indeed, Ottaviano considered calling the English police, his own lawyers, or the newspapers. Instead he decided to call Matthew Carver in Kentucky.

Matthew blamed himself with as much agony as Jean Whyte had done. His only excuse was that drug addiction was something

340

entirely unknown to him. As far as he knew he had never seen an addict. He did not know what they were supposed to look like, how they were supposed to act. He dimly remembered something about the pupils of their eyes — dilated or unnaturally small — but he had never noticed anything odd about Jamie's eyes.

After some trouble and a lot of expensive calls, he got Liz's new telephone number in London.

'Oh, my God,' said Liz. 'I knew he was on something, but I didn't know it was that.'

'Why didn't you tell me?'

'Your mind was on other things,' said Liz, in the clear accusing upper-class English voice which Matthew had never got used to from his own daughter.

Liz agreed to get Jamie on to an aircraft to Chicago, by whatever force was necessary.

'I think I'd better bring him,' she said.

'I'd be very happy if you did,' said Matthew. 'Do you want to come?'

As it happened, Liz did want to come. Her actor had been kidnapped by his mother, who was very rich, and taken to South Africa for the winter. He had given in with shameful readiness to blackmail. Liz was loveless, shortly to be homeless, and fed up with London.

'Can you run to two tickets?' she said.

The telephone rang again and again in Matthew's empty house. There was nothing in the timbre of the ring to convey that at the other end of the line was a very angry Italian. Matthew was out, arranging a cure for Jamie. In the intervals he struggled to keep abreast of the work with the horses.

'This is a double-edged weapon, Squire,' said Lee V. Lowe to George Whyte.

They were both holding photostats of an edited version of Gareth Rhys's report. It was not a two- but a three-edged weapon. Carver was an addict, but there was no doubt that he was the victim of an older boy, a stronger character.

George had no wish to antagonise Ottaviano di Vianello, an important shareholder in Cragrock and the single most important man in Italian bloodstock.

'There'll come a time,' said Lee V. Lowe. In his voice for

making jokes he said, 'Old man bluebird will sing on that old magnolia.'

Gareth Rhys's report went into a folder with the transcribed tapes and photographs from Fox Hill.

Matthew finally got Rosie on the telephone.

'Come,' she said. 'Here. Now. The dust is all settled. Nobody cares anyway.'

'I can't,' said Matthew. He explained about the Mungos and Fay Candy.

'Then I can come to you.'

'You could have. You could be here today. But not tomorrow. My kids . . .'

'I see,' said Rosie. 'Okay. That does beat me. We're together again and we can't get together. Is it parallel lines that never meet? Goddam geometry. Goddam geography, you so far away.'

Her voice was unsteady and she hung up.

Sir Merivale Lucas came, yet again, on what sounded a spurious errand. He had heard from George Whyte a guarded reference, an intriguing reference, to tapes made at Fox Hill. He thought Peach could enlighten him. But Peach was in a trance-like state, and no sense could be got out of him.

Rosie, in the bitterness of her separation from Matthew, was brutally rude to Lucas. He went away in a rage.

Liz settled into the house where she had spent her early childhood. She became companionable, though there were large no-go conversational areas. She was intermittently vehement about keeping the house clean. Her cooking verged on the over-ambitious. Matthew taught her to drive. She began at once to meet people and to go to a few parties. She and Matthew saw Jamie as often as possible. They were cutting him down pretty quickly and he was having a bad time.

Jamie said he had abandoned any idea of going to an English university. He would come back and live with his father and work on the farm, and try for a new sense of direction. Matthew was not sure if he would still have this idea when they let him out, but he welcomed it meanwhile. Matthew warned himself not to let the seesaw toss him too far: not to brood over his younger children like a hen.

Rosie was still barred from the place, with Liz and Jamie

342

around. Matthew's relationship with them remained fragile. Their rehabilitation was young. The impact of Rosie would torpedo the one and therefore the other. He burst out laughing, all by himself in a stall he was mucking out, when he remembered her in blackface. He thought with a kind of awe of her covering herself with black gunk in order to make him laugh. He missed her terribly.

Sir Merivale Lucas went back to England. His wife mocked him for his failure with Rosie Phillipson. She was an ill-natured woman; she had a lot to be ill-natured about. Lucas made his stay at home as short as possible, and caused business to cause him to go to Kentucky in November.

At Cragrock he observed Jean Whyte's preoccupation, but they were coy about the reason. He was aware of the new ferocity of George's attitude to Matthew Carver. He shared it. He admired Alice Harding. He knew that Carver had had her and could probably still have her, as well as Rosie. He was a child with no lollypop looking at a child with two lollypops.

After dinner, in George's study, with highballs, the two men sat talking. The conversation circled like a greedy but nervous fly over a custard.

It began to come out: George's desire to give Carver leprosy.

Lucas cleverly said, 'If we were writing a thriller, this would be easy. We'd set it in England.'

'Why?'

'Bent bookmakers, bent stable-lads, strict rules, a super laboratory.'

'You can find all of those in America.'

'In your backyard, George. In your shoes I'd prefer remote control.'

Improvising the plot of a thriller, Lucas gave his victim a novice steeple-chaser trained in England by an ex-jockey, a horse certain to run during the coming winter and probably fancied to win. This horse could be backed, anonymously and at long range, so that it started hot favourite. A likely danger also to be heavily backed so that it started clear second favourite. The favourite doped, the dope-test positive after the favourite badly beaten, the doping palpably an inside job. A heavy bet on the second favourite traced to the favourite's owner. Order for the doping traced to the owner. Banco.

343

'A little elaborate,' said George. 'A little fanciful. You have to hypothesise a lot of crooks in the right places, and they have to be agreeable to manipulation.'

'This will cost. Given the bread, your problems disappear.'

George pondered. He said, 'I never much liked that trainer Carver picked, that Fred Cottle.'

'A rough diamond, certainly.'

'But I never heard he was, uh, amenable to this kind of thing. His staff, too. He's pretty much of a disciplinarian there. He doesn't hire crooks.'

'He would for a thousand quid.'

'I don't think so. He must have money saved. He wouldn't risk his reputation for, uh, a douceur.'

'If you can't join them lick them. Have you got a big stick?'

'No. I guess to the world he's clean, cleaner than Carver. But I imagine we can find one. He was a jockey. All jockeys ride funny races sometimes. He's been around in racing a very long time. There must be blots.'

'That's very nearly true. Have you got a blot researcher?'

'As a matter of fact,' said George, 'I have.'

Initially it was office work for the Cornhill Detective Agency: the *Racing Calendar* for the entire period of Fred Cottle's career. The stewards of various meetings had enquired into his riding of horses that were expected to win but didn't, that were not ridden out to be placed, that were needlessly boxed in to create the presumption that he let himself be beaten on purpose, that were beaten by disqualification or objection. Cottle was cautioned a few times for excessive use of the whip, and twice suspended for short periods for rough riding. As a trainer, he was asked half a dozen times over the years to explain discrepancies in running. His explanations were mostly 'accepted', but on two occasions 'noted', which meant that he wasn't quite believed but nothing could be proved.

It didn't add up to a row of beans. It was the profile of the career of a man who was impetuous when young, careful when old, and fairly nearly completely honest throughout.

Reminiscence, widely and tactfully canvassed, confirmed the picture.

The Cornhill Detective Agency had seldom earned so large a fee for so small a result.

344

Semi-legal use was made of a police computer. Offences dealt with in magistrates' courts were mostly expunged from all record, but with certain exceptions where a moral risk was involved, especially to children. In April 1948, in Lambourn, Frederick Cottle was charged with indecent exposure to three schoolgirls at a bus stop. He was acquitted owing to conflicting evidence.

'If a man does this once he does it again,' said Gareth Rhys.

Operatives went to Wantage, Lambourn, Malton and Newmarket, to study the files of local newspapers for the periods when Fred Cottle had been based at each of these training centres.

There was an unsolved case at Newmarket: an indecent exposure committed late at night, by a small elderly man who appeared drunk, the previous October. Gareth Rhys compared the reported description of the culprit with a photograph of Cottle taken at the Houghton Sales and printed in *Horse and Hound*. He was not surprised at the prodigious trouble somebody was taking to nail this horrible man. The thought of his own young daughters being subjected to such a thing filled him with anger and revulsion. Psychological damage could be permanent, emotionally crippling. It was just as bad as drugs. Poor little girls.

Gareth Rhys arrived in Newmarket very early in the morning. He found out from the office of the Jockey Club Agent that Fred Cottle's first lot was being galloped on the Bury Side at eight. He drove along the Norwich road, parked, and confirmed from a journalist that Cottle was with his string and would be there for another half hour. He went to Cottle's yard and to his house, and presently into his kitchen, where Mrs Cottle was sleepily making breakfast.

He was Dr Rhys, originally from Brecon, as his card proved. When he pulled it out of his wallet, the sheaf of photographs of his children fell on the kitchen floor. He picked up a picture of his daughter Gwynneth, taken when she was twelve, in a muslin party frock.

'I am concerned, as a medical man you understand, not from a moralistic standpoint and certainly not from a legal standpoint, about the effects of certain traumatic episodes on the emotional stability of a child like this.'

Mrs Cottle stared at him blankly over the bacon in the pan. Gareth Rhys was sure she knew exactly what he was talking about.

'I am doing research into the motivation, you understand,' he went on, rapid, chanting, beaming, 'why a respectable married man, a man of position and status in the world, a respected professional man, should be driven to display his anatomy to young schoolgirls. That of course is why I am here.'

Mrs Cottle was staring at him like a bird at a cat.

'You understand that this is all in the most perfect confidence,' he lied. 'The seal of the confessional, you know. Oh, absolutely. The quest for scientific knowledge to guide the psychiatrists of the future. I am sure that if it is put to him like that, Mr Cottle will not withhold his assistance. He will not deny the help he is in a position to give to generations yet unborn.'

The bacon began to smoke. Mrs Cottle exclaimed, and took the pan off the burner. She put the bacon on a plate set to heat. She turned her back on Gareth Rhys so that he could not see her expression.

He put a miniaturised radio transmitter in a bowl on a shelf.

Regaining control, Mrs Cottle turned. She cut a slice off a loaf and put lard in the pan.

'Fried bread, by jingo,' said Gareth Rhys. 'Lucky Mr Cottle, that's what I say.'

'Mr Cottle has never done anything at all like what you're talking about. You must of come to the wrong house. It's somebody different you're after.'

'I think not, ma'am. You and I both know better than that, eh? I'll be back to see him after he's had his breakfast.'

'You stay away from here. You stay out of this house.'

'Ah, now, don't be like that, don't be difficult. It only makes for unpleasantness. It only makes for pieces in the newspapers. I don't want to have to come back with a policeman, but if I have to I will. It is the Home Office I'm working for, you understand? Did I not mention that? I am legally entitled to demand co-operation, you understand.'

'Oh God,' said Mrs Cottle.

Gareth Rhys bowed, smiled and made a long farewell speech.

He sat in his car, out of sight of the arch into the yard. He had earphones, a radio and a tape recorder. Earphones and recorder were both plugged into the radio.

Fred Cottle stopped his car and got out. Soon afterwards the first of his string clattered towards the arch.

On headphones came the noise of pans, cutlery and sobbing.

346

Fred Cottle disappeared towards the house. Gareth Rhys switched on the tape.

'So you did it again, you dirty old man,' came Mrs Cottle's voice, thick with anger and terror.

For a time he pretended not to understand her. She said the doctor would be back, with a policeman if Fred wouldn't see him.

'A policeman. Jesus Christ! Those girls. They saw me under the light. It's all that bastard Carver's fault.'

Fred Cottle broke down. Gareth Rhys listened with indignation, with satisfaction. Bitter disappointment about the Mill Reef colt. Drinks, too many drinks. A walk through back streets, to get some air before bed. Girls in the street, leaving a party. Something made him do it, the drink, the disappointment, anger. Doctor. Police. Prison. Ruin.

He went out of the room, away from the transmitter. It seemed he did not want his bacon and fried bread. The bacon was overcooked, but Gareth Rhys could have done with it. He switched off tape and radio. He made no attempt to return to the house. One or more of his bluffs might be called. He made them a present of the radio in the bowl. He turned his car and started back to London.

Doris Bernard heard Jean Whyte say that Liz Carver was now with her father. The moment she was alone Doris called the Carvers. She spoke to Liz, a sugary twittering, the call of a lover.

'Oh, shut up,' said Liz, at her most English. 'I've completely outgrown all that. You make yourself sound ridiculous.'

Alicia, just home from school, submitted to Doris's embraces after her tub. Gentleness, butterfly fingers and tongue, an explosion of sensation which she had missed since early September. For a little while she was Doris's slave: for long enough.

She told her parents that she had been seduced by Liz Carver during the summer, that they had had a Lesbian affair. That, sickened by the memory and believing Liz evil, she had decided to come clean.

'Is there no limit,' said George, 'to what that family do to us?'

Jean stared at her daughter in shocked disbelief. Alicia stared back. Alicia looked sullen and herself a little shell-shocked.

George went away, his hands trembling, to dictate a confidential memorandum to Lee V. Lowe.

'Orchestrate,' said Doris Bernard.

Jean would have turned for comfort to Alice Harding, but Alice was away for the weekend. Jean went to Will Stevens, impetuously, too impetuously, needing him as never before. She wept as they embraced, calling herself names, demanding that he contradict her self-accusations, shutting him up when he contradicted her. She was not far from hysteria, and she made too much noise. Will tried to hush her. She pulled off his clothes and her own, in the shed behind his house.

Mary-Jane Stevens heard the noise, the sobbing and the banging about. They thought she was out marketing. She came to the shed and found them.

Mary-Jane went straight to the big house and asked for George.

Jean was silent when George faced her. There was plenty she could have said. She had plenty of answers to his charges, good answers to questions he meant as rhetorical. She looked round the beautiful room, and the pictures and drapes and antique furniture; she looked at the heavy gold Dior bracelet on her wrist, and beyond it to her Gucci shoes. She thought she could keep it all if she held still. She could have her cake even if she couldn't eat it, not that cake, not at once, probably not that particular cake. It was terribly tempting to spell it all out for George, but the game was not quite worth the candle.

George went away to the telephone. He sent Doris Bernard out of the office while he telephoned. He used the private line that had no extensions anywhere in the house.

Burying all manner of hatchets, he called his ex-brother-in-law Frank Harding on the coast.

Frank was delighted to hear from George, surprised but unaffectedly pleased. He had no hatchets to bury. He bore no grudges against anybody. He was a ray of California sunshine. He understood that he had made Alice sad and George sore, and he had kept out of their way.

He immediately agreed to do as George asked. He was as affable and obliging as could be. He owed the Whyte family a good turn after the ill turn he had done them, and he was happy to be given the opportunity. He understood exactly what was wanted of him. George offered to pay for the whole thing, but

Frank said the money was unimportant, it was part of the reparations he owed the Whytes.

George could not bring himself to face Will Stevens. He sent a message to him by Harold the butler.

Alice came back into the turbulence left by these events. She found herself once again Jean's comforter, which was not easy. She had known Jean had somebody. She had seen that Jean needed somebody, although she herself was strong on fidelity. She had never guessed at Jean doing something so *outré,* so rash, so squalid as screwing the farm manager. Any kind of affair seemed out of character for someone so cool and classy; that one seemed a deliberate plunge into the swamp.

The Alicia business, which had triggered the Jean business, made much the same demands on Alice and equally shocked her. She had never had anything approaching a Lesbian experience, and could not imagine the attraction. She tried not to be prurient when she got Alicia to talk about it. Alicia was vague.

George probably needed comforting, too — a third patient for Alice Nightingale — but he had locked himself away. Alice pictured him licking his wounds. Maybe Doris Bernard was licking his wounds. George's massive but fragile pride, the lifelong performance of which she was pityingly aware, would take a knock out of any disloyalty by Jean. But if the man had been a Mellon, a Whitney, a Stewart of Baltimore, a Combs or a Hancock in Kentucky, the shock would have been dulled, the wound balmed. The help was something else.

Coming away from the office, where George was closeted with Doris, Alice saw a stack of mail waiting to go out. On top was a letter to Lee V. Lowe Associates. Of course Alice knew about Lee V. Lowe. She knew George had had ideas, crazy vengeful ideas, of somehow smearing Matthew, punishing him for his treatment of herself. She had a premonition. She did something she had never done before. She took the letter, went to her room, steamed the envelope open over a kettle.

She went straight to Alicia, who was reading in the small library. Alice was startled to notice that she was reading Booth Tarkington's *Penrod*. She was recapturing the sweetness of childhood, taking shelter from these sad adult storms.

Alice remembered that she herself, the morning after her first precocious and disastrous heavy sexual experience, had found herself playing with a doll.

'Look,' she said, 'do you realise that you're being manipulated? You and Hal both, I guess. Me too, if I let them.'

'What do you mean, Aunt Alice? Nobody manipulated me.'

'Doris Bernard. Your father. One or both. It would make me very mad, if I were you. I shouldn't let you see this but I'm going to.'

Alice read the memorandum and the covering letter. She finished aloud, 'Not for immediate use, but as a quick follow-up to the main story we shall have in the near future. Then anything about that damned family will be news. More of that anon. Cordially, Doris B. Bernard, Secretary to Mr George . . .'

'What really did happen in the summer, Alicia?'

'Doris had me a year ago. She kind of took me off guard. It was disgusting but it was, you know, terribly exciting. We both had Liz in the summer. She was new to it. This document is crap. Liz liked it all right, but I think she'd had enough by the time she left.'

'Come tell your father that.'

'I can't possibly. I daren't.'

'You have to. Otherwise a horrible injustice is going to be done, a horrible lie spread.'

'Yes. Okay. This is very sick, this material.'

'It's a lie,' screamed Doris.

Nobody had ever heard her scream before. It was a startling noise from such a little, prettyish, fluttering person.

'You had no right to read that letter,' said George to Alice.

'I know it, but it's lucky I did.'

'She's lying! Can't you see she's lying?'

'Oh, get that woman out of here, George,' said Alice.

'Yes. Go. I'll give you half an hour to pack. If you think I owe you any money, sue me.'

'I'll sure as Christ sue you. I'll spill all the dirt about you.'

'There is no dirt about me,' said George.

'Your son's a hophead, your daughter's a dyke, your wife's a whore, and you're paranoid.'

'Rubbish,' said Alice. 'Who's going to believe you?'

'They'll believe Mary-Jane Stevens,' said Doris. 'She's mad enough to tell anybody anything. Ha, big shot, suckered by the hired hand.'

Doris shot out of the room, before George could once again order her to leave.

'What's that about Mary-Jane Stevens?' asked Alicia after a pause.

'Nothing, darling,' said Alice. 'Delirium.'

Doris ran out of the house and round to where her car was parked. She raced the half-mile to the manager's house.

She saw there were no drapes in the windows. The front door stood open. She ran in. Her footsteps clattered on bare boards and echoed from bare walls. The house was empty. She saw furniture which belonged to the farm, not to Will and Mary-Jane. There was not much of it. The house looked despoiled, looted.

Doris collapsed on to a chair and planned revenge, and realised there was nothing in the world she could do. Warned of all this in advance, she could have taken a trunkful of papers to prove the things she said. Now the papers were locked in the files and George had the key. She had a key and she left it behind in the office, in her rush to see Mary-Jane. She had lost job and love and power and she had to go back to New York to start all over again. She lay across the arm of the chair and wept, until she got too cold to sit there any more.

Frank Harding acted fast. He called the President of the Fedora County Fair and Exposition Inc., which owned the small Sandhills track in northern California. They had a fifteen-day meeting, starting the second week in January. Frank asked for barn space for four horses. It was a late and irregular application, but he thought he could swing it and he did. Places like Fedora were always short of horses. That was why California permitted drugs which would have horrified the East. Then Frank asked his trainer, at Santa Anita preparing for the racing just after Christmas, to send his four worst horses to Sandhills with a groom and a work-rider. The men had written discharges from the trainer, post-dated, without which they would not have been able to take jobs with a different trainer. From the California Horse Racing Board in Sacramento, meanwhile, Frank arranged for a provisional licence enabling a new trainer, from outside the state, to prepare horses at Sandhills and enter them in races. Full authorisation would go through by the time racing started.

Woody Stevens and his wife arrived from Kentucky, and moved

into a big trailer provided by Frank at Sandhills. Woody was William Woodward Stevens; he used his second name. His wife Bea was Mary-Jane Beatrice; she used her second name, too. Nobody at Sandhills had ever seen them before or ever heard of them. They fitted in okay, he better than her, and Woody knew something about horses. He was paid an awfully big salary by northern California standards, where the racing is a stepping-stone to, or a refuge from, the rich tracks of the south.

Matthew was wondering when Poetaster, his young English 'chaser, would see a racecourse. The expected letter came from Fred Cottle. Poetaster had had a minor setback in training, but would be fit and ready to run in the New Year. He was entered in a novice 'chase at Sandown.

Jamie came home, wobbly, clear-eyed, determined. He began at once to help on the farm, and Matthew paid him. He was more use as his strength returned. He and Liz bickered, but on the whole the family rubbed along pretty well. Matthew and Jamie had a few talks about Jamie's future. By some magic for which Matthew had not even prayed, he became interested in horses. He re-learned to ride. He liked grooming them. He particularly liked the young stock, the weanlings soon to be yearlings. He began to wonder about working for Tom Kavanagh in Ireland, as a trainee stud manager.

Fred Cottle wrote again. Poetaster would definitely run at Sandown, on the 9th of January.

'Go,' said Liz. 'You need a break. You're exhausted. We can look after everything here. There's nothing to do at this time of year. Jamie can feed the horses. We've got the vet's number.'

'I can't leave you here.'

'Of course you can. We won't give any wild parties. We might give a tame one.'

'I'll get somebody in.'

'If you feel you must, but it's really quite unnecessary.'

Fred wrote a third time. Poetaster was jumping out of his skin. He was a natural leaper — had hardly needed schooling — and showed a touch of speed on the heath. There was no reason he shouldn't win first time out.

'There you are,' said Liz. 'You must go.'

Sir Merivale Lucas saw Poetaster in the Calendar. He tipped

the horse to a journalist, inventing a conversation with the owner in Kentucky. The journalist followed up the tip by talking to Fred Cottle in the unsaddling enclosure at Lingfield Park. Fred Cottle was perfectly open. His was not a betting stable and Matthew Carver was not a betting owner. Poetaster at Sandown became one of the writer's 'Long Range Forecasts' in his Saturday column.

Lucas had heard, not once but a thousand times, Lord Goring's story of the perfidy of the Carver family in the matter of Ghalib's stud. He knew that Goring was short of money, as anybody did who looked at Goring's clothes. He knew that Goring had intimate contacts with bookmakers, though he did not know which.

Lucas offered Goring a lot of George Whyte's money, though Goring did not know it was George Whyte's.

Goring accordingly met his friend Trevor Plimsoll, on a non-racing day, in a pub near Victoria. Trevor Plimsoll owed Goring a favour, for getting him Ghalib's custom directly and Rosie Phillipson's indirectly. In a deeply shocked voice, Trevor Plimsoll acknowledged that he knew a man who knew a man in a Newmarket racing stable who would do anything for a few quid. Goring said he wanted this stable-lad to apply for a job with Fred Cottle.

'Cottle won't touch 'im wiv a barge-pole, Lordy.'

'Oh yes, he will.'

'Why will 'e?'

'I don't know,' Goring admitted. 'But I'm told he'll do as he's told.'

Goring had a message from Lucas. He telephoned Trevor Plimsoll. Plimsoll gave him another number and the name Sidney. It was a Newmarket number. He spoke to Sidney. Some papers already delivered to Sidney were to be shown to Fred Cottle. Goring was explicit. He wanted no mistake.

Old Lady Goring, next door in the kitchen, was trying to get burnt sugar off the bottom of a saucepan. She heard every word that Bobbety Bobs was saying, because it was impossible not to. She was puzzled. She was sorry for Bobbety Bobs, working so late into the night.

Nigel Hughes, Lord Hadfield's affable but slap-happy trainer, was rather pleased than otherwise when a stable-lad called Darren Finn gave notice. Finn had never done anything wrong, as far as

Nigel Hughes knew, but he gave you an uncomfortable feeling. Some of the other lads, the older men, steered clear of him. Nigel hated firing people — had not considered firing Finn — had no real grounds for doing so. He might be taken to an Industrial Tribunal and made to pay heavy compensation. All things considered, he was glad to see the back of the boy.

A man in a fur hat went to see Fred Cottle, and saw him privately in his office. He had a photocopy of a transcript of a tape. He said the tape existed and the sound quality was excellent. The voices were perfectly recognisable.

Fred felt sick. He was terrified. There was something so humiliating, so pathetic, so childish about his single weakness. Everybody would be disgusted, but everybody would laugh, too. It was like a grown man being a bed-wetter, or a nose-picker, or a pocket-billiards player.

He expected to be asked for thousands of pounds, but he was simply asked to give a job in the yard to a lad presently employed by Nigel Hughes and with a satisfactory reference from him.

Fred Cottle thought Nigel Hughes a friendly bloke but an amateur. He trained better horses than he deserved because he had friends and relations among the nobs. A reference from him was only worth hanging on a nail in a shit-house.

The whole deal stank. The purpose might be inside information, for punters or ring, or it might be more sinister.

To his wife Fred said, 'I won't do it. I won't be blackmailed. This lad must be a wrong 'un, or why would they go this way about it? I won't risk my horses. What I done ain't so terrible. I never laid a hand on a girl, never touched a one, done 'em no harm, just a bit of folly with drink taken. I'd hate like hell for it all to come out, but I'd rather that than I-dunno-what in the yard.'

'Oh no, you wouldn't,' said Ivy Cottle. 'You know what my family will say, when you're standing in the dock for this? They'll say, "I told you so", they will. They'll say, "That's what comes of marrying a jockey, marrying beneath you like we said you shouldn't." They'll say, "We warned you," they will. They'll sneer at me. My sisters will. My nieces will. They'll laugh. I can't bear it. I won't have it. It's only taking on a lad from Nigel Hughes, and he's a gentleman. Where's the harm in that? What's all the fuss about? Nigel Hughes never pulled out his prick under the nose of a schoolgirl.'

'Stop,' said Fred Cottle. 'For Christ's sake, stop.'

'You do like I say, then.'

'Yes.'

Darren Finn went to work for Fred Cottle, sharing a room in the lads' house with two others, riding out in clothes scruffier than Fred liked, skiving a bit when there were straw-bales to be carried. He still saw his mates at Nigel Hughes's, and he still saw the man in the fur hat, who promised him more lolly than he'd ever heard of.

There was no need to rig the market as Lucas had planned. The morning papers, informed by the biggest office bookmakers, forecast Poetaster as clear favourite at prices varying between 2 to 1 and 7 to 4. There was a clear second favourite, another six-year-old from a powerful Middleham stable, called Green Bay Tree. David Cawley was down to ride Poetaster, a popular twenty-five-year-old professional, recently married, based near Cheltenham. He had ridden Poetaster on the gallops and asked to ride him in public. This was reported and in itself a hot tip. Eight racing correspondents selected Poetaster and three napped him.

'It's not really dishonest,' said the man in the fur hat. ''Cos it's orders from the owner hisself.'

'Bugger that,' said Darren Finn, folding away five ten-pound notes.

'I'll show you the letter.'

Goring telephoned a man who called himself a turf commissioner and was called a pro backer. He said that £10,000 was to go on Green Bay Tree at best odds. Bill or cheque was to be sent to a New York bank, to be debited or credited to an account of which Goring provided the number. Goring identified himself with a number.

Old Lady Goring, on her knees on the kitchen floor, nearly had a heart attack from the shock.

Nobody understood why the new fellow Finn came with Fred Cottle's two runners to Sandown. He said the governor was giving him a day at the races. It was a surprise for the horses' lads, the travelling lad and the driver.

There was nothing like it anywhere else in the world, Matthew thought. Sandown, Cheltenham, Doncaster. Leopardstown and Fairyhouse too, no doubt, but he had never been jump-racing in Ireland. A crowd as big and excited as for the flat, but looking different. Sheepskin coats, quilted Huskies, fur-lined boots, leather-faced old ladies with regimental brooches in their hats, white moustaches above regimental ties. Lots of girls in Hermès scarves. Fug in the bars, cold and clear outside. There had been a little hoar-frost on the lush grass-blades, but there was no bone in the ground. The going was perfect.

There was a four-year-old hurdle, a novice hurdle, a handicap hurdle, a novice steeplechase, a conditions 'chase, and a three-mile handicap 'chase. A normal card and a high-class entry. Many of the runners were bound for the National Hunt Festival at Cheltenham in March, and some of the staying 'chasers were entered in the Grand National. The novice 'chase was the fourth race: two miles, stiffish brushwood fences, not as big as some but needing to be jumped, including open ditches and water; a sharp uphill finish.

Fred Cottle's first runner ran a good third in the four-year-old hurdle, a nice each-way bet at 12 to 1. Neither Matthew nor Fred himself backed it, but the horse's own lad had a bit on for himself and the rest of the yard.

Poetaster drifted in the market. Green Bay Tree hardened. People guessed at smart brass from Yorkshire, or something wrong with Poetaster. He didn't look wrong. Fred Cottle was known to be confident. People observed the betting, and, according to temperament, either took with pleasure a better price than they expected about Poetaster, or switched their interest to Green Bay Tree.

Matthew saw his horse saddled, then went into the parade ring with Fred Cottle. Fred was edgy and uncommunicative. Matthew knew one of the stewards and a few trainers. It was a field of twelve. They walked round in their rugs. The jockeys came in, in wool instead of silk. Matthew met David Cawley for the first time, and liked him.

The ITV cameras followed Poetaster round the paddock. The commentator said that the owner had flown over specially to see it. That was obviously significant. But Poetaster was taking a walk in the market, presumably in response to support for the Yorkshire candidate, which was also significant. Fascinating contest. Stars of the future.

The jockeys mounted. The horses went down the steep tan path under the rhododendrons, and out on to the course. Matthew wondered as always at the differences between here and home. Did American racehorses really need all those pony-boys and outsiders to get them safely to the start?

No draw for any jump race. A webbing tape, held down against springs, for the start. The starter on his rostrum. The white flag up. The lever pulled. The tape whipped up. 'They're off.'

The usual adrenalin, the hands shaking almost too much to hold the binoculars. Climb. Right-hand turn. Steeply downhill, and a jump there. Poetaster labouring. Something wrong. Right again, and into the railway straight, three fences close together, still a mile to go. Poetaster losing his action, struggling to keep in touch. Poetaster down, a crunching fall, seemed to land across the jockey. Ambulance on the move at once. St John's men already there. Horse up, trotting on, seeming sound, weaving. Jockey motionless.

Green Bay Tree won. People who had backed him shouted with a glee unalloyed by the distant accident.

The jockey had concussion and multiple fractures.

Poetaster, glassy-eyed, was led in. A dope-test was ordered and samples taken.

Sick, Fred thought about his licence. Matthew thought about the jockey. The jockey's wife thought about her unborn baby. Neither David Cawley nor Poetaster was capable of thinking about anything.

CHAPTER 17

The laboratories at Newmarket normally took several days over tests. Sometimes they hardly needed minutes. Poetaster had been given a heavy dose of barbiturates shortly before his race. The timing explained why he had seemed all right in the paddock and on the way to the start.

It seemed proper to the Jockey Club Disciplinary Committee and to Racecourse Security Services, its technical and professional arm, to delay announcement of the result of the test, until the normal period had elapsed. This enabled enquiries to be made into things which nobody knew were being enquired about.

The Stewards of the Jockey Club requested the owner of Poetaster, if it were quite convenient, to remain in Britain pending the result of the test. They had, of course, no power to make him stay. He called Liz, was reassured by her that all was well at home, and accepted an invitation to stay with Lord and Lady Hadfield.

The ex-senior police officers employed by R.S.S. established that no unauthorised person could have entered the racecourse stables from dawn onwards. It followed that the drug was administered by an authorised employee either of the racecourse or of a licensed trainer. The signing-in book was scrutinised. Fred Cottle had sent three stable-lads, as well as his travelling man, with two horses. One was not the regular lad who did either of Cottle's runners. This man had joined Cottle's staff only eleven days previously, from Nigel Hughes.

Hughes was interviewed unofficially. He had no idea why Darren Finn had left him. He tried to be loyal to his ex-employee, but he revealed that, without firm grounds, he had never quite trusted Finn.

Cottle was interviewed unofficially. He was visibly uneasy.

This was to be explained without reference to any possible guilt, but other things were unexplained. He was able to show the investigators the reference Finn had brought from Nigel Hughes. He was not able to explain why he had recruited an extra lad into a fully-staffed yard at a time of the year when he had few horses running. He was not able to explain why he had sent an extra lad to Sandown, though he was perfectly entitled to send as many lads as he liked. He was not at this stage obliged to answer any questions at all, and he answered few. He was a bad liar and he made a bad impression.

Nobody thought Fred Cottle had been a willing party to the stopping of one of his horses by dope. It seemed possible that he had been terrified into it.

Darren Finn was interviewed. He was cocky. He said he moved jobs because Mr Cottle was a better trainer than Mr Hughes. He said his record in racing was clean and he wanted to keep it that way. He admitted his year in Borstal, and said he had gone straight ever since. He had not gone near Poetaster at the races and had given him nothing. He was at this point tricked by men cleverer than himself. He was told he had been seen with Poetaster. A statement was read to him that he was seen giving something to the horse. The statement purported to come from a security guard who was watching a close-circuit television monitor.

Finn changed his story. He said he now remembered, as he had previously forgotten, giving the horse a peppermint. Horses usually loved peppermints. Peppermint wasn't a drug. Finn was sharing his peppermints with the horse, as any horse-lover would.

The investigators thought he was a right little villain. They were surprised that either Hughes or Cottle should have employed him.

The bookies were asked, discreetly, to cooperate. Everything was regular. Nobody had laid heavily against Poetaster and failed to hedge, which would have created the presumption that they knew he was being got at. Substantial bets were reported on Green Bay Tree, placed with three London offices by a professional backer. The backer said he had received his instructions by telephone, the client number, used for confidentiality, being that of Prince Ghalib al-Jilani, who sometimes employed him to get money on quietly. Cheques totalling £27,000 had already gone off to New York, to the credit of an account of which he had the number.

A coded Telex to New York elicited a surprising and unwelcome answer. The depositor with that account number was Mr Matthew Carver. The New York bank properly refused any information beyond this, but the money was already credited to Carver because the cheques had been cleared.

Prince Ghalib had gone to Halat al Bhudi in mid-December and was there still. The pro backer did not think the call he received came from so far away.

Carver was Ghalib's partner. It was feasible that he should have known the number used by Ghalib to his pro backer.

The investigators got hold of Darren Finn again, with difficulty. He had left Fred Cottle and was working on a building site. They frightened him. He repeated that he had given Poetaster a peppermint, just a peppermint. He had not bought the peppermints. He had been given them. He did not know the name of the man who gave them to him. They seemed like ordinary peppermints. He had not eaten any himself. He did not fancy peppermint. He did not know, and could not guess, why a stranger had suddenly given him a packet of peppermints in a Newmarket pub.

'There wasn't any man, lad, and we know it and you know it and you know we know it. And we all know ruddy well why you didn't eat any peppermints. This won't be just a bother with the Stewards, you know. This is criminal charges. Where did you get the stuff? Nick it from a chemist? Forge a prescription? There's a lot of offences you're going to be charged with. Make it much worse, it will, the jockey being hurt so bad.'

Darren Finn changed his story into something that might have been the truth. The man in the pub showed him a letter. It said to see that Poetaster had a peppermint just before his race. It was a kind of superstition, the letter said. It was the owner of the horse wrote the letter, signed it as large as life, so Darren Finn did like the owner said.

The Disciplinary Committee of the Jockey Club called before itself, in a panelled room in Portman Square, Matthew Carver, Fred Cottle and Darren Finn, all of whom were supported by lawyers, and a considerable number of witnesses.

Matthew sat like a stone, unable to believe that any of this was happening to him. His start of astonishment, hearing that he was

360

$51,000 richer in New York, was regarded as creditable acting.

His own evidence consisted of blank, blanket denial. He was swamped by circumstantial evidence. He was swamped by the screamingly obvious fact that Fred Cottle and Darren Finn had lied and were lying still.

Fred Cottle lost his licence to train. Matthew Carver and Darren Finn, prettily bracketed, were warned off the British turf.

Matthew Carver was automatically disqualified from setting foot on any racecourse in any country.

Criminal proceedings were not contemplated against Darren Finn, because he was evidently a tool, an ill-educated youngster. Carver might be charged with obtaining moneys by fraud, and with criminal responsibility for the shocking injuries to the jockey.

What astonished everybody was that Carver thought he could ever get away with it. There was never the slightest chance of him doing so. It was almost as though he wanted to be found out.

He had to stay in England, until the Director of Public Prosecutions decided whether to prosecute.

Ralph Hadfield sent a message to say he was no longer welcome.

The secretary of the London club of which he was a visiting member said that he could no longer be vouchsafed use of the club, according to a rule which dated from the expulsion of a member, on similar grounds, in 1809.

Matthew hid in a nasty hotel in West Kensington.

Few racing scandals had ever achieved such lurid and global publicity.

Liz saw it. Matthew called her. She said she and Jamie were leaving, and did not want to see him again.

Clare saw it. She would not talk to him.

Lee V. Lowe came in under the mushroom cloud, and this time they wanted everything he had for them:

The son's heroin addiction.

The daughter's Lesbian affair with a Cragrock employee now dismissed.

The successful conspiracy to defraud Lord Goring.

The successful conspiracy to defraud M. Henri de Cheminade.

The unprofessional purchase of a bad and expensive yearling as a means to the seduction of its owner.

The unprofessional siting of an important stallion as another means to the seduction of the farm's owner's sister.

The seduction of a woman, in her own brother's house, while her adoring and dependent husband lay chronically sick in hospital.

The financing by that husband of his entertainment while he was seducing the wife.

The deprival of the wife's support for that husband, by her removal to the fleshpots of Southern Europe.

The responsibility for his own wife's death, by his constructive desertion of her, which obliged her to undertake hazardous physical tasks.

The profane and obscene brawls at that wife's funeral.

Of course. That kind of man. It all fits in. No wonder he needed $50,000.

Jean said to Alice, 'All this stuff George's man is putting out is pretty rancid, but . . .'

'But it seems Matthew had a pill given to that horse.'

'I'm afraid it does, darling.'

Old Lady Goring read the newspapers, when she had time. She saw the news about Poetaster, some days after the event. The name Matthew Carver meant nothing to her.

Then she saw his photograph, taken outside the magistrates' court where he was remanded on bail. Then she knew him.

He had made her sit down, at Newmarket races, when she had badly wanted to sit down. He had been kind and friendly. Though American, he was a gentleman, a gentle man. She remembered him with gratitude and admiration. She was quite sure that he had not put a young jockey's life at risk, and his wife expecting a baby too.

Then Lady Goring remembered telephone calls, early in the morning and late at night, Bobbety Bobs about his mysterious business. She read all that the newspapers said about the case, and she put the telephone calls against it. It was impossible to doubt that somebody had done something unfair.

Fair play. Lady Goring had learned it in the nursery, and it was her religion still. Greater than faith or hope or charity. Greater than her love for Bobbety Bobs.

She was almost a whole day considering where her duty lay, but really she knew all along.

She pulled on a knitted hat bought from a jumble sale, and took a bus into the West End. She walked to Portman Square and the offices of Messrs Weatherby.

She said, 'I want to see someone in the Jockey Club.'

'Perhaps you can help us, Mr Carver,' they said in Portman Square. 'If we're going to get to the bottom of this we need an idea of the motive. It wasn't money. You've got that. Who'd *want* to land you in this? What's the *point*? Look at the *trouble* somebody took. Does *anybody* hate you that much?'

Matthew shook his head slowly. He was not expert in hatred. He had never felt it. Like everybody else, he understood what had happened; no more than anybody else could he understand why.

Lord Goring cleared himself, more or less.

The calls his mother had heard had been made on instructions he believed came from Prince Ghalib. He had thought the instructions odd, but suspected nothing sinister. A man like Ghalib went about things in a strange, devious way. All Arabs did. Nothing was ever straightforward. Ghalib was a very clever man, but over-subtle. Goring did everything Ghalib asked, because the Prince was an important client of the Agence Fille de l'Aire, but of course he would never have done anything illegal or unsporting, even for Ghalib. Now Goring accepted that he had been duped, that Ghalib had nothing to do with it. He was sorry for the trouble he had unwittingly caused.

It was possible to believe that Goring really thought his instructions came from Ghalib. It was impossible to prove otherwise.

Sir Merivale Lucas was one of very many well-known racing personalities who were glad to assist the enquiry. He might have been helpful, because of his knowledge of the American scene. But he knew nothing of use. He knew no one with any grudge against Matthew Carver, whom he himself greatly liked and esteemed, and at whose complete vindication he was overjoyed.

George Whyte's name was not mentioned in this or any other connection.

Trevor Plimsoll, answering with public spirit a circularised questionnaire, said truthfully that he had never had any dealings with Carver, personal or professional, and had never exchanged a word with him spoken or written.

Nobody traced the man in the fur hat. Perhaps he had stopped wearing it, and so become unrecognizable.

Matthew withdrew all the money he had inadvertently won on Green Bay Tree. With the approval of the bookmakers who had paid it out, he gave half to David Cawley and half to the Injured Jockeys Fund. The bookmakers, who had been defrauded, came well out of this; they sought and gained wide publicity for their generosity. Incidentally the publicity spotlit Matthew's generosity, too, and he became still more of a popular hero. All the bookmakers had made money on the race because the favourite had fallen.

He was welcomed back to the Hadfields' and to the club.

George Whyte said publicly and often that he had never believed in Matthew Carver's guilt. It did not occur to his wife or his sister that he was telling the truth.

Dame Ninette, Matthew's mare, was at Cragrock waiting to foal to Beausoleil. She was there because there was nobody at home competent to help her with the foaling. Her foal would be the first of Beausoleil's get.

She foaled without trouble, under the eye of the new farm manager. The mare was a sensible old thing. The foal was grand. He was a bright bay with a white blaze and one white sock. Almost exactly Beausoleil's markings. This was highly encouraging. It suggested that Beausoleil was prepotent — that he stamped his stock. Other breeders whose mares he had covered asked for nothing better — George Whyte, Epi Makropulos, Ghalib al-Jilani, Luis Valdes, Ottaviano di Vianello, Lord Hadfield and the rest. There was jubilation among them, a happy suspense as they waited for their foals.

Cheered by news of his foal, dumb with joy at the turn-round of his fortunes, Matthew flew to Ireland for Clare's wedding.

The date, long chosen, had seemed monumentally disastrous. It turned out disastrous only in the number of photographers who wanted pictures of bride, bride's father, bride's brother (once branded as drug-addict; this calumny now disbelieved) and bride's sister (once named Lesbian; this also now discredited owing to established innocence of father). The venue might more obviously have been Kentucky or England. But Kavanaghs in large numbers could not afford to go to America. Clare preferred her new Irish relatives to her existing English ones, few of whom she knew. A large London wedding accorded with no one's preference. A wedding at the church in Wiltshire, the merry-makers treading on the fresh earth of Mollie's grave, seemed inappropriate. After the publication of the Jockey Club's first findings, a quiet little ceremony somewhere seemed best. After publication of their second findings, a very noisy wedding in the public eye seemed inevitable.

Matthew met Liz and Jamie at Shannon, and they drove to Ballycardeen. Jamie looked transformed. Liz irritated him sometimes, by motherly fussing. The first person they saw was Ghalib, in tweeds and Old Harrovian tie, perfectly versed in social usage and Christian rites. They were in good time for drinks before lunch.

Noon at Ballycardeen; seven in the morning in New York. Epi Makropulos was there, being a banker. He had sent two cables to Matthew; he sent one now to Clare.

He took a call from the farm in Virginia where he boarded his American mares. One of the two due to Beausoleil had foaled during the night.

The foal was grey.

In the recorded history of the thoroughbred horse, there is not one single reliable record of a grey foal without at least one grey parent. Beausoleil was bay. Epi's mare was chestnut. The thing was impossible. Epi set off immediately for Virginia.

The big house at Ballycardeen was habitable, though the renovations were incomplete. All the Carvers were staying there. Tom's immediate family were in his house. The two parties mingled after lunch. Ghalib took Matthew round the stud. Clare showed Liz her wedding dress. Liz wanted to get married, at once, to anybody.

Luis Valdes was in Washington, to see operas at Kennedy Center. He took a call from Virginia. One of his mares due to Beausoleil had foaled in the early morning. The foal, incredibly, was grey.

Ghalib gave an immense dinner party. Clare looked beautiful and happy. Photographers were flushed out of the new rose beds which, had it been summer, they would have damaged. They got stable muck, spread by Tom's orders over the roots of the roses, on their feet. Ghalib gave them whisky, and Matthew his thirtieth impromptu press conference. Goodwill bathed him like the very nicest and most fragrant soup, nourishing and laced with liquor.

George Whyte was disturbed late at night, by his new farm manager. He had a Beausoleil foal. He was nonplussed. Breeding history had been made. A bay and a black had produced a grey. It seemed typical of the topsy-turvy nightmare of the previous few days.

Both Epi Makropulos and Luis Valdes called Cragrock early in the morning. Both spoke to George Whyte. All agreed on an immediate visit to Fox Hill. They made a rendezvous at the Farmington Club. George flew, airstrip to airstrip. The others drove. All three made it by mid-morning.

At which time Matthew Carver was giving away his elder daughter in marriage. She was attended by children, girls with flowers in their hair and boys in sailor suits. She wore a tiara lent by Viscountess Wincham, who herself wore a purple sombrero.

George and the others went to Fox Hill. On the way to the house they stopped at the farm. They saw Beausoleil, magnificent in a paddock by his barn, circling, lord of the place, shortly to be coupled with some of the best broodmares in the world. A few mares that had already foaled were out in the weak sun. In a big field yearlings raced. The scene was beautiful and the place was in beautiful order.

They looked for the farm manager. He was nowhere to be seen.

He was said to be around, but he was invisible.

They went on to the house.

Epi greeted Rosie as though he had never paid her gambling debts and she had never drugged a stallion. Luis Valdes had not met her before; he hummed the phrase from *Rigoletto* which introduces the last-act quartet. They asked about Beausoleil and the breeding.

Rosie said, 'You have to talk to Matthew Carver about that. Beausoleil lives here, but we don't have anything to do with managing him. Of course we look after him. He looks great, don't you think?'

Rosie did not know what mares had visited Beausoleil the previous spring, except for those boarding at Fox Hill. She knew his fertility was high. She heard he was tough to handle, but she had not seen him breed. She could be of little help to them.

She looked beautiful as she spoke to them in the beautiful Fox Hill portico. Epi thought she was a girl who had come out of the valley of the shadow of despair: Matthew's despair.

Peach said, 'If you desire congress with Carver, gentlemen, you must choose another meeting-place than this.'

Peach offered George Whyte a candy-bar, a personal sacrifice and a mark of esteem he had almost never before allowed himself. George declined.

The three of them went back to the farm. They found and questioned a groom whom Epi had met. The groom knew no more about Beausoleil's breeding than Mrs Phillipson. Seemed like he was a funny character. Needed privacy. The groom never heard of a stallion being bashful, but that was what Rick Field said. Rick handled the whole thing behind the closed doors of the breeding-shed, not practically out in the open as they usually did it. He didn't let anybody in — just Rick and the big twins from Mount Malcolm. They were a pretty good choice. Adrift in the head, but mighty strong and with a beautiful feeling for animals.

'Rick Field?' said Epi. 'But where was the old black man? Where was Ed Lindsey?'

Epi heard for the first time about Ed's accident.

It became urgent that they see Rick Field. His disappearance was unaccountable. He had been around; he had vanished.

'He doesn't want to see us,' said Luis Valdes. 'He doesn't like your face, Epi.' He hummed '*Ah, che musa*' from *L'Italiana in Algeri*.

'I think I don't like his face,' said Epi. 'We must talk to those twins.'

They went to Mount Malcolm. Miss Viola Biggs was puzzled but welcoming. She took them to where Luke and John Field were digging a drainage ditch.

'No use askin' 'em,' she said. 'They just make bird noises. They do signs, though.'

George was shocked at the sight and sound of the twins. He thought they should have been in an institution. Luis Valdes hummed the giants' leitmotiv from *Rheingold*.

They took the twins to Fox Hill. Miss Viola Biggs came along, because she was often able to interpret chirrup or gesture. Epi pointed at the breeding shed. Nods, beams. Yes, the twins knew it well. Epi pointed to Beausoleil. Luke gestured 'large'. John mimed 'fierce'. Epi pointed at mares. He tried to get gestured or chirruped confirmation that Beausoleil had covered mares. It was a long time coming. It did not come. The twins pointed to another barn. A head poked out over a half-door, a friendly old grey head, Corporal's head.

'For years an' years that ol' fellow's been breedin' here,' said Miss Viola. 'The twins helped Ed Lindsey hunnerds of times, before Rosie an' Peach come back. It's what they'd expect. They wouldn't see nothin' strange in Corporal breedin'.'

'Where is Rick Field?'

'Here's his wife,' said Miss Viola. 'Hi, Janice. You seen Rick?'

Janice stopped her used V.W. Rabbit. She had been to market. She had not seen Rick. She knew nothing about Beausoleil's breeding.

She went on to her house. She put her car in the garage. The others faced one another helplessly. The twins crouched in the dirt and played with twigs.

They heard Janice scream. They hurried towards the garage. Janice came out of the garage. She had stopped screaming. She would not scream again. Her face was lop-sided, as though she had had a stroke.

Rick had hanged himself with a halter-rope from the roof of the garage.

'He bred some of the mares, maybe all of the mares, with the teaser, with old Corporal,' said Miss Viola Biggs.

Luis's mouth dropped open. George began to compute a

financial loss so staggering that his internal computer blew.

'For God's sake, why?' said Epi.

'He was scared,' said Janice Field. 'That stallion scared him shitless.'

'He must have known he would be found out. Grey foals.'

'Hopin' for a miracle, I guess,' said Miss Viola. 'If a foal wasn't grey it might be Beausoleil's. One or two grey foals, that could be a mistake, the teaser slippin' it in. He didn't think ahead, I guess. Didn't dare to, I guess. Needed to keep the job. Keep Janice. Right, girls?'

'Yellow,' said Janice.

'Kept ever'thing together for a year. Hoped for a miracle at the end of it. Lot o' folks done the same kind of thing, like fellows takin' money from the till in the bank, hopin' for a miracle at the end of it, earthquake swallowin' the bank, ground crackin' open. Rick had the grey foals instead of his miracle. He had you, comin' to ask questions.'

'I don't understand,' said George Whyte. 'A professional farm manager, a horseman, how could a man like that be frightened of a horse to such abject folly?'

''Cause he was scared shitless,' said Janice, 'that's how.'

'Thirty more foals are due,' said Luis Valdes. 'How many by Beausoleil?'

'Tell you one that is,' said Miss Viola. 'Matthew's own, if it's born.'

'It's born,' said George Whyte.

'Colour?'

'Bay. White face and sock.'

They looked at Beausoleil in his paddock.

'Matthew handled that breeding himself,' said Miss Viola. 'I remember he had the twins up. I dunno who else he had.'

'Not Rick,' said Janice. 'He was shammin' a gut-ache.'

'One Beausoleil foal in thirty-five,' said George. 'And that one Carver's.'

'There may be others,' said Epi.

'I reckon the twins are trying to tell us,' said Miss Viola, 'that there won't be no others.'

They were all in the marquee which Ghalib had had put up behind the house. It was warmed by charcoal braziers, lined with banded material that looked like silk, and full of flowers which must have come from a long way away.

Ghalib had insisted on paying for the marquee and the flowers. Matthew was paying for the champagne which came now and the music which would come later.

There was no godfather or paternal relative of the bride to propose the health of bride and groom. Matthew had few relatives, and those few too frail or idle to cross the Atlantic in February. Lord Wincham had expected to be asked to make the speech — had, indeed, prepared his remarks and rehearsed them in front of his shaving mirror. But in Matthew's absence, preoccupied in London, the Kavanaghs had taken it upon themselves to ask Ghalib. He was very elegant in his morning coat. He made a conventional speech. He was better than Wincham would have been, and briefer. An unrehearsed reference to Matthew's recent vindication brought a ripple of applause. Wincham joined in the clapping, although he looked as though he did not know why. 'My lords, ladies and gentlemen, I ask you all to raise your glasses to Clare and Tom.'

'Long life and happiness. God bless them. Clare and Tom.'

'Thank you all very much,' said Tom, on his feet and scarlet. 'Is that enough?'

'No,' said Clare. 'But almost.'

Tom thanked Prince Ghalib for his speech and his hospitality, Matthew for the reception, all those present for being present and for their presents (Clare prodded him as he stumbled over unintended puns), Clare for marrying him. Cheers, laughter.

Ghalib was called away to the telephone.

He came back and signalled to Matthew. Matthew joined him, leaving the party unobtrusively.

When Matthew heard what Ghalib had heard from America, he said, 'I'd better write out a cheque for this party now. After tomorrow I won't be able to.'

'Will you come with me to Virginia, now at once?'

'Yes.'

Barring unlikely accidents, there would be thirty-four live foals putatively sired by Beausoleil. Some were certainly Corporal's, and it seemed likely that thirty-three were Corporal's. Corporal was a thoroughbred, a stud-book stallion, and his get out of good mares would not be completely valueless. Just very, very cheap.

Nominations to Beausoleil in his first season had sold at widely varying figures, according to the commercialism of shareholders and the optimism of the owners of mares. The cheapest nomination had been sold by Epi Makropulos to Lord Hadfield for $50,000; the most expensive was $125,000. The average was $87,500. This was accordingly the average sum lost by purchasers of nominations and by shareholders who had believed they were using their shares. The total lost to breeders on this calculation was $2,887,500. Other factors had to be considered. The thirty-three mares successfully impregnated by Corporal had, effectively, lost a year of their breeding lives. If seven live foals was a good average for a mare, and $500,000 was the average value of the high-class mares involved, then each mare's owner had lost on average $71,485, and the thirty-three mares represented a loss of $2,359,005. Again: shares in Beausoleil had been valued at $500,000, giving him a value of $20,000,000. One share in the great Lyphard had been sold in July 1981 for $900,000, giving him a value of $36,000,000. Beausoleil might or might not rival Lyphard, but he had certainly been expected to join that league. The value of his shares was practically certain to increase. But not if he had no foals, no yearlings, no runners. His value might still increase, under proper management, but not for another year. All the shareholders had been deprived of a year's rise in the value of their shares. Perhaps $100,000. The total loss from this source therefore $4,000,000. The total loss from all sources therefore $9,247,010. A tiny fraction of this sum — one fortieth part of the presumed increase in Beausoleil's value, $100,000 — Matthew Carver had himself lost. He had not lost a year of his broodmare's career, nor wasted his share of Beausoleil. The total owing was further reduced by the value of Corporal's foals. Possibly $300,000. Reduced by these sums, the money owed was $8,847,010.

Different attitudes were taken concerning this balance. Some interested parties expressed desire for immediate payment in full. These included George Whyte, Lord Hadfield, the duc de Montfermainbrey and il Conte Ottaviano di Vianello. Epi Makropulos waived payment; Ghalib al-Jilani and Luis Valdes consented to indefinite postponement.

Matthew valued his foal by Beausoleil out of Dame Ninette at $1,000,000. He was offered, and was obliged to accept, $750,000. Dame Ninette was aging. Two more foals were the most that could be expected from her. She was valued at another $750,000.

Matthew's share in Beausoleil raised $600,000. His other mares and young stock realised $1,860,000 in total. His wholly-owned horses in training in England, Dandy Dinmont and Poetaster, were sold privately, the former to the Agence Fille de l'Aire for £6,500 and the latter to the MidAtlantic Agency for £8,250, both agencies acting on behalf of unnamed clients: a total of £14,750 or $28,025. All these sales were at a bad time for the vendor and a good one for the purchasers. The encashing of securities on the New York Stock Exchange realised $1,694,161. The farm sold for $480,000. That was it. That was $7,502,186. The absolute generosity of Epi Makropulos, which Matthew was not in a position to refuse, reduced the debit by $317,970. The qualified generosity of Luis Valdes and Ghalib al-Jilani reduced it by a further $1,294,925. Matthew owed them this money. He was able, when all the sales were through, to pay them $278,000 on account. This left him with $71.

He handed over the keys of his house to the purchaser, the Californian manager of the new local electronics factory, whose wife thought the place darling. He took a ride into a town and a bus westwards.

'Where did he go?' said Alice. 'How can I help him if he disappeared?'

'Would you help him?' asked Jean.

'Oh, yes.'

A new manager was installed at Fox Hill, an experienced stallion-man from Upperville. He had some trouble with Beausoleil, but he stood no nonsense. Beausoleil served forty-five mares, of whom thirty-six were tested in foal.

George Whyte extended a stallion-barn, mentally earmarking for the purpose the money he had been paid by Carver. He intended to move Beausoleil to Cragrock in time for the next breeding season. Most shareholders approved of this decision.

'How can we help him if he disappeared?' said Clare.

'He disappeared because he doesn't want help,' said Tom.

Ghalib wrote off the remainder of Matthew's debt to him, which was $410,153, but he was unable to tell him so.

With Ghalib's approval, Tom engaged Jamie Carver as a

working pupil. Jamie no longer had any kind of allowance. He began to save up for a car.

The Winchams were shamed by their relatives into paying for a secretarial course for Liz. She lived with a family in Holland Park, a bedroom and two meals a day in return for light housework and baby-sitting. She was aiming at a job in publishing.

Rosie Phillipson went to see Tim once a week, sometimes twice. Her face was thinner but the rest of her was fatter. There were new lines round her eyes.

At Maxwell Park, the only thoroughbred racetrack in western Nebraska, Barney Stutt had his dozen horses in the barn in time for the twenty-six-day meet beginning April 4. His assistant was kicked in the groin by a sassy two-year-old, and they took him away in an ambulance. A guy came looking for a job, any job, without references or money. He was growing a moustache. The moustache was going to be streaky grey, though his hair was still brown. It was going to make him look older. He said he knew about horses, but he had never worked for a trainer. Desperate, Barney hired him on a strictly provisional basis. He seemed a respectable guy, not a lush or a burglar on the run. He was twenty years older than Barney, but that made no difference to their relationship. Barney was boss. Mike Smith accepted that. He worked hard. Barney's horses were pretty bad. He bought them out of claiming-races, and sold them again. He couldn't afford to get fond of any horse. He couldn't afford much of a salary for Mike. He had to pay a basic wage to grooms, work-riders and hot-walkers, but an assistant trainer wasn't covered by any code.
Barney thought Mike Smith had walked out on his wife, but Mike said his wife had died. Obviously he was on the run from something. That explained the moustache and what was probably a phoney name. He did the work fine. The provisional employment became permanent. They moved east at the end of the meeting, to Ak-Sar-Ben, on to Lincoln, Columbus, Atokad. Barney began to respect Mike's judgement, about what horses to claim and about the way to work them. But Barney remained boss. You had to have it clear who ran things. They had a pretty good year. Mike sent away all the money he could spare out of his

salary. He said he was paying off two debts. He never would pay them off but he had to keep trying. He was a loser, but he was useful. Barney imagined the two of them circling Nebraska for ever, with Mike sending off little dribbles of money at the end of every week.